CN00926133

FAIR GAME

DAVID J. GATWARD

WEIRDSTONE PUBLISHING

Fair Game
by
David J. Gatward

 Created with Vellum

To Michael and Jean Forster, and to Glen.

Grimm: nickname for a dour and forbidding individual, from Old High German grim [meaning] 'stern', 'severe'. From a Germanic personal name, Grima, [meaning] 'mask'. (*www.ancestory.co.uk*)

CHAPTER ONE

LUCA'S STOMACH GRUMBLED LOUD ENOUGH TO STOP HIM dead, a skeletal statue cloaked in shadows draping from trees furred with moss. The sound reminded him of the rumbling from the quarry close to where he'd grown up, but that was now such a long time ago, and so very far away, that the memory was little more than a dream. He patted his stomach as if to comfort it, remembering when it had been considerably larger.

The evening was full dark, no stars, the distant lights of the heavens shut off by thick clouds. Gloomy autumn weather had refused to move on after a few days spent brooding over the Dales, hanging around to release the occasional shower and dampen any spirits daring to lift.

Luca breathed in air rich with the scents of damp woodland, the sweet and savoury notes of tree, leaf and soil, then moved on.

He had parked his car at the end of the track and under the shadow of some overhanging branches, far enough away from where he now was, as well as from the local population, not to arouse suspicion. Now all he had to do was focus on the task ahead.

On his back, in a small rucksack he'd had with him for years now, he carried the simple tools of the night's activities: a worn and oily hessian sack he had found left behind a market stall, a wooden rolling pin, and a catapult he'd managed to make himself.

He'd crafted the catapult from a thick V-shaped branch and some elastic exercise bands he'd helped himself to a couple of weeks ago from the back of an open car boot belonging to a woman far too interested in her phone to notice what he was doing. Ammunition was a handful of steel ball bearings liberated over several evenings from various old vehicles rusting behind a local garage. He doubted they would be missed.

As for light, this was provided by a small torch. He had covered the lens with a thin layer of red transparent plastic, held on with an elastic band. The plastic had previously been wrapped around chocolate; a taste Luca rarely experienced these days, and the thought of it made his mouth water.

Creeping through the thick undergrowth and navigating a careful path through the trees, the torch provided just enough light to show him the way, but not enough to give away his location. The red plastic also ensured that his night vision wasn't compromised by the bright bulb. Not that Luca thought anyone knew where he was or had followed him, but he'd grown to be wary over the past year. He trusted no one.

Ahead, the trees thinned a little and Luca paused, his breathing calm. He was able to make out a large pen, built from chicken wire and thick wooden staves. On the other side, he saw plastic feeder tubs. The pheasants were no longer kept inside, having been released for one of the many gameshoots run up and down the Dales, but some always came back, drawn by familiarity and food and security. He had been here once before, but only because he'd followed another in secret. And this time he would not be going home empty-handed. Kindness and handouts were all well and good, but he still had his pride; he would feed his own, otherwise what kind of man was he?

For a moment, he despaired at what his father would say if he saw him now, if he knew. But the old man was long gone, taken by the hardships Luca had been sure he was escaping from. How wrong he had been.

Inching forward, Luca settled down close to where the birds, fat on grain and good husbandry, meandered in and out of the pen, their clucks and squawks loud in the quiet quilt of night.

With the catapult pouch loaded, he knew all he had to do now was wait. Then, all being well, he could head back home in a couple of hours with enough good meat to bring a smile to the tired faces of his wife and daughter. Thinking of them brought a smile to Luca's face, and he allowed himself to enjoy what he was doing, hunting for food in the dark.

It wasn't long before movement in the shadows betrayed a bird's approach. Luca watched as the creature made its carefree way out from beneath a heavy clump of fern, pecking at the ground, oblivious to any danger. They would roast it, he thought, lifting his arms and stretching back the band of the catapult, anchoring the ball bearing against his cheek, stuff the bird with onions and stale breadcrumbs, serve it with potatoes, boil up the carcass for soup. His stomach rumbled once more, and he was aware then of how loose his trousers were about his waist, how much weight he had lost.

Just a few metres closer and Luca knew there was no way he could miss. A finishing blow from the rolling pin and he could then sit back and wait for a few more to wander into range to help fill the sack in his bag.

The sharp crack of a twig sent the pheasant squawking and flapping in panic back into the dark. Luca instinctively snapped round to see what had caused it, only to see two large shadows racing towards him.

Half falling as he scrambled to his feet, his legs stiff from how he'd been sitting on the soft woodland floor, Luca bolted into the dark, his catapult and ammo scattered, but he managed to keep hold of his bag.

Branches whipped at him, brambles reached out to snatch at his legs, but he powered on. Behind him, he heard heavy feet crashing through the undergrowth, mean voices swearing into the night, rich with threat. Whoever they were, Luca didn't care. All he knew was that he had to get away, get home, be safe. He'd find other ways to feed his family.

The woodland seemed to crush in as he raced on, his heart pounding. His pace was rapid and yet the treacle-thick darkness lurking amongst the trees made it seem as though he was barely moving at all.

Luca guessed that his car wasn't too far away now, at least he didn't think it was. The woodland all looked the same, but he'd always had a good sense of direction, so trusted in it. Then something slammed into the back of his head, his thoughts shattered like a glass thrown at a brick wall, and Luca fell hard into the thorn-toothed mouth of darkness.

When Luca came to, he was blind, and his breaths were

pulling in something foul-tasting. A sack was over his head, his arms tied behind his back, and he was lying on the ground on his side. He could feel earth beneath him, and the air was still that of the woodland. Most of all, though, his body felt like he'd been thrown off a cliff to smash into the rocks below. Every breath, every movement hurt. He knew bones were broken and he tasted blood in his mouth.

'He's awake.'

'Good. Don't want him missing what's coming, now, do we?'

The voices were gruff and mean. He didn't recognise them, but their accents reminded him of a soap opera he'd seen on TV, where no one smiled and there was a lot of shouting in a pub called the Queen Vic. Panic reached out its icy fingers and squeezed as he struggled to free himself from his bonds. But it was hopeless.

'What is it you want? Who are you? I have done nothing wrong.'

Laughter as cruel as a storm-ripped sea made him shudder.

'You need to know your place.'

'I don't understa—'

The hard toe of a boot hammered into Luca's side, killing his voice. Pain shot through him so sharply that the cry he let out was half strangled by shock.

'You know the rule. Talk to no one. And there's no other rule, now, is there? No. Not unless you've decided to make one up. Well, is that it? Is that what you've done?'

'I ... I have n...' Luca said between gasps as he sucked in breath, trying to stay calm.

He sensed a body close by, someone leaning in. Then a voice whispered in his ear.

'And yet, here you are. So, how's about you start telling us what exactly it is you've been up to?'

Luca didn't want to say anything. He couldn't. But maybe, if he said just enough, but not too much, he'd get out of this.

'I followed someone,' he said.

'Followed who?'

'I don't know. I never met them. A customer.'

It wasn't exactly the truth, and it wasn't exactly a lie, either.

Another boot, harder this time, and Luca cried out in agony, sure that a rib had snapped with the impact.

'We need a name.'

'I ... I don't have a name.' Luca was crying, his body on fire. But he spoke anyway, forced out the words, knowing that he couldn't give a name. 'I just want to feed my family.'

Laughter, but Luca ignored it.

'I work. Seven days a week. No stop. No rest. But the money ...'

He stopped himself before he said too much.

'Yes?'

Luca kept what he was going to say to himself.

'You were going to say something about the money?'

This time, something crashed into his face. A slap so hard Luca tasted blood as lightning burst in his brain.

'It is not enough!' Luca said. 'We cannot live! It is impossible!'

Another slap, on the other side of his face this time, making his ears ring.

'Time for your lesson.'

'What are you talking about? What lesson?'

Hands grabbed Luca's right foot and something hard and

cold was dragged under his leg. He kicked out, thrashed around as hard as he could, but he was held fast, the hands on him like the jaws of a vice.

'What are you doing? Let me go! My family, I have to be with them! Please!'

Once again, a voice whispered into his ear.

'I'm afraid to say this is going to hurt just a little.'

'What? What are you doing? Please, whatever it is, I—'

A metallic snap sounded out, the slam of a steel door in an abattoir.

For a moment, Luca's brain was unable to process exactly what had just happened. He'd heard the sound, sharp and incongruous in the woodland, then felt something so violent happen to him that he just couldn't make sense of it. The shocked gasps from his attackers hadn't helped either.

Then the pain hit Luca with the force of a tsunami and he knew then that something was catastrophically wrong.

'What have you done to me? What the ... What have you done?'

Luca's voice came out of him in shreds as he cried out in agony, nausea hot on the heels of the pain. He retched, emptying his stomach of what little it contained.

'Yeah, that hurt, didn't it?'

Laughter then.

But Luca wasn't listening. All he could think about now was the pain in his leg and how cold he was, as though heat was just draining away from him.

'Boss wants a photo. Smile for the birdy!'

Luca's screams faded to sobs. He tried to roll away from the pain, but his leg was caught in something, and the movement was like rolling in broken glass. The sweet scent of the woodland had been replaced by the acrid stink of his own vomit, dripping down the sack on his head, coating his face.

'Well, I'm afraid to say that we'll be leaving you now.'

'Please, don't leave me,' Luca said. 'My ... my family ...'

'Don't worry yourself about them. They'll be fine. We'll make sure of it, I promise.'

More laughter and Luca could do nothing but lie there and listen to it, screaming into the night, as they rolled him onto his side and cut his hands free.

'There you go,' said one of the voices, rich with amusement. 'You've a fighting chance now, I think. It's only fair. And if you manage to crawl back to work tomorrow, all is forgiven.'

The two men said nothing more and Luca listened to them walk away as he pulled the hood off his head, sucking in clean air.

He sat up, woozy with everything that had happened. He felt down his leg only to find that below the knee, something had almost severed it completely. It was a metal blade, like some kind of giant mousetrap.

Ignoring the pain, Luca tried to prise the jaws of the contraption apart, to pull himself free, but they were stuck fast. And it was impossible to get any grip, slick as they were with his blood.

Luca saw his bag just an arm's reach away. He dragged it over and pulled out his phone, knowing he couldn't call the police. The phone contained only two numbers. One for his wife, the other his only chance out of this. He tapped on the number and held the phone to his ear. As he waited, the woodland started to swim in front of his eyes and Luca knew that soon he would drown.

CHAPTER TWO

GRACE BLACK WAS SITTING AT A SMALL KITCHEN TABLE opposite a man whose face was etched as much with worry, as it was with scars. On the table between them were various documents for him to sign and the details of a modest, though hardly reasonably priced, house in Gayle at the top end of Wensleydale. They'd both read everything through several times, but as yet no ink had been set to dry on the paper. Underneath the table, quietly snoring, was a black Labrador.

A bottle of wine, half drunk, sat just to her left. She reached for it and topped up both of their large glasses. It was a decent drop, too, she thought, which had been the point; a good bottle of wine and a takeaway to make this important moment much more of an event. Unfortunately, she wasn't all that sure it had worked.

Grace took a sip of her wine.

'Well?'

'Well, what?'

'You've read the documents, sorted the deposit, you know you can afford it, so ...'

Grace arched an eyebrow, took another sip.

She had known Harry Grimm a good while now, having met the detective chief inspector during one of his investigations, which had involved the rather sad loss of her dad's young dog, Jake. At some point, she'd noticed a spark between them and had taken the first step in seeing if getting to know each other a bit better was a good idea. And it had turned out to be a very good idea indeed. It was all still very early days, true, and she wasn't one for reading too much into things, but as her dad had told her a few weeks ago, it certainly seemed to have legs. An odd phrase, for sure, but true enough all the same.

Harry picked up his glass, stared at it, put it down again, then started to shuffle through the papers again.

The sound of someone half falling as they stumbled through Harry's flat interrupted the moment. Grace looked up to see Ben, Harry's younger brother, standing behind him, a few too many boxes piled up in his hands.

'Nearly there,' Ben said, the strain of the weight in his hands squeezing his voice. 'Just a few more to go and then that's it.'

'Excited?' Grace asked.

'Of course he is.'

The reply came from behind Grace as Liz Coates, Ben's girlfriend and one of the two Police Community Support Officers on Harry's team, walked over to help him. She had returned from her place to pick up the last remnants of Ben's life from the flat he'd shared with Harry for the best part of the last twelve months.

Liz grabbed one of the boxes.

'How much is there left to go?'

'Just these and half a dozen more,' Ben said. 'One

carload.'

'What I don't understand,' said Liz, 'is how someone who was in prison not that long ago can accumulate so much crap.'

Ben did his best to look shocked.

'Crap? How can you say that?'

'Did I say crap? Sorry, I meant to say junk.'

'Ha ha.'

'Do you even know what any of it is?'

'It's ... important,' Ben said. 'And it's not all stuff from here. Harry looked after things for me while I was inside, so most of it is from down south.'

'You're blaming your older brother then, is that it?'

At this, Harry lifted a hand. 'Don't go bringing me into this. I've more important things to be worrying about than why Ben here thinks keeping all the Lego he had when he was a kid is a normal thing to do.'

At this, Grace saw Liz's eyes widen.

'Lego? You've got to be kidding me! These boxes are filled with Lego?'

'Harry used to buy it for me,' Ben said. 'And no, not all of them. Just two.'

'And you want to keep it?'

'Of course I do.'

'Why?'

'Like I said,' said Ben, 'Harry used to buy it for me.'

As he said this, Grace saw Ben glance at Harry.

'You know, I still have a few things around from when I was young,' she said. 'Bits and bobs from my mum. Doubt I'll ever throw any of it out, even though it's just in boxes in the loft.'

Ben smiled at Grace, then moved off to take his boxes out

to Liz's car, Liz following behind.

'He's too sentimental for his own good,' Harry said once they were alone.

'And there's nothing wrong with that,' said Grace. 'Now, where were we?'

Harry went to answer, but a ring from Grace's phone cut him off.

Grace picked it up and looked at the screen.

'It's Dad,' she said, standing up. 'He's probably forgotten I'm staying over here tonight and ringing to find out where I am.'

Harry laughed.

Grace answered her phone.

'Now then, Dad,' she said. 'What's up? I'm round at Harry's like I said, remember?'

'Grace? It's your dad.'

Grace sighed.

'I know,' she said. 'That's why I said, *now then, Dad*, just a second ago.'

'You psychic or something?'

'Yes, I'm psychic,' Grace said. 'So, what's up, then?'

'I'm down at the pens. Well, I'm not actually at the pens. Not yet. I'm down where we park, you know, just off the road, like. But I'll be heading to the pens soon enough. That's why I'm calling.'

Grace, like her dad, was a gamekeeper. She'd followed him into the business after a childhood spent outside, rearing pheasants, keeping the rabbit population down with ferrets and a shotgun, and was now responsible for a number of shoots, large and small, up and down the Dales.

'You're calling to tell me you're off to the pens?' Grace shook her head. She loved her dad dearly, not least because the man had brought her up single-handedly after her mum had died when she was a baby. But he wasn't one for taking it easy. 'Which pens, though, Dad? There's a fair few of them.'

'The ones up by your place, out the back of Carperby.'

'But they're fine, Dad,' said Grace. 'I checked them yesterday, remember?'

'Did you?'

'I did.'

'Well, anyway, it's a good job I'm here, regardless. There's a car, Gracie. Just parked here like it's a normal thing to do.'

'You're not making any sense, Dad,' Grace said.

'But there's a car. And it's parked up where we park up. Can't be right, that, can it? Only folk I know who park here are me and thee.'

'And the landowner,' Grace said.

'Well, it's not his either. No way would he be seen in this, that's for sure. That pillock wears shirts that cost more than this. God knows why, mind. Have you seen some of them? All flowers and swirls. Stare at them too long and you start seeing things, like in those 3D books you had years ago, remember?'

Grace looked over at Harry, who was now leaning back in his chair and listening in, an amused look on his face.

'It could be a walker,' Grace offered.

'It's the middle of the night!'

'It's late evening, Dad,' Grace said. 'And people do go walking at night.'

'Why the hell they'd do that and call it fun, I don't know. Anyway, it's not a walker. No one parks up here, you know that as well as I.' There was a pause. Then, in a hushed tone, 'Could be a poacher, Gracie.'

Grace moved the phone away from her face and covered it with her other hand.

'He's found a car,' she said to Harry.

'Well, you best tell him it's not finders keepers,' Harry said. 'Where is he?'

'Back over by Carperby at the shoot I manage there. It'll be nowt to worry about, but you know what Dad's like when he gets something in his head.'

'I do,' Harry said. 'He'll be out there all night watching it, waiting for the owner.'

Ben and Liz dashed past to grab the last few boxes from Ben's room. When they came back through she watched as Ben leant over and gave Harry a hug. Harry, still sitting at the table, and clearly unsure how to deal with such an open display of emotion, patted Ben on the back. Then Ben and Liz were gone.

'I'm on my way,' Grace said to her dad.

'I'll stay here and keep an eye on it. The car, I mean. Just in case. You never know, do you?'

'No, you won't,' Grace said. 'You'll head back to my place and I'll see you there. You're heading there later anyway to check on the dogs.'

'But what if they get away?'

'Dad, if it's not poachers, then it doesn't matter, does it? And if it is, then I don't want you tackling them on your own.'

'What are you saying? That I can't handle myself? That I couldn't take them? Is that it? I know I'm old, but—'

'I'll be there in twenty minutes,' Grace said, refusing to respond, and hung up.

'Poachers?' said Harry.

Grace gave a nod as she fetched her coat off the back of

her chair and pulled it on. 'Dad's a bit paranoid at the moment. There's been a few birds go missing over the last few weeks, lights seen out in the fields, that kind of thing. We've not managed to catch anyone, but he's a bit on edge with it all.'

'Probably best you don't try to, either,' Harry said. 'If you find something, you call me, all right?'

'Yes, Mr Policeman,' Grace said, offering a salute.

Harry growled.

'You know what I mean,' he said. 'Like you just told your dad, I'm telling you the same. If you find anything, or if you see anyone suspicious, you stay clear and call.'

Grace nodded.

'Don't worry, I will,' she said. 'But I'm not going to be bothering you over the occasional bird or rabbit.'

Harry stood up. As he did so, movement from under the table had Grace look down to see Smudge, Harry's dog, push herself to her feet, to go and stand by her owner's side.

'You want me to come along? It's always entertaining to have a natter with Arthur.'

'No, I don't,' Grace said, a little more pointedly than she'd meant to. 'Look, I'll be fine. Honestly. I've seen cars up there before. Tourists are nosy buggers and they'll park anywhere, usually where signs tell them not to. Could be someone wild camping. Anyway, you've got things to do.'

'Have I?'

Grace walked over to stand in front of Harry. She lifted the pen off the table and held it up in front of his face, then gave him a kiss.

Harry took the pen.

'I'll give you a call later,' she said, heading out towards the front door of Harry's flat. 'Now sign those documents!'

CHAPTER THREE

THE JOURNEY OVER FROM HAWES WAS A QUIET ONE. Grace didn't have her own dog, Jess, a Cocker Spaniel that, around a year ago, had given birth to a litter of pups. She'd been out all day with her, and Jess was now resting in the run back home. Her dad would check in on the dog later. He would give her a bit of fuss, make sure she had enough water, and let her have a run around before securing her in the run for the night. There was always the risk he'd end up falling asleep on the sofa with her as well, but that didn't matter too much. And it was always funny to find them cuddled up together and then listen her dad make his excuses and blame the dog.

The evening was gloomy, the sky low and dark. Yet, below it, Grace noticed, as she always did, how Wensleydale still rippled with beauty. Dark greens of field and tree, the rich mottled greys of ancient walls and homely dwellings, and above them, the sweeping, drifting clouds of purple heather lay sleepily across the moors.

Dashing along the road out of Hawes and along to Bainbridge, pinpricks of light twinkled amongst the fields, a tiny star system of lives resting in front of televisions and warmed by fires. Grace had hoped for an evening with Harry, but her dad's naturally suspicious nature had put an end to that. Still, he was probably right to call her.

Poachers were the bane of her life and on the off chance there was evidence here to help her put a stop to it, she'd be happy with that. Also, she wasn't about to let her dad head off and deal with it on his own. Not that he wasn't a tough old goat and couldn't handle himself. In fact, that was more the worry; that he could handle himself very well indeed and she didn't want someone else coming off worse because of it.

The village of Bainbridge swung by in quiet stillness as she made her way on towards Carperby. She caught sight of the village green, saw a few folk hurrying along, no doubt on their way to or from the Rose and Crown. She'd not been in there for a while herself. Might be somewhere to drag Harry along to, she thought. The promise of good food would be enough to persuade him.

Rolling into Askrigg a few minutes later, Grace saw the stained-glass windows in the church all aglow, like a handful of boiled sweets thrown up into the brightest sun, and wondered what Anna, the vicar, was up to, and if her partner, and Harry's Detective Inspector, Gordanian Haig, was with her. Their little romance seemed to be going from strength to strength as well, she thought. Perhaps it was something in the air, the Dales working its mystery and magic on the people who called it home.

From Askrigg, the road straightened out and Grace sped up just a little. Window down, she listened to the hum and drone of the tyres on the road and bathed in the cool evening air as it swept into the cabin to wash over her. With only four miles to go, the journey was soon over, and she slowed down as she arrived in Carperby, a place she'd called home for a good while now, having eventually moved out of her dad's house over in Redmire and into a place of her own.

The village was small but perfect, Grace thought, with its little green and its own pub, and a community of folk who all looked out for each other. Well, not all, perhaps, she laughed to herself, thinking of one or two who she'd trust about as far as she could kick them, but that added to the flavour of the place; everywhere needed a rogue or two, just to spice things up a little.

Passing her own house, Grace drove on and took a left halfway through the village to head along a single-track lane lined by high dry-stone walls. The darkness gave her the impression that they were closing in ahead of her. Ahead, dark slopes rose towards the brooding sky, which would soon give way to the moors, thick with heather and bracken, hiding places for pheasant and rabbit, deer and hare.

At the end of the lane, Grace pulled up into a small area of land, two sides of which were lined by woodland, the whole of it corralled by walls. The remnants of an old stone barn sat in one corner, the roof collapsed and baring broken teeth of ancient wooden rafters to the sky. She was surprised to see three vehicles, having only expected to find two, her father's and the supposedly suspicious one he'd called her about.

Parking up, Grace clambered out into the embrace of the evening's chill breath. Two old men walked over to greet her. One was her father, the other a small man with no hair and, as always, a pipe clenched between his teeth. She caught the scent of his tobacco before they arrived in front of her, a sweet woody note with a hint of almond just behind it.

'Hi, Dad,' she said. Then she turned to the other man and said, 'Just passing by, were you, Phil?'

Phil Thwaite was one of her dad's oldest friends, having known each other since primary school. Apart, they were trouble enough when they wanted to be, but together they were a force to be reckoned with, not least because, more often than not, there was mischief in the air. Though Grace doubted that was going to be a problem right now.

'Arthur called me,' Phil said, taking the pipe from his mouth, a metal-stemmed thing with a wooden bowl. 'Said he was out hunting poachers. And you know my views on those thieving little sods. Vermin, they are.'

Grace, hearing a surprising amount of venom in Phil's voice, snapped her eyes back around to her father.

'Dad! I said—'

Arthur raised his hands in an attempt to dampen Grace's admonishing tone.

'What you said was that you didn't want me facing anyone on my own, so I gave Phil a call and he popped by. Just while I waited on you, that's all.'

'But hunting poachers? Really?'

'They need hunting, if you ask me,' Phil said, jabbing his pipe at Grace, emphasising the point he was making. He spat on the ground. 'Like I said, they're vermin.'

'I didn't ask you,' Grace replied, without looking at the man. 'So, that's the car, then, is it?'

She walked over to where the vehicle was parked, deep in shadow beneath the heavy tree boughs hanging low over a wall.

'I bought one of my pies over, if you're interested, Grace,' Phil said, his voice cheering with the change of subject. 'I was just settling down for some supper, you see, so thought, why not just bring it over with me to share with Arthur?'

'Very kind of you, but I've eaten,' Grace said, perhaps a little too quickly. Phil's pies had a reputation, none of it good.

'You know, your dad here said the same,' said Phil. 'Doesn't matter; all the more for me. You don't know what you're missing.'

Oh, I do, Grace thought with a shudder.

She stood back to have a good look at the car.

'Bit of an old banger, isn't it?' Phil said, standing beside her with her dad. 'Hardly looks roadworthy.'

Phil had a point.

'How long do you think it's been here?'

'The bonnet was still a little warm when I turned up,' her dad said. 'That's what? Maybe an hour and a half ago now? So, maybe two, two-and-a-half hours?'

If it was walkers, Grace thought, then where were they walking to? There was a footpath not too far away from where they now stood. It led up onto the moors and then on, over into Swaledale. Maybe they were out doing a bit of not-entirely-legal wild camping, like she'd suggested to Harry earlier before heading out.

'It's open,' Arthur said.

'What is?'

'The car. I tried the door handle when I arrived, and it just popped open. There's nowt in it. Even the boot's empty.'

Grace stared at her father.

'Dad, you can't just go around helping yourself to cars you don't own. You do know that, don't you?'

'I'm not helping myself. I'm carrying out a bit of an investigation, aren't I? Harry would approve.'

'Would he now?' said Grace, shaking her head. 'And this is something you know because?'

Her question was left to float off into the darkness, unanswered.

'Is he coming along, too?' Phil asked. 'I can save a bit of my pie for him.'

'No, he isn't,' Grace said. 'Not unless all of this is considerably more serious than it currently looks.'

Grace headed back to her vehicle to return with a torch. She shone a bright beam into the car. There was nothing she could see inside to give away anything about the owner, other than the fact that they just didn't care about their car. As knocked and scratched and covered in dents the outside was, the inside was no better, the carpets dirty and worn, the seats threadbare.

'We could get Harry to run the plates,' Phil suggested.

Grace laughed.

'Run the plates? Really? Been watching a few police dramas, have we, Phil?'

'It's what they say, isn't it?' Phil replied. 'Anyway, we could, couldn't we? Harry wouldn't mind.'

'No, we couldn't,' Grace said. 'Harry and the rest of his team have more important things to be on with than a clapped-out shed of a car parked out here.' She raised the beam of her torch to the woodland. In the darkness beyond, were the pens her dad had come out to check. 'You've not been in yet, then?'

'No, I've not,' Arthur said. 'Waited, like you told me to.'

Grace eyeballed her father, looking for the lie behind his deep-set eyes.

'Did you now?'

Arthur turned to Phil.

'See? Never believes a word I say.'

'Can't say I blame her, either,' said Phil, pipe back in his mouth and held fast by a grin pinned to his face, a glint in his eyes.

'Well then,' said Grace, moving away from the car. 'No time like the present. Best we get on and have a look, don't you think?'

'I'll get my gun,' Phil said.

'No, you bloody well won't!'

'What if we see someone?'

'If we see someone, the last thing any of us want is you waving a twelve-bore in their face.'

'It wouldn't be loaded.'

'Oh, well, that's okay then, is it?'

'What use would it be if it wasn't loaded?' Arthur asked.

'Plenty, I reckon,' said Phil. 'Bit scarier than a stick, that's for sure.'

Grace breathed deep and let it out, long and slow.

'No shotgun, Phil,' she said. 'And that's final. Now, come on, the pair of you. The sooner we're done, the sooner we can all head home.'

'Or to the pub,' said Arthur.

'Cracking idea, that,' Phil agreed.

Grace wasn't listening. Instead, she was striding off to the small gate that led through to the woodland. She'd installed it herself, having made use of a gap in the wall where a few stones had, over the years, slipped out of place.

On the other side of the gate, the beam from her torch had its work cut out, breaking through the oily blackness which seemed to ooze around and between the trees. A small path lay ahead, and Grace knew the way so well she could probably walk it blindfolded.

'Shall we spread out?' Arthur called from behind.

'No, let's just get to the pens and see if there's been anything going on,' Grace replied.

'But what if there has, and the buggers responsible for it are trying to sneak around, like?'

'We stick together,' Grace said. 'Either that, or you head back to the vehicles and stay there until I come back. Your choice.'

There was no argument.

A few minutes later, Grace noticed something on the path up ahead. It was too far away for her to work out exactly what it was, but she slowed her pace just enough to have her father and Phil catch up.

Pausing, she rested her torch beam on what she'd seen, which was a lump of something she couldn't make out, blocking the way about fifty paces ahead of where they now stood.

'What do you think that is?' she asked.

'Haven't the foggiest,' said Phil.

'Whatever it is, it isn't moving,' said Arthur.

'Could be a deer,' Phil suggested. 'Maybe it's tired and laid down for a nap.'

'Yes, they're well known for doing that, are deer,' said Grace. 'Taking naps right in front of people.'

'Maybe it's just not heard us yet.'

'We could throw something at it,' said Arthur.

'We could, but we won't,' said Grace. 'Come on ...'

She headed off again, her eyes on the mysterious object.

When she was about twenty metres away, the shadows which had disguised the shape so well until that moment could no longer fight against the light from Grace's torch and for the first time, she saw what it was.

'That's … It's a body,' she said, and broke into a quick jog. 'Come on, they might be injured.'

It was only when she was almost on top of what she assumed to be an injured walker that the reality of what she was racing towards came into stark focus.

At once, Grace skidded to a stop, only to stumble and fall, landing hard in the dirt and only just managing to stop herself from falling on …

Dear God, she thought, *what the hell is this*? What the hell had they found? And who?

When she tried to push herself back up onto her feet, she saw that her hands were slick with blood.

CHAPTER FOUR

In the time since Grace had left, Harry hadn't exactly got much further on with signing the documents for the house. It wasn't that he didn't want to, more that his hesitation was born from a deep-seated mistrust of change. He'd had more than enough of that during his forty-odd years on Earth, and it hadn't always been good. The thing was, though, the way his life had changed since being placed in the Dales was actually *only* good, and in so many ways. And yet, still he hesitated.

Maybe it wasn't change, then, he thought, but that this change is considerably more permanent than any of the others I've been through.

In the Paras, he'd lived out of a bag. Moving into the police, that habit had been hard to kick. With few possessions to his name, he'd seemingly always lived in transit. Even now, he had a grab-bag packed and ready by the door, just in case. Though, just in case of what, he hadn't the faintest idea.

A deep sigh from beneath the dining table caught his attention and Harry looked down to see Smudge resting on her back, all four paws in the air, the very embodiment of contentment. He reached down and gave her stomach a rub, then stood up and headed over to the kettle to make himself a coffee. It was late in the day for caffeine, but he was in no mood to go to bed, not yet.

It wasn't just the house that was bothering him, either. Ben had moved out, which was great, and he couldn't be happier about where his brother's life was heading. But the flat was quiet, and to Harry, the silence of the place seemed to have moved in all too quickly and made itself very much at home.

The kettle clicked off, and he reached for the fresh coffee, throwing a few spoonfuls into the French press. The bitter chocolate aroma of the dark liquid slipped through the air as he stirred it before gently easing down the plunger. Then, with a mug of it poured, thick and black, he moved from the kitchen into the lounge and lowered himself into the sofa.

He reached for the remote and switched on the television, spent a few moments flicking through the channels, then switched it off again. There was nothing on. Even if there was, he couldn't be doing with all the adverts.

Sipping the coffee, Harry watched Smudge roll over, push herself to her feet, then come over and join him. She rested her head on his leg and thumped her tail lazily on the floor.

'So, what do you think, then?' Harry asked, staring into Smudge's deep brown eyes. 'And don't go pretending you don't know what I'm talking about, either.'

At the sound of Harry's voice, Smudge's tail thumped a little harder.

No, it wasn't change that was bothering him. Far from it,

he thought. Instead, for the first time in his life, he was taking the step to put down some roots, and that was just a little unnerving. And the soil in the Dales was fertile stuff, wasn't it? His Wensleydale life had already grown into something he could never have imagined, gifting him with a dog, a serious relationship with Grace, and perhaps strangest of all, work colleagues he didn't just like, but regarded as friends.

Not that he hadn't liked work colleagues before, but this was different. There was a depth to everything, to every moment. Harry was reminded, then, of his earlier days in the Dales and of a swim he'd taken in the shimmering chill of Semerwater, a local lake of haunting beauty, its waves constantly lapping the shores with its own tales and myths. He'd felt a change then, too. A shifting of things in his life, as though the water itself had ...

No, Harry thought, don't go overthinking things. Better to just face it all head-on and get those documents signed.

Decision made, Harry drained his coffee, stood up, and headed back to the kitchen table to pick up his pen.

His phone rang. It was Grace.

'If you're phoning to check up on whether I've signed the documents or not—'

'Harry, we've found a body!'

Harry wasn't quite sure he'd heard her correctly.

'Say that again, Grace. You've what?'

'There's a body, Harry, in the woods, where the pens are, but it's not there. I mean, it's just down the path a way, and there's blood, Harry, just everywhere! I couldn't see what it was at first but then, when I got close enough, I saw it and I fell and it doesn't look right because there's this thing, and the leg, I've never seen anything like it—'

Grace's words were tripping over themselves as though

each and every one of them thought they were by far the most important and had to be heard first. Her voice was riven with shocked panic, and Harry could tell she was working hard to keep herself calm.

'Where are you now?'

'Back at the vehicles. I need to get cleaned up ... there's blood just ... Anyway, Dad and Phil are keeping an eye on things while I head back to mine.'

'I need a location, Grace.'

'Meet me at mine.'

'I'll see you there.' Harry went to hang up, but said, 'Are you okay?'

'Yes, I'm fine,' Grace said. 'I know I don't sound it and no doubt at some point it'll hit me, but right now, I'm okay, honestly.'

'You said Phil was there?'

'Dad called him,' Grace explained. 'He was here when I arrived. He's saved you some pie.'

Despite the subject of the call, and Grace's obvious and understandable agitation, Harry laughed.

'I'm on my way.'

Conversation over, Harry put the pen down and was in the hallway heading to the front door, Smudge at his heels. Grabbing a coat, and clipping the dog to a lead, he headed out into night, striding off through Hawes' marketplace to his old RAV4. On the way, he put a call in to his detective sergeant, Matt Dinsdale, who was on duty and hopefully not too far away.

'How do, Boss.'

'You busy?' Harry asked.

'Depends who's asking and why,' Matt replied.

'I'm asking,' Harry said. 'Remember me? Your DCI?'

'Then it's definitely the *why* that's bothering me. What's up?'

'I've just had a call from Grace,' Harry said. 'She's found a body over Carperby way. No idea who it is yet, or what's happened, but she sounds fairly shaken. I'm heading over now. Probably best if there's two of us there, just in case.'

'Where are you?'

'Outside,' Harry said.

'I'll be out in a sec.'

Harry clipped Smudge into his car's backseat and started the engine. Matt arrived and jumped in beside him.

'A body, then,' he said, clipping in his seatbelt. 'How did she find it?'

Harry explained about the phone call from Arthur.

'Could just be an accident,' Matt said, as Harry pulled away, heading out of the marketplace to head down dale.

'The blood is a concern, though,' said Harry.

'Head injuries bleed like crazy,' said Matt. 'I've dealt with a few falls in my time with the Mountain Rescue Team and I'm always amazed by just how much of it can gush out of a crack to the skull.'

'Well, we'll just have to see, won't we?' Harry replied.

The trouble was, Harry had heard something in Grace's voice that had him concerned. There had been a hint of her wanting to say more about what she'd found, and she'd mentioned something about a leg not being right. Yes, someone tripping in a woodland at night could fall badly and snap a bone or two. Harry's gut, however, was telling him that whatever Grace had found wasn't going to be quite that simple.

The journey went by quickly and quietly, Harry driving

just fast enough to have Matt holding on, and Matt offering little in the way of conversation.

When they arrived at Grace's house, Harry knocked and walked straight in, Matt close behind.

'Grace? It's Harry.'

'Of course it is,' came Grace's reply from the kitchen. 'Who else would it be?'

She came out and met them in the small hallway.

Harry noticed immediately just how pale she was. There was no smile on her face, just a wildness in her eyes from what she'd experienced.

'Right, best we get going,' Grace said and made to push past Harry to get to the front door.

Harry didn't budge.

'First, I need you to tell us exactly what it is you found,' he said.

'I can do that on the way.'

'You can also do that sitting in the lounge so DS Dinsdale here can take a few notes.'

'We're wasting time,' Grace said, as Matt waved his little black notebook in the air.

'Lounge,' Harry said, his voice firm. 'Now.' Then he softened his tone and added, 'We just need to know what it is we're dealing with. Always best to have as much detail as we can before we arrive at the scene.'

Grace hesitated, but then Harry saw her shoulders drop and she turned and led the way into the lounge.

Once they were all sitting down, Harry asked Grace to explain what she had found in the woods. He watched as she clasped her hands together, interlocking her fingers, her thumbs fidgeting with each other as though engaged in an impromptu thumb war.

'I headed over because of what Dad had said about that car, remember? He thought it might be a poacher and I figured it was probably just some walkers out for a night-time stroll.'

'Or camping,' said Harry, remembering what Grace had said just before she'd left.

'Not the best night for it, though,' Matt said.

'How do you mean?' Harry asked.

'No stars. You go for a walk at night, you usually do it on a clear night with the moon high and bright. Means you can see where you're going for a start, and you also get to see a place with a completely different view. You should head up Penn Hill on a clear night. Amazing stuff.'

'You're right,' Grace said. 'And to be honest, when I saw the thing, the car I mean, it struck me as a bit odd.'

'How so?' asked Harry.

'Not sure, really, just that it looks like it belongs at the scrapyard. I'm not saying walkers can't have knackered cars, but they usually look like they can at least get you home. And there was nothing in it that suggested it was a walker's, either. No maps or outdoor equipment inside at all.'

Harry looked up at this.

'Inside?'

Grace gave a nod.

'Dad had already tried the doors. The car was open. He said the boot was empty. I just shone a torch through the windows to have a look. I told him he shouldn't be going around opening cars that aren't his.'

'And he's well known for listening to advice, is Arthur,' said Harry.

'What did you do then?' asked Matt.

'Headed off into the woods. We've had a few birds go

missing here and there, and a few farmers I know have said they've seen lights out on their fields.'

'Lamping,' said Matt.

'Soon as they get out there, whoever it is, they've scarpered,' said Grace. 'I've some pens in the woods for a shoot. I wanted to check them over. The birds have been released, but they still come back.'

'And that's when you found the body,' Harry said.

For a moment, Grace didn't respond.

'Grace?' Harry said. 'You okay?'

'There was something on his right leg,' she said.

'He?'

'Definitely a man,' Grace acknowledged. 'I was more than close enough to tell the difference.'

'And how do you mean by there was something on his leg? Like a branch had fallen on him or something, trapping him?'

Grace shook her head.

'No,' she said. 'It definitely wasn't a branch.'

'What was it then?'

For a moment, Grace was quiet, staring into the middle distance. When she turned back to Harry, he saw that her already pale face was now ghostly white, the shock of what she'd seen written in the silent horror hiding deep in her eyes.

'What was it, Grace?' he asked, his voice calm and quiet. 'What did you see?'

When she answered, she spoke with the voice of someone staring in disbelief at images burned into her mind.

'His leg, something had cut it off,' she said. 'Severed it below the knee.'

CHAPTER FIVE

Following Grace's directions, Harry parked up at the end of the lane to see Arthur and Phil leaning against Phil's old long-wheelbase Land Rover. The vehicle had at some point in its life been blue, but the old thing was so beaten and mud-covered that it was hard to tell. The canvas hood covering the rear was grey with age, rather than by design. Harry also noticed a large sprig of what looked like heather stuck in the grill and held on with a twist of wire.

Grabbing a torch and climbing out of his RAV4, Harry headed over to greet the two old men, Matt and Grace coming along behind.

He'd decided to leave Smudge back at Grace's with her dog, Jess. They tolerated each other, and it made more sense than having her along at what Harry was already thinking was a potential crime scene.

Harry nodded at the heather jammed into the front of Phil's Land Rover.

'Drive through the moors to get here, did you, Phil?'

Phil glanced over to where Harry was gesturing.

'Why do you ask?'

'The heather,' Harry said, a little confused now.

'That's not heather,' said Phil.

'It's not?' Harry looked a little closer. 'What is it then?'

'Bog Myrtle,' Phil said. 'It's from the Highlands. Gill gave it to me a while back. Smells wonderful.'

'But why've you stuffed it into the grill?'

'Why not?' Phil said. 'Anyway, I rather like it. Gill does the same, you see, and I'd seen it on his old truck and commented on it and he gave me some.'

'And who's Gill, then?'

'Does a bit of shepherding and other farm work around and about,' said Arthur.

'And he helps me and Dad a bit, too, with our work,' Grace added.

'Part-time gamekeeper as well, then, is he?'

Grace gave a nod.

'He helped us build the pens up in the woods. Bit of a perfectionist, but there's nowt wrong with that.'

Phil frowned then and scratched his head.

'Something the matter?' Harry asked.

Phil looked up and stared at Harry.

'I thought I remembered something just then,' Phil said, 'with you mentioning Gill.'

'I didn't, you did,' Harry said. 'I'd never heard of him until you mentioned him.'

Phil shrugged.

'Well, whatever it was, it's gone.' He tapped his skull. 'Like a sieve these days. Sometimes I swear I can hear things land on the ground after falling out of my head.'

'Well, I hope it wasn't important.'

Arthur laughed.

'And what's so funny?' Phil asked.

'Nowt at all,' Arthur said, then smiled at Harry and rolled his eyes just enough. Clearly, Phil had a reputation.

Harry decided to extricate himself from whatever conversation this was and get them all back on track.

'Grace told me what she found,' he said. 'I'm assuming you can both confirm it?'

Arthur stepped a little closer to Harry and leaned in, staring at him.

'You're not suggesting she's lying, are you?'

'Of course I'm not,' Harry said, his voice jumping a few decibels. 'It's simply a fact that the more witness testimonies we have, the better. And if your own stories corroborate Grace's, then we have a good starting point, haven't we?'

Matt said, 'What say you both have a quick chat with me here, while Harry and Grace head into the woods? Just so we have all the details down, okay? How does that sound?'

'Well, if you think it will help,' Phil said.

'It will,' said Harry, then looked at Grace. 'You good to show me where everything is?'

'Probably not, but I can't have you tramping through there not knowing where you're going, can I?' she said. 'No telling what damage you'd cause.'

'Plenty,' said Arthur, but Harry saw the flicker of a grin on his face.

'I'll have a look at the car as well,' Matt said. 'Might save us a bit of time.'

Leaving Matt with Arthur and Phil, Harry stepped back to allow Grace to take the lead. He followed her away from the vehicles and through a roughly made narrow gate in the wall.

'Made this myself,' Grace said as she clambered through first.

'Better than anything I could do,' Harry said. He was very good at breaking things, but actually building something? Not a strength. Though, he'd not really ever had the opportunity. Flatpack furniture was as far as he had ever got.

On the other side of the gate, the woodland closed in almost immediately, the gloomy murkiness of the night replaced by a thick, impenetrable darkness pulled in close by the trees. Grace flicked on her torch, and Harry did the same. At once, shadows danced in front of them, the torch beams chasing them from tree to tree. The air was heavy, Harry noticed, rich with the perfume of the natural world folding itself into the next season, leaving summer behind and embracing autumn.

Harry had always loved woodland, and even though the reason for them being there right then was terrible, he couldn't help but appreciate the place.

The thin track they followed threaded its way through the trees in a relaxed meander, bending left and right as it navigated around trees both young and ancient. He heard scuffles and calls of animals invisible to them as they strode on, watching them warily, no doubt. The ground was a mottled blanket of numerous browns, roots breaking the surface to plunge again into the earth, the mulch of leaf and bark and twig now welcoming the greens of fresher falls from the quiet, swaying limbs above.

A call from Grace broke Harry from his almost meditative state and he saw she had come to a dead stop.

'Everything okay?' he asked when he reached her.

'It's just ahead,' she said. 'The body, I mean. Just beyond that old oak tree.'

Harry lifted the beam of his torch to show the way forward.

'You stay here, then,' he said, and pulled some white, disposable covers for his shoes and a pair of gloves from a pocket. 'There's no need for you to see it all again.'

'If you're sure ...'

Harry's answer was to move slowly off towards where Grace had pointed. The tree she had mentioned was another ten metres or so, and as he approached it, he saw nothing untoward ahead, no sign of the violence Grace had described. Then, as he followed the path around the trunk of the old tree, the bright light of his torch came to rest on a scene so alien to the surroundings that Harry paused, just to allow himself a moment to take it all in.

The body was lying on its back, lifeless eyes staring up into the canopy of the trees. Whoever he was or had been, he was wearing dark clothes. That would explain how Grace had not seen him before she was almost on him, Harry thought. He had only spotted the body himself because he'd known exactly where it was; it would be easy to simply mistake the shape for yet more of the woodland's cunning tricks played with shadow and leaf.

Edging closer, though maintaining enough distance so as to cause as little disturbance to the scene as possible, Harry saw how the ground around the lower part of the body shimmered, the wetness of the blood lost from the terrible wound he was now unable to pull his gaze from.

Harry remembered what Grace had said, about how something had cut the leg right off below the knee. That description was scant on detail and did nothing to communicate the true horror of what had taken place.

Going no further, Harry rested the beam of his torch on

the awful wound which had taken this man's life in such a violently catastrophic way.

The large metal jaw of a man trap, glistening with blood, was clamped below the man's right knee. To Harry it looked like the giant, fleshless, bony jaws of some prehistoric creature had thrust itself out of the ground, like a shark bursting through the surface of the sea to take a fatal bite. He could see the bottom part of the leg, trapped in the jaws, the blade having cut through not only beneath the knee, but right through the foot as well, the shoe it was wearing providing no protection at all to the mean teeth.

From the way the body was lying in relation to the section of the leg in the trap, Harry guessed that the man had tried to pull himself free. He could only imagine the pain that he had felt, the panic taking hold as the body, through a catastrophic loss of blood, went into shock. There was a bag close by and it looked to Harry as though the man had dragged it over in his last moments, though he didn't know why.

There was a temptation to move nearer to the body for a closer look, to collect evidence, clues about what had happened and why, but Harry held off. He'd seen plenty of strange things in his time, the most bizarre deaths imaginable, but this was a new one for him. He wasn't about to risk contaminating what was clearly a crime scene. He had to make a call.

Walking back to the vehicles, Harry said little to Grace other than to assure her that there was nothing she could have done and that calling him had been the right thing to do.

Leaving the woodland, Harry headed over to Matt.

Grace walked over to stand with Phil and Arthur, who were leaning up against Phil's Land Rover, chatting away.

'Well?' Matt asked. 'What have we got?'

'You wouldn't believe me if I told you,' Harry said.

'I believe everything you say and never question it,' said Matt. 'Except all that rubbish when you first turned up in the Dales about not liking cheese.'

'That wasn't rubbish.'

'You just needed persuading, that was all.'

'You wore me down.'

'Gently.'

'Well, we have a body,' Harry said, moving on from one of Matt's favourite subjects. 'Leg caught in what looks to me like a man trap. Cut it off just below the knee. Blood loss would've been fatal.'

'Did you say a man trap?'

Harry heard the disbelief in Matt's voice.

'I did,' he said, pulling out his phone.

'But why the hell would there be one of those out here? It's not the eighteen-hundreds, is it?'

'Not the last time I checked, no,' Harry said, and having flicked through his contacts, lifted his phone to his ear.

'I'll give the rest of the team a call,' said Matt.

Harry nodded his agreement as his call was answered.

'Sowerby.'

'It's Grimm,' Harry said.

He heard a sigh.

'I'll get my gear,' she said. 'And tell Mum.'

CHAPTER SIX

Rebecca Sowerby was standing in the kitchen and stuffed her phone back into her pocket. She was very aware that the evening had left its youth far behind, and that she was now encouraging it to embrace old age with the help of a large gin and tonic.

Well, that had been the plan anyway, but she'd only just poured herself the drink and it was now going to go to waste. Which was a shame, because the gin itself was a new one on her and one of the best she had ever tried in her life.

She'd never really been into the explosion of people making small-batch gins in their kitchens and sheds, seeing it as little more than a fad. This one, though, from down in Exmoor, was too good to waste. Well, if she wasn't going to be able to drink it now, then the very least she could do was save it for later, but not as a drink.

In a trick she'd stolen from her mum, she opened the freezer and poured the liquid into the empty spaces in an ice tray. It made complete sense really: gin and tonic ice cubes for gin and tonic. She wondered why more people didn't do it.

'Mum?'

'Have you poured me that gin and tonic, yet?'

The voice called through from another part of the house, loud and clear enough, Rebecca thought, to probably be heard outside.

'That was Harry.'

'What was?'

'My phone.'

Rebecca heard footsteps and a moment later her mum, Margaret Shaw, strode into the kitchen. She was smaller than Rebecca, but somewhat sturdier-built. Sometimes, when Rebecca watched her out in the rather substantial vegetable garden at the back of the house, she reminded her of a general commanding his troops. She would bark orders at the plants, commanding them to grow and produce a good harvest, marching around armed with a garden fork and a pair of secateurs, giving weeds no quarter in the battle.

'So, no gin and tonic, then?'

Rebecca shook her head.

'And I'm assuming by the look on your face that our presence is required?'

'I'm afraid so.'

'That man treats us like we're a package deal,' Margaret said with a smile.

'He'd be hard-pushed to find a better one,' said Rebecca. 'He's over in Carperby, so not exactly far. I reckon it's best if we head down and have a look first before I actually call it in.'

Margaret cocked her head to one side and frowned.

'So, is Bennett a full member of the team now, or just standing in while another is on extended sick leave?'

Rebecca shook her head. The man her mum was referring to could rub everyone he worked with up the wrong way, even Harry's DS, Matt Dinsdale, and that was one hell of an achievement.

'Bennett's just covering the position,' she said. 'If he was made permanent, I think I'd have to replace the whole team. Or leave myself. Perhaps both.'

'Try not to let him get to you,' Margaret said. 'And if that doesn't work? We can always dispose of him, can't we? It's not like we wouldn't know what we were doing, is it? And we would do a very fine job of covering our tracks. No one would suspect a thing.'

'Or care,' Rebecca said. 'You good to go?'

Margaret looked herself up and down.

'I'm wearing my dressing gown,' she said.

'Harry wouldn't mind.'

'I would.'

Margaret turned and left the kitchen.

Rebecca, once again alone, saw her empty glass on the table, shrugged, then headed off to get herself ready for whatever it was Harry had waiting for her down the road.

BACK AT THE WOODLAND, Grace had borrowed her dad's Land Rover and headed back to her house to grab some supplies. Harry had said it wasn't necessary, but she'd insisted and, encouraged by Matt and both her dad and Phil, had then returned with a couple of flasks of tea and a decent slab of cake.

'Made this one myself,' Arthur said, as Grace handed Harry a slice.

'He's a better baker than me,' said Grace. 'I never say no when he turns up with something fresh out of the oven and still warm in a tin.'

Harry took a bite, only to be interrupted by the sound of an approaching engine. Then headlights flooded the area, and a car pulled up. Pathologist Rebecca Sowerby was at the wheel, her mother in the passenger seat beside her. He walked over to meet them.

Sowerby lowered her window.

'So, was this all a ruse just to have us come over and join in a picnic?'

'Is that one of Arthur's?' Margaret asked, leaning over her daughter.

'It is,' Harry replied, cake in hand. 'Though you'd better hurry if you want some. Matt and cake are rarely seen in the same place at the same time, if you know what I mean.'

Sowerby opened her door and climbed out, and her mother did the same.

'Where's the body, then?'

Harry pointed into the trees.

'About a ten-minute walk through there. I'll take you as soon as you're ready.'

'When are we ever anything else?' Margaret said as she came to stand with them.

'How's Grace?' Rebecca asked.

'She's okay,' Harry said. 'The shock from what she found seems to have eased, anyway. We have the rest of the team heading over, so they should start arriving soon enough.'

Harry saw Sowerby's jaw harden just a little.

'You're that confident this is a crime scene?'

'I think you need to see it for yourself,' Harry said. 'But yes, I am.'

Rebecca walked to the back of her car. When she returned, she was wearing the all-over white PPE of her trade and had a bag hung from her shoulder.

'Come on then,' she said. 'Lead the way.'

Heading back into the woodland, Harry was acutely aware of what awaited them at the end of their short walk. He had deliberately said little to Sowerby because he wanted her to take it all in firsthand. This was her speciality, and it was best to just let her get on with it.

Just before the old oak tree, Harry pulled them to a halt, as Grace had done with him earlier.

'It's just ahead,' he said. 'It's not a pretty sight, either.'

'It never is,' Sowerby replied. 'I'll have a quick look at what we're dealing with, then call in the team. I'll have Mum do her district surgeon bit and confirm death, so she can head off home.'

'By then, the rest of my lot should be here, too,' Harry said. 'Matt will sort them out, put on a scene guard, the usual.'

'What about cordoning all this off?' Sowerby asked.

Harry pulled a roll of tape from his pocket.

'Never go anywhere without it. I'll get on with that while you head on.'

Sowerby walked on and Harry unrolled the end of the tape, tying the end to a branch. He then swung out wide, looping the tape from tree to tree, until he'd come full circle, the body and the man trap in its centre. With that done, he headed back over to join the pathologist. She was crouching a short distance away from the body.

'Quite something, isn't it?' Harry said.

'Why do you think he was here in the first place?' Sowerby asked.

'Grace's dad was out here to check on her pheasant pens,' Harry explained. 'There's been some poaching apparently, not that they've kept us abreast of it.'

At this, Sowerby looked up. She was wearing a facemask, but her eyes were all she needed to communicate her surprise.

'I know,' Harry said. 'But ignoring that, if he was here poaching, then someone really didn't want him to be.'

'Which puts us all in a bit of a quandary, doesn't it?' Sowerby said.

'How's that, then?'

'Who else comes up here to check on the pens other than Grace and her dad?'

'You're not suggesting they're suspects.'

Sowerby stood up.

'I'm not suggesting anything, just saying what I see.' She pointed at the body. 'Whoever this was, if they were out here poaching, and if that man trap was put down as a deterrent, then—'

'Then nothing,' Harry said, his voice snapping at Sowerby's suggestion like a crocodile lunging at its prey. 'Grace didn't do this.'

'Of course she didn't!' said Sowerby. 'We both know that. But someone did and with where it's placed, anyone could've walked into it.'

'I don't think this woodland is public access,' Harry said.

'Not sure that makes much difference to some. Mum has people walk through her garden all the time thinking they can just go anywhere because they're on holiday.'

'And I'm sure she's very happy to inform them otherwise.'

'You could say that, yes.'

Sowerby came over to stand with Harry.

'I've tried to call this in, but there's no signal, so I'll do it when we get out of the woods to fetch Mum.'

'It's pretty obvious he's dead,' Harry said. 'Quite the way to go, isn't it?'

'He wouldn't have lasted long, so that's some small mercy. Oh, and I found this ...'

Sowerby opened her hand. In her palm, inside a small, plastic evidence bag, Harry saw a small steel ball.

'Looks like a ball bearing,' he said.

'Looks a bit knocked about,' Sowerby said. 'Smells of engine oil, too. Any idea what it would be doing out here?'

'Not the foggiest,' Harry said. 'Anything else?'

Sowerby stowed away the steel ball.

'This,' she said, and this time brought out something Harry wouldn't have guessed at in a million years.

'That's—'

'A rolling pin,' Sowerby said.

And Harry, for once, could think of nothing to say.

CHAPTER SEVEN

'THAT'S A ROLLING PIN,' SAID MATT, STARING AT A PHOTO on Harry's phone.

'It is,' Harry replied.

'And you found that up in the woods?'

'Sowerby found it lying next to the body. Think it must've spilled from his bag.'

'But it's a rolling pin,' Matt repeated. 'I mean, that's what it is, isn't it? A bloody rolling pin!'

'It wasn't the cause of death, either,' Harry said. 'And I've seen just how much damage one of these can do in the hands of someone who means business.'

'So, what on earth was it doing out there?'

'Right now, I have no idea.'

Matt was thoughtful for a moment. 'Well, I don't think it's because whoever that is out there was on his way to Cockett's to sort out pastry for tomorrow's pies.'

'As assumptions go, I think I'll allow that one,' said Harry.

Police Constable Jadyn Okri had arrived and was already

set up as scene guard, patiently waiting at the end of the lane for the forensics vans to arrive. Liz was obviously otherwise engaged with helping Ben move in, which left Detective Constable Jenny Blades, PCSO Jim Metcalf, and Detective Inspector Gordanian Haig. However, with things as they were, Harry had told Matt to leave the rest of the team as they were; there were enough people on-site now to manage it. A late night spent standing around not doing much, except perhaps patrolling a perimeter on the off-chance of bumping into someone taking a night-time stroll, was pointless. He would need everyone fresh over the next few days as the investigation took hold.

Sowerby had headed back into the woods with her mum, who, as district surgeon, had the job of signing off on the fact that the person in the man trap was officially dead. Everyone knew it was a formality, but having everything done properly was vital. Harry had been involved in investigations before where errors and missteps early on had led to an entire case falling apart later in court. Following procedure may have made him want to smash his head into a brick wall on more than one occasion, but he understood the importance of it.

'A rolling pin,' Matt said again, clearly unable to move on from just how incongruous the object was under the circumstances, and shaking his head as though trying to dislodge the thought from his mind.

'What about the car?' Harry asked, if only to make Matt think about something else.

'Well, the reason it looks like it belongs on a scrap heap is because that's exactly where it should be.'

'How do you mean?'

'All I can find linked to that number plate is a certificate of destruction from two months ago,' Matt said. 'I put a call through and all they could give me was the address of a scrap dealer over Richmond way.' He handed Harry the address. 'Only, as you can see, the car was clearly given a stay of execution by someone.'

'Could be that's who we found in the woods.'

'No way we can know, really,' Matt said. 'We can send someone over to check in the morning with the scrap dealer. Also, I had a quick nosy around on the inside, but nothing stands out. Maybe forensics will find something.'

Then, as if the mention of the word worked like some magical summoning, Harry saw two large, white vans and a car roll along the lane towards Jadyn, who held up a not entirely necessary hand to bring them to a halt in front of him. Jadyn directed them where to park and then, while the driver of the first van spoke to Jadyn, a figure climbed out of the passenger side and was joined by the driver of the car.

'Ah, bollocks,' Harry grumbled when he realised who they were.

One was the photographer, Simon Parks, a man with what struck Harry as a little too much enthusiasm for his job. The other had the kind of personality that repelled him like an opposing magnet, his bald head glinting in the headlights from the vans.

Matt narrowed his eyes and leaned forward as though trying to get a better look at who it was.

'It can't be.'

'It bloody well is.'

'Then I find myself with no option but to support what you just said,' said Matt. 'Bollocks indeed, with a generous dusting of *ah, shite*.'

After Jadyn waved them through, the two men came to stand in front of Harry and Matt.

'Good evening,' said the bald man, while the photographer wrestled with his bags of kit.

'Oh, now, I wouldn't go saying that,' said Matt.

The photographer laughed unexpectedly and rather loudly at this, and the three other men all swept their eyes round to stare at him.

Harry then watched the man he'd spoken to go to say something, but decided to jump in first before he had the chance.

'Didn't know you were still on the team,' he said. 'Not now that Sowerby's back.'

Sowerby had been away from work for a good while due to injuries sustained during a previous investigation. The pathologist now in front of them, a man Harry found to be one of the most noxious individuals he'd ever had the displeasure of working with, was a certain Dr Ian Bennett, who had filled in for her in the meantime. Harry had assumed Sowerby's return would have sent Bennett scurrying on his way back to whatever little hole he lived in.

'Unfortunately, another member of the team has taken ill,' Bennett said. 'I stepped in. You know me, always willing to help.'

Harry wasn't convinced that was true at all. With Bennett, there always seemed to be an ulterior motive to whatever help he was providing, that generally being his own advancement or comfort, and he had a habit of expecting others to buy him provisions, which hadn't exactly gone down well with the team.

'Of course,' Harry said, as convincingly as he could.

'And Sowerby certainly needs the support at the moment, as I'm sure you both understand.'

'No, I'm not sure that I do. Looks to me like she's fully

recovered and firing on all cylinders. Wouldn't you agree, Detective Sergeant?'

'I would indeed,' Matt said.

'And where is she, if you don't mind my asking?'

'At the crime scene with the district surgeon,' Harry answered.

'I'll head up straight away then,' the photographer said. 'Where am I going?'

Harry directed the man to the gate.

'Just follow the path on the other side.'

As Simon walked off, Bennett said, 'I'll head up there myself, too, actually. I'm sure there's been too much waiting around already.'

He turned to leave, but Harry caught the hook in the oily man's last comment.

'Not sure what you mean by that,' he said. 'There's certainly been no delay on our part.'

'No, of course, of course,' said Bennett.

'And I doubt very much if Sowerby's been late for anything in her life, do you, Boss?' said Matt.

Harry shook his head, but his eyes were on Bennett.

Then, with the kind of smile a murderous rattlesnake would be proud of, the man turned away and headed off to where the two forensics vans were now parked.

'You know,' Matt said, 'that man is possibly the easiest person to not like that I've ever met in my life. It's effortless, isn't it?'

'It's a talent, I think,' said Harry.

'Not one that would get you on the telly, though.'

Matt checked his watch.

'It's getting late,' he said. 'Or early, depending on how you want to look at it.'

'I was going to send Jim out to knock on a few doors when he arrived,' Harry said. 'But like I said, we don't need anyone else here for this, and I think all of that can wait till morning. No one wants someone in uniform knocking on their door at this hour, do they?'

'No, you're right,' agreed Matt. 'That happens, you just know it's bad news. Always. So, what do you want to be on with next?'

Harry looked around and his eyes fell on Grace, who was still standing with her dad and Phil.

'Liaise with the forensics team,' he said. 'They'll want a wider area cordoned off, I should think, and just keep your ears and eyes open for anything they find. I know we'll get the report from Sowerby soon enough, but as we're already into tomorrow, we'll be waiting another whole day at least for that and the photographs. And I'd rather be cracking on with this as soon as we can.'

'What do you think this actually is?' Matt asked. 'What the hell's been going on for someone to use a man trap? And where the hell did they get it in the first place?'

'Right now, I've not the foggiest idea about any of it,' Harry said, then nodded over at the two white vans. 'Just let me know if you learn anything from that lot, okay?'

With a nod of acknowledgement from Matt, Harry then wandered over to Grace.

'I think you can all head home,' he said as he came to stand in front of the small group. He looked then at Arthur. 'You were right to be suspicious, though, that's for sure.'

Arthur, Harry noticed, puffed his chest out a little at this.

'You hear that?' he said, looking over at Grace.

Grace shook her head and glanced up at Harry.

'Please, don't encourage him.'

'If you need a deputy, you just let me know,' said Arthur, sending the sharpest of winks at Harry.

Harry laughed.

'This isn't the Wild West, Arthur,' he said.

At this, Phil said, 'You know, someone once said I looked a bit like Clint Eastwood.'

Ignoring him, Grace asked, 'Do you think whoever that is in there was out here poaching, then?'

'I should be asking you that,' Harry said. 'But right now, we don't know what we're dealing with. Which reminds me, who else, other than you and your dad, has access?'

'The landowner,' Grace said.

'The farmer, you mean?' Harry asked.

'That's not what I said. He's my employer. And other than that, no one, really.'

Harry heard both Arthur and Phil let out clear huffs of contempt.

'Something the matter?'

'Like Grace just implied, he's no farmer,' Phil said.

'How so?'

'Oh, he owns the farm, right enough,' Arthur said, 'but that's about as far as his involvement in the land goes.'

'Why's that, then?'

'Haven't a clue. Soon as he arrived, he rented out every acre to pasture and employed Grace here to set up a shoot on the land.'

'Sounds expensive,' said Harry.

'Oh, it is,' said Grace. 'I'm probably the cheapest part of the whole operation in some ways. Gamekeeping isn't exactly something you get into for the money.'

'Money isn't everything.'

'I think he'd disagree.'

'So, who is he, then?' Harry asked.

'Vince Walker, that's who,' said Arthur. 'Moved here after winning the lottery, would you believe? Or at least that's what he tells everyone. It's not like it's something you can check up on, is it? He's certainly rich, anyway. And that kind of money, with that kind of man, is never going to be a good thing, you mark my words.'

'I'm getting the impression you don't like him,' said Harry.

Arthur looked thoughtful for a moment.

'To be honest, I don't know him well enough to say either way,' he said. 'But you know how it is with some people. How there's just something about them that you just don't like, even though you've only ever really seen them driving around, or down at the supermarket. He's like that.'

'He is,' Phil said. 'Worse, maybe. I wouldn't put any of this past him.'

Harry remembered then what Matt had said about Bennett. Still, he didn't want anything to colour his judgement before meeting Walker. He glanced then at Grace.

'You work for him,' he said. 'What do you think?'

Grace shook her head.

'He's not a fan of people trespassing, that's for sure,' she said. 'He's had me putting up dozens of Private Property signs all over the place. And there are footpaths all over his land that he's doing his best to get redirected if he can.'

'Any reason?'

'Yes,' said Phil. 'He's a rich bastard who thinks he's better than everyone else.'

Harry didn't respond, just waited for Grace to speak again.

'It's just the way he is, I think,' Grace said. 'As far as he's concerned, he owns it, so no one else should be allowed on it without his say-so.'

'And I'm guessing his say-so is to either be on the shoot you've set up for him or one of the farmers renting out the land.'

'That's about it, yes. And anyway, he'd never come down here to do something like this. Doubt he even knows where it is.'

'You have his address?'

'I'll send it to you,' Grace said, but then a look of concern flashed across her face. 'You're not thinking of going round now, are you? I mean, it's the middle of the night. He won't like that at all.'

Harry shook his head.

'Don't worry, I'll leave it till tomorrow. Gives me something to look forward to.' He pointed down the lane. 'Now, you three head home.'

Grace smiled.

'You're not the boss of me.'

'No, you're right there, I'm not,' Harry said. 'But I am a detective chief inspector and right now you're standing around making my crime scene look very untidy. So, if you don't mind buggering off, it would be very much appreciated.'

'You always talk so sweetly,' Grace said, and reached up to gently squeeze Harry's arm. 'I'll see you later, then?'

'You will,' Harry said, then stepped back and watched Grace climb into her dad's old Land Rover and then head home.

CHAPTER EIGHT

As Harry waved them off, a familiar voice called his name. He turned around to see Margaret Shaw striding over to him, powering forward as though wading through deep grass.

'For someone who clearly enjoys giving the same first impression as a battle-scarred Rottweiler with a bad temper, you're actually a bit of a soft bugger at heart, aren't you?'

Harry ignored the comment.

'So, what do you think?'

'About you and Grace? You've seen Beauty and the Beast, I assume?'

'No.'

'Oh,' said Margaret. 'Why not?'

'Why would I have?'

'Fair point,' Margaret said with a shrug. 'Anyway, that's what I think.'

'And it was very interesting, I'm sure. Now, what about the crime scene?'

'In a word, bizarre. Never seen anything like it in my life.

Actually, that's not quite true.' Margaret paused, her thoughts causing her to frown. When she spoke again, the frown had gone, replaced by an urgency to unload the story she'd managed to drag up from somewhere deep in her memory. 'There was this one idiot who'd decided the best thing to do with his weekends and evenings was to spend a good deal of his free time in his garage making a sword.'

'You're kidding.'

'It was still jammed hard in his leg when the ambulance brought him in.'

Harry shook his head in disbelief.

'Really?'

'When it was finished, he decided that the best thing to do was to head out into his garden and give it a test run against a tree that had spent a few too many years looking at him a bit funny.' Margaret mimed giving a sword a good old swing in mid-air. 'The blade hit a particularly hard knot in the tree, bounced back and sliced right into his leg. It cut straight through his fibula, then came to a stop by embedding itself at the top of his tibia. It may not sound it, but he was lucky.'

'Ouch.'

'Just a bit. Managed to save the leg, so that was something. Police confiscated the sword, thankfully. That chap in there, though?' She gestured over her shoulder with a thumb at the woodland. 'He didn't have a chance with that man trap.'

'Well, that was the point of them, I guess,' Harry said.

Margaret, Harry noticed, didn't look so sure.

'I've seen vintage ones before,' she continued. 'The jaws have teeth, but they're designed to maim, aren't they? To trap someone so that they can be caught and prosecuted.'

'And the one here is different?'

Margaret nodded.

'You'll have to speak with Rebecca about it, but the jaws on it are razor-sharp. They went through that poor sod's leg like the proverbial hot knife through butter. I'm surprised the shock alone didn't kill him within seconds of it happening.'

'Hell of a price to pay for poaching.'

'Hell of a way to exact it from him, if you ask me,' said Margaret. 'Anyway, Rebecca asked me to say that you might want to head up there and give her a hand with things.'

Harry paused at this. There was a tone to Margaret's voice that was saying more than her words were on their own.

'Bennett?'

'Bennett,' Margaret said, then leaned in a little too obviously. 'I've already suggested to her that between the two of us, she and I could probably ... No, we absolutely could, get away with murder. Now, if you were able to lend a hand ...'

'My guess is you'd have to get in line,' said Harry.

Margaret laughed.

'True enough, I'm sure.'

Conversation over, Margaret headed off, leaving Harry to take a stroll back into the woods. On the way, he stopped to check on Jadyn. He was, as ever, immaculately turned out.

'So, how are things over here?' Harry asked.

'Quiet,' PC Okri said. 'Not much for me to do right now other than stand around and make sure we don't have anyone turn up who shouldn't.'

'It's an important job,' said Harry.

'Forensics doesn't seem to think so. Weren't at all happy when I stopped them to sign in. Said I could just check them in afterwards, but that's not how you want me to do it, is it?'

'You're doing your job, that's all,' Harry said. 'Not everyone will appreciate it.'

'So, what's happening, then? I know there's a body, but that's all, really.'

Harry gave Jadyn a very brief run-through of what he knew so far.

'Poaching seems like a lot of effort for not much reward,' Jadyn said, once Harry had finished. 'Dangerous, too, by the sound of it. Poor bloke.'

'You'd be surprised.'

'How?'

'Poaching isn't always a case of just one for the pot,' Harry said. 'There are people out there who take that approach for sure, but there are plenty of others who do it for the sheer hell of it. No thought given to anyone else, the landowners, those who make a living from shooting game, even the danger of it all.'

'Like with the sheep rustling that happened at Jim's?'

Harry gave a nod.

'Where there's money to be made, you'll find organised crime gangs. With poaching, all they have to do is send a few lads out in a couple of vans, all armed with air rifles, and they can easily bag hundreds of birds and a good few rabbits in a night. Sell it all the following morning, and they've made some quick money and had a bit of fun in the process. And there's not really much risk; it's not like the police are out patrolling the countryside, is it?'

'So, you think that's what this is, then?' Jadyn asked.

'Between you, me, and the devil himself? I bloody well hope not,' Harry said, and with that, he turned away from the constable and headed back into the woods, his thoughts as dark as they were private.

Arriving at the crime scene, Harry was met by the photographer coming the other way. Behind him, the crime scene itself was floodlit, courtesy of several bright directional lights placed on poles.

'That's me done,' he said. 'Fascinating one this, isn't it?'

'Horrifying, if you ask me,' said Harry.

'That too, yes. Can't imagine the kind of person who'd do a thing like this, can you?'

'Yes,' Harry said. 'I can. And that's the problem.'

Harry pushed on past the photographer to where the body was now hidden from view by a white tent. Various people busied themselves around the site, all dressed from head to toe in white PPE. There was an otherworldly feel to what was going on, Harry thought. For a moment, the scene put him in mind of a cheap re-enactment of the discovery of an alien artefact or some other such nonsense, the kind of television programme he'd found himself staring at in disbelief on more than one occasion after late nights on the job.

One of the white-clad figures waved to him. He waved back and headed over, relieved when he arrived to find that it was Sowerby, not Bennett.

'How's it going?' Harry asked.

'Do you mean what have we found, or have I managed to resist the urge to throttle a certain Dr Ian Bennett?'

'Both.'

'So so,' Sowerby said, holding a flat hand out in front of her and wiggling it.

Harry smiled, folded his arms, and stared at the tent.

'What've we got, then?'

'Over here,' Sowerby directed, and led Harry over to where various bits of evidence had been collected in labelled evidence bags. She removed her facemask now that they were a distance away from the crime scene itself.

'You don't usually show me anything until you're done,' said Harry, wondering what it was he was looking at.

'You're a distraction,' Sowerby said. 'Also, Bennett won't like it, so ...'

'Your mum said something about the man trap,' Harry said.

'Yes, it's been sharpened. Razor's edge on the thing. With the power of the spring on it, his leg didn't stand a chance. Died in minutes of massive blood loss.'

'Someone sharpened it, then? Anybody could've put their foot in it, even a kid!'

Harry's voice was barely able to hide his anger as it threatened to boil over. What the hell was wrong with people?

'Not so sure about that,' Sowerby said.

'What?'

'From how the trap is positioned on the victim's leg, it doesn't look like he stepped on it. More like his leg was dropped in there on purpose.'

'But it's a man trap,' he said, confused. 'The whole point of it is that you hide it under some leaves and some poor bastard who you don't want taking your pheasants steps in it and WHAM!' Harry clapped his hands together to emphasise the horror of having the jaws slam shut. The sound of his hands crashing into each other was louder than Harry had expected in the quiet stillness of the woodland. He saw some of the forensics team staring at him.

Sowerby crouched down and pointed to just below Harry's knee.

'And if that's what had happened, we would expect the

jaws of the device to have bitten here with its front teeth, if that makes sense.'

'It does,' Harry said. 'But that's not what this is, then?'

Sowerby shook her head.

'The jaws have cut through his leg here and here.' She pointed again at just below Harry's knee, but also at his foot. 'So we think he was lying on the ground, on his back, when the man trap was triggered.'

'But that doesn't make any sense at all.'

'No, it doesn't, does it? Because you don't just lie on the ground and drop your leg into something like that. Add the fact that we've found no evidence to suggest that the device had been hidden in the first place—'

'How do you mean?'

'It's clean,' Sowerby said. 'If it had been buried, it would be covered in everything we're standing on; mud and leaf mould, that kind of thing. And if it had been out for any amount of time, there would be evidence of weathering, corrosion. But there's none of that. It's as though it was brought out here tonight specifically to do this.' She pointed over to where the awful event had taken place.

Harry frowned and rubbed his forehead.

'You know what you're suggesting, don't you?' Harry said.

'Yes, I do,' Sowerby replied. 'But why don't you say it for the both of us?'

Harry really didn't want to, because if he did, then it meant that whatever dark hole this killing was pulling them into was darker and more frightening than either of them could have imagined.

'Someone did this to him,' Harry said. 'Came out here, caught him—'

'And dropped his leg into the trap,' said Sowerby, finishing what he was going to say.

'Bloody hell.'

'Figured you might say that. Also, we found this ...'

Sowerby reached for one of the bags. Inside, Harry saw a phone.

CHAPTER NINE

'IT'S FULLY CHARGED, STILL UNLOCKED,' SAID SOWERBY.

'He was going to make a call?'

'My guess is he was probably attempting to call for help, but ...'

'As soon as that man trap had him, he had seconds left,' Harry said. 'By the time he'd pulled it out of a pocket, he was probably already dead.'

He held up the bag for a closer look. The phone had a small screen and actual buttons to press, rather than a large touchscreen.

'Don't see many like that now, do you?' said Sowerby.

'In this line of work, more than you'd expect,' answered Harry. 'Looks like a burner, though it could be a pay-as-you-go. Anyway, something like this, it's usually used by someone who either hasn't got much cash or doesn't want to use something else for privacy reasons. Or both. Has anyone checked it yet?'

Sowerby shook her head.

'No. At this stage, we just bag and tag everything.'

Harry checked the phone's most recent calls. As far as he could tell, there were only two numbers on the phone, and one had been used and answered that same evening. He looked at Sowerby, hit the little green telephone button to make the call, and lifted the phone, still in the bag, to his ear.

'What the hell are you doing?'

'Following my gut,' Harry said as the phone rang.

'And it knows what it's doing?'

Harry shrugged. 'Sometimes.'

The ringing stopped.

Sowerby mouthed, 'Someone answered?'

Harry gave a nod, waiting to hear a voice, but there was nothing.

'Hello?' he said.

The line went dead.

'Who was it?'

'Someone who didn't want to speak to me,' Harry said, pulled up the other number, and dialled it.

'Your gut is a persistent bit of biology, isn't it?'

Harry said nothing, just waited. At last, the dial tone cut, and Harry heard a female voice at the other end of the call, desperation in every word.

'Luca? Where are you? What's happened?'

Harry decided to just go with it.

'Hello? Luca asked me to call you.' He heard a gasp, then the line went dead.

'Hung up on you?'

'I'm used to it,' Harry said. 'But that was a female voice. And she used a name. Luca.'

'Luca? That's not a British name,' Sowerby said.

'No, it isn't. And her voice, it sounded Eastern European, but that's all I can say about it at the moment.'

'At least you have a name.'

'Only a first name, though,' Harry said. 'And whoever that is, they clearly didn't want to speak to me. She sounded scared. Terrified actually.'

'Doubt they were expecting you on the other end of the call.'

'No, what I mean is there was more to it than that,' said Harry, but decided to say no more on the matter for now. 'I just don't know what.'

'What about the first number?'

'Didn't even speak,' said Harry. 'Didn't even hear a breath. But this is a priority,' he added, holding up the phone. 'If there's anything your team can get me on those numbers tomorrow—'

A cough interrupted the moment.

Harry turned from Sowerby to see Bennett in the shadow of a nearby tree. How the man had managed to remain hidden, despite being dressed entirely in white, was beyond him.

'What?' said Sowerby, her voice switching from inquisitive to a sharp crocodile's snap.

'I've called an ambulance for the body,' Bennett said.

'Of course you have,' said Sowerby. 'But why are you telling me?'

Harry realised immediately that Bennett had not come over to share that news at all. The man was staring at the evidence bag in Harry's hand.

'The evidence,' Bennett said, now looking at Harry. 'This all needs to be examined first, to be run through the normal procedures, before you're allowed to handle it.'

For the moment, Harry kept a hold of the bag.

'You know you're absolutely right,' he said, doing his utmost to sound contrite. 'My sincere apologies.'

Surprise lit a small fire behind Bennett's eyes.

'Oh ... yes, well. That's good. No harm done.'

'I'm sure you have a lot of evidence from a crime scene like this,' Harry said.

'An awful lot, yes,' Bennett replied.

'Then we're lucky to have someone as organised as you to look after it, aren't we?'

Harry saw the man's chest puff out a little, like a strangely proud pigeon. If pigeons were slimy, wee bastards dressed in PPE.

'The details are important.'

Harry wasn't sure if it was really this easy to hook Bennett in like a fat, lazy carp, but he ran with it anyway, just to see.

'Some weird stuff with this one, though, isn't there?' he said. 'I mean, how do you log it all? What do you call things?'

'We call them what they are,' Bennett said. 'As clearly as we can. I mean, there's the rolling pin, and that's very clearly what it is. But some things take a bit of thinking.'

'Such as?'

'Well, the slingshot, obviously,' Bennett said.

'You mean catapult,' Harry said. 'If you're going to call things what they are, then use the correct name.'

'Well, I call them slingshots.'

Harry looked at Sowerby.

'What do you think?'

'Explains the ball bearing we found, doesn't it?' she said.

'It does, but it doesn't go any way at all to explaining why someone was killed for carrying one.'

Before Bennett could say anything else, Harry handed

him the phone and and added, 'Well, I don't want to keep you any more from your work.'

With a slight look of confusion on his face, Bennett trudged back to the crime scene.

'He's like a really bad smell,' Sowerby said. 'Even when he's not near you, it's almost like you can just sense him.'

'How long is he staying on the team?'

'Too long.' Sowerby sighed. 'Actually, it's only a couple of weeks, but that seems like an absolute age.'

'I'd best leave you to get on,' Harry said.

Sowerby yawned.

'I'll do my best to get at least a few details over to you tomorrow,' she said. 'Not the full autopsy, though. That will probably be the day after.'

'Well, anything will be helpful,' Harry said. 'And it'll give Jadyn something to write on the board.'

Sowerby smiled at that, then she pulled her facemask back over her mouth and headed back over to the white tent.

When Harry arrived back where all the vehicles were parked, he was greeted by a white-faced Matt who had panic in his eyes.

'I was just about to come up and see you,' the DS said.

'What's wrong?' Harry asked. 'What's happened?'

'Joan just rang,' Matt said. 'Mary has been having some breathing problems lately.'

'You never said.'

Matt wasn't listening, and he was moving from foot to foot, unable to stay still.

'Joan ... She called me as the ambulance arrived.'

'What?'

'They're on their way to hospital now. It's probably nothing, I know.'

'Get in your car, right now,' Harry said, cutting in. 'And none of your bollocks about everything probably being fine.'

'It probably is, though,' said Matt.

Harry shushed the DS with a raised finger.

'Move! Now!' Harry said and handed him the keys to his RAV4.

Matt hesitated, but not enough for Harry to have to give him a boot up the arse, and turned and ran. As he was about to climb in behind the wheel, he paused and shouted over, 'But how will you get home?'

Harry said nothing, just stared, then pointed at the lane.

Matt climbed in and headed off. Harry pulled out his phone and made a call.

'Hi, it's me,' he said when the call connected, and that was enough.

CHAPTER TEN

When everything was finally done in the woodland, the body removed, the forensics team having taken everything they could from the site for testing, Harry's arrival at Grace's had been considerably closer to his normal waking time than he'd either expected or desired. But he'd managed to get his head down for a few hours more.

With Matt still at the hospital with Joan and their daughter, he had sent Jadyn home with clear instructions that he would not be needed the following day and should get his head down. That he didn't listen to his own advice wasn't lost on him. Or on Grace.

'You do know you're impossible, don't you?' she said, standing in the doorway, as Harry left her house just after eleven that morning.

Jim had popped over to pick him up and was waiting outside. He'd also passed the message round for a meeting at midday and for everyone, bar Jadyn and Matt, to be there.

'You've barely had four hours' sleep. It's not enough. Gordy can manage without you. They all can.'

'I'll be fine,' Harry said, realising then that Smudge was still standing behind Grace.

He understood where Grace was coming from, and he wasn't quite sure how to deal with someone genuinely caring for his wellbeing. So, he dealt with it in the only way he knew how. He ignored it.

Grace, however, was clearly not about to give up.

'Shall we ask your blood pressure about that?'

'There's nothing wrong with my blood pressure.'

'Yet.'

Harry walked over to Jim's vehicle and climbed in. Fly was lying in the back and greeted him with two gentle thumps of his tail against the seat. Harry offered Grace a wave. She returned it, though added a shake of her head, then closed her front door.

'Smudge not coming, then?'

'I'm beginning to think she prefers Grace's company.'

'Fair enough,' Jim said, then realising exactly what he'd said, and to whom, immediately started to apologise. 'Oh God, that's not what I meant, I was just ...'

Harry laughed.

'No, it is fair enough,' Harry said, then pointed at his own face. 'I mean, you've seen this, right?'

Jim said nothing and pulled away from Grace's house to drive them up the dale to the community centre in Hawes.

Sitting quietly in the passenger seat, Harry saw how what was left of the morning laid out before him was everything autumn should ever be, only more so. The fells seemed to stretch themselves out to the horizon, great slumbering giants of quiet beauty keeping watch over the lives played out at their feet. Their deep green slopes were bathed in mottled sunlight breaking through clouds as light and white as freshly whipped meringue.

With the window down, Harry allowed himself a moment to enjoy the breeze, drinking in the scents whipped up in it. He wondered if this view was one that he could ever tire of. Such a thing didn't seem possible.

Every day was different, every season, the weather working as the most gifted artist's brush to paint the Dales afresh with such relentless and vivid brilliance he'd given up trying to find the words to describe it. Instead, he just allowed himself a moment, the fresh air on his damaged skin, his eyes soaring over this ancient vista like a hawk riding the thermals.

'—you okay?'

Harry caught Jim's voice, but not what he was saying.

'What was that?'

'You drifted off there for a moment,' laughed Jim. 'I thought you were asleep.'

'Grace thinks I probably should be,' Harry said, a yawn cracking through his words. 'But we have things to be getting on with, haven't we? If I need a nap, I'll nip to the flat later this afternoon and get my head down.'

'I can drop you there first if you want, like?'

'No, we have a meeting to be had,' Harry said. 'One where we have to somehow manage without Jadyn doing the boards.'

'Don't see how we will,' Jim said, smiling to himself.

A part of Harry wondered if there was a little bit of truth in that.

Arriving in Hawes, Jim parked them up in the market-place. Plenty of folk were milling about, he noticed. Hawes constantly proving that despite its size, and its somewhat isolated location, it was a place full of life. It managed to support a good number of independent shops, pubs, and businesses, not only during the tourist season, but throughout the year, and was a vital hub and a lifeline for many who lived in the Dales. Harry's mind drifted to the documents still unsigned in his flat, but he didn't have time to think about that now.

Walking into their small office in the community centre, an expectant team greeted Harry and Jim, with Fly to heel. They all knew enough about what had happened the night before for the information to be fuelling their discussions already. Harry noticed that a clean board was front and centre. Also, DC Jenny Blades was fiddling with a pack of drywipe pens, ready to spring into action in Jadyn's absence.

Detective Inspector Gordanian Haig walked over to meet him. She presented him with a steaming pint mug of tea.

'Hello there, Mr Sleepy Head,' she said, her soft Highlands accent making her words almost sound like musical notes.

'Morning, Gordy.'

'My guess is you very much need that,' she said, as Harry took the mug, narrowly avoiding scalding himself with it. 'There's a tin of flapjack on the table over there,' she added, gesturing behind her. 'Anna made it a couple of days ago, so it's had time to mature. You'll love it. Assuming your body lives through the massive sugar rush, that is.'

Harry took the mug, then walked over to the flapjack and took a slice. His eyes widened at the first bite.

'What the hell is in this?'

'She refuses to give me the recipe,' Gordy said with a shrug. 'It's not exactly a traditional recipe, that's for sure, seeing as its rammed full of raisins, cashews, and chunks of chocolate, but I do know that she doesn't just use golden syrup to sweeten it, but some honey as well that she has sent to her from friends over in Wales.'

'It's ...'

Harry was lost for words.

'It's the only flapjack I've ever had that I can taste behind my eyes, if you know what I mean.' Gordy laughed. 'And I grew up on my mum's tablet, so I know what I'm talking about, trust me. But then she was a woman who grew up on eggy bread dipped in sugar. There's a lesson there, I think.'

Harry knew exactly what she meant, though perhaps not about the eggy bread, took another bite, then washed it down with a glug of tea.

'Just so you know, Jadyn rang in just before you arrived,' Gordy said.

'He's supposed to be asleep.'

'Well, he sounded like he still was.'

'He's not coming in, is he? Because if he does—'

'No, he's not.' The soft Highlands lilt of Gordy's voice hardened as she spoke, and was enough for Harry to know that she'd made sure of that. 'Any news from Matt?'

'None that I've heard,' Harry said. 'But then I've not been up that long. No messages on my phone, though.'

'Must be a real worry for them.'

'No doubt.'

There was little else either of them could say on the matter, so Harry took another mouthful of tea and made his way to the board. Jen was there, along with Liz.

'How's Ben settling in, then?' he asked, looking at Liz.

'Too early to tell,' Liz said through a yawn, which Harry thought was born of more than just moving boxes.

'Well, he's house-trained, so that's something.'

Liz laughed and headed off to wash her mug in the sink. When she was far enough away, Jen leaned in and spoke in hushed tones.

'It's the first time she's lived with anyone, you know that, right?'

'What?'

'Seriously,' Jen said. 'She's had a few boyfriends, but Ben seems to have got under her skin.'

'Sounds painful.'

'Anything heart-based usually is.'

'On that, how's Steve?'

Jen's laugh was bright and warm.

'Keen to meet you again,' she said through a smile put there by more than a little mischief.

Harry remembered the first and only time he'd met Steve, having stumbled in on a set-up that had struck him as not too far removed from owning a pet dinosaur. He'd popped around to Jen's to pick up some stuff to drop to her in hospital after she'd been the victim of a hit-and-run while on duty, only to find himself in the presence of Jen's huge and somewhat lazy monitor lizard. The creature had defined the term "lounge lizard," with Harry finding it relaxing on the detective constable's couch.

'I'm sure he is,' Harry said. 'You ready, then?'

'Just say the word,' said Jen.

Harry finished off what was left of Anna's flapjack, put down his mug, then turned to the rest of the team. Before he even had a chance to gather them around, they all stopped what they were doing, the chatter died, and they took their seats.

'You see the power you have?' said Gordy, with a smile.

Harry looked at the team in front of him.

'First of all, I know it's almost lunchtime, so we'll get through this as quick as we can. That way, we can all head off and grab food on the way. Hope that suits.'

The team all gave approving nods and murmurs.

'You all know what Matt, Jadyn, and I were on with last night,' he began, 'But I'll go over it again just so as we're all clear.'

Harry then quickly described what Grace had discovered, and the actions taken since, including the surprise arrival of a certain Dr Bennett.

'I mention that only because I think it's fair that you're all pre-warned. He's not the easiest to deal with, even less so if it comes as a complete surprise. So, pre-warned is pre-armed.'

'So, this is a murder, then?' Jim asked.

Harry paused before answering.

'Even if the trap was left there to maim, with no specific individual as the target, it's hard to see it being regarded as anything else,' he said, his words unrushed and heavy. 'This is clearly a situation where someone was killed by a person, or persons, who set out to cause either death or serious injury by what they did. There's just no getting away from the fact that the device, the man trap, is lethal.'

'If this is about poaching, could they not argue it was there to catch animals?' asked Liz.

'You mean to try and reduce the charge because they'd put out a trap capable of cutting a deer in half?' Harry asked. 'Not a bloody chance of it.' He then remembered something Sowerby had said to him about the wounds the victim had suffered. 'The victim didn't sustain the injury by stepping into the man trap by accident. It looks as though his leg was dropped into it on purpose, while he was lying on the ground. Which leads me to think that this is all about poaching. However,' Harry continued, 'that doesn't mean we have a local farmer or whatever meting out their own form of justice. We need to stay open-minded.'

For a moment, no one spoke.

'A man trap, though,' Gordy said, breaking the silence and shaking her head. 'There's dealing with poachers, and then there's that.'

'Some would say they have it coming,' Jim said.

Harry snapped round at this and stared at the PCSO.

'You mind explaining that statement to the rest of us, PCSO Metcalf?'

Harry watched as Jim squirmed a little in his seat, clearly caught out by Harry's question. Perhaps he'd rounded on him a little too quickly. Then again, it was good to keep them all on their toes, and he wasn't about to let a throw-away comment like that slip by.

'Sorry, that came out wrong,' said Jim, his tone clearly apologetic, but with a hardened edge that spoke of something else. Personal experience, perhaps? Harry wondered. 'What I meant was that poachers, well, let's just say that there's farmers all across the Dales who've had run-ins with them, and they can be proper bastards. The poachers, I mean, not the farmers. Though, to be honest, the same could be said of some of them, too, that's for sure.'

'Go on,' Harry said, wondering now if perhaps Jim's farming background would provide a different take on what had happened.

'I'm not on about the few who take a rabbit here and there,' Jim said. 'That's still not right, not by any means, but the others, though. That's where the problem is.'

'You're talking from experience, then?' said Harry, who was well aware that Jim and his Dad had been the victim of sheep rustlers last year. That they'd also had run-ins with poachers was news to him, though.

Jim gave a nod.

Just as he'd expected, Harry thought.

'Dad doesn't have a shoot on his land. Don't think he can be arsed with it all. He does shoot, though. Everyone does.'

'Get to the point, Jim,' Harry said.

He knew just how popular shooting was in the Dales, and that included the members of his team, too.

'It was a few years ago,' Jim explained. 'Dad was out in some of the top fields, up by the Roman Road, you see, and he saw some lights, like, and went to investigate. Something like that is usually a lost walker, though how anyone gets lost up there is anyone's guess. Anyway, he heads off to investigate and finds there's a gang of blokes, their four-by-fours all parked up, and Dad sees that the back of one of them is just full of what they've been shooting. Not just rabbits either, but a deer as well. There's even a buzzard in there, though God knows why they killed it, never mind taking it back with them. A trophy or something, maybe.'

Jim paused, the memory of what he was telling them all clearly harder to relive than he'd realised when he'd started. Harry was about to tell him to stop, when he started up again.

'Dad was livid. I know that because he called home to say what he'd found. I told him not to do anything, but he went over to challenge them anyway. I drove up but by the time I arrived they'd gone. Dad was in a bad way. They'd given him a beating, though I think he gave as good as he got. They'd also shot a sheep, just for the sheer hell of it. Left it next to

Dad just to rub it in that there was nothing he could do about any of it.'

'Did he report it?'

'No,' he said, shrugging. 'Got pretty angry about it when Mum said we should. I think they threatened him as well, if you know what I mean, though he never said as much.'

Harry knew exactly what Jim meant. If you want someone to do something, or to warn them off in the first place, you don't threaten them, you go for the family.

'Well, I'm really sorry to hear that you all went through that,' Harry said.

'I'm only telling you because it's easy to understand why someone might take a harder line with poachers than they should. Though, I'll admit, killing someone with a man trap is beyond anyone I know, that's for sure.'

'Which is why we need to find whoever did this, and quickly,' Harry said. 'Because in my experience, things like this never happen in isolation.'

'How do you mean?' Liz asked.

'They'll feel emboldened,' Harry said. 'If this is someone working alone, they're dangerous. If it's an organised crime gang sending a message to another for trespassing on their territory, then this could easily escalate, and quickly. Either way, if whoever did this thinks they got away with it, then there's every chance—'

'They'll do it again,' Liz said.

'Exactly.'

CHAPTER ELEVEN

HARRY DECIDED TO LEAVE IT THERE AND TO GET cracking on what they would all be on with for the rest of the day. Jen had already jotted a few notes down on the board, but as yet there wasn't much to go on.

'We won't be hearing anything from forensics for a while,' he said. 'Probably not till tomorrow now, seeing as it was a late one. Though knowing what Sowerby's like, she'll probably send something through earlier if she can, or she'll call me.'

'Even more likely with Bennett involved,' said Gordy. 'She'll be working to keep that man out of this as much as possible, that's for sure.'

'Which he won't like,' said Harry. 'But that's not for us to worry about. What we need to do is get cracking with what we've got and see if that leads us anywhere. I'm sure there are a few jobs in the Action Book, but unless it's desperately urgent, this is the priority.'

'That man trap,' Jim said. 'I've been wondering where it could've come from.'

'Not really an everyday item on the high street, that's for sure,' said Gordy.

'Exactly,' Jim agreed. 'But you can still buy them, can't you? Not new ones, obviously, but antique ones.'

'You can?' Harry asked.

Jim gave a nod.

'They're rusty old things usually, but a few scrapes with a wire brush and a bit of black paint and they look okay. If that's what you're into. Never really understood why people buy old farming stuff, like ploughs or pitchforks, and paint them and have them in their garden or hanging on a wall.'

'At what point does a man trap ever look okay hanging on a wall?' Liz asked.

'What I mean is, they're sold for display purposes, aren't they?' Jim said. 'The kind of thing you only ever see in museums and stately homes and houses belonging to people with too much money and not enough sense, that kind of thing.'

'You mean you're allowed to buy and sell those things?' Jen asked.

'What I'm thinking,' Jim said, 'is that someone could buy one and renovate it, couldn't they?

'Or use it as a basis to then build their own,' added Liz.

'That makes some sense, actually,' Harry agreed. 'Sowerby said that the man trap had been sharpened to a razor's edge.'

'Tell you what, then, I'll head over to the auction rooms in Leyburn,' suggested Jim. 'They sell all kinds of crazy stuff over there. And rich folk will buy anything, won't they? Maybe they've had something like that come through in the last few months.'

Harry was impressed with the PCSO's line of thought. He

was also wondering about the landowner, Vince Walker, especially after learning of Phil and Arthur's clear dislike of him.

'That's you sorted, then,' he said. 'And while you're on with that, how about following up on the car found at the scene?'

'You've got an address, you mean?' Liz said.

Harry shook his head.

'Not exactly. Matt checked up on it last night. We've got a hit on a scrap dealer over near Richmond. Might be something we can learn there, you never know. Why don't the two of you go? Safety in numbers and all that.'

'So, what else have we got to play with?'

The question was from Gordy.

'We need to rule out the landowner, a Mr Vince Walker,' Harry said. 'Grace's dad mentioned something about him last night. Doesn't sound like he's too highly thought of, at least not by Arthur and his mate, Phil.'

'In what way?' asked Gordy.

'Sounds like someone with a stack of money who just enjoys spending it. From what I understand, he won the lottery, bought the farm, rented the land out, and then hired Grace to set up a shoot on it.'

'It's an expensive one,' Jim said.

'You know of it?'

'It's been talked about a bit. Costs a grand a day per gun, at least.'

Harry did a double-take at that.

'Seriously? That much money to go shoot a few birds?'

'It's big money if you want it to be,' Jim said. 'But you can imagine the kind of people who go to something like that, can't you?'

'I can indeed,' Harry growled.

'Anyway, that's not even the most expensive. Some grouse shoots up in Scotland are thousands. But that's for oil barons and billionaires, people who spend more on a gun or two than any of us would ever earn in a year.'

'Well, whoever he is, he sounds an absolute delight,' said Gordy.

'Glad to hear you think so,' said Harry. 'Because even though I was thinking of heading there myself, I'm going to send you instead. His name is Vince Walker.'

Gordy laughed.

'Vince? Sounds like a dodgy London gangster from the eighties.'

'You're heading out to inform him about what happened last night, but you're also there to see if he knows anything, trips himself up, that kind of thing. If the shoot is running the kind of numbers Jim just suggested, then I can't imagine someone like Vince being all that happy about poachers buggering it all up.'

'If Grace works for him and runs the shoot, what does she have to say about it?' Gordy asked.

'She seemed to think Mr Walker wouldn't even know where the woodland was, which only makes it even more confusing, doesn't it?'

'It does.'

'That leaves just me, then,' Jen said.

'And me,' said a voice from behind Harry, and he turned round to see DS Dinsdale standing in the doorway.

'Before you say anything,' Matt said, stepping into the room and holding up his hands to calm any chance of a storm, 'yes, I've had some sleep.'

'But I thought you were all still at the hospital?' Harry said.

'Joan and Mary-Anne are, but there's nowt I can do just sitting next to her getting a backache in a chair, is there? So, I headed home and grabbed some shut-eye.'

'And you'll be heading straight back to the hospital,' Harry said. 'I'll hear no arguments either.'

Matt shook his head.

'Everything's okay,' he said. 'Mary is being kept in for observation. Joan has to be there, for obvious reasons, but I'm just a spare part. Much better to have me busy with what you're up to. I'm certainly more useful here.' He shrugged. 'And there's only so many journeys I can make to the vending machine or café.'

Harry still wasn't sure.

'You know my views on family,' he said.

'I went to them last night,' said Matt, 'and now I'm here. So, what do you want me on with? There's that rolling pin for starters, isn't there?'

'Rolling pin?' said Gordy. 'You've been here not even five minutes and you're already thinking about food?'

Harry shook his head.

'No, he means this,' he said, and brought up the photo he'd taken of the object in question. He showed it to Gordy and Jim leaned over for a look.

'That's not a rolling pin, it's a priest,' he said.

'No, it's definitely a rolling pin,' said Matt.

'Yes, I know, but it's been used as a priest, hasn't it?'

Gordy said, 'Assume for a moment that I don't know what a priest is, other than someone who wears a cassock and says Hail Mary a lot. What's that got to do with a rolling pin?'

'A lot, actually,' said Jim. 'It's called a priest because it's for giving last rites.'

Harry knew then what Jim was getting at.

'You mean it's for killing game,' he said. 'Which reminds me of what I was going to mention next. Bennett said that they found what they think could be a catapult at the scene.'

'There you go, then,' said Jim. 'That's your poaching weapon, isn't it? They're surprisingly effective at close range, assuming you've had a bit of practise and aren't just shooting pebbles at tin cans.'

'They found ball bearings at the crime scene as well,' Harry said.

'Sounds like whoever the victim is, they were definitely out there poaching,' said Jim.

'Unless someone planted all of what we've just talked about,' added Liz.

'Sounds a bit elaborate to me, does that,' said Matt. 'Luring someone to a woodland, dropping their leg into a man trap, then surrounding them with the tools of a poacher's trade.' He paused, frowned, then looked over at Harry. 'But how did they do it, then?' he asked.

'Do what?'

'Get the victim's leg into the man trap? You couldn't, unless they were unconscious or subdued in some way.'

Thinking back to what he'd seen in the woodland, Harry agreed.

'You'd struggle, wouldn't you? No way it would just happen,' he said. 'There's clearly much more to this than we can see right now. Forensics will hopefully give us something, once they get back to us with the photographs, report, and autopsy.'

Harry glanced over at the notes Jen had made on the

board, lines connecting bits of information, jobs delegated to the team, though Matt's name, like Jen's, was yet to be put next to anything.

'There was one other thing,' he said then. 'A phone was found with the victim. Unlocked, and with only two numbers stored. A call had been made to one of them earlier in the evening. Obviously, forensics is looking into the two numbers, but I called both.'

'Anyone answer?' Matt asked.

'The first number, the one that had been called, someone answered but hung up before saying anything. The second number was answered by a woman, and she used the name Luca. She sounded worried, too. Accent was Eastern European I think.'

'Girlfriend or wife, maybe?' Gordy suggested.

'Could be,' said Harry.

'Swift won't like that you used the phone before forensics had a look at it,' said Jen.

The name of their Detective Superintendent had Harry clenching his jaw and grinding his teeth.

'My hope is that Sowerby will be able to get me something on those numbers sooner rather than later,' Harry said. 'By which time, what Swift does or doesn't like won't matter, now, will it?'

Harry's phone buzzed in his pocket. When he looked at the screen, he almost swore out loud. He looked over at Gordy.

'You mind taking over and sending everyone on their way?'

'Of course,' Gordy said. 'Everything okay?'

'I'll let you know,' Harry said, and quickly left the office and made his way to the small interview room down the hall.

CHAPTER TWELVE

Matt had lied. Something he rarely did, and yet was surprisingly good at. So much so, even the ever-perceptive Harry had believed him. Yes, Mary was doing fine. And yes, he'd headed home to grab some shut-eye, that much had been true, but sleep he had not. Whether it was due to the amount of caffeine he'd consumed over the past twelve hours, the deep, aching worry for his child, or a dire mix of the two, he wasn't really sure. Regardless, he was wide awake right now, and sitting at home being busy doing nothing wasn't going to help him or anyone else. So, work it was.

With Gordy on her way to speak to the landowner, it had been decided to split up Jim and Liz's tasks, so they were on their way over to the auction house in Leyburn, and he and Jen were now on their way to find out what they could about the car. They had the address of the scrap dealer and that was it.

With Matt doing the driving, Jen had suggested she do a bit of research herself into their destination.

'You know how some places just look dodgy?' she said, staring at her phone.

'How do you mean?' Matt asked, as he took them out of Bainbridge and on towards their destination.

For years he'd fancied living in one of the houses looking out on the village green there, but not only could he not afford it, but he also wondered if it might not be as great as it looked. Bainbridge was a popular place and the green would quickly fill up on a hot day, wild with tourists busy taking photos and covering the place with litter. He'd often thought how that old set of wooden stocks, which had sat in the same place for goodness knew how many hundreds of years, could do with being brought back into use now and again.

'Let's start with the name,' Jen said. 'Karz, spelt with a K and ending with Z, then there's a four, as a number not as a word, and then Kash, again spelt with a K. Karz4Kash.'

'It's just a business name.'

'But why use that K and Z? What were they thinking?'

'Trying to stand out,' Matt suggested.

'Listen to this, then,' Jen continued. 'The company has two straplines; "*It ain't crap, it's scrap!*" And, "*Your crap is our scrap!*"'

Matt laughed.

'I rather like that.'

'Really, do you?' Jen asked, and Matt could see her shaking her head out of the corner of his eye. 'Come on, Matt.'

'It's catchy,' Matt said, and repeated what Jen had said to emphasise the point.

'There's even a picture gallery.'

'For a scrap dealer? It's not like you don't know what a knackered car looks like.'

'All it's filled with are screengrabs of random cars from the internet, most of them badly cropped, out of focus, or pixelated.'

'So, it's a cheap website,' said Matt. 'It's not like their line of business needs something all shiny and clever, is it? Anything else?'

'Ignoring the numerous spelling mistakes littering the site, there's a small *Testimonials* section, too.'

'You mean people have actually reviewed a scrap merchant? What have they said?'

'Prepare yourself,' Jen said, then read from her phone, '"Karz4Kash are friendly and I have recommended them to all of my friends. Amazing!"'

'Well, that's nice, isn't it?'

'No, it isn't,' Jen said. 'It is, as Harry would say, horseshit nonsense. There's just no way it's a legitimate review. Who recommends a scrap dealer to all of their friends? I mean, do all of this person's friends also have cars they all want to scrap? Seriously?'

There was more headshaking as Jen continued to look through the website.

'Is there anything of use, though?' Matt asked. 'Details about the owners, that kind of thing?'

'Not a thing,' Jen said. 'Just an address and a phone number.'

'Mysterious.'

'You say mysterious, I say dodgy.'

For the next few miles, neither Matt nor Jen spoke. Matt was happy to roll along behind the wheel, enjoying the countryside he felt blessed to call home. The imposing bulk of Penn Hill rose from the valley floor, thrusting its flattened summit up to the sky as though trying to keep it up there. A mountain it certainly wasn't, but that did nothing to diminish its grandeur, Matt thought. He then remembered a recent case the team had been involved with, where a severed foot had been found up there by someone out running.

In his time as a member of the Swaledale Mountain Rescue Team, and when just out on the hill for fun, he'd certainly found a few strange things. From garden gnomes and a tennis racket to a full set of the Encyclopaedia Britannica, all stacked neatly on a small bookshelf and sitting at the summit of another of the Dales' fells.

Rumour was that this particular find had been an art installation. Matt, on the other hand, had thought it to be total bollocks having set off to have a look at it with a few friends. They had then quickly dismantled it, worried that the weather could turn and scatter the moors with pages of information about everything from aardvarks to zebras. Art had its place, but that, to Matt's mind, hadn't been it.

'So, how are Joan and the little one?' Jen asked, the question dislodging Matt from his thoughts, which had moved from weird art to the rumbling in his stomach. It was a sound he'd been considering doing something about as they were now driving through Leyburn and lunchtime was drifting by a little too quickly.

'Oh, they're fine,' he said, realising too late that he'd already driven on through the town's marketplace, home of a rather excellent bakery.

'Asthma, right?'

Matt gave a nod. He didn't really want to talk about it, if he was honest. The worry of the previous night was something he was trying to forget.

'What have they said? The doctors, I mean.'

'Not much.'

'It's manageable, though,' Jen said. 'If they get it all sorted, with the right drugs, then—'

'I know!' Matt said, realising too late his reply had been more biting than he'd meant it to be. 'I'm sorry,' he added. 'I didn't mean to—'

'Of course you didn't,' Jen said. 'You're worried, and despite what you said back at the office, you didn't sleep at all, did you?'

Matt shook his head.

'Anyway, all I'm saying is that with asthma, you learn to live with it, to manage it, some even grow out of it. I mean, I didn't, but I'm okay with it now. Have been for years.'

Matt was rather taken aback.

'You have asthma? But you run ultra-marathons.'

Jen smiled.

'I'm like an asthma superhero. No cape, though.'

'That is a shame.'

'I know.'

'Thanks, though,' Matt said.

'For what?'

'Making me feel better about it. As a parent, it's easy to panic.'

'I'm sure,' said Jen. 'There's a fee, mind. You're hungry, right? I heard the lunchtime rumble.'

'I am,' said Matt.

'Then turn round and you can buy us a pasty each. I've got a feeling we'll need a full stomach to deal with Karz4Kash.'

'What makes you say that?'

'Everything,' Jen said. 'But the K and the Z, mainly.'

Matt indicated into a side road, then took them back into Leyburn.

.   .   .

WHILE MATT and Jen were deciding on what to have for a late lunch, Gordy was now winding her way down a recently metalled lane towards a grand-looking house near Carperby.

The first warning she'd had that the person she was about to meet would not be to her liking was the preposterously huge electric gates she'd had to drive through after leaving the main road. The next had been the gilded lions sitting on top of the pillars on either side of the gate. Together they presented an air of rude arrogance, the kind Gordy associated with those whose wealth was dwarfed only by their stupidity and self-centredness. A part of her was not looking forward to meeting the person responsible for the gates. However, as the thrum of the tyres led her on, she knew that there was also a part of her that rubbed its hands together in glee at the prospect, and she found herself grinning a little in anticipation.

About halfway along the lane, she saw a black car approaching. It slowed down, then pulled over just enough to let her by. As she slowed down, Gordy saw the driver's window slip down into the door. Maybe I just caught the owner leaving, she thought, and pulled up alongside.

'Good morning,' she said.

The man in the car turned to face her, a toothy smile beneath black hair and keen eyes.

'You're here to see the owner,' the man said, as though stating a fact.

'I am,' Gordy said.

'You'll find him up at the house. Is there a problem? Has something happened?'

'Just need to ask him a few questions.'

'Whenever the police say they want to ask someone a few questions, there's never anything good behind it, is there?'

Gordy decided to not respond to that. 'And you are?'

'Heading home, actually,' the man said. 'But I'm sure Vince will make you welcome and help you with your enquiries. I do hope he's not in any trouble.'

Gordy wasn't sure if she heard sincerity in the man's tone, or just a very well-rehearsed example of it.

'I'd best get on,' Gordy said.

'Me, too,' the man said, and with that, he pulled away.

Well, that was odd, Gordy thought, but shrugged the chance meeting off and continued on her way. She'd ask Vince who the man was, just so she had his details.

At the end of the lane, Gordy pulled up in front of a house which had, for a good part of its life, obviously been a traditional Yorkshire Dales' building of grey stone and slate. Now, however, it stood seemingly trapped between two large extensions, one comprising mostly of glass on a metal frame, like a giant's greenhouse, the other of wood, all beams and large windows. She had no doubt that the architect had sold the idea to the owner as some attempt at marrying the old and the new and had probably used a phrase like *genuinely unique aesthetic* and charged a fortune for the pleasure.

Climbing out of her vehicle, Gordy stared at the building, unsure whether she liked it or wanted to burn it to the ground. It was that kind of building, one which elicited extreme views in anyone who saw it.

Gordy walked up to the front door to find that it was already open. She reached out to press the doorbell when she heard a growl from somewhere inside. The sound froze her to the spot just long enough for her to see, walking towards her, the largest dog she had ever seen, its jet-black fur giving it an unnecessarily demonic edge. In fact, she was fairly sure she'd seen smaller horses. Not ponies, *horses*. As yet, the creature hadn't bared its teeth, but she didn't want to hang around to see if it would.

Backing slowly away, Gordy returned to her vehicle and climbed in. As she pulled the door to, the dog strode over, sat down on the other side, and stared at her through the window, its eyes shouldering heavy eyebrows. The dog's gigantic mouth dropped open, its tongue lolled out, and a string of drool started to make its slow, stretchy way to the ground.

'Nice doggy, good doggy,' Gordy said, not believing a word of it, convinced that it was now staring at her with hunger in its eyes. She had no idea what kind of dog it was, and right now, she really didn't care.

If there had been any chance of the house's owner making a good impression, that was long gone now. And if he didn't appear soon, Gordy would have no option but to turn around and come back later with reinforcements, perhaps even a suit of armour.

A shout from the house caused the dog to turn from Gordy, then lollop slowly away, its hugely muscled body rippling as it sauntered off. Then it stopped halfway up the path to the front door as its owner came out of the house. A man Gordy couldn't yet see clearly. The dog rose up on its rear legs and rested its paws on the man's shoulders, blocking him from her view entirely. She saw the man's arms reach around the dog, as though hugging a bear. Then the dog flopped back down onto all four of its huge paws and continued onwards, back into the house.

The owner approached, and now that Gordy could see him, in many ways she really wished that she couldn't.

The first thought that came to mind upon seeing him quite literally in the flesh, was that someone had taken a very overweight bear, shaved it, then dressed it in a pair of very tight jeans. And nothing else. Because other than the jeans, the man was naked.

As he closed the distance between himself and Gordy, she saw how the toes on his bare feet looked like cocktail sausages that had been left under the sofa for a few weeks to collect dog hair. The man's belly wasn't so much fat, as it was bloated like a balloon, and Gordy wondered if she tapped it with a spoon, if it would sound hard and hollow like the sound of a drum.

Strangely, and somewhat incongruously, considering the rest of his physique, his arms were well-muscled, as though he knew the meaning of exercise, but only saw the importance of biceps curls. And then there was his head, a great bowling ball of a thing, with a well-crafted beard, the hair so black it was obviously as dyed as that on his head, which was scraped flat with hair product, and skulking there like it was hiding and ready to pounce at any moment. To finish the look off, he was wearing aviator sunglasses and enough gold around his neck and wrists and on his fingers to make Gordy wonder if the Bank of England should check its gold reserves.

The man stood where his dog had been, slowly bent over, braced his hands on his thighs, and stared in at Gordy.

'Private property,' he said, his voice echoing her own accent, but with a considerably harder edge, a thing forged in the crucible of urban landscapes and factories rather than the Highlands. 'So, why don't you just turn around and sod off?'

Gordy dropped her window into the door.

'Mr Walker?'

A frown lowered itself onto the man's face with consummate ease, as though he was pulling on a very comfortable sweater.

'You heard what I just said about this being private property, didn't you?'

'I'm Detective Inspector Gordanian Haig ...'

'Because if you did, then you'll have also heard that little bit at the end about you sodding off.'

Gordy ignored what the man was saying and just continued, as politely as she could.

'I need to come in and discuss something with you, Mr Walker, so before I get out of my car, I need you to ensure that your dog is safely shut away.'

'You takin' the piss out of my accent?'

Gordy could feel her grin starting to give way to a stony grimace.

'Mr Walker ...'

The man took a step back.

'So, you are actually Scottish, then?'

Gordy gave a nod.

'Of course.'

'You're Highlands, though. It's like I can hear those mountains and all that rain, not forgetting those bloody midges. Glasgow myself, born and bred.'

'The dog, please, Mr Walker?' Gordy said.

Walker laughed, but the sound was a mean one, the kind of laugh reserved for finding the comedy in people getting hurt, accidentally or otherwise. Not that she was one for judging a book by its cover, but Mr Walker certainly had an air about him which made Gordy think that quite a large number of people who came into contact with him may well have ended up hurt, and very much on purpose.

Walker whistled and the dog stood up and turned around to pace back towards the house.

'Thor's a big softy,' Walker said, as the dog's rear-end disappeared into the darkness. 'You've no worries there now that I've sent him inside. And he'll stay there ...' He paused just long enough for the silence to become awkward, then added, 'Until I need him.'

Gordy wondered if she was picking up on stuff that wasn't there, but she was pretty sure there was a veiled threat in the way that sentence had ended.

'You going to get out of that car of yours, then?' Walker asked.

Gordy, not wishing to give the man any more control of the situation by thinking she was nervous, opened her door abruptly, forcing him out of the way, and pulled herself out and up to her full height. She wasn't exactly tall, but then it turned out that neither was Mr Walker and, to his very obvious surprise, she was now eye-to-eye with him.

'Can we talk inside, please?' she asked.

'Why? What do you want?'

'I think it's better if you're sitting down, that's all.'

'Sounds serious,' Walker said, narrowing his eyes and leaning in just a little too closely. 'Who sent you?'

'My boss sent me,' she said, and gestured to the house with a hand. 'Please, Mr Walker, if you would be so kind as to lead the way?'

With a huff, Walker turned on his heel, his enormous belly brushing against Gordy as he did so, and walked back down the path into the house. Gordy followed, very aware that somewhere inside, the huge beast, Thor, lurked.

CHAPTER THIRTEEN

With the team on their way with the first stages of their investigation, Harry was now sitting in the small interview room at the community centre, phone to his ear, and trying to take in what he'd just been told.

'You still there, Grimm?'

The voice of Detective Superintendent Graham Swift barked down the phone.

'Yes, I'm still here,' Harry said. 'You said that you're retiring, then.'

'I did and I am.'

'Well, that's good then, sir.'

'And what do you mean by that?'

'I don't mean anything by it,' Harry said, shaking his head even though no one was in the room with him. 'Other than I'm sure that it was a big decision to make, and that you did so for the right reasons.'

'The reasons for the decision are not important right now,' Swift said.

Harry, however, wasn't so sure. When the man delivered

the news, he had heard something behind it. It was as though Swift was hiding something, suggesting to Harry that the decision wasn't simply because the man fancied spending more time in the garden, or actually being able to go on a proper holiday rather than just spending a week or two recovering from the day job. No, there was something else going on, but what, he hadn't the faintest idea. Not yet, anyway. And it wasn't his place to ask; he'd have to wait for that information to be offered.

'So, when will you be leaving?' Harry asked.

'As yet, a date hasn't been set,' Swift said. 'And as soon as it is, I will, of course, inform you.'

'I'm just wondering why you rang, that's all,' Harry said.

Swift waited just a little too long before he replied, arousing Harry's suspicions even further that there was more to it than he was currently being told.

'I'm informing everyone who needs to know, that is all,' Swift said. 'Efficiency is key at times like this. I don't want anything or anyone to be missed.'

'No, I understand that completely,' Harry said. 'Anyway, congratulations, sir. Any plans, then?

'Plans?'

'Retirement is a major life change. All that free time, something you've not had much of after all those years on the force. Just wondering if you've given any thought to what you'll be doing with it.'

'Not right now, no, I haven't,' Swift said, offering nothing else on the matter.

'I'm not really sure what I'll do when I retire,' Harry said. 'I'm so used to working I can't imagine just stopping and having all that time on my hands. I'd have to keep busy, I know that. I'm just not sure at what. Never really been good with hobbies or joining clubs, anything like that.'

'I can assure you,' Swift said, 'that I will have no problem at all in filling my time when I get around to it.'

Harry still wasn't sure why Swift had called. News of retirement, particularly when a date for it starting hadn't even been decided on, was hardly the kind of thing he would have expected the man to call him about. It just didn't make sense.

'Is there anything else, sir?' he asked.

Another moment of silence, then Swift answered.

'What is the team on with?' he asked. 'Anything important?'

'We have a few things to be getting on with, yes,' Harry said. 'I've just sent them out, as it happens.'

'You've sent them out? Has something happened?'

Harry heard an urgency and perhaps even some very uncharacteristic excitement in his boss's voice.

'It has,' he said, then added, in as convincing a tone as he could muster, 'I was planning to call you later today, actually, just to give you an update. But I can do that now, if you wish.'

'Yes, tell me now,' Swift said. But then as Harry went to speak he jumped in again with, 'No, better still, I'll come over tomorrow! Yes, that's what I'll do. Perfect. And in the meantime, if you could send me a quick update when you get a moment, that would be much appreciated.'

'You're coming here?' Harry said, not exactly doing a great job at disguising his surprise. 'Tomorrow?'

'I'll be there first thing,' Swift said. 'Sounds like this is important and you need my help.'

'Does it?'

Harry shook his head and stared at the ceiling as though Swift's imminent arrival was its fault.

'Yes, absolutely.'

'Honestly, sir, we're fine,' Harry said, becoming increasingly confused now by Swift's behaviour. 'If I need you, I promise I'll give you a call.'

'I'll be there at nine sharp.'

'Yes, sir. Of course,' Harry said, but the line was already dead.

Harry gave himself a few seconds of quiet before muttering, 'Bollocks,' under his breath. Then he stood up and went back through to the main office.

The room was empty, the rest of the team now on task. He had a quick look at the board, running through the scant information they'd gathered so far, only to realise that in taking Swift's call, he'd managed to leave himself without a job to do.

Of course, he could take a stroll through town to the flat and sign those documents, maybe catch up on a bit of much-needed sleep, perhaps even get started on the insane amount of paperwork that an investigation always generated, but right now he wasn't really in the mood for any of it. The combination of the investigation and Swift's news would have his mind buzzing for a good while yet. So, when his phone rang once again, he was almost thankful for the interruption. And when he saw who it was, even more so.

'I wasn't expecting to hear from you so soon,' he said, turning away from the board to go and stare out of the window for a moment. Grey clouds were gathering, as though they knew something bad had happened in the dale below.

'Are you busy?' Sowerby asked at the other end of the line.

'You know, I'm not actually. So, in many ways, I'm hoping that your call is about to change all of that.'

'It is,' Sowerby said. 'First off, there's been a delay with the photographs, some software issue or something I think, though I'm not sure, but it's technical and it means we won't be able to get any of that to you quite yet. So, in light of that ...'

'What?'

'I think you should pop over,' Sowerby said.

'Pop over? You do know that your place of work isn't exactly down the road? You're an hour away on a good day.'

'I'll put the kettle on.'

A couple of minutes later Harry was back on the road and once again driving down the Dale, this time for a date with a corpse.

WHEN THEY ARRIVED at the Karz4Kash scrapyard, Matt had a fairly clear idea of what to expect. A yard of cars in various states of decay for sure, probably a guard dog or two wandering around just because that seemed to be the kind of thing such a business would have, if only to add to the sinister air of the place. What he hadn't expected, however, was an archway built from the bodies of four brightly painted 1980s Ford Cortinas.

'Well, you don't see that every day, do you?' he said to Jen, as he slowed down to turn into the yard, rolling through the arch, half convinced it was about to collapse in on them as they did so.

'How do you think it stays up?' Jen asked. 'Those cars don't seem to be held together by anything at all.'

'Probably best to not think about it,' Matt said. 'And ignore that cloud of rust shaking off them if you can.'

On the other side of the arch, he pulled up outside a small Portakabin. The only other vehicle was a white Range Rover Sport—which was very shiny indeed, he noticed—and attached to it was a vehicle trailer carrying an old Vauxhall Astra, the red paintwork of which had weathered to a sort of greyish pink, like a bad steak in a cheap hotel restaurant. Some way off, he spotted a pale blue plastic cabinet faded by the sun, a Portaloo, the kind usually seen at festivals.

Above the Portakabin door, in flashing neon lights, Matt read the words *Karz4Kash*. When he opened the door, there was music playing. He thought he recognised it, but because it was such a blatantly poor version of something very popular, hammered out on a cheap keyboard, he just couldn't place it.

'I'm beginning to feel like we've arrived at the worst theme park in the world,' said Jen, coming to stand next to Matt.

Looking back at the yard, Matt saw that it was laid out very neatly indeed, clear lanes divided by stacks of cars, car parts, and various other piles of rusting metal, the origins of which were not entirely obvious.

'After you, then?' Jen said, nodding at the open door into the Portakabin.

Matt took the hint and walked up a couple of rickety steps and on through the open door. Inside, he was hit immediately by a cocktail of smells all mixed together by someone who clearly had no olfactory sense at all. There were notes of strong coffee, stale sweat and engine grease, alongside overpowering cherry-scented air freshener, dog food, microwave food and, to really make it something super special, off milk.

'Holy crap,' Jen said, her hand going immediately to her nose.

'Yeah, I've smelled better crime scenes,' Matt said.

He looked around the small office to see a tired desk piled high with paper, scant other furniture other than a couple of chairs leaning together like drunks, and a cupboard on which sat a microwave, a kettle, and a toaster. There was also a fridge tucked into the space in the lower part of the cupboard, from which a worrying stain was making its slow progress across the thinly carpeted floor.

As Matt was about to reach into his pocket for some vapour rub for him and Jen to dab under their nostrils, a cough sounded from behind them. He turned to find a woman staring at them from the bottom of the steps. She had a hard face beneath a perm so tight it looked like a burst bag of springs. Her hair, unlike her eyebrows, was the brightest of reds, and she was wearing dungarees. He wanted to say she was in her late fifties, but it was rather hard to tell underneath all the makeup. She opened her mouth and blew out a great cloud of raspberry-flavoured vapour, which momentarily hid her from view.

'It's supposed to be healthier than cigarettes,' the woman said, lifting what looked like a USB stick to her lips. 'I only started so that I'd stop smoking, but it hasn't worked. I'm still on at least ten a day, sometimes more. It's just that I do this too now. What's the point of that?'

She took a deep drag on what Matt could see now was a vape pen and then, as she emitted yet another huge cloud, she walked up the steps and pushed between him and Jen to park herself behind the desk like the captain of a cruise ship.

Staring at them from the chair, she continued to leak vapour from her mouth, and Matt thought she looked rather like a dragon guarding its horde.

'So, how is it I can help you?' the woman asked, as she put down the vape pen and opened a drawer. 'I heard you pull up while I was in the loo. Had a curry last night. Can't say that it agreed with me. I wouldn't go in there for a while, if you know what I mean.'

'We're from the police. My name is Detective Sergeant Dinsdale,' Matt said, showing his ID and doing his best to move on from the image the woman had just painted. 'And this is Detective Constable Blades.' But then his voice caught in his throat as the woman pulled from the desk drawer a packet of cigarettes and a small handgun.

'Is that right?' she said, pointing the handgun directly at Matt, and pulling the trigger.

CHAPTER FOURTEEN

WHEN JIM ARRIVED AT THE AUCTION ROOMS IN Leyburn in his old Land Rover, Fly clipped in next to him with his head sticking out of the window to enjoy the many scents swimming in the breeze, Liz was already waiting for him. It wasn't that she'd gone hugely fast on her motorbike, more that any race against an old Land Rover was usually already won before it had even begun.

'You took your time,' Liz said, as Jim clambered out.

Behind him, Fly settled down for a nap.

'Hard to do anything else in this old thing,' Jim said, strolling over to her. 'Anyway, it's nice to not rush everywhere.'

'I didn't rush. The roads were clear and here I am.'

'And what have you done with those spare few minutes while you waited?' Jim asked.

'This,' Liz said, and revealed a couple of brown paper bags sitting on the seat of her motorbike. 'It's lunchtime, if you hadn't noticed. Hungry?'

She handed one of the bags to Jim. He opened it and pulled out a large, filled roll.

'Nowt special, I know,' Liz said. 'But you can't beat a cheese and onion roll with salad.' She reached into a pocket and handed over a bottle of water.

Tucking in, Jim looked around the car park of the auction rooms. There were a few cars parked here and there, but what drew his eye was how the most expensive one there, a very shiny red Porsche, was parked across two spaces.

'I know we're PCSOs,' he said, 'but sometimes, I feel that bad parking should be an arrestable offence. Or at the very least a fine.'

'Private car park, so not really our business,' Liz said, devouring her roll. 'And yes, we are PCSOs, but we end up doing more than most, don't we?'

'True,' Jim said, walking over to a badly parked car. 'But just look at it! Who parks like that? And why? I just don't understand it.'

Liz laughed.

'The car park's empty,' she said. 'It doesn't really matter, does it?'

'It's the principle of the thing, though, don't you think?'

'I do,' Liz said. 'But right now, I think we've got other things to be on with.'

Giving the car a final look of disgust, Jim turned back to Liz and asked how things had gone with Ben moving in.

'He's got two boxes of Lego,' she said, shaking her head.

'Really? That's Awesome!'

Liz groaned.

'Not you too.'

'I'll have to come round!'

Liz narrowed her eyes.

'I'm not sure whether you're being serious or not.'

'Oh, I'm being serious,' said Jim. 'We could do a Lego evening. Get some takeaway and a few beers in.'

'You don't think it's a bit odd, then, that he has it, a grown man?'

'Just because we grow old doesn't mean we have to grow up.'

Liz laughed at that.

'Can't argue with that, can I?'

Jim saw a man wearing jeans and a dark brown leather jacket walk out of the auction room. He walked straight over to the Porsche and climbed in. When he started the engine, the roar of it barged its way across the car park like a pack of invisible lions chasing their prey.

'Now that sounds fantastic,' said Liz, as the Porsche reversed, then sped out of the car park.

Jim watched the car as it headed off into the day, away from whatever the driver had been interested in inside the auction rooms. Probably something hugely expensive and of very bad taste, he thought. Not that he had any real idea of what constituted good or bad taste. Fashion, of any sort, had never really been his thing.

'Come on then,' said Liz, scrunching up her paper bag and stuffing it in a pocket. 'Let's get on with it.'

Jim quickly checked on Fly, then fell in beside Liz as they walked into the auction rooms.

Inside, and once through the lobby, they found themselves in a large hall filled with row upon row of items ready to be sold later in the day. A number of people were milling around, checking things over, measuring them, and jotting notes. Jim saw furniture and paintings, odd bits of refurbished farm implements, and glass cabinets filled with taxidermy. Against one wall stood a number of fireplaces, a horse brass display, a collection of flags, and some old leather luggage and travelling trunks.

In some ways, Jim had always found rooms like this to be rather sad. These items all had tales to tell. They had been owned by various people over the years, loved and cherished, and were now simply waiting to be reduced to nothing more than a list price, before being whisked off to who knew where. Everything in front of him brought with it the invisible baggage of memories lost and forgotten, and the worst thing that could happen to any of it was proudly displayed in one corner.

Jim led the way and stopped in front of various items that to him made no sense at all. There were lamps made out of everything from a pair of old football boots to whisky bottles, bits of an engine, and even a food mixer. He saw coat racks for the wall where the hooks were simply bent bits of cutlery screwed into a plank. What had once been the table for an old sewing machine was now bright purple and being advertised as 'a unique incidental table'.

'Upcycling,' Jim said, shaking his head. 'I mean, would you?'

'Would I what?' said Liz.

'Buy any of this? It's just junk bought from a house sale for a song, given a lick of paint and then sold for—' Jim's voice stuck in his throat as he saw the price of the purple sewing table. 'Holy crap, that's crazy!'

'Far too much?' Liz said, finishing off what Jim had originally been about to say.

'Now then,' said a voice, pulling Jim out of his shock.

Jim turned to find himself facing a tall, slim man with a goatee and a warm smile, dressed in moleskin trousers and a checked shirt. His brogues, Jim noticed, were polished to a mirror finish.

Jim introduced himself and Liz.

'Don't get many visits from the police,' the man said. 'Which is probably a good thing, right enough. I'm Rob, by the way. Rob Sharp. I'm assuming you're not just here to browse?'

Jim laughed a little too quickly at the question.

'No,' he said. 'Not right now, anyway.'

'Pity really,' Rob said. 'We've some cracking lots today. Always worth throwing a bid in. Some stuff goes for a song, but other stuff, well, it's hard to believe sometimes what folk'll pay for something, isn't it?'

Jim's eyes were once again drawn to the purple sewing table.

'You're not wrong,' he said.

Rob laughed.

'Not for you, then?'

'Can't really see how it's for anyone, if I'm honest.'

'Horses for courses,' said Rob. 'It's not for me, either, like, but it would be a bit dull if we all liked the same things, wouldn't it? I've always had a leaning towards vintage weapons, that kind of thing. And a bit of taxidermy. No idea why, can't explain it. I just like it.'

Jim remembered then a case a while back where some taxidermy owls had been used to hide cameras in plain sight.

'Well, we're not here for stuffed animals,' he said.

Liz then asked, 'Do you ever sell things like man traps?'

Straight out with it, then, Jim thought. Well done, Liz. Never one for mincing your words.

'You'll be wanting the vintage farm implements section,' Rob said. 'Come on, I'll take you there myself.'

Rob didn't wait, and instead just turned on his heel and headed off towards a side door.

Jim followed, with Liz behind, Rob setting up quite the pace as they snaked their way through row upon row of furniture and ornaments and goodness knew what else in the main auction room and on into a smaller, pokier side space. This area was full of lovely vintage furniture, all old tables and huge wardrobes.

'Lovely stuff this, isn't it?' Rob said, pausing for a moment. 'Brown furniture, though, it's really fallen out of fashion, so it's as cheap as you want. Mad really. You can buy something handmade and a few centuries old, a real work of art if you ask me, for bugger all. Makes no sense, does it, that this stuff costs less than some flatpack crap that'll fall apart in a year or two.'

From the furniture room, they headed through a small corridor and then came to another room, this one filled with everything from pitchforks and stone planters, to battered feeding troughs, old wood-and-brass tools, and even a small section of vintage kitchen items.

'Up there,' Rob said, pointing at the wall.

Jim looked up and saw, hanging from a number of hooks on the wall, various traps of different sizes, all in varying states of decrepitude.

'We don't get as many in as we once did,' Rob said. 'I don't think people like them as much as they used to, though why they did in the first place is anyone's guess, isn't it? Hardly works of art, are they? Anyway, those are mole traps, obviously, over on the left there, then we move on to the larger gin traps for foxes and whatnot, and then, right at the end, we've the larger types.'

'Bloody hell,' Liz said, looking at where Rob was pointing. 'They're horrific.'

'You're not wrong there,' Rob agreed. 'Had a bear trap in once, and that thing was terrifying. Massive it was. Hard to imagine anything like that would be put to use.'

'They're all absolutely terrifying,' said Liz.

'Which is why most traps are now banned,' said Rob. 'Obviously, mole traps are still in use, but the rest? You get caught with one of these and there's no hole or well deep enough that you should be thrown down. Not as far as I'm concerned, anyway.'

'So, why do you sell them?' asked Jim.

Jim had noticed that at the end of the line of traps was an empty hook and wondered what it had contained.

'Well, the mole traps, they can still be used, so we kind of just move them on, really,' Rob explained. 'The rest? They're little more than museum pieces, aren't they? None of them are usable anymore, that's for sure. Too rusted or corroded. Some are even welded shut so that they can't be used again, like with old firearms being deactivated. Same thing, I suppose. Even had a poacher's gun in once.'

'You mean like a folding 410 to shove down your trousers out of sight?' Jim asked.

Rob shook his head.

'We've one of those coming in tomorrow actually, but no, not like that; this thing was crazy. Basically, it was a blunderbuss on a swivel spike. You'd set it in the ground with tripwires. If you were unfortunate enough to pull one of them, the gun would swing round in your direction and fire.'

'Seriously?'

Rob gave a nod.

'Anyway,' he said, 'why are the police interested in these, then?'

Jim saw the unasked question in Rob's eyes.

'Not for catching poachers or anyone else, in case that's what you were thinking,' he said.

'Then what?'

Jim knew he couldn't say much about the case.

'Just part of an investigation,' he said. 'Wondered if you'd have access to anything like a man trap, for example, or anything similar that might have been sold over the past few months.'

'Well, we've not sold one in over a year, I know that for a fact,' Rob said.

'You remember it, then?' Liz asked.

'Not as such, no,' Rob said, then pointed up at the empty hook Jim had noticed. 'We had one up there, and that was a man trap. I wasn't here the day it was sold. All I know is that it was a rusty old thing, no use to anyone, but someone bought it anyway. God knows why. Takes all sorts, doesn't it?'

'Is there any way you can look back and find us the details of the purchaser?'

'Don't see why not,' Rob said. 'Might take a while, mind. Busy day today.'

'How long?'

'Well, we've got an auction on this afternoon, but I can have a look after that, no bother. You're based over in Hawes, right? I can give you a call and let you know if I find anything or not. Either way, it's no bother.'

'That would be really helpful,' Jim said. 'Thank you.'

Rob then led Jim and Liz back outside.

'If there's anything else I can help with, you just let me know,' Rob said. 'I'll be in touch later, as promised.'

With Rob heading back inside, Jim thought back to what they had seen on the wall.

'So,' Liz said, 'that empty hook, then.'

'Exactly what I was thinking,' said Jim, but noticed Liz was shaking her head. 'Something up?'

'Who'd be daft enough to buy a man trap from somewhere like here, then use it just down the road? The paper trail is too easy to follow, isn't it? I mean, if you're a criminal and you want a gun, you're not going to buy one legally, are you? It's the same with this.'

'Well, it's the best we can do for now,' Jim said.

He was about to jump back into his Land Rover when his phone buzzed. It was Harry.

'Yes, Boss?'

'I'm just over with Sowerby,' Harry said. 'There's a missed call on my phone. Wondered if you and Liz could deal with it once you're done at the auction rooms.'

'No problem,' Jim said. 'We've just finished. What is it?'

'More of a who,' Harry said. 'Phil Thwaite.'

'Arthur's mate? What does he want, then?'

'Not a clue,' Harry said. 'Must've got my number from Grace. Didn't leave much of a message other than to give him a call. But I reckon my two favourite PCSOs could head over and have a natter with him.'

'Your two favourite PCSOs?' said Jim. 'We're your only two PCSOs.'

'Exactly.'

Jim shook his head, a smile in his voice as he asked Harry to send Phil Thwaite's number through.

'I'll do that now,' Harry said, then hung up.

'So, what are we on with now, then?' she asked.

'Phil Thwaite left a message with Harry to give him a call. But Harry is over with Sowerby and has asked us, his two favourite PCSOs I might add, to do it.'

'But we're his only—'

Jim held up a hand.

'I know,' he said, then quickly called the number Harry had given him. When the short conversation was over, he stowed his phone and gave Liz the address.

'I'll see you there, then,' she said.

And with that, she was on her bike and off before he'd even had a chance to get behind the Land Rover's wheel.

CHAPTER FIFTEEN

Harry put his phone away and looked up to see Sowerby waiting for him outside one of the many doors which lead into the labyrinthine corridors of the hospital.

'Thanks for coming over,' she said.

'Oh, I'm always happy to pop over for a good old nosy around a morgue,' Harry said. 'The sights, the smells ... Really makes my day.'

'It's not as bad as people think.'

'Oh, it is. And you'll have to work hard to convince most of them otherwise.'

Sowerby did a good impression of looking deep in thought, then asked, 'Will biscuits help?'

'Biscuits always help.' Harry said. 'Unless all you've got is those bloody awful pink wafer things. Those are definitely not biscuits.'

Sowerby laughed.

'No pink wafers, I'm afraid. Plenty of Chocolate Bourbons, though, and some Custard Creams, a Ginger Biscuit or two, and an unopened packet of Rich Tea.'

Harry grinned.

'Now you're talking. Bloody love a Rich Tea.'

Following Sowerby into the building, he immediately noticed the air change to something sharp and clinical, the smell attacking his nose and raking at the back of his throat.

Sowerby led him down several corridors, executing various sharp turns without warning, clearly on autopilot, until, after a number of heavy doors and various sets of stairs had been negotiated, they strode into the reception area of the mortuary itself. It sat on the ground floor at the rear of the hospital, and Harry knew why: being here allowed undertakers to drive to it without the risk of the public seeing a body, or having them accidentally walk into the building.

'Home sweet home,' Sowerby said.

The reception contained a small number of seats, a water machine, some fresh flowers and a collection of leaflets on dealing with grief and various counselling services. Harry found himself picking one up to browse through as he followed Sowerby on through another door and into the viewing room.

'I usually come in through the staff entrance,' Sowerby said, making small talk. 'That one opens straight into the fridge room which helps keep things secure and confidential, if you know what I mean.'

'I do,' Harry said, having dealt with at least one that he could remember where someone had attempted to steal a body during a case many moons ago.

The viewing room was dimly lit with more flowers on display, a coffee table, and some seats. Harry spotted a box of tissues as well, tangible evidence of the grief this room had witnessed, either when viewing a body wheeled in from the fridge room, or through the large window in one of the walls, which looked into another smaller room.

Those viewings, with the distance between victim and relative or friend, had always struck Harry as worse somehow. A body may have already started to decompose, perhaps there was a forensic or infectious reason for the body only being viewable through the window, and that all made sense. But that cold, clinical and very necessary reasoning did nothing to ease the pain of being separated, even at such an awful moment, from someone you loved.

'Why are we in here?' Harry asked.

Sowerby paused, then shook her head as though dislodging a thought.

'Auto-pilot,' she said. 'Sorry.'

Sowerby led Harry back out into the reception area and through another door into an office. Here Harry saw a small kitchen, a bed, a desk, and a locker room with showers.

'I'll get the kettle on,' she said. 'Can't remember how you take it.'

'Splash of milk, no sugar,' Harry instructed, looking around the office. 'Cosy.'

'That's one way to describe it.'

The room was barely large enough, not only for the bed and the desk, but the various filing cabinets it contained, never mind the two humans now standing inside it waiting for a brew and a biscuit.

'Not exactly homely, I know,' said Sowerby, waiting by the kettle.

Harry smiled. 'It's an office in a mortuary. Not sure something like that could ever be described as homely, or that it ever should be, for that matter.'

'Gets a bit quiet sometimes.'

'Sometimes? I'd hope all the time, wouldn't you? It's not like you want to come to work one day and find everyone in here having a good old chinwag and helping themselves to your Custard Creams, is it?'

Tea made, Sowerby handed Harry a mug, then pulled a few packets of biscuits out of a drawer in her desk. She opened the packet of Rich Tea.

'Fateful I know,' she said, offering them to Harry. 'Once they're open, I just can't stop eating the damned things until they're all gone.'

Harry reached in, grabbed four.

'Don't know what you mean,' he said.

Harry lowered himself onto a small, clear section of the very busy desk.

'So, you've called me out here for a reason, which means I'm intrigued as to what it is.'

'I've a few, actually,' said Sowerby.

Harry took a hefty glug of his tea to wash down the biscuits.

'I'm ready when you are.'

Sowerby stared at him a little open-mouthed.

'But you had four biscuits in your hand barely seconds ago.'

'Magic,' Harry said, taking four more. 'Come on.'

He pushed himself up from the desk and gestured to the office door.

Sowerby placed her mug down and handed Harry some PPE, then pointed to a row of Wellington boots against a wall. 'We should have your size.'

Kitted up, Harry followed Sowerby once again, through the transition area and into the fridge room. Here, they walked past several steel tables, one of which was holding a body draped in a white sheet. Harry saw a trolley to the side of the body, various implements of surgical steel lined up like the instruments of a mediaeval torturer displaying the tools of their trade.

The bright white walls were made all the brighter by the stark light blasting out from the lights in the ceiling. Everywhere Harry looked, the glint of steel shone back, and he followed Sowerby over to the body still hidden from view. She took hold of the edge of the sheet and carefully folded it back. Harry immediately saw the wounds of a fresh autopsy. The pale, wax-like skin cut with the sharpest of blades.

As he always did in cases like this, Harry wanted to make a connection with the victim, and he made a point of coming around to stand opposite Sowerby to look at the face of the victim, whose name so far they only knew as, or at least assumed to be, Luca. He had been a living, breathing human only hours ago. Someone with hopes and dreams, worries and plans, friends and family. There had been a life ahead of him, violently snatched away by a person or persons who Harry was damned sure going to find and throw every book he could at them.

'I've done everything,' Sowerby said, 'so in case you're squeamish, you don't need to worry about any of that.'

'I'm not,' Harry said.

'Too long in the job?'

'Something like that.'

Sowerby picked up a clipboard from a metal trolley to her side.

'As always, we started with the external examination. Obviously, we're able to do some of that at the crime scene, take samples, that kind of thing. But the bulk of it is done here, followed by X-rays, internal examination, testing body fluids, brain examination, and so on, until we have a report. I've not written that up in detail yet, so this is just the notes stage.'

'Where do we begin, then?' Harry asked.

'Here,' Sowerby said. Placing the clipboard back down, she lifted the left hand of the victim. 'As you can see, the skin is damaged.' She opened the fingers to allow Harry a closer look. 'The fingers, between them, chemical and water damage.'

'How do you mean?'

'Detergent,' Sowerby said. 'And this damage is from regular exposure to water. What my mum would call dishpan hands. Basically, excessive exposure to soap and water, and you've got dry, red, flaky skin.'

'So, he worked in a kitchen, then.'

'That's a strong possibility.'

'And spent his free time poaching.'

'Takes all sorts.'

'Doesn't it, just? But how does poaching lead to this?'

Harry's question was left to float off unanswered.

'You can see the Y-Incision in the torso,' Sowerby said, resting the hand back down to point at the chest. 'We found bruising on the chest, three cracked ribs.'

'Three? Bloody hell,' said Harry, unable to hide the shock in his voice at what the man in front of them had suffered. 'It looked like he'd taken a beating, but this was more than that.'

'Definitely more,' Sowerby said. 'This was vicious. Even without his leg cut off, he'd have been lucky to have survived the night in that woodland with this damage. Whoever did this to him, they really meant business.'

'No, they meant more than that,' Harry said. 'This isn't just a beating, it's a warning to others. Word gets round that this was done to one person who stepped out of line, or got on the wrong side of the wrong people, and everyone else gets in line sharpish.'

And that was worrying, Harry thought, because that meant there were others out there who were potentially now terrified that what happened to Luca could happen to them. But why? That was the question that bothered him.

'Also, I think there were at least two attackers,' Sowerby said, then pointed at the various bruises and lesions on the body. 'A lot of the damage on the arms is clearly self-defence and it very much looks like he was being attacked simultaneously from both sides. He's been punched, kicked, and beaten. Stomped on, too, which actually gave us the best evidence to support the theory that there was more than one attacker.'

She rolled the body onto its side and pointed at large marks on the back and legs.

'See?' she said. 'You can clearly make out tread marks here, here, and here from the footwear of the attackers.'

'And they're not all the same, are they?' Harry said.

Sowerby shook her head.

'Completely different treads. Also, we've checked the organs,' she said, moving on. 'They've been knocked around as well, which is hardly surprising. His stomach contents were nothing to write home about. Just a simple meal of vegetable soup and bread.'

As Sowerby was speaking, Harry was then struck by the build of the man on the slab.

'Thin, isn't he?'

'Yes, very,' said Sowerby. 'I'm amazed he was able to put up any fight at all. But then adrenaline is a powerful stimulant.'

'I'd even go so far as to say that he looks emaciated.'

'Well, he's definitely malnourished. A man of his age shouldn't be this weight, not unless he's a professional long-distance runner. But even then, muscle mass has quite an impact.'

'What's his weight, then?'

Sowerby checked her notes again.

'We put him in his mid to late twenties,' she said. 'Five eleven, and at that height and age, your normal weight can be anything from 136 to 172 pounds.'

'That's quite a range.'

'It is,' Sowerby said. 'But he was well under that. The low end of that is around nine and a half stone, and he's lying here at barely eight and a half.'

Harry let out a faint whistle.

'Last time I weighed that I was probably barely a teenager.'

'You sure you've ever been that weight?'

'No,' Harry said. 'So, he's showing water and soap damage to his hands, hasn't eaten a proper meal for what seems like an age, weighs about the same as a sparrow on a good day, and ended with the shit kicked out of him before having his leg dropped in a man trap.' Harry shook his head in despair. 'Makes you wonder about this world sometimes, doesn't it? Anything else?'

Sowerby gave a nod, then picked up the left hand once again, this time focusing on the wrist.

'He was tied,' she said.

'But when we found the body, his hands were free.'

'Also, there's this …'

Harry followed where Sowerby was pointing, which was at a point some way above where the right leg had been so violently severed. He saw a bruised line wrapping itself right around the leg like a thin snake and recognised it immediately.

'Tourniquet.'

'And I doubt very much if he did it himself,' Sowerby said.

'What was used?'

Sowerby shrugged, shook her head.

'Haven't a clue. Nothing was found at the site. But it looks like it was done by someone who knew what they were doing.'

'How can you tell?'

Harry had asked the question but knew the answer; he just wanted confirmation from Sowerby.

'If this was someone who didn't know what they were doing, then the tourniquet would most likely be much closer to the wound, just because that's what you would think—to stem the bleeding, you need to be close to it—but that's not the case, is it?'

Harry shook his head but didn't interrupt.

'As you can see,' Sowerby continued, 'this is much further up and closer to the groin; better chance of stopping the bleed.'

Harry had used tourniquets himself and understood exactly what Sowerby was saying.

'That call he made,' Harry said. 'I'd be willing to put money on whoever that was being the person who came out and did this to try to save him.'

'Whoever it was, they didn't have a chance,' Sowerby said.

'No, you're right, they didn't,' Harry said. 'But they still tried, didn't they? And that tells us something.'

At this, Sowerby looked directly at Harry, the only expression visible on her masked face being a frown. 'Does it?'

'Yes,' said Harry.

'What?'

'They cared.'

CHAPTER SIXTEEN

Inside, the house was a car crash of ideas and styles that Gordy had to work very hard to not just stop and stare at, her mouth agape. The furniture was a bizarre mix of traditional English furniture, most of it dark brown, sitting alongside the kind of modern affair that she would have to spend a good few moments working out what it was for, and then how to sit at or on it, or not, just in case there was a chance of being injured.

Then there were the walls, or to be more accurate, what they were hiding behind. And fair enough, too, Gordy thought, because if she was covered in any of it herself, she would feel nothing but shame and embarrassment. Wherever she looked, the walls were covered in pieces of what she assumed to be art, the likes of which she'd never laid eyes on before.

Some were massive swirls of colour; others were little more than empty frames with a few dots of black on them. One piece seemed to be an exercise in things you could do with egg boxes but had never tried, and probably would never want to, either. Another piece was a broken mirror, and behind the shattered fragments were words like hate, despise, loathe, and abhor.

Further on were sculptures, though of what Gordy didn't even want to guess, most of them designed to either induce the most horrific nightmares or were the product of such. One or two looked positively pornographic.

'All originals,' Walker said, and Gordy heard the pride in his voice. 'The art, I mean. I invested, you see. I may have a decent pile of money to my name, but I've not been a complete idiot with the money. I've worked hard for it, but I'm not about to waste it.'

Gordy wasn't sure that she could entirely agree. Then again, perhaps she was a philistine, and Walker here knew what he was talking about. Something told her, though, that he really didn't.

'I heard that you won the lottery,' she said.

Walker laughed, that mean sound even colder when trapped by the walls of his house. Though there was a nervousness to it as well, Gordy thought, as though it was something the man did when he wasn't exactly sure what was going on.

'That's what I tell people, gives them something to talk about, doesn't it? Stops them asking questions. And I don't like questions.'

Maybe it does, Gordy thought, but why would Walker not want people to ask questions? Was he hiding something? Or was he, as she suspected based on the very strong evidence so far, simply just a dunderheid with all the charm and warmth of a funeral director's freezer?

'I'm a businessman,' Walker said. 'That's all. And business, as they say, is booming.'

'What business would that be?'

'My own,' Walker said.

Gordy decided to change tack and turned back to the art.

'Choose all of it yourself?' she asked, searching hard for something to say that didn't commit her to giving an opinion.

'Yes. I mean, no,' Walker replied, his answer an odd mix of confidence, confusion and disdain at that mere suggestion. 'What I mean is that I paid someone to do that.'

That explains a lot, Gordy thought, as she followed on behind the man until they were in the section of the house almost completely made of glass. Still, though, it had been an odd answer.

Walker stood in the middle of what was little more than a huge, empty space, bar two enormous sofas, a coffee table large enough to play pool on, and a plain, white rug, so thick Gordy thought that if she trod in it, she might be eternally lost in a world of wool and dust.

What wall space there was had once been the side of the original house. It was painted white and on it hung various old farming implements. Gordy could see a couple of pitchforks, a wood rake or two, even a couple of shotguns, but the display looked a little out of balance, like something was missing from one end.

'Sit down,' Walker said, distracting Gordy. 'Drink?'

'I'm fine, thank you,' Gordy said, pulling her gaze from the wall. 'Interesting collection you have up there, isn't it?'

'And what do you mean by that?'

'Nothing at all,' Gordy said. God, this man was touchy. 'Just an observation.'

'Not really my kind of thing, I'll be honest, but the guns I like. And before you ask, they're decommissioned. I'm not a complete idiot.'

Gordy wasn't so sure about that.

'Where's it all from?' she asked.

'Not a clue,' Walker said. 'Now, I asked if you wanted a drink, not how you are. So, do you want one?'

'No, thank you,' said Gordy.

'You sure about that?'

'Very.'

'What about water?'

He wasn't going to give up, was he? Walker was clearly someone who didn't take no for an answer and who also really liked to be in control.

'Okay, yes, water. Thank you.'

Walker strode off, leaving Gordy alone. When he returned, he was carrying two glasses, both large, both filled with water and rattling gently with ice.

'Cheers,' Walker said, handing Gordy her glass, then sitting down opposite. 'Now, how can I help?'

Gordy said thank you and then, to stop her throat from drying out as she moved on to asking questions, took a glug from her glass.

Fire burst in her mouth, torching her throat, and she gasped, coughed, spluttered.

'What the hell ... What is this?' Gordy managed to say, her words barely a rasp.

Walker looked at his own glass as she continued to cough, took a sniff, then shook his head.

'Goodness, I am sorry,' he said. 'I think I gave you the wrong glass. Here ...' He handed Gordy his glass and took hers for himself. 'Nice bit of vodka. None of your cheap crap either. You've probably just coughed up fifty quid's worth onto my rug.'

Gordy wiped her eyes, took long, deep breaths, mainly to

calm herself down and stop her from grabbing the man by his smug chin and dragging him outside to put him in handcuffs.

'It was an honest accident,' Walker said, though Gordy was fairly sure she could detect a thick note of sarcasm coating his words. 'My bad, as they say, right?'

Gordy looked up to see Walker raise his glass to her. She coughed some more, then with her voice almost back to itself, thought it best to just get on with the reason for her visit. The sooner she did that, the sooner she could leave.

She placed her glass, which she made sure was filled with water by taking a tentative sip, on a slate coaster on the enormous coffee table sitting between them.

'Mr Walker, I need to tell you that last night the body of a man was found on your property. It is our belief that he was murdered.'

Mr Walker stared at Gordy, no emotion in his eyes, no visible sign in his body language as to how he had taken the news. Instead, he just stared back, sipping his vodka.

'I also need to ask you where you were yesterday evening, between the hours of approximately eight and eleven pm.'

'Where on my property, exactly?'

'A small woodland, outside Carperby.'

Walker gave a shrug.

'Where's that then?'

'Carperby?'

'No, I know where that is, don't I? I've only been here a couple of years, though, and I can't just memorise every square metre of the estate, can I?'

Gordy explained where the woodland was, astonished that the man didn't know his way around his own land, then added, 'We understand that it is part of a shoot you run on your property.'

'I've someone who runs that for me. Best you ask them about it, not me.'

'It was your gamekeeper who found the body.'

'Well, there's plenty of signs up around the place to tell people to sod off, so if they were trespassing, it's not my fault they've come to harm, now, is it?'

'Are you able to confirm where you were between the aforementioned hours?' Gordy asked again.

'What if I decide I don't want to tell you?'

Walker placed his glass on the table and stared at Gordy.

Gordy did her best to look relaxed and approachable. Trouble was, Walker was rapidly becoming the kind of person she wanted to throw in a cell just to shut him up.

'All we're doing at this stage is trying to establish the whereabouts of people of importance to the investigation.'

'And that's what I am, is it? A person of importance? What about my gamekeeper?'

'We've already established her whereabouts. Are you able to do the same?'

'I am, but I'm not going to.'

'I would advise—' Gordy began, but Walker interrupted, holding up a finger to stop her talking.

'I've had more than a few dealings with the police in my time,' he said. 'And right now, I'm going to contact my ... solicitor.'

Gordy noticed the pause in Walker's words as he leaned forward and pulled a mobile phone from a back pocket in his overly tight jeans.

'There's really no need,' Gordy said. 'You're not under arrest. This is simply to help us with our enquiries.'

'You know, I've helped the police with their enquiries

before,' Walker said. 'Got properly stitched up I did, too. You probably saw him, by the way.'

'Your solicitor?'

'He'd just left when you arrived.'

'Ah, the man in the car,' Gordy said. 'Yes, I did.'

Walker put his phone to his ear.

'Mr Walker ...' Gordy began, but Walker once again held up a finger to shush her. She had to really force herself to not reach over and snap the damned thing off at the knuckle.

'It's Vince.'

The name Vince really suited Walker, Gordy thought. Not that there was anything inherently wrong with the name, just that for some reason, there were names that could, quite easily, conjure up the image of someone less than law-abiding.

'Yeah, I know you saw her when you left. She's right in front of me, drinking my vodka, too, if you'd believe it.'

Walker stared over at Gordy as he spoke, his eyes narrow and hard. He was nodding now, listening. Either that or falling asleep. It was hard to tell.

Walker turned then from Gordy, his voice a whisper. Part of her wondered if he was actually having a conversation at all, and not just faking the call to keep her on edge.

Walker nodded a few more times, then hung up.

'Useful?' Gordy asked.

'Very,' said Walker. 'My solicitor says you need to speak to him and that right now I shouldn't comment, just in case.'

'Just in case of what?'

'I say anything incriminating.'

'All I'm asking is where you were, that's all,' said Gordy.

'I'm a private man, officer,' Walker said, his already

narrow eyes narrowing even further until they were little more than thin slits of meanness.

'I'm sure you are.'

'And what do you mean by that?'

Gordy bit her tongue.

'I will need your solicitor's details, then, so I can speak to him. That is, unless I can't persuade you now to give me your whereabouts?'

'Here you go,' Walker said, and handed Gordy a gold-coloured business card. 'Posh, right?' he added. 'That's because I can afford the best. Though he did say that he would be over tomorrow to give a statement on my behalf.'

Gordy smiled thinly. That would be something to look forward to.

'That must make you very happy.'

'Who was it, anyway?' Walker asked. 'And how was he killed?'

'We are currently working to formally identify the victim,' Gordy explained, giving little away, and certainly not approaching the modus operandi of the murder. 'However, we do believe that he was poaching. Is that something you've had a problem with in the past?'

Walker gave a shrug. 'I leave all of that to the game-keeper. That's what I pay her for, don't I? Otherwise what's the point?'

Gordy stared at Walker for a moment. His response was a little odd, she thought. Everything he said was guarded or camouflaged somehow, but why? Maybe he was just the kind of person who always had something to hide. It wasn't exactly making her job any easier.

'Can I ask you if the name Luca means anything to you?' Gordy asked.

'You can, you have, and it doesn't,' Walker replied. 'Luca? Doesn't sound very local to me.'

'Are you able to recall if your gamekeeper has mentioned anything to you about poaching in the past?'

Walker shook his head, gave a disinterested shrug worthy of any teenager.

'Just so long as any on my property are dealt with accordingly,' he said, and Gordy heard teeth in his words. 'And it sounds like this one was, doesn't it?'

'How do you mean?'

'How do you think I mean?'

'I don't know,' Gordy said, and threw the question back. 'That's why I asked.'

Walker stared at her for a moment.

'Just out of interest,' Walker said. 'If we did catch any poachers, what would the police do, exactly?'

'The poachers would be arrested and dealt with accordingly,' Gordy said.

'You'd go soft on them, wouldn't you?' Walker said, then leaned back against the sofa, spreading his arms wide as he did so, bracing himself with them on top of the plump cushions. 'Makes me wonder why I even bothered to report that break-in.'

Gordy's eyes widened at this.

'Break-in? What break-in?'

'A few weeks back,' Walker said. 'I was out one evening, and when I came back, someone had been in and had a bit of a rummage around, shall we say?'

Gordy frowned. Hadn't he taken more than a little pride in telling her about all the art he'd invested in? If the house had been broken into, what had been taken? And what about security?

'What did they take?' Gordy asked.

Walker laughed, leaning his head back as he did so.

'Nothing of real value,' he said. 'Walked past everything and just took electronic stuff, things you can shift quickly for cash. TVs, music system, that kind of thing.' He shrugged. 'Nothing important.'

'No art, then?'

'Of course not,' Walker said, as though Gordy had just said the stupidest thing ever. 'That stuff is much more difficult to move. You have to know people, and you can't just sell it, because it has to go to someone who knows about art, or someone who knows someone who knows about art, if you know what I mean?'

Gordy had almost lost track there, but yes, she knew what Walker was getting at. She was also thinking that the man knew rather a lot about what to do with stolen goods.

'And your security?' Gordy asked. 'Your dog?'

'Thor was at the vets and he's the only security I have. Don't believe in it. Waste of money. It's cheaper to replace what was nicked, than to install and run a decent system.'

Gordy wondered if those who had broken in had known then that Walker and his dog would be off-site.

'And you say you reported the incident?'

'I did,' Walker said. 'Well, my solicitor did. He was here to meet whoever it was that came out to have a look, not that there was much to see.'

'I'll check our records when I get back to the office.'

'No point,' said Walker. 'Insurance is all sorted.'

'There's a good chance that those who broke in here are involved in other crimes in the area,' Gordy said.

'I've a list somewhere of everything that was taken,' Walker said. 'Put that together just so I had a shopping list.'

'That could be useful,' Gordy said, doubting it rather.

'If I find it I'll send it through. Can't promise anything, though.'

'Thank you,' Gordy said, and with nothing much else to discuss, she finished her water and stood up.

'Thank you for your time, Mr Walker. Very much appreciated.'

'Where do I send that list of stolen stuff? If I find it, that is?'

Gordy gave him the email address of the community centre in Hawes, then walked back through the house the way she'd come. Her eyes were once again drawn to the horrifying art and sculptures on display, and she found herself wishing that money could be a little more discerning as to who it decided should have lots of it.

'I'll be in touch if we need to speak to you again,' Gordy said, climbing into her car.

'I don't think you will, do you?' Walker replied. Then he let out a piercing whistle. A moment later, the huge bulk of Thor sauntered up to him and sat down at his side. The dog's jaw fell open, and his tongue lolled out. Walker reached out and stroked its head. As he did so, the dog bared its teeth.

You know what, I bloody well hope not, Gordy thought. Then she pulled away from the house to head back along the drive towards those idiotic electronic gates, hoping against hope that they would let her out again. Because if she stayed here any longer, only one of them would be leaving alive.

CHAPTER SEVENTEEN

A TINY FLAME BURPED OUT FROM THE END OF THE small handgun.

'Bloody hell!' yelled Matt, and before he could stop himself, he slapped from the woman's hand what he could see now was nothing more than a novelty cigarette lighter. It crashed into the wall of the Portakabin, then fell to the floor with a clatter. Her cigarette followed the same arc to land beside it.

'What the—?' the woman began, but Matt didn't give her a chance to even think about questioning what he had just done.

'We're the police!' he yelled, stamping on the still lit cigarette to put it out. 'What part of that did you not understand? Was it my ID, which clearly shows who and what I am? Was it the use of words like police and detective sergeant that caused you some confusion?'

'Sarge ...' Jen said, but Matt wasn't listening. He was, instead, channelling his inner Harry, or that's certainly how it seemed.

'No? Then perhaps it was the very bloody obvious police car we parked outside?'

'You slapped me!'

'And you pointed what looked very much like a handgun right at my face!'

Matt pointed a very firm finger at his own face.

'This one, right here! You do see it, don't you? And does it have anywhere on it at all a big sign saying *please point a gun at me*?'

The woman's mouth fell open and her jaw just sort of bobbed up and down for a moment, like it was attached to Matt's finger by invisible elastic.

'But you—'

'Don't,' Matt said, his voice a warning bell. 'Now, sit!'

'I've a good mind to call the police.'

'We *are* the police! And you went right on ahead and pointed a weapon at me. And before you argue that point, yes, I know it's a cigarette lighter. But that's now, isn't it? Not two minutes ago when I damn near had a heart attack! You're bloody lucky you're not right this minute pinned to this grimy floor of yours while we cuff you.'

'You wouldn't dare!'

'SIT! DOWN!'

The woman sat.

'You okay, Sarge?' Jen asked.

Matt was definitely not okay. His heart was racing, and he was fairly sure that his blood pressure had taken a near-fatal jump into the red. He hadn't seen his life flash before his eyes, but he had seen shock turn to fear, then rage in less time than it takes to blink.

Matt allowed for a moment of quiet, took a few deep,

slow breaths, then spoke again, this time his voice a little quieter.

'Shall we start again?' he asked.

Matt stared down at the woman, daring her to challenge him. She glanced over at the floor to where her lighter had landed, the squashed remnants of her cigarette by its side.

'Can I vape?'

'What?'

The woman held up the vape pen she had been using.

'Can I ask why you use both?' said Jen.

'I took this up to try and stop smoking,' the woman said.

'And how's that going for you?'

'How do you think?'

She didn't wait for Matt to answer her earlier question and stuck the vape pen into her mouth, then released a plume of vapour a power station would be proud of.

'Let's start again, then, shall we?' Matt said. 'You know who we are. Can we have your name, please?'

'Carr,' the woman said. 'Mrs Margaret Carr, with two Rs. In Carr, I mean, not in Margaret. Though, there are two Rs in Margaret, aren't there?'

Margaret stopped speaking.

'Right then,' Matt said. 'Now that we have all of that sorted at last, would it be okay if we asked you a few questions?'

'Well, I don't know,' Margaret said. 'I am rather busy.'

'We won't take up too much of your time, I'm sure,' Jen said.

'So, what's this about, then? Can't be my husband, so that's something, isn't it?'

'What can't be your husband?' Jen asked.

'This,' Margaret said, gesturing at Jen and Matt with her

vape pen. 'Whatever it is that you're here for. It can't be about him.'

'And why's that?'

'Because he's dead,' Margaret said. 'Jeff's been gone about six months now. So, like I said, this can't be about him, can it?' She smiled then, her eyes narrowing to such a degree that the crow's feet in their corners grew like the roots of an old tree. 'You know what they say, every cloud, right?'

That Margaret was suggesting the silver lining to the cloud of her husband's death was that the police turning up on her doorstep couldn't be due to him, had Matt wondering about just what kind of relationship they'd had before he'd died. Not a good one, he guessed.

'I'm sorry for your loss,' Matt said.

'I'm not,' Margaret sighed. 'Now I'm left with running this place, aren't I? And do I look like the kind of person who wants to spend her time running a scrap dealer? No, of course I don't. Driving around in my lovely white Range Rover picking up knackered old vehicles is not my idea of a good time.'

If he were honest, Matt wasn't entirely sure what it was that Margaret looked like she should be doing instead. And he shuddered a little as he momentarily wondered what her idea of a good time was exactly.

'The reason we're here,' Jen said, 'is that we're trying to trace a specific vehicle in relation to an ongoing investigation.'

Margaret took another deep pull of her vape pen and when she spoke again, every word drifted from her mouth on a sweet-smelling cloud of white.

'Can't help you there.'

'We've not told you what the vehicle is yet,' said Matt.

'Doubt it'll matter,' said Margaret, shaking her head. 'Jeff's paperwork was little more than this desk and a rubbish bin.'

'But what about your accounts? He would've kept full records for those, surely.'

'Not a clue,' Margaret said. 'I'm trying to get things together now, for the new owner. I can't have this place fall apart now, otherwise, that will all fall through, and I'll not have a thing to live on, will I? All Jeff left me with was debt and the joy of being woken up in the morning by bailiffs. And nothing says happy marriage like a debt collector, now, does it?'

Matt had a photo of the car on his phone and showed it to Margaret.

'Do you recognise this?'

Margaret leaned forward and shook her head.

'You've seen this place, right? How am I supposed to remember every knackered heap of rust that turns up here?'

'Which is why I asked about your records.' Matt remembered then a detail about the certificate of destruction that might help. 'Your husband died six months ago, correct?'

'He did,' Margaret said. 'Had a heart attack while watching the darts on the telly. Most of the players look healthier than he ever did, which says a lot, I think, don't you?'

'There's a certificate of destruction attached to this vehicle,' Matt continued. 'From a couple of weeks ago. So, if you are trying to get things into better shape, isn't there a chance that you have the relevant records?'

At this, Matt saw a flicker of something in Margaret's eyes.

'Two weeks back. That's what you said, isn't it?'

'It is,' said Matt.

'We had a break-in around then. I say we, it's only me here now. Gets lonely, you know.'

Margaret stared at Matt and sent a wink his way on a cloud of more vapour.

'You said there was a new owner?' Matt asked.

'I did, but they're very hands-off. No idea why they wanted the place, but I wasn't about to complain. Probably sell the land off for development. Still, I'm okay for the moment. Hardly something for me to be worrying myself about.'

'This break in,' said Jen, stepping in. 'You reported it?'

Margaret shook her head, laughed, then mimed picking up an invisible phone.

'Hello, is that the police? Yes, I'd like to report the theft of a car worth absolutely nothing to anybody and about to be ripped apart for scrap.'

Jen looked at Matt and shrugged.

'Not sure what you're getting at,' she said.

'Of course, I didn't report it,' said Margaret, her words tripping over the bitter laugh in her voice. 'Like any of you lot have the time to go looking into the theft of a car worth barely a hundred quid!'

'What about CCTV?' Jen asked.

'Now that I do have,' said Margaret, much to Matt's surprise.

'Really?' he said, unable to disguise the shock in his voice.

'Of course,' said Margaret, looking momentarily down her nose at him. 'And it's all recorded on the computery thing in that room at the back, there.'

Matt and Jen both looked behind them and saw nothing.

'What room?'

Margaret stood up, slid around the side of her desk, then walked over to the back of the Portakabin. She pushed at a section of wall and it made a faint click, then sprang back a little.

'Jeff had this put in a few years ago,' Margaret said, then laughed. 'Called it his panic room, would you believe? No idea why, though I do feel a little panicky when I'm in there. Like that old, dead bastard is somehow haunting the place. Gives me the shudders.'

Me too, now you mention it, Matt thought.

'Walls on this place are as thin as a slice of processed cheese and offer less protection,' Margaret continued. 'Some days I'd come looking for him and he'd be nowhere to be seen. Then I'd hear snoring coming from in there. God knows what he was up to. Probably best you don't think about that, though. I know I try not to.'

Matt walked over to the space in the wall, Jen behind him. After what Margaret had just said, he wasn't entirely sure he wanted to venture in without full PPE.

'In you go, then,' Margaret said, and she reached out and took hold of Matt's arm, dragging him into the room in front of her.

When Jen joined them, there was barely enough room to breathe.

'There you go,' Margaret said, and pointed at an ancient desktop computer, the plastic grey and stained, the image on the screen out of focus because of the dust. It was sitting on top of another desk, only this one looked even worse than the one in the main room.

The black and white image was of the front gates. It changed to show another part of the scrapyard. A few seconds later, it changed again, showing more busted and broken vehicles.

Margaret leant over the keyboard. She clicked through a few folders and pulled up a file and set it to playing.

'This is from the night of the theft,' she said.

'You've looked at it, then?' Jen asked.

'Oh, I come in here a lot when we have customers,' said Margaret. 'You wouldn't believe what people get up to when they think no one's watching.'

Matt shuddered at the thought of being spied on by Margaret. So, he focused his attention on what was on the screen. Which, for now, was nothing.

'Can we fast forward?' he asked.

Margaret moved the cursor and the image stuttered forwards until he saw something moving.

'Stop ...'

Margaret stopped scrolling.

Matt and Jen watched as on the screen, and in surprisingly high definition, a vehicle pulled up outside the scrapyard and someone climbed out of the passenger side. The car then drove off and whoever it was that had just climbed out, then squeezed in through the gap between the front gates. They disappeared off-screen, the image changed, and they saw them again, now in another part of the yard, checking out a few cars that looked almost roadworthy, one of which Matt recognised from the night before. The image changed again, and this time they saw the car being driven towards the gates.

'How did they get out without smashing through?' Jen asked.

The person climbed out of the car and again dashed off-screen. When they returned, they were carrying a length of piping. They jammed it between the gates, gave it a twist, and the chain fell to the ground. A few seconds later, they were gone.

'That chain gave up easily,' said Jen.

'Because Jeff was cheap,' said Margaret. 'It was probably nothing more than a plug chain from a bathroom. I replaced it with something a little more substantial. Oh, and it's electrified now, too. So, if they come back ...' Without any warning at all, Margaret rounded on Jen, grabbed her arm, and made a sound rather like a rubbish electric razor.

Jen snatched her arm away.

'We'll need this,' Matt said, pointing at the flickering image on the screen.

Margaret opened a desk drawer and, after a quick rummage around, pulled out a handful of USBs.

'No idea what's on any of these,' she said, and jammed one of them into the computer. A moment or two later, and having demonstrated a rather surprising degree of savvy with working on a computer, handed the USB to Jen.

'Hope it's useful,' she said.

'I'm sure it is,' Jen said. 'And thank you for your help.'

Outside, Matt went to climb into their car, but his eyes came to rest on the white Range Rover. The vehicle seemed just a little incongruous considering their current surroundings and the state of the Portakabin they'd just left. He turned back to Margaret.

'Nice motor,' he said.

'Thank you,' Margaret said. 'I like to keep it looking nice, you know. It was my treat when I sold the place. I wash it once a week, without fail. Well, I don't, obviously. I take it to a place in town.' She then rested her eyes on the car Matt and Jen had driven over in, popped back into the Portakabin, and returned to hand a card to Matt. 'Looks like yours could do with a bit of spit and polish too, if you ask me.'

Matt looked at what Margaret had given him to see that it was the business card of a local car wash.

Stowing the card in a pocket, he looked back up at Margaret.

'A word to the wise,' he said.

'What's that, then?'

'Buy a new lighter.'

Margaret smiled and popped another cigarette into her mouth.

'Yes, officer,' she said, and lit it with the end of her replica pistol.

CHAPTER EIGHTEEN

'Big, isn't he?'

Phil Thwaite's voice was full of the kind of pride that only a farmer can display when showing off a prize beast.

Liz had to agree, staring up into the Shire horse's enormous brown eyes to give its nose a rub. It let out a soft neigh, and she scratched the white line of coarse hair that ran between its eyes and up through its ears. Bar this, and the white feathering on its lower legs and covering the hooves, the horse was black. Its coat glistened, a testament to how well cared for it was.

'He's just a touch over seventeen hands and around a thousand kilos in weight. I know that's average for a Shire, but there's just something about old Harry, isn't there? Like he has this presence that fills whatever space he's in at the time.'

That Phil owned a Shire horse called Harry was quite something in itself. That the creature was as imposing as their boss could be, almost on demand, was a little disconcerting. Despite this, and as with DCI Grimm, Liz couldn't help but be drawn to Phil's Harry. I'll have to bring Ben out to meet him, she thought, and then had an image of Ben sitting atop the horse and looking not exactly at home with it.

Liz noticed that Jim was standing a little way off, arms folded.

'Come and say hello,' she called over.

'I can do that well enough from here,' Jim replied. He waved. 'Now then, Harry.'

The horse stomped one of its front hooves, scraping it across the gravel of Phil's yard.

'That means he wants you to come over and say hello properly,' Phil said.

'I just did.'

'No, you didn't,' said Liz, smiling. 'Come on, you have to actually stroke him to say hello. Isn't that right, Harry?'

The horse leaned its head on Liz's shoulder and let out another soft neigh.

Jim made to step forward, but hesitated.

'I'm not one for horses, if I'm honest,' he said. 'Went to Blackpool years back and got bumped off by a donkey on the beach.'

Once again, the horse tapped a hoof on the ground.

'Come on, now,' Phil said, walking over to Jim and taking a hold of his arm. 'Let's get you over.'

Before Jim could react, he was standing beside Liz and up close and personal with Harry's huge head.

'Yes, he's, well, he's lovely, isn't he?' Jim said, stepping back.

The horse leaned its head over towards Jim and nibbled gently at his clothes, before rubbing the side of its head against his arm.

'Just stroke him,' said Liz. 'That's all you have to do. Give him a pat, go on.'

Liz watched as Jim reached up a hesitant hand, only to have Harry meet him halfway and nuzzle it.

'See?' she said.

Jim smiled.

'He's not too bad, I suppose.'

'He's looking extra smart right now because I'd just finished giving him a good old brush over when you rang,' Phil said. 'I like to keep him in top condition.'

'Just out of interest,' Jim said, 'why do you have a Shire?'

'Why not?' Phil answered, and Liz heard the finality in it, as though nothing else needed to be said.

'So, we're here because you left a message with Harry,' she said. 'The other one.'

'I did,' said Phil, 'and I'm glad you've come over. Definitely got something to go over, that's for sure. Come on ...'

With Harry happily secured in the yard and munching on some hay, Phil turned and walked across the yard and through the front door of the farmhouse.

It was a small house, but not exactly tiny, Liz thought, and she wondered if anyone else had ever shared it with Phil. Though, having seen how much he loved Harry the Shire, she was quite sure he was more than alright living on his own.

Inside, they followed Phil through to a kitchen recently updated and smelling of roast beef. An old radio was on in the corner, tuned to something classical. A table sat centre stage.

'Sit yourselves down and I'll put a brew on,' Phil said.

Liz did as they were told, and Jim sat down opposite. A

couple of minutes later, Phil was over with a large, brown teapot, three mugs, and a plate piled with cake.

'One more thing,' Phil said, and jogged off through another door to return with something wrapped in waxed paper, a small jug of milk and three small plates. He unwrapped it, placed it on another plate, and grabbed a couple sharp knives from a drawer. 'There we go; cheese and cake. Nowt better with a mug of tea, am I right?'

Liz wasn't about to disagree as Phil proceeded to cut large slabs of cake and cheese and hand them out on the plates.

'Thank you,' she said, after finishing her first bite.

'You'll be wondering what it was I called Harry about, then,' Phil said.

Liz saw Jim place his mug down and pull out his notebook and pen.

'Well, it's about something that happened at a pub a couple of weeks ago ...'

Phil's voice faded just enough to have Liz lean forward.

'Which pub?' she asked.

'Oh, that was the Fox and Hounds, over in West Burton,' Phil said. 'Love the place. Possibly my favourite pub in the Dales, it is. I've a few old friends there from my school days, so I sometimes head over for a pint or three and a chance to put the world to rights.'

And I bet you do, too, Liz thought, just about managing to stop herself from smiling at the thought.

'So, what happened?' she asked.

'Well, I was in there, you see, sitting with Trev and Mart, having a bite to eat, that kind of thing. They do homemade pizzas, you know, so we'd all had one of those each, plus some of that garlic bread. Delicious! And it was getting on a bit towards last orders, like, so I headed over to the bar to get us in another round or two.'

Phil, Liz could see, was a man who loved to meander a little when telling a story, rather than get straight to the destination. She was surprised that he liked pizza. She had heard tell of his notorious pies, so hadn't expected him to be so cosmopolitan. Not that eating pizza was, but it was a little more adventurous than a pie.

'And something happened then, yes?' Jim said, obviously trying to prompt Phil to get to the point.

'You could say that, yes,' Phil said. 'So, there we were, the three of us, sitting in the corner of the pub, bellies full, pints topped up, and there's nowt better than that, is there? Except a pipe after, like, but anyway, like I was saying, that's when it happened.'

Liz glanced over at Jim to find him giving her the same confused look she was sending him.

'What happened, Phil?' she asked.

'The fight!' Phil said. 'Did I not say that bit?'

Liz shook her head.

'No, I'm afraid you didn't.'

'Well, there was a fight. Not right away. First there was a fair bit of shouting, and that sort of got louder, then there was some shoving about, and everyone involved seemed to just get a little carried away with it all, if you ask me.'

Jim said, 'And you think we should look into it, is that right?'

'Of course, I do,' Phil said. 'I mean, it's connected, isn't it, like I said?'

'But you've not said it was connected to anything yet,' said Liz. 'Just that there was a fight at the pub.'

Phil leaned back in his chair and took a glug of tea.

'Gill was there,' he said. 'That's the connection, isn't it? Like I said to Harry in that message I left him. You can see it now, can't you?'

'Gill?' said Jim. 'You mean as in Gill Mitchell? That Gill?' He looked at Liz and added, 'If it's the same Gill, he does a bit of shepherding and other jobs for folk, up and down the Dale, including for my dad.'

'Is there another?' Phil said.

Liz hadn't heard of anyone called Gill, but then she wasn't from a farming family, so it sounded like he was the kind of person she probably hadn't had a reason to bump into.

'I don't think there is, no,' Phil said, looking thoughtful. 'Anyway, he doesn't like poachers, does he, so there we are, then, aren't we? And that's why I called Harry, because something we'd chatted about last night reminded me, and then I'd forgotten. He'd seen the bog myrtle. I'd mentioned Gill, who had given it to me, and right then my memory had tried to remind me, but it didn't, until a couple of hours ago now, and there you go. Simple.'

Liz scratched her head, hoping that would help her get to the point of what Phil was telling them. It didn't.

'I'm not sure that Gill not liking poachers, and you seeing him in a scuffle in a pub, is a connection to what happened last night over in Carperby,' she said.

'But it was poachers he was having a go at, wasn't it?' said Phil. 'In the pub. That's what the argument and the fight were all about.'

'Was it?' Jim asked.

'Of course it was!'

Phil leaned forward, as though what he was about to tell them was very important and very secret.

'Gill wasn't the one who started it, though,' he said. 'There were a couple of farmers there, you see, and I think they recognised these two lads at the table. They were minding their own business, quiet as you like, but then one of these others, he's over there and shouting at them. Then his mate ups and heads over to join in. It's all getting properly heated, like, and these two lads at the table look terrified, I don't mind telling you. Which was when Gill waded in.'

'The two lads at the table, they were poachers?' Liz asked.

'That's what those others were yelling at them,' said Phil. 'Calling them all kinds of names, they were. Telling them they'd give them what for if they ever caught them on their land again. The barman shouted at them to give over, but they just kept on.'

'And what did the ones they were accusing say?'

'I'm not sure, actually,' said Phil. 'They looked pretty bloody terrified, mind. Not from round here, that's for sure.'

'How do you mean, not from round here?' Jim asked, and Liz fully suspected Phil to say that they were from *down south*.

'They spoke English well enough, if a little broken, and their accents were from elsewhere.'

'Anywhere in particular?' Liz asked. 'Did you recognise them?'

'Sounded a little like Bond villains from the seventies, if you know what I mean. But not exactly that.'

'You mean Russian?'

'A bit like that, yes.'

Liz remembered what Harry had said at the meeting about the phone found at the scene. He'd said the voice on the other end had sounded Eastern European and had used the name Luca.

Phil was talking again, pulling Liz away from her thoughts and back into the conversation.

'Then, out of nowhere, Gill strides over, doesn't he? Just wades in and tells these two blokes doing all the shouting and threatening to bugger off and that he'll deal with it. That done, he grabs those two from the table by the scruff of the neck like they're two bad lads caught skiving school, and marches them outside, quick as you like. And the voice on him when he gets going—it's like being barked at by a sergeant major—we could still hear him bellowing at them even though they were outside.'

'And what happened after that?' Liz asked.

'Nowt,' Phil said. 'Gill walks back in, the whole pub staring at him, heads to the bar to pay for whatever he'd had to eat that evening, apologises, then off he goes, like nowt has happened and it's just a normal evening.'

For a moment, no one said anything, and the only sound was that of Jim mopping up the crumbs on his plate.

'Look, I'm not saying Gill is the one who's responsible for what happened yesterday,' Phil said. 'No one likes poachers around here, including me, but I just wondered if Gill and those others might have an idea as to who those boys were at the table, the ones they were shouting it. It's a lead, isn't it? That's what you call it. Maybe they knew the one Grace found in the woodland. You never know, do you?'

Liz was actually impressed, because when Phil had first started with his tale, she'd wondered where on earth they were going to end up. Turned out, the destination was worth it.

'Don't suppose you know where they live, do you?' she asked.

'The poachers? Not a clue,' said Phil.

'No, I mean the ones who accused them,' she said.

'I know where Gill lives,' Jim added. 'He's done a bit of work for my dad over the years.'

Phil clapped his hands then, the sound like a shotgun blast.

'This detective lark's a bit of a laugh, isn't it?' he said, pushing his chair back and standing up. 'But I've things to be getting on with, and you've criminals to catch, haven't you? Now, do you want to take anything with you? Cake? I've some pie somewhere, too, I'm sure.'

Outside, and having declined Phil's offer of food, Liz headed over to give Harry the Shire horse another pat. Phil had taken him back into his stall and was already on his way himself, having then jumped into an old tractor to trundle off out of the yard.

'What do you think, then?' Jim said, coming over to stand with her.

Harry tapped a hoof on the floor of his stall. Jim reached up and gave his nose a scratch.

'I think it's something we have to look into,' Liz said, and reminded Jim what Harry had said about the voice on the end of the phone found at the crime scene.

'You're right,' Jim said, but he was shaking his head. 'Can't be old Gill, though. Not a chance of it.'

'Doesn't sound like he's a fan of poachers, though, does it?' said Liz.

'Neither am I,' said Jim. 'Anyway, Gill's all bark and no bite, if you know what I mean. I've seen him care for lambs at death's door, staying up all night with them, feeding them by hand. He wouldn't do something like this.'

Liz glanced at her watch to see that there wasn't much of the day left for either of them.

'Looks like it'll have to wait till tomorrow anyway,' she said. 'Let's get back to the office, put in a few calls, and then we'll see what's what, won't we?'

'That we will,' Jim said.

CHAPTER NINETEEN

AFTER THE MEETING WITH SOWERBY OVER AT THE mortuary, Harry had headed home, then thought better of it, because he missed his dog, and he missed Grace. Not necessarily in that order, but sometimes it was a close-run thing. He wasn't about to tell anyone that, but the fact that he was thinking it at all was a huge surprise. He still wasn't quite used to it.

There was also the knowledge that Ben wouldn't be home either. Not that he'd actually been home all that much these past few months, with his romance with Liz blossoming, but his absence was now a permanent fixture. Harry had grown used to the possibility of bumping into him in the evening, having a chat, maybe going for a pint, things they'd rarely ever done together in their lives before. It seemed strange that it was now gone.

Approaching Carperby, Harry shook his head and swore under his breath, telling himself that he needed to pull himself together. What the hell was wrong with him? Was it age? He wasn't exactly ancient, was he? He was happy for

Ben, more than, so it was time to stop being a fool and crack on.

Come on, Harry ...

Arriving at Grace's house, Harry parked up and was on his phone, catching up with Matt and Gordy, who updated him as best as they could on what everyone else had been on with. The details he would deal with tomorrow, however, so he asked them both to make sure that the team would be at the office for eight-thirty, passing on the news that the DSupt would also be turning up. That would give them all time for a natter and then they could get on with business at nine.

The front door opened as Harry put out his hand to knock and out bounced Smudge, using her head like a battering ram against his legs, before jumping back onto her hind legs to reach up with her front paws.

As Harry patted the dog, he looked up to see Grace. He smiled, but the smile was broken by a yawn.

'Tired, then?' she said through a smile.

'A little. Been a good day, though. How are you doing, yourself?'

'The shock's worn off,' Grace said, 'so that's something, isn't it? Kept myself plenty busy with other jobs. Dad's been like a proper mother hen, though. I've only just sent him back up home to Redmire.'

'He's just being a dad.'

'He's also being a mum, and sometimes the roles get confused.'

Harry followed Grace inside.

'How do you mean?'

'Have a look for yourself,' Grace said, and nodded through to her kitchen. On the side, Harry saw various trays and dishes filled with food and stacked up on the floor were four bags of logs, on top of which were a couple of magazines and a bottle of wine.

Grace picked up the magazines.

'He grabbed these in a panic,' she said. 'This one is puzzles, and I really don't do puzzles, and this one is all about horoscopes, I think. Had a flick through earlier and if I want to, I can order various crystals, book a call with a medium, even pay to have past-life regression. Oh, and there's a piece about ghosts, too.'

'Don't knock it,' said Harry. 'There's that house out beyond Hawes that's supposedly haunted. I had a fair amount of trouble there just before we met.'

'You mean Black Moss House?'

'I do.'

'So, you saw the ghost then, did you?'

Harry paused for effect, remaining serious.

'Numerous times,' Harry said, his voice a little quieter now. 'It followed me home, I think, back to the flat.'

'What?'

Another pause.

'There was a presence,' he said. 'Corner of the bedroom. I'd wake in the night, and I'd swear there was someone standing there, staring at me. Took to sleeping in the lounge for a while. Even had Anna come out and do an exorcism in the end, which was a bit strange. I mean, she was keen and everything, but the Church of England isn't really into exorcisms, are they? That's more of a Catholic thing. She did a good job, though, that's for sure. At least, I think she did. I've heard a few odd things over the last few weeks. Knocks and bangs and this voice, just calling my name ...'

Harry held Grace's gaze just long enough, then winked.

'You absolute bastard,' Grace said, laughing and letting out a relieved breath. 'Had me going for a moment there.'

'Joking aside, there was definitely something odd about that place though,' Harry said, and picked up the bottle of wine that Grace's dad had left with her. 'Anyway, shall I do the honours?'

Later that evening, Arthur's food and the wine working together to send Grace to sleep, Harry stepped outside into the cool night air. Smudge upped and followed him and they stood at the front door staring out into the darkness beyond.

In front of him, even though it was hidden by the still shadows of night, Wensleydale breathed slowly and deeply, a breeze skipping along and with it came the sounds and smells of what Harry guessed was as near to Heaven as anyone could wish for. Behind him, the warm glow of Grace's house, the comforting aroma of burning wood and cooked food slipped out of the open door and rested upon him like a thick, comforting blanket.

Harry reached down and patted Smudge on the head. Tomorrow would be a busy day and he and the team would be dealing with the darker side of living. For now, though, he gave a thankful nod to the world at Grace's doorstep, turned around, and stepped back inside.

HAVING SLEPT LONG AND DEEP, Harry had arrived the next day at the office in Hawes refreshed and alert. A good breakfast of bacon and eggs with toast had certainly helped, as had the fresh coffee, but sharing it all with Grace had been the crowning glory. Now, with Smudge away in the corner play-fighting with Fly, and the rest of the team sitting in front of him ready to run through everything they had from the day before, he was about to start the meeting at dead on nine am, when a knock at the office door was followed by it being pushed open and someone walking in.

'Morning everyone,' Graham Swift said, stepping into the room.

Harry, along with everyone on the team, swivelled round to see their Detective Superintendent standing in front of them. In one hand was a large carrier bag and the other a battered briefcase.

'Good morning, sir,' Harry said, mustering up as much enthusiasm as he could.

Swift edged into the room and the door swished shut behind him. And then he smiled.

At first, Harry wondered if the man was having some kind of attack, his face contorting out of its usual look of mild irritation and into one that showed far too many teeth.

'Good to be here, actually,' Swift said, the grin turning down in intensity a notch or two from manic and terrifying, to awkward but means well.

Jadyn, who was standing with Harry up front, and on the other side of the board Jen had done such a good job with the day before, said, 'I'll get you a chair, sir.'

Swift was given no opportunity to argue as Jadyn jogged across the room, grabbed a chair, then placed it at the end of the row, next to Matt.

Swift sat down, then turned to Matt and asked how Mary-Anne was doing.

Matt, Harry noticed, looked a little stunned to be asked, but offered enough of an answer to satisfy the DSupt.

'Oh, I almost forgot,' Swift said, and stood up again. 'Thought I'd bring you all something to help with the day, keep your strength up, that kind of thing. I wasn't sure what to get exactly, so I just got two of everything. I do hope that's okay.'

From the bag, Swift proceeded to pull out various brown paper bags, all of them with dots of grease from their contents, and place them on a table.

'I saw that Cockett's was open when I drove past, so I dashed back. I've never once been in there myself, but you're all such fans of it, I thought you would approve.'

'That's ... Well, that's very generous of you,' Harry said, staring at the still hidden food now on the table.

'I'll get the kettle on, shall I?' Swift offered.

'We were just about to start the meeting,' Harry said, then saw the looks of longing in the eyes of his team. 'But we can delay that a while, I'm sure.'

'Good,' Swift said, and before Harry could say anymore, he was over at the sink filling up the kettle.

As the team busied themselves with refills and the tough decisions of which unhealthy thing to eat, Harry gently guided Swift away from the others for a quiet chat.

'Everything okay, sir?'

'Of course it is,' Swift said, the familiar snap in his voice returning with vigour. 'Why would you think otherwise?'

'Well, it's just that ...' Harry paused, trying to find the words, which wasn't easy when he wasn't exactly sure what he was trying to say. 'The food, it's very kind. As you can see, everyone is very appreciative.'

'That's good, then,' Swift said. 'Shall we get on?'

'And there's nothing you want to tell me?' Harry asked. 'Or shall we just leave that till after the meeting?'

'Why?' Swift said. 'I'm here to join in the investigation. To help. Wasn't I clear when we spoke yesterday?'

'No, you weren't, sir,' Harry said.

'I think I was.'

'And I said that we were more than fine.'

'Well, another pair of hands can't hurt now, can they?' Swift said, and before Harry could argue, he turned on his heel and headed over to join the rest of the team.

Harry decided to not follow. Instead, he just watched, as Swift picked something from one of the bags, a pastry laden with glistening currants, then patted Fly on the head, and started to chat with Jim.

As bizarre and unexpected ways to start the day, this was a winner, Harry thought, and with little other choice, headed over to join in.

CHAPTER TWENTY

'Well, Vince sounds a treat,' Matt said, as Gordy finished running through her notes from her meeting with the man the day before.

Gordy gave a short laugh.

'Not someone I'd be looking to see on an episode of *One Man And His Dog*, that's for sure. I think that great, demonic brute of his, Thor, would probably eat the sheep rather than round them up.'

'Demonic?'

'Very,' Gordy said. 'Looked like it had been carved out of Hell's darkness, its fur was so black.'

'Definitely a person of interest, though,' said Swift. 'Evasive, wasn't he?'

'Very,' Gordy said. 'Though I got the impression that was just part of his nature. Not the kind of man to have anyone know his business.'

'Has he sent that list of stolen goods yet?'

Gordy shook her head. 'But that solicitor of his, the one I met briefly on my way up to the house, is supposedly popping in today to give us a statement. No idea of when, though.'

Swift looked up at Harry.

'Then if it's okay with you, I'll take a trip out there to have a chat with him about it, jog his memory, that kind of thing.'

'And I'll have a look through the system to see what was actually reported,' Jadyn said. 'Can't say I remember anything about it right now.'

Although they'd only gone through Gordy's notes so far, plus a couple of things from the Action Book, it hadn't escaped Harry's attention that Swift had been almost overly engaged with what was going on. He'd offered plenty of *um*s and *ah*s and even at one point, when Jadyn had stood up to start doing his thing with the board, provided a light burst of applause.

Something was going on, of that Harry was certain, but what? It hadn't escaped the notice of the team either, and he'd exchanged confused looks with both Matt and Gordy.

'Yes, why not? It could be useful,' Harry replied.

'Even if not with this investigation, then that break-in might link to something else,' said Swift. 'And I can't sit here and let that go.'

With Gordy done, Harry turned everyone's attention to Jim and Liz.

'Man traps, then,' he said. 'What've we got? And I'm assuming you've not stumbled across a little cottage industry in the things, someone in their garden shed knocking out a couple a week for the occasional disgruntled landowner.'

Liz spoke first.

'No, but we do have something a little interesting, I think.'

'She's not lying,' said Jim, and Harry saw a smug look on the young PCSO's face.

'Out with it then,' Harry said.

'The auction house does get traps through now and again,' Liz explained. 'They're classed as historical items and either too old and rusted to be of any use, or decommissioned, you know, welded together or something, so that they can't be used, even if someone wanted to.'

'Mostly mole traps I think,' said Jim. 'But other ones, too, for animals. Awful things, like. That's no way to be catching anything.'

'What about man traps, then?' Harry asked.

'They're rare, but they do get them,' answered Liz. 'Not sold one in over a year, though. However, ...' She pulled something from her pocket. 'This was dropped off late yesterday afternoon by the man we spoke to, Rob Sharp.'

'And what is that, exactly?' Harry asked.

'It's a bill of sale,' she said. 'For the man trap.'

'And?'

'And it might be of interest to our detective superintendent: the buyer was and is a certain Vince Walker.'

'Seriously?'

'Seriously,' Jim said. 'The last man trap to go through the auction house was sold to Vince Walker.'

Swift rubbed his hands together.

'Looks like it's going to be an interesting conversation,' he said.

'Before that, they'd not sold one in years,' added Liz. 'Rob checked and could find nothing till about five years ago.'

'Vince has this big display of old farming equipment on one of his walls,' Gordy said. 'No man trap, though.

Although it did seem like there was a gap in his display,' she added.

'So either our man Vince decided to use it on a poacher,' said Jadyn 'or someone nicked it off him because they somehow knew he had one?'

Harry nodded thoughtfully at Jadyn's words.

'It certainly looks that way. But we still have to keep an open mind. We can't assume one thing has anything to do with anything else. All we can do, and all we should do, is investigate further, and if there is a connection, we'll follow it.'

'Still though,' said Jadyn, 'it is a bit of a coincidence, isn't it, and you—'

'Don't believe in coincidences, I know,' said Harry. He looked back over at Liz and Jim. 'Anything else?'

'Not from that, no,' Liz said. 'But there's our chat with Phil as well.'

Harry held up a hand to stop her before she launched into what had happened with that.

'Let's hear from Matt and Jen first.'

Matt said, 'Not much to tell really, is there, Jen?'

'We've some footage from a security camera at the scrap merchant's,' said Jen, and held up a USB stick. 'I had a look through it all yesterday, but will have another look again today. Plus, there's various files on here that I might take a peek at, too.'

'Are they relevant to this case?' Harry asked.

'Probably not, but if you'd seen what we saw at that place, you'd want to look at them, too.'

Matt was staring at Harry.

'You weren't there, man,' said Matt, shaking his head with just a touch too much drama. 'You weren't there ...'

A ripple of laughter bounced around the team.

'It was a lighter,' Harry said, remembering then what Matt had told him the night before. 'A novelty lighter.'

'A novelty lighter in the shape of a pistol,' Matt said. 'Very realistic it was, too, and she pointed it at my face.'

'You'll get over it.'

'I thought I was going to die.'

'No, you didn't.'

'No, you're right, I didn't.' Matt sighed. 'But it still gave me one hell of a shock.'

Jen laughed.

'I don't think I've ever seen our DS look or sound so shocked or angry. For a moment there, it was like he was you, Boss; positively terrifying.'

Harry wasn't sure whether to take that as a compliment or not.

'What was on the security footage, then?'

'The car we found at the scene being stolen,' said Matt. 'Someone broke in, found it, and just drove it away, cool as you like.'

'And you think this someone is our victim?'

'Hard to say for sure,' said Liz. 'But I think so, yes.'

'And you think he was looking for that car specifically?'

Matt gave a nod.

'I do, actually, because he was in and out pretty sharpish, didn't exactly go mooching around trying other vehicles. He went in there, nabbed the car, and left. Someone dropped him off as well.'

'But why get a vehicle from a scrapyard?' Harry asked. 'Why not steal an actual, road-legal car?'

'I've been thinking about that, too,' said Jen. 'If you nick someone's car, there's a lot more paperwork with it, isn't there? Insurance and all that. All this had was a destruction certificate, so once destroyed it's kind of off the system. Use it for short runs here and there, and in the meantime, keep it well out of sight, and no one would be any the wiser.'

Harry thought about that. There was some sense to it, but it wasn't risk-free. And no vehicle was ever truly off the system.

'Well, let's think on that while we go through everything else,' Harry said, and looked over at Jim and Liz. 'So, how was Phil, then?'

'You'll be relieved to hear he didn't give us a pie to bring back,' Liz said.

'Thank God for that,' said Harry.

'What he did give us, though, was a very long version of a story that probably could have taken just a couple of minutes. But anyway, it's relevant.'

Jim then told the team what Phil had shared with them about the altercation at the pub.

'He said he nearly told you back at the crime scene, but then forgot.'

Harry had listened intently, but the main thing that had stuck with him was that Phil had seen two men have a go at these supposed poachers. If they were that angry then, in a public place, who was to say what they were capable of in a dark woodland with their victim cornered?

'I'm assuming you have the addresses of those involved?'

'I know where Gill lives,' said Jim. 'The poachers, we've nothing on, but by their description from Phil, I think there's a good chance one of them was our victim. The two blokes who went for them in the pub we'll follow up on today, after we've spoken with Gill, as he probably knows them.'

Harry was impressed. Everyone was thinking and

working things through. The team was unlike any other he'd ever worked with, but somehow, they were turning into one of the most effective.

'Sounds like those two are the ones we really need to speak to,' he said. 'And if Gill's our way to them, then that sounds great.' He coughed to clear his throat. 'The victim, then,' he said, but was interrupted by Swift.

'What about the crime scene photographs?' he asked.

'They'll be with us at some point today, I'm sure,' Harry said.

'I'll give them a call. Hurry them along a bit. Who should I speak to?'

Harry was about to say Sowerby, when another name floated to the top of his mind.

'Bennett,' he said. 'Best you speak to him, I think.'

A murmur of agreement rippled through the office from the rest of the team.

He had a suspicion that Sowerby wouldn't take kindly to being hurried along. Also, of all the people in the room, he figured Swift would be the best to deal with Bennett.

Harry moved on to what he had found out from his visit to the mortuary. He explained first about the tourniquet.

'So, someone went out there, then?' Jim asked.

'Our victim made a call,' Harry said. 'I assume whoever took that call went straight out and tried to save them, even though it would've been clear that it was a lost cause and our victim was no doubt already dead. Hopefully, forensics will get us something from the phone, but we'll just have to see.'

'So, why try?' Jim asked. 'To save him, I mean, if he's already dead? That doesn't make sense.'

'Because in that kind of circumstance, it's difficult to just stand back and accept death,' Harry said. 'Trust me, I've been there.'

He didn't dwell on that point and quickly moved on, deciding to use the victim's name, to emphasise the point that they were now trying to find someone who killed a living, breathing person, someone with a life, someone just like everyone else in that room.

'Luca's body was badly beaten. He'd been tied up before his leg was dropped into the man trap, then released.'

'Why release him?' Jen asked.

'To be cruel,' Harry said. 'That's my guess, anyway. After the damage his body had taken, those who did it to him knew he was going to die. That was the point. By cutting his bonds, they gave him an empty hope he'd survive. And from the damage sustained, it looks like there were two attackers, instead of just one.'

Gordy let out a long sigh.

'What is wrong with people?' she said.

'Also, his body showed signs of extended malnutrition,' Harry continued. 'He was severely underweight, and his most recent meal had just been soup. Sowerby also identified chemical and water damage to his hands. Flaky skin, some-thing she referred to as dishpan hands. Something you get from excessive exposure to soap and water, that kind of thing.'

'Worked in a kitchen, then,' said Matt.

'Possibly, yes,' said Harry. 'Which means the lengthy process of checking up on every restaurant and café in the area. We still don't actually know where Luca is from, but if he was at that scrapyard you and Jen visited, Matt, then my guess is the same area, so Richmond way.'

'Could be a car wash, though.'

Jadyn's voice cut through Harry's thoughts and he turned to look at the constable.

'What was that?'

'A car wash,' Jadyn said. 'The soap and water damage. If you spend a few days cleaning cars, you're going to get sore hands, aren't you? I worked at one myself a few years ago now. Got paid in cash, too.'

Matt was on his feet and Harry saw him pull something from his pocket.

'Her Range Rover,' he said. 'Remember, Jen?'

'It was white,' Jen said. 'Goodness knows why she was using it to tow old bangers to the yard.'

'You mentioned that when we spoke yesterday,' Harry said.

'And it was really clean, too,' continued Matt. 'She said how she got it washed every week, looked at the state of the car we'd driven over in, then gave me this ...'

Harry took what Matt was handing him. It was the business card for U-WAIT-WE-WASH. An idea grew in his mind, then.

'You said she was using the Range Rover to tow?' he asked.

Jen gave a nod.

'There was a trailer attached with an old Astra on it.'

'What are you thinking?' Matt asked.

Harry held up the business card.

'I'm thinking that if your pistol-wielding friend Margaret is having that posh Range Rover of hers washed every week at the place on this card here, then there's a good chance that sometimes she's towing a vehicle at the same time, on her way back to the scrapyard.'

Harry saw a lightbulb spark behind Matt's eyes.

'Which means,' said Matt, 'that someone at the car wash would see the vehicle and know just where to go to nick it.'

'Someone like Luca,' said Jen.

Harry gave a nod.

'Exactly.'

CHAPTER TWENTY-ONE

THE MORNING WAS ALREADY GETTING ON AND DIVVYING up the jobs wasn't any easier with Swift deciding to join in, but at least he had already given himself a job to do. Harry tried to pull the senior officer to one side at the end of the meeting, but Swift seemed very keen to be off to visit Vince.

'But I thought you were here to explain a little more about what we discussed on the phone yesterday?' Harry asked, as Swift pulled on his jacket to head out the door.

'This is much more important, I think,' Swift replied, with an energy to the man Harry had never seen before. 'I'll give forensics a call on the way about those photographs. Then I'll go and chat to this Vince about that theft of his. Perhaps, later on, we can go for a chat in a café or something. How does that sound?'

Weird, Harry thought, but out loud he said, 'Sounds great.' Then added, 'Looking forward to it already,' and immediately worried that his insincerity had been too obvious.

Swift didn't seem to notice though, and was out the door and heading off even before Harry had finished speaking.

Liz volunteered to be the office manager for the day. Someone had to do it, to be available to keep everyone up to date with any new developments, and be a point of contact for any other business coming in from the local community. She would also do a walk around Hawes, just to be that obvious police presence. There was also the promised visit by Vince Walker's solicitor, so she would be on hand to deal with that as well.

Gordy and Jadyn were tasked with heading off to the car wash. Harry had thought about going along, but had decided to head off with Jim to meet Gill instead. He wanted to not only know what had happened at the pub from Gill's perspective, why he'd waded in, but also to get a better understanding of just how bad, or not, poaching was in the area. He could ask Grace, true, but that didn't seem right, as she was closely involved with the case. Much better to speak to someone like Gill. Also, with Jim knowing Gill, they'd maybe have a chance at having him give up more information than he would to someone he didn't know.

Harry had sent Matt and Jen to chat with the pub owner where the scuffle had taken place, and to knock on a few doors to check if anyone had seen or heard anything. There was also the chance that the landlord would be able to give them the names of the ones who'd had a go at the two poachers, and they could then follow that up, too.

As for the dogs, well, they both seemed very happy indeed to be travelling together, clipped in as they were in the back of Harry's RAV4, and currently play-fighting.

'It's such a shame that they don't get on,' Jim said, swishing across his seatbelt.

Harry laughed and shook his head.

'It's like having kids in the back.'

Almost as though they knew they were being talked about, both dogs looked at Harry as he stared at them in the rearview mirror and started the engine. They had one last playful snap at each other, then settled down as Harry pulled out of the marketplace and headed off down dale.

'So, where exactly are we heading, then?' Harry asked as Hawes faded behind them. The day was a little overcast, but surprisingly warm, though a cool breeze had followed them out to the car to rush them in as they climbed into their seats.

'Gill lives out beyond West Burton, Walden way,' Jim said. 'It's pretty remote; one of those places where the road soon becomes a track, then just ends in a field and the fells. He's lived in this tiny cottage down there as long as anyone's known him.'

'And he's worked for your dad, is that right?'

'He's a professional shepherd. Well, some of the time he is,' Jim said. 'He's never had a farm of his own, but he's always been around to help out.'

Onward they rolled, through Bainbridge, its village green quiet, then on until Aysgarth greeted them, sat as it was at the top of a long, steep rise in the road which climbed out of the valley floor like the greying branch of a vine.

'Didn't realise there was such a thing, if I'm honest,' Harry said, speeding up a little as the road straightened ahead, pulling them on towards Bainbridge.

'He does other stuff, too,' said Jim.

'Such as?'

'He's handy with a chainsaw for a start. Just seems to be someone who can turn his hand to most jobs, you know?'

'Not sure I've ever been like that myself,' Harry said.

'No, I know what you mean.'

Aysgarth seems as asleep as always, Harry thought, as they drove through the village. Rarely had he ever actually seen anyone walking around. The pub looked good though and was one of many he had yet to try.

Out the other side of Aysgarth, they dipped down again, heading back towards the valley floor, soon to turn right to head towards West Burton.

'So, why's he never had his own farm, then?' Harry asked.

'They're not easy to come by for a start,' said Jim. 'We're lucky, I guess, because we own ours. A good number are tenanted, and they don't come up much. Anyway, it's different with Gill.'

'Is it? Why?'

Jim was quiet for a moment, thinking about what to say.

'Likes his freedom, I think,' he said at last, as they came into West Burton. 'He's getting on a bit, like, I mean. He's probably in his seventies now, but you wouldn't know it. Fit as pins, as my dad would say. And sometimes, he just buggers off, just like that; gone. And he'll not be seen for a few weeks, then he'll be back like nowt's different.'

'So, where does he go, then?' Harry asked. 'Holiday?'

'Travels a lot, I think,' said Jim. 'You get him talking, and he certainly seems to know the world better than most around here. He's quite unique, is Gill.'

'Sounds it,' Harry said.

West Burton came and went, but not before Harry had allowed himself a moment to slow down enough to look at the place. He wondered then, as he saw the old Methodist chapel, the pub, the houses staring at each other across the village green, if there was such a thing as an ugly patch to the

Dales. He guessed that there had to be, just by the law of averages, but so far, he'd not spotted anything other than picture-postcard-perfect views and scenes wherever he went.

Out the back of West Burton, Harry followed Jim's directions, and soon enough they took a left and headed down a single-track lane. And, as Jim had said, the metalled road eventually gave up the ghost, and they were rumbling along over gravel, grit, and stone.

'That's Walden Beck, just down there,' Jim said, pointing out the window and down to their left.

Harry saw lush green fields dipping their grey-walled boundaries into the waving arms of trees, which marched together in a long line along the valley floor. They passed a couple of fields with caravans in them as well, an activity Harry had never really seen the attraction of. A campervan was something he'd maybe consider one day, because that struck him as a little more adventurous. But parking a plastic box in a field to just sit in and watch the telly? What was the point of that? Obviously, there was more to it, he was sure, but it still struck him as odd.

'And that hill up there on our left, that's Brown Haw,' said Jim.

'It's an impressive sight,' said Harry.

'It's bleak up there, though,' Jim said. 'Nowt much around once you get up there. Anyway, we're here; that's Gill's place just ahead on the right.'

Harry saw the house and slowed down. As he did so, both dogs in the back sat up, tails wagging with excitement to be at their destination, and barking.

'Give over!' Jim shouted, turning round at the dogs. 'Fly! Smudge! Down!'

As one, and to Harry's surprise, both dogs stopped

barking and dropped to the seat, lying beside each other, and staring at the PCSO.

'Bloody hell,' Harry said. 'What are you, the Dog Whisperer?'

Jim laughed.

'Fly's coming along with his training, and Grace seems to be doing well with Smudge, too.'

Harry narrowed his eyes at Jim.

'Are you saying I've nothing to do with it, is that right?'

'No, I'm sure you're doing a grand job,' Jim said.

There wasn't much Harry could say to that, because he knew Jim had a point with what he hadn't said as much as with what he had. Grace was responsible for Smudge being such a good dog. But then, why not? She was the game-keeper, training dogs was part of her job. The only dogs Harry had any experience with were police dogs, and even then only as an officer arresting whichever poor sod it was they'd dragged to the ground.

'And this lane leads nowhere, then?' Harry asked, climbing out of the vehicle.

'It's just a farm track, really,' Jim said. 'Not used much, other than by farmers in tractors, or the occasional idiot in a four-by-four thinking they can just go off-roading wherever they want to.'

Harry looked over at Gill's house. It was small, as Jim had said, and Harry wondered if it had always been a house or, at some other time in its life, little more than a stone shelter for sheep. The ground floor held the front door and a single window to one side. Above were two windows. There was a tin-roofed lean-to on the right of the property, a small front garden comprising two small patches of lawn, and to the rear, Harry saw a huge tree leaning over the place, like a drunk frozen in time mid-collapse. Leaning up against the house was an old, rusting bike, but Harry noticed that the chain was well-oiled, so it clearly saw regular use. Just off to one side, he spotted the front end of an old, red Suzuki 4x4 poking its nose out, as though afraid to reveal itself in full.

'Probably best if you knock, seeing as Gill knows you,' Harry said.

Jim stepped forward, lifted his knuckles to the door and gave a sharp rap-tap-tap-tap.

'And you're sure he's in?' Harry asked.

'I am,' said Jim. 'I gave him a call to check he'd be here.'

'Seems dead though, doesn't it?'

'Lives quietly, does Gill. Not one for television or radio. If he's not out on the fells, or working with someone somewhere in the Dales, he's usually at home either gardening or reading.'

Harry frowned.

'I thought you said he travels a lot?'

Jim shrugged.

'No one really knows what he gets up to when he's away,' he said. 'He's a private man, is Gill. You'll like him, I promise.'

'And why do you say that?'

The door opened and in the space it had occupied stood a man a head shorter than Harry, trousers tucked into Wellington boots, a faded denim shirt rolled up at the elbows. He was tanned as only someone who lives their life outside can be, and he stared up at Harry from beneath a roughly sewn hat of soft, brown fur. He pulled it off to scratch grey hair buzz-cut short, like his own, then replaced the hat.

'Is that Jim?' the man said.

'It is,' Jim replied. 'How you doing, Gill? I rang, remember?'

'I do,' Gill said. 'And you've arrived just in time.'

'For what?'

'A brew,' Gill said, then he looked up at Harry, stared for a moment through narrowed eyes, gave a nod, then turned back into the house, leaving the door open.

'See?' Jim said.

'See what?' Harry asked.

'I said you'd like him, didn't I?'

'You did, yes, but why?' Harry asked.

Jim laughed.

'You go to the same barber!' he said, then followed Gill inside.

CHAPTER TWENTY-TWO

JADYN HAD FOUND THE PREVIOUS DAY A LITTLE frustrating. It was all very well following procedure, but sometimes he thought the best thing to do was ignore it. After what had been discovered by Harry's girlfriend, Grace, on Tuesday night, he'd been itching to get involved with the investigation, but Harry had insisted, and Gordy had made it more than clear on the boss's behalf, that he wasn't on duty and coming in had not been an option.

He'd spent the day mooching around his flat over in Catterick, either dozing on the sofa, listening to random selections from his vinyl collection—the day had been all about Earth, Wind and Fire, for some reason—or eating. Not a bad day, all in all, but he'd have rather been out doing something useful. He'd been to the gym, so that was something, wasn't it? Keeping that regular wasn't easy, but so far, he'd managed pretty well with it. And now he was sitting next to Detective Inspector Haig as she sped them along through Wensleydale, their destination a car wash.

Jadyn looked again at the business card for where they were heading.

'Catchy name,' he said.

'Not half as bad as the one for the scrapyard Matt and Jen visited yesterday,' Gordy said. 'Well done on making that connection, by the way.'

'How do you mean?'

'This was your idea, remember? You made the link between the victim's hands and washing cars.'

Jadyn couldn't help but smile at this, smugly, too.

'Could still be that they worked in a kitchen, though,' he said, attempting a little bit of modesty, but not too much.

'It could,' said Gordy. 'But this feels right, don't you think?'

'Do you?'

'Very much so, actually. That was some sharp thinking, if you ask me. We could've found ourselves traipsing around every restaurant, hotel, and café in the area if it wasn't for you speaking up.'

'I sometimes think Harry's view is that I speak up too much.'

'Don't be daft,' said Gordy, a laugh in her voice. 'You're keen. He likes that. And so do I, as it happens. So, don't you go losing that.'

Neither spoke for the next few minutes, and Jadyn spent the time trying not to yawn. But it was no good and one escaped a little too loudly.

'Sorry about that,' he said.

'Didn't rest much yesterday, then?'

'I did. Well, I tried,' Jadyn said. 'Guess I was just thinking about what everyone else was doing.'

'Their job, like you are now, that's all. And being off duty *to rest* is as important as it is being on duty. Never forget that.'

'I won't.'

'Good.'

The journey continued in relative silence, the only sound that of the wind hissing in through the vents. Jadyn knew the route well, as it was one he took most days, travelling over to Wensleydale to work. And even though it was a lovely drive, he was beginning to wonder if he should move a little closer. Catterick was all very well, but he was really getting to know the team now, having joined around a year ago. And it wasn't as though he was tied to where he was right now. Maybe I should chat with Jim about it, he thought.

It wasn't long before the view of green, rolling fields was replaced with the urban sprawl of Richmond, though that description didn't quite fit the historic town, Jadyn thought, as they breached its boundary, heading over a bridge, the castle rising above the river on their right.

'It's a beautiful place, Richmond,' Gordy said, as she drove them on. 'Loads of lovely little shops and cafes.'

'Never really been,' Jadyn said.

'Well, make sure that you do. We can't have a visit to that place being your only memory of it, can we?'

'What place?'

Gordy pointed out through the windscreen, and Jadyn saw their destination just ahead.

'We're here,' she said.

Jadyn was out of the vehicle as soon as the DI had parked up and was struck with how professional the set-up seemed. He had seen plenty of car wash places, particularly at home in Bradford, and most of them looked nothing like this. He had been expecting to find a rough scrap of ground, perhaps a derelict petrol station forecourt, repurposed for washing cars, buckets and hose pipes strewn everywhere, with the staff milling about in what were clearly their own clothes, doing their best to get through as many vehicles as possible in a day. Not here though, not at U-WAIT-WE-WASH.

The colour scheme was orange and black, the staff all decked out in black overalls with orange flashes down the arms and legs. The site had clearly been a petrol station at some point in its life, but it had been renovated and cleaned and polished, with the business sign clear for all to see, and a large board displaying prices according to what service you required, and for what vehicle you drove.

And it was busy, Jadyn thought, with a good number of cars and vans lined up waiting their turn. Once washed, the vehicles would either head back out into the traffic or take a little detour for a full valet of the interior. This place was thorough.

It was already difficult to see how the crime scene from two nights ago could be connected to this place at all. But then, as Gordy called him over to join her, Jadyn couldn't help remembering Harry's words of wisdom, which seemed ever-present in his head: *to always keep an eye open for something that shouldn't be there, but is, and something that should be, but isn't.* He wasn't sure if those were his exact words, really, but it was close enough, and the sentiment was always on his mind when he was at work.

'Let's go have a word with the management,' Gordy said, and pointed over at the office behind where the vehicles were being washed.

They entered through a door that rang a little bell as it opened.

Inside, the office was all motivational posters and the

aroma of coffee. Jadyn read some of the posters as they made their way to a glass desk at the other end of the office, behind which sat a middle-aged woman, smartly dressed, her very shiny black shoes just visible beneath the desk.

One of the posters was the picture of a rowing team, and beneath it read, *There is no I in team*. Beside it, and above the word *Perseverance*, there was a poster of a kitten hanging onto a thick piece of rope. Another had the words, *Dreams don't work unless you do,* emblazoned across a sun-kissed horizon. The last one Jadyn glanced at was just words on a black background, *Don't stop when you're tired, stop when you're done*. He read that one a few times and wasn't sure whether it was motivational, terrifying, or an awful, bullying mix of both.

The woman at the desk stood up, her face full of bright white teeth set in a holiday tan.

'Good morning,' she said.

Gordy, Jadyn noticed, was already wearing her most disarming smile.

'Isn't it just?' Gordy replied. 'And how lucky we are to be enjoying it, wouldn't you agree?'

'Very much so,' the woman said, her eyes flicking over to Jadyn, probably because he was the only one of the two of them wearing a uniform. 'How can I help?'

Gordy pulled out her ID.

'Detective Inspector Haig,' she said. 'And this is Police Constable Okri. Ms—?'

'Knight,' the woman said. 'As in Michael.'

At this, Gordy laughed, though Jadyn had no idea why.

'I like that,' she said.

'Obviously, that's not actually me,' Knight said. 'Though my parents did call me Michelle. Fans of The Hoff and with a terrible sense of humour to boot. Can I ask why you're here?'

'We are making some enquires with regards to a current investigation and wondered if we could speak with your staff.'

'What investigation?'

Jadyn heard concern in the woman's voice.

'This is all routine,' Gordy said. 'We are simply trying to work out the movements of one or more of those involved.'

'Will it take long? As you can see, we're rather busy.'

Gordy glanced out of the window and then back at Knight.

'We will do our upmost to be as quick as we possibly can, I promise. Is there somewhere we can use to chat to your staff?'

'Not really, no,' Knight said.

'What about here?' Gordy asked, gesturing at the room they were in.

Knight was quiet for a moment, then said, 'And this has to be done now?'

'It does.'

Knight let out a frustrated sigh.

'Excuse me a moment, please.'

For the next minute or so, Jadyn watched as the woman made her way around the room, locking up filing cabinets and then shutting down her computer. She then picked up a set of car keys from her desk.

'I have an errand or two to run anyway,' she said. 'So, you can use the office while I'm out.'

'Perfect,' Gordy said, then turned to Jadyn. 'Perhaps you could ask them to come in?'

Jadyn turned to head for the door but Knight strode past him.

'I'll just let everyone know what's happening and send in the first two,' she said.

'Thank you,' Gordy replied.

Jadyn watched as Michelle Knight strode out of the office and called her staff over. Jadyn had no idea what she was saying, but it was clear that they were all listening, all of them staring at her, almost without blinking.

Knight pointed at two men, then behind her at the office, before climbing behind the wheel of a black Mercedes-Benz and heading off. Jadyn had no idea as to what model it was, just that it looked expensive.

The bell on the door chimed and in walked the two men, nervous eyes darting between himself and Gordy.

'Please,' said Gordy, gesturing to two chairs in front of the desk, as she settled down in Knight's on the other side.

Jadyn was about to join her when she held up a hand and he paused.

'Perhaps it would be useful to have a look around outside?' Gordy suggested. 'I'm sure I'll be fine in here.' She looked at the two men then and said, 'Coffee?'

The men looked at each other, and Jadyn could see that they were surprised by the question. Their sleeves were rolled up, probably in some attempt to keep a part of their clothing dry, he thought. He noticed as well that there were bruises on their arms, easy enough to acquire from washing cars all day.

'There's a pod machine thing over there,' Gordy said, pointing to the far corner of the office. 'Why don't you grab yourselves one each, and one for me while you're at it? Nothing fancy though, just a flat white, if that's available.'

One of the men headed over to the coffee machine. He stared at it for a moment, glancing occasionally back to his friend, sitting in front of Gordy.

After a rather awkward moment or two of nothing happening, Jadyn walked over.

'Here,' he said, picking a pod from a selection to the left of the machine, then demonstrated how to use it.

'Thank you,' the man said, and Jadyn noticed the accent straight away; Eastern European, the same as the one Harry had heard on the phone Tuesday night.

'No problem,' he said. 'They're always a bit confusing if you've not used one before.'

The man followed Jadyn's instructions, using the machine with a mechanical slowness and stiffness in his movements. Standing closer to the man, Jadyn saw that the bruises looked a little worse than he'd originally thought, which was odd.

The man smiled in thanks. Jadyn turned and headed out of the door.

CHAPTER TWENTY-THREE

The house was functional, Harry thought, as he and Jim sat down with Gill in the lounge. Gill had brought in a pot of tea and a packet of biscuits and laid them on a small table in the centre of the room. He'd sat down and once again looked Harry over, his eyes on the scars, but said nothing about them.

The room itself provided all that Gill required, but nothing to give it the impression of comfort. That wasn't to say that it wasn't comfortable. Far from it, Harry thought. The wood-burning stove was already lit, the small sofa and armchair more than comfortable. It's just that was about it. No television was the main thing Harry noticed. He was so used to seeing them in every house in the land, to not see one seemed strange.

The walls were bare, bar a few rather excellent photos of Highland scenery. He saw no ornaments on shelves or windowsills, nothing really that didn't serve a function. There was, however, a large bookcase. Harry gave it a glance and saw that it would provide anyone with more than enough to read, just so long as all they wanted to read about was mountaineering.

As to the rest of the house, Harry had seen nothing of it bar the small hall just inside the front door, which led straight through to the lounge and the stairs to the first floor.

'So, Jim,' Gill said, 'what is it that brings you out here to see me, then?' He turned then to look over at Harry. 'You'd be Grimm, right?'

Harry was hard pushed to place the accent. It was clearly one that had travelled, he thought, its origins erased by time and experience to give little away. There was Yorkshire in there for sure, but only a dusting of it, Harry thought, just enough to add a bit of local flavour, but no more.

'I am,' Harry said. 'Thank you for giving us a bit of your time this morning, Mr Mitchell.'

'Not a problem at all,' Gill said. 'And it's Gill, so you can stop with all that Mr Mitchell rubbish.' He turned back to Jim. 'Well then, are you going to tell me what this is all about, or do I have to guess? How are your parents, by the way? Had a lot of fun helping your dad out with lambing time earlier in the year, didn't we?'

'They're fine, thanks, and yes, we did,' Jim smiled. 'Can't beat lambing time.'

'Couldn't agree with you more.'

Harry saw Jim glance over at him, clearly expecting him to take over proceedings. Harry had other ideas though. Seeing as Jim and Gill knew each other, he decided to give the PCSO the lead. No, it wasn't exactly procedure, but then Harry had quickly learned that being a PCSO in the Dales wasn't quite the same as it was down in Bristol. Here they had to be a jack of all trades. Plus, they were a key part of the team, and no matter how different or strange that team was compared with others, it worked. Harry wasn't about to pop the hood and start tinkering with the engine.

'We're here to speak to you about something that may be linked to an investigation,' Harry said, Gill turning once again to face him. 'Jim is probably better placed than I am to talk to you about it, which is why he's here.'

Gill's eyes were now back on Jim and the man leaned forward, hands clasped, the muscles in his tanned forearms flexing like steel wire.

'I was over with Phil Thwaite yesterday,' Jim said.

'Phil? How is that silly old sod?' Gill asked. 'Still got that giant horse of his, hasn't he? Never really been sure what he uses it for other than a bit of company. I've seen him riding it about a few times; looks like a child sitting up there on the thing, it's that big.'

'He's still got it,' Jim said. 'Anyway, he mentioned something that happened in the pub in West Burton a couple of weeks ago, I think.'

'Did he? And what was that?'

Jim briefly explained what Phil had told him about the events of that night.

Gill was quiet for a moment.

'Ah, that,' he said at last, and sat back. 'Phil was there, then, was he? I'm sorry he saw me get like that, all angry, but you know how it is sometimes, when your blood just boils over, you see red, that kind of thing.'

'So, what happened?' Jim asked. 'Obviously, we know what Phil saw, but your side of things would be very useful. And any names, if you have them.'

'And this is relevant to an investigation, is it?' Gill asked.

'It is,' said Harry, stepping in momentarily so that Jim

didn't give too much away. 'So, if you can tell us what happened, that would be very useful.'

Gill rubbed his chin thoughtfully, took a sip of tea.

'It was late in the evening,' he said. 'I'd been out working on a farm over Kettlewell way. It had been a good, long day, lots of tree work, that kind of thing, so I was having a few pints and a steak and kidney pie. Food's good there, as you know, Jim.'

Jim gave a nod. Harry remained still, staying out of proceedings as best he could.

'Anyway, I'd had a couple, and I was tired, so I was good for another pint and then a stroll home. I take that old bike of mine to the pub, you see. Anyway, I was about to head to the bar when these two big lads, who'd been in there most of the evening I reckon, judging by how loud they were, just got up and started having a go at these other two sitting at a table.'

'Did you recognise them?' Jim asked.

'They were John Bell's sons,' Gill said.

'You mean the twins?'

'I do. Few years older than you, Jim, I think. Everyone knows them by sight.'

'Also by reputation,' said Jim.

Harry picked up on this and asked him to clarify.

'Like Gill said, they're big lads and usually where you see one, the other's not too far away.'

'And this reputation?'

'They've been known to like a scrap or two,' said Jim. 'Sometimes with each other, if they have a falling out, like. I've seen them leathering the hell out of each other at the auction mart before, right in the middle of a sheep pen. Took a good few blokes to drag them apart.'

'They sound like fun.'

'Well, that's one way to describe them,' said Gill. 'They can be a handful, that's for sure. They're alright, really, just get a bit carried away. And they're thick as thieves, even with their disagreements.'

Harry allowed Gill to continue.

'They do most of the work on the family farm now, rather than their mum and dad,' he said. 'Can't remember their first names right now. Anyway, they're usually good lads, but with a few too many jars inside them, they can be hard to handle, if you know what I mean.'

'What about the two at the table?'

'They'd not been in long,' said Gill. 'They were chattering away, nice and quiet, minding their own business. And they were nursing those beers they had like they'd not had a drink in years.'

'You didn't recognise them, then?'

Gill shook his head.

'They weren't local,' he said. 'And suddenly they're being yelled at and pushed around by the twins, one of whom then tries to drag them out of their chairs.'

'And that's when you intervened?' Jim asked.

Gill gave a nod.

'There was a lot of swearing,' Gill said. 'I'm glad there were no children in the pub at that point, not fit for their ears what those two brutes were saying. But once I'd filtered that out, I could hear what the problem was.'

'And what was that, then?' Harry asked.

'Poaching,' said Gill. 'That's what.'

'So, these two at the table were poachers?'

'That's what the Bell lads were accusing them of, anyway. But there's a way to deal with things, isn't there, and that kind of stupidity, and in public, just isn't it, is it? Which is why I had to do something, seeing as no one else was. Not a surprise, though. Those Bell lads are pretty terrifying when they get wound up.'

'And what was it that you actually did?' Jim asked.

'I may be small and a few years past my best, but I can still handle myself,' Gill said. 'So, I went over and sent those two great idiots back to their seats. I made it absolutely clear I'd be on to their parents about their behaviour. No, they're not teenagers anymore, far from it, but round here, family still means something, doesn't it? Didn't look happy about it one bit, either of them. They squared up to me, but I've taken on worse. They backed off.'

'And the two at the table?'

'I took them outside and you might say that I had a word ...'

Phil said he could hear you shouting at them from inside the pub.

'That would be right,' said Gill. 'I challenged them on it. What they'd been accused of, I mean. And they admitted it. Straight out with it, they were. Even showed me what they'd caught, which was nothing but a couple of rabbits and a pheasant. Even so, I made it bloody clear what I, and what everyone else in the Dales, think of poaching. And that if they didn't want to end up having blokes like those two Bell lads after them, then they needed to be careful.'

'What did they say?'

'Not much. Just took it. Said they had just stopped at the pub for a drink, that's all, were sorry for the trouble, that they'd never do it again, that kind of thing.'

'And that was it?'

'I sent them on their way, yes,' said Gill. 'And I let them

keep the rabbits and pheasant as well. Mainly because the pair of them looked like starved rats, the poor sods.'

'Do you think the two poachers could've been part of a larger gang?' Harry asked.

'How do you mean?' asked Gill.

'Poaching isn't always one for the pot, is it?' Harry explained. 'Sometimes, it's gangs coming out in vans to spend a few hours killing as much as they can, then taking it back to flog for a quick profit. I've dealt with them before. They're organised and violent and not to tangle with.'

'Can't really say,' Gill said. 'There could be others, I suppose, but these two hadn't had a big haul that night, so if they were with a gang, they were heading back fairly empty-handed.'

'Is there anything else you can tell us about them?'

'Well, like I said, definitely not from round here. Their accent told me that much. Slovakian, I think.'

The conversation paused for a second or two as Harry and Jim exchanged looks.

'We also need to ask where you were Tuesday evening,' Harry said.

'I was out getting one for the pot myself,' Gill said. 'Legally though, I hasten to add.'

'Is there someone who can confirm your whereabouts?'

'Of course there is,' Gill said, and looked at Jim. 'Your dad, as it happens.'

'Dad?'

'I was out shooting on his land, those fields just up by the Roman Road. Rabbits have gone a bit mad up that way, as I'm sure you know.'

'He didn't mention it,' said Jim.

'I gave him a call to let him know where I'd be, just so he

wouldn't go thinking there was someone out there without his permission. I know what he went through that time, years ago, don't I? Last thing he needs is to be worrying that the same thing is happening again.'

Harry remembered the story Jim had relayed to the team the day before.

'You were alone, though, yes?' he asked.

'I was,' Gill nodded.

'What time did you get back?'

'Haven't the faintest idea. Did okay though. Freezer is a little fuller now, that's for sure. The skins are useful, too.' He pointed at the fur hat he was wearing.

Harry realised what he was implying.

'You made that yourself, then?'

'I did,' Gill said. 'I can make you one, too, if you want. More than happy to.'

Harry had no response to that, having never been offered a handmade rabbit fur hat before. Then, just as he found himself about to politely turn down the offer, he noticed Gill was looking at him and Jim, his brow creased, expression serious.

'There's something you're not telling me, isn't there?' Gill said.

'There is,' Harry said. 'A body was found two nights ago. A poacher, we think.'

Gill's jaw clenched.

'Who the hell kills someone for that?'

'Right now, we don't know,' said Harry. 'Which is why we had to come over and talk to you about what happened that night at the pub.'

Gill sat back.

'And you think the Bell lads did it?'

'After what you've told us today, I definitely need to speak to them,' Harry said, careful to not give away his suspicions. 'And soon.'

'I can give you their address easily enough. I can't see it being them, but you never know, do you? They were pretty riled up that night, that's for sure. Took me some handling to get them to back off. Best you go speak to them, like you said.'

'The address would be very useful, yes,' nodded Harry.

'What about the victim?' Gill asked. 'Do you know who it is?'

'We don't have an identity yet, but there's a very good chance one of those you dealt with that night in the pub—'

'Ended up dead in a woodland on Tuesday night,' said Gill. 'Right?'

Harry's silence was answer enough.

CHAPTER TWENTY-FOUR

BACK OVER IN RICHMOND AT THE CAR WASH, JADYN WAS feeling a little bit awkward. The day was getting on, and lunchtime had rolled by unsated. In the office, DI Haig seemed to be doing rather well with chatting with all the staff. After she had finished with the first two, having managed to get them to relax enough to actually speak, she had sent them back outside with what was left of their coffees, and asked Jadyn for another two to join her.

Jadyn had done exactly that, though it hadn't been easy; few of them spoke anything other than broken English, so Jadyn was left with only hand signals, his killer smile, and little else. Which had him confused as to what exactly the DI was getting from them.

They had been there getting on for an hour now and Jadyn had done his best to look useful, wandering around the site, offering nods here and smiles there if anyone happened to look his way. At one point, he'd even gone over to help a young couple with their toddler, as they struggled to rearrange everything in the boot and on the back seat before having the staff do a full valet. The car had definitely needed one, thanks to the toddler's unrefined eating habits, the footwells in the back a smorgasbord of snacks including rice cakes, raisins, and goodness knew what else.

Now, having sent the last two in to chat with Gordy, and having run out of ways to look interested in what was going on, or to attempt communication, he decided to have a bit more of a mooch around the site. Everyone was busy, and no one seemed to care where he was wandering.

Heading around the back of the building containing the office, Jadyn found himself in a yard penned in by various other office buildings. It was little more than a small industrial unit of various buildings and offices. None of them looked in use, but he had a nosy anyway, because it was better than heading back round to where all the cars were being washed and standing there like a smiling idiot.

The first office was boarded up. Jadyn tried the door, but it was locked. The second unit was identical, except this time the door was open. He poked his head inside, saw a room full to the ceiling with boxes of sponges and car wash detergent, and moved on. The next two units were also open, the first empty except for a rat trap or two, but the second was a break room of some kind. And compared with the office, it was a little more down market, to say the least.

A collection of mismatched and rickety chairs were pushed up against the walls. At one end sat a single fridge, the door scratched and stained. A small unit next to it contained a sink and a kettle, the draining board piled with washed mugs, all of them chipped. The walls of the room were in dire need of a lick of paint, and the whole thing was gloomy, thanks to the window being boarded up and the single lightbulb blinking in the ceiling above.

Jadyn saw a door in the far wall. However, he was unsure about the protocols of just walking in and having a proper look, so thought it best to go and chat with Gordy first. Which was when the door opened and someone in the same overalls as the rest of the staff at the car wash pushed their way backwards, out into the room, their dark ponytail bouncing on their back as they struggled with whatever it was they were carrying. Jadyn was about to say something, or at least cough, to announce his presence, when the person turned round and he came face-to-face with a young woman carrying a baby.

Jadyn froze, unable to find any words to make his presence seem entirely normal. Then, at last, his mouth came unstuck.

'That's a baby,' he said.

The woman continued to stare and Jadyn was relieved that his opening gambit hadn't scared her off with its ridiculousness.

'My name is Constable Okri,' he said. 'I'm a constable, with the police, I mean.'

'Hello?' the woman said, and Jadyn heard the clear question of confusion in her tone.

'Sorry, I didn't mean to disturb you. I'm … I mean we're … just here to have a chat with everyone, that's all, as in me and Detective Inspector Haig.'

The baby struggled in the woman's arms, and Jadyn saw the briefest flash of fear in her eyes.

'Don't worry, you're not in trouble or anything,' he said. 'Honestly, we're just here to—'

The woman started to edge back into the room on the other side of the door.

'Do you work here?'

No response, just eyes staring at him.

'Would it be okay if we had a little chat? I tell you what, I'll go and get my DI, you'll like her, she's lovely. And I'll bring you a coffee?'

The woman was almost fully in the other room now, the door closing in on her.

'I'll go and get her now,' Jadyn said, but the door was already closed.

Jadyn stood there for a second, very aware of the frown on his face. Whoever she was, she hadn't exactly been keen to talk to him, that was certain. Perhaps she was squatting, he thought. But that didn't make sense, not with her wearing those overalls and this being the break room for the staff at the car wash. Who was she, then? And why was she here with her baby?

Jadyn left the room and marched back around to the main office, arriving just in time to see Gordy coming outside.

'We're done here, I think,' Gordy said. 'Not much to go on, I have to say. Talkative they are not. But I'll tell you more in the car on the way back, because I think—'

Gordy paused and Jadyn noticed she was staring at him.

'Something up, Constable?' she asked.

'I don't know,' Jadyn said. 'No, I do, but I don't know if something is up as such, it's just that I'm ...'

'You're rambling and getting nowhere is what you are,' Gordy said. 'Out with it, then.'

'I need you to follow me, round the back,' Jadyn said.

'You've found something?'

'Yes,' Jadyn said, leading the way.

'What?'

Jadyn pointed across the yard to the break room.

'In there,' he said. 'A woman. She had a baby.'

Gordy stopped.

'A what?'

'There's a woman with a baby in that room,' he said. 'She's wearing the same overalls as everyone else.'

'Maybe they've a crèche then,' Gordy said. 'A lot of workplaces provide those nowadays.'

'It's definitely not a crèche,' Jadyn said. 'You need to look for yourself, though, I think.'

A few steps later and Jadyn opened the door to allow Gordy to enter first.

'Ah,' Gordy said. 'Definitely not a crèche, then.'

Jadyn pointed at the door in the other wall.

'She's through there,' he said.

'Doing what?'

'I've no idea. But she just seemed really scared when she saw me.'

'She probably wasn't expecting to see a police officer in here.'

'No, it was more than that. I'm sure of it,' Jadyn said. 'Shall I go and knock?'

Gordy shook her head.

'Might be best if I do that. We don't know what she's doing on the other side, do we? You sure it's not the bathroom?'

'I'd not thought of that,' said Jadyn.

Gordy walked over and gave a gentle tap on the door.

'Hello in there,' she said, her voice calm and cheery. 'My name is Detective Inspector Haig. Just popping in to say hello. And to apologise for my colleague giving you a bit of a scare.'

There was no sound at all from the other side of the door.

Gordy tried again, called out, still nothing. Then, she reached down and turned the door handle, pulling the door open.

'Hello?'

She pulled the door fully open.

'It's empty,' she said. 'Look.'

Jadyn peered over Gordy's shoulder to see a small room with no way out. On the floor, he saw a thin mattress and blanket and some baby toys that looked years old and well used.

'She must've come out through the main door after I left,' Jadyn said.

'Looks that way. And you don't know who she was?'

'She didn't say a word. But she had a baby, that much I do know.'

With nothing else to see in the room, Jadyn followed Gordy back out into daylight and then round to the front of the car wash. As they made their way over to their car, the owner returned. She climbed out, armed with a killer smile and purpose in her every step.

'So,' she said, clapping her hands together, 'I hope everyone was helpful?'

'Very polite, all of them,' Gordy said. 'Though there is one member of staff we saw but were unable to chat to. I think she left before we had a chance.'

The woman looked genuinely confused.

'Really? That's most unlike the staff here. Do you know her name?'

Gordy shook her head.

'My constable here saw her.'

'She was round the back,' Jadyn said. 'With a baby.'

'A what?'

'A baby,' Jadyn repeated. 'You know, small human, cries a lot, about this big?' He put his hands in front of him as though holding up an invisible baby. 'She was in the room that I'm guessing is where everyone goes for a break.'

At this, Knight's face faltered a little.

'That old place? I'm sorry you had to see it in that state. I am in the process of having it completely renovated. Not easy to get money from the owners, but I'm doing my best.'

'So, do you know who she is?'

'The staff here come and go a lot,' Knight said. 'It's that kind of job, you see. I'll have to check my records. It's hard to keep a track of all names.'

'And what about the baby?' Gordy said.

'Well, babies and children are absolutely not allowed on site. This is a dangerous environment, isn't it?'

'It most certainly is.'

'So, I will be looking into this myself, I assure you. I can only thank you for bringing it to my attention. Now, will there be anything else?'

'Not at the moment, no,' Gordy said. 'I'm sure we'll be in touch, though, if we have any further questions.'

Conversation over, Jadyn followed Gordy back to their vehicle. Once inside and buckled up, Gordy started the engine and pulled them out of the car wash.

'What did you find out?' Jadyn asked.

'Not much, and perhaps just enough,' Gordy said.

'Not sure I understand.'

'You heard their accents, for a start, and that corresponds with the woman's voice Harry heard on the phone. They're all Romanian.'

'So, did any of them recognise the name of the victim, then?'

'Luca?' Gordy shook her head. 'Apparently not, no. Not that they were going to say so, anyway.'

'What about the manager, Michelle Knight?'

At this, Gordy glanced over at Jadyn.

'Answer me this,' she said. 'If every single person I spoke to did their level best to tell me that they had been working here for months, some for well over a year, why, then, would she tell us that it's the kind of job where the staff come and go a lot?'

Jadyn shook his head.

'I don't know,' he said.

'I do,' said Gordy. 'Because, for whatever reason, she was lying.'

CHAPTER TWENTY-FIVE

WITH THE ADDRESS OF THE FARM THE BELL TWINS RAN with their parents, Harry and Jim headed back down towards West Burton. With lunchtime having already passed, they drove on into the village itself to grab a sandwich from the small shop, giving themselves a decent half an hour to just eat and to give the dogs a run on the green. Harry remembered lunches on the hop had been a little different down in Bristol, usually just something greasy pushed into his face while sitting in yet more traffic. That life was a world apart from this.

Lunch done, and early afternoon now welcoming them, they then headed back out of West Burton to take the main road, Temple Lane.

'Bit of an odd name for a road,' Harry said, pleased to have something in his belly. 'I mean, I'm not seeing many temples around here, are you? Though there is that odd place up Temple Bank, if you're heading on towards West Witton, isn't there?'

'The Folly, you mean?' said Jim. 'Yeah, weird place, that.

Creepy. Lots of roads around here have odd names, though. The Dales are old though, aren't they? Names can be centuries old, but whoever came up with them or why, that gets forgotten.'

Harry looked over at Jim.

'Sometimes, and considering you're only in your twenties, you speak like someone decades older.'

Jim laughed.

'That'll be my dad's influence,' he said. 'Gets this mystical look on him sometimes, like he's older and wiser than the hills he's lived alongside his whole life.'

'Anyway, where are we heading now?' Harry asked.

'Up Walden. It's a hamlet, I suppose, as well as a dale. Nowt much there, really, just a few small farms. It's pretty, though. Nice and quiet. The Bell twins, their farm is right at the end of the lane. Never been there myself.'

'And you know them?'

'Like Gill said, only by sight. But then everyone knows the Bell twins. Mainly because you can't miss them.'

'Why's that, then?'

'Big lads,' Jim said. 'My dad has a few old annuals of the Dandy comic at home, from when he was a kid. His favourite character was Desperate Dan.'

'Never heard of him.'

'Basically, he's this bloke with a massive chest who's really strong and lives on cow pies.'

Harry shook his head.

'Must've passed me by,' he said. 'Never was one for comics.'

'Well, that's what they're like,' Jim said. 'You'll see what I mean when we meet them.'

'I'm already looking forward to it.'

Jim laughed.

'Oh, I wouldn't go that far,' he said.

Driving on, Harry stared at the road ahead, a thin line of grey at the bottom of a small valley, working almost like a bit of stitching to hold everything in place. Drystone walls lined the lane, shooting off to form small fields populated by sheep. The summit of Brown Haw was even more imposing now, rising to their immediate left.

'Just drive to the end and you'll see the farm, I think,' Jim said.

A couple of minutes later, Harry slowed down to pull in through an open gate and down a gravel track, leading to a collection of farm buildings, all gathered around a farmhouse like chicks around a mother hen.

'This must be it, then,' he said, and pulled up in front of the house.

'Prepare yourself,' said Jim.

Harry was about to reply when movement caught his eye and he looked up to see a large man standing in the now open front door of the house. His arms were folded across his chest. Harry put him in his mid to late fifties. He was ruddy-cheeked, and his bare forearms were large and well-muscled.

Harry climbed out of his vehicle. The farm was tidy, he noted, a place run by someone who liked order and a freshly swept yard. He spotted two large brooms leaning up against the wall of one of the farm buildings. Another was stacked with bales of hay. Some of the buildings were clearly old stables, though he doubted that they still housed horses. In another building, the front of which was fully open, he saw a couple of tractors, a quad bike, and an old Subaru pickup.

'Don't see many of those around now,' Jim said, nodding

over at the pickup. 'Dad said everyone had them back in the eighties. Can't get them now. Shame really.'

Harry turned his attention to the man in the doorway.

'Morning,' he said, offering a polite wave.

'It is that,' the man said, then looked at his watch. 'Though not for much longer.'

Harry was surprised at how quickly the morning had gone by.

He walked over to the house, Jim at his side, having left the dogs in the RAV4.

'I'm Detective Chief Inspector Harry Grimm,' he said.

'I know who you are,' the man said, then looked at Jim. 'And this is young Metcalf, from up Burtersett way. How's your father, then?'

'He's good, thank you,' Jim said.

Harry looked at the PCSO.

'There's no such thing as a stranger in the Dales, is there?'

Jim gave a shrug.

'We're actually looking to have a chat with your sons, Mr Bell,' Harry said. 'Do you know where they are?'

'Not in trouble, are they?' Mr Bell asked.

'Just need to ask them a few questions, that's all.'

'Because if they're in trouble, that'll be for me to sort out, won't it? I'm their father and I'll not be having anyone doing my job for me, that's for sure.'

A voice called out from inside the house and then a woman pushed past Mr Bell. She had her hair pulled up into a bun, and was wearing a denim dress cinched in at the waist with a leather belt. Harry figured she was probably around the same age as Mr Bell.

'Who's this, then?' she asked.

'It's young Jim, from up Burtersett way,' Mr Bell said. 'He's here to have a chat with Daniel and Robert.'

'Why's that, then?'

'Haven't the faintest.'

'You've not asked?'

'I have.'

'Not in trouble again, are they?'

'They won't say, will you, Mr Grimm?'

Harry introduced himself to Mrs Bell, then said, 'We just need to speak to them, that's all. Do you know where they are?'

'Yes, but what about?' Mrs Bell asked. 'We're their parents. We have a right to know.'

Harry looked at Jim and hoped that was enough for the PCSO to see if he could do any better with persuading Mr and Mrs Bell to help them locate their sons.

'I've not seen Danny and Rob for a while,' he said. 'How are they both doing?'

'Very well, actually,' Mr Bell said, and Harry saw the man inflate with pride a little. 'Healthy lads. Strapping, if you know what I mean. Built themselves a gym in one of the barns a while back. When they're not out on the farm, they're in there lifting weights. Strongest boys in the Dales, if you ask me.'

Jim laughed, and the sound was genuine, Harry noticed.

'Weights? Really? Aren't they big enough already?'

'Well, we're not about to discourage it,' Mrs Bell said. 'Nice for them to have a hobby or two, if you ask me. They've even got into wildlife, would you believe?'

'Wildlife?' Harry asked. 'In what way?'

'Cameras,' Mr Bell said. 'It's their money, so who am I to say what they do with it? Can't see why they need so many, though. I mean, surely, once you've seen one stoat or buzzard, you've seen them all, haven't you?'

'You know, I've often wondered about doing it myself,' Jim said. 'Weights, I mean, not wildlife photography.'

'You should talk to them about it, then,' Mrs Bell said. 'They'd be happy to help, I'm sure.'

'That's a great idea. Are they around?'

Mrs Bell pointed up the dale behind the farm.

'Just up in the high pastures, checking on the sheep up that way.'

Mr Bell looked over at his wife, shaking his head.

'We don't yet know what they want them for, do we?' he said.

'Well, Jim here wants to talk to them about weight training, so I think that's fine, don't you?'

'Yes, but that's not why they drove all the way over here, is it?'

'We're just following something up,' Harry said. 'And we think they can help us with our enquiries. The sooner we can find them, the sooner we can be on our way.'

Mr Bell turned his eyes back on Harry.

'Well, they're up there for the rest of the day, I should think,' he said. 'So, the only way you're going to be able to chat to them is by either staying here and waiting for them, or heading up there yourself.' He looked over at Harry's vehicle. 'Good little motors, those are. You should be fine.'

'Fine how?'

'Well, I'm not about to give you a lift, am I? I'm not a taxi service. Just head up out the back there. You'll see there's a track leading through the fields. It's a bit boggy in places, and you'll most likely have a bit of fun getting there. But I think you'll be alright. If not, just give me a call and I'll come out with the tractor to give you a tow. That might not be for a while, though; jobs to do myself, you know. I can't be pulling the police out of fields day in and day out, can I, now?'

'No, you can't,' Harry said, and turned back to his vehicle. 'Just out the back of the farm, right?'

Mr Bell pointed to his left.

'That way,' he said. 'You can't miss it. You'll be with them in about twenty minutes, give or take.'

Back behind the steering wheel, Harry started the engine.

'Every day's an adventure in the Dales, isn't it?' he said.

'It is indeed,' said Jim, and Harry slipped the RAV4 into first and slowly rolled them out of the farmyard towards the fields and fells ahead.

CHAPTER TWENTY-SIX

Jen and Matt had arrived at the pub in West Burton just a few minutes after Harry and Jim had driven through the village to see Gill. Jen stood for a moment to take in the scene before her of the perfect green and the cosy houses surrounding it. West Burton was not a place where houses came up for sale very often, and when they did, she wondered at those who could afford them.

Probably not local, she thought with a sigh. Her place over in Middleham, was hardly a picturesque house of old stone and mullion windows, the kind of house which had looked after generations of Dales folk, seeing their lives unfold inside the safety of its walls. But it was home, and she was happy there. Plus, Middleham was a beautiful place in its own right. Then again, it was hard to think of somewhere in the Dales that wasn't.

With a deep, cleansing breath, sucking in the taste of the fells high above, Jen was about to head over to the pub to give the door a knock when Matt's phone rang. She stopped and glanced back at the DS. He held up an apologetic hand, mouthed that he'd be just a couple of minutes, and turned away.

Jen headed over to the pub anyway and as she drew closer to the building, caught a waft of something delicious from the kitchens inside; notes of meats roasting and fresh herbs. It was mid-morning, but the smells immediately made her hungry. She had a run planned for the end of the day, a quick half marathon, so she would probably easily burn off most of the calories from a roast dinner. And she knew that Matt would be easy to persuade to have a quick lunch at the pub if they were still around.

With that tempting idea in her mind, she turned to see Matt jogging over towards her, a worried look creasing his face.

'Everything okay?' Jen asked. 'What's up?'

'That was Joan,' he said. 'Mary has had another attack. I'm sure she's okay, and the doctor's on their way, but she's in a panic, and—'

'Go,' Jen said. 'I'll ring Liz and have her get someone from the team to swing by and pick me up.'

'You sure?'

'Yes, of course I'm sure,' said Jen. 'Harry and Jim are up Walden way, so they'll be passing back through here soon enough. And Jadyn and Gordy can always pop in on their way back from Richmond, can't they?'

Matt hesitated.

'Go!' Jen said.

Matt said nothing more, turned on his heel, and ran back to the car. A few moments later, he was gone.

Alone now, Jen turned back to the pub. The front door was locked but she saw movement through the frosted window set in it and gave a knock.

'We're closed!'

'This is Police Constable Blades,' Jen said, her face close to the door. 'Just wondering if you could spare me a few minutes?'

Jen heard swearing, stomping feet, the rattle of chains, and a lock being turned, then the door was heaved open. In front of her stood a middle-aged man with next to no hair, dressed in a scuffed and holey boiler suit. He was holding a mop and bucket.

'Just getting the place cleaned up and sorted for opening time, and that's only a few minutes away,' the man said. 'So, no, I don't have a few minutes to spare at all. Not after the disaster of last night, with the power going off, which meant we lost a load of stuff in the freezers, plus they leaked everywhere, didn't they? Thankfully, the chef was able to get enough food in, but even so.'

'You look like you could use a hand,' Jen said.

The man looked confused.

'Are you offering?'

Jen gave a nod.

'What say I help you get ready for opening, and then you give me a few minutes of your time when we're done? How's that?'

A smile dared to break through on the man's face.

'Very kind,' he said, and handed Jen the mop and bucket. 'Know how to use these?'

'I do.'

'Then follow me.'

BACK AT THE other end of Walden, Harry and Jim were creeping up through the fields to where Mr and Mrs Bell had directed them to find their twin sons, Danny and Rob. Though he wasn't about to admit it, Harry was very much enjoying himself, as the RAV4 picked its way up the rough track and through the fields, towards the open moorland ahead.

They'd passed some small crags and rocky outcrops a couple of minutes ago, which had at some point spilled a good number of boulders and rocks onto the fields below. Navigating through them had been fun and Harry had been very careful to make sure that he didn't drive over anything that could potentially cause damage to the undercarriage. Now they were driving along a slope, the vehicle at a slightly unnerving angle, a small ravine down to their left staring back up at them hungrily.

'You've driven off-road before, then,' Jim stated.

'Not since I was in the Paras,' Harry said. 'Did a few driving courses back then. A lot of fun, actually.'

Jim pointed ahead.

'That must be them,' he said.

Harry looked to see where Jim was pointing and saw a vehicle far off, though what type it was, he had no idea.

'Weight training, then?' said Harry.

'Making conversation,' said Jim. 'Can't see it being my kind of thing, really. That's more Jadyn than me, I reckon.'

'You should give it a go. I've done it myself and I've often wondered about getting into it again. Does you a lot of good. Makes you realise just how weak you are, too, when you start, which is always a bit of a shock.'

'We could put an office gym together.'

'With all that space we've got,' Harry smiled.

They were closer to the vehicle now and Harry could see that it was another pickup. It was painted yellow and looked somewhat beaten up.

'Toyota Hi-Lux,' Jim said, as Harry pulled them up alongside. 'Bombproof, these are. Dad won't get one, though.'

'Why's that?'

'Thinks they're a bit showy, if you know what I mean,' said Jim, shaking his head.

Harry climbed out. The land about them was empty of livestock, but full of a wildness only open moorland and the silent presence of the rising fells could impart.

'Let the dogs out,' he said, calling over to Jim. 'Reckon they could do with a run. I'll have a look at the pickup.'

Harry wandered over to the vehicle. The cabin was empty, but the keys were still in the ignition, so Danny and Rob were obviously up here somewhere and not too far away, either. He looked around, staring out across the vast swathes of emptiness in front of him, and walked away from the pickup, breathing in the beauty of the moors.

This was a bleak place, he thought. Yes, there were a few farms back down the valley, but up here, the wind spun and twisted around, tugging at heather and fern, swishing through grass and reed, as though the landscape was setting itself to prove just how lonely things actually were and how distant civilisation was. But by God it was beautiful, Harry thought.

Something nudged at his leg and Harry looked down to see Smudge sitting at his heel. He reached down and gave the dog's head a pat. Her tail wagged hard.

'You like it up here, don't you?' Harry said. 'Can't blame you, either. It's something else is what it is.'

'Harry?'

Jim's voice snatched Harry back into the moment and he turned round to see Jim standing at the rear of the pickup.

'What is it?'

'Best you have a look for yourself,' Jim said.

Harry walked over.

'Well?' he asked.

Jim pulled back a faded sheet of grey canvas tarpaulin covering whatever was in the back of the pickup.

'This,' he said.

Harry looked down to see what had been revealed. He saw what at first glance looked like nothing more than a pile of rope and wire and bent bits of metal, a small box of 4.10 shotgun cartridges, plus some wooden stakes, a sledge-hammer and, in a cardboard box, at least four wildlife cameras.

'Well, Mrs Bell did mention the cameras,' he said. 'Seems they've enough to start their own television show.'

'But what about all this?' Jim said and gestured at everything else.

Harry had another look inside the back of the truck. 'Not sure what I'm looking at, if I'm honest. Why don't you enlighten me?'

Jim reached in and picked something up. He held it out for Harry.

'Those over there, they're mole traps,' Jim said, 'but this is a snare.'

'You mean for rabbits?' Harry said. 'But isn't it a bit big?'

Harry had seen rabbit snares before, used them even, back during survival training many years ago now.

'Exactly.'

'Exactly what?'

'If this snare isn't for rabbits, then it's for something bigger, isn't it?'

'But no one snares deer, do they?' Harry said.

Jim dropped the snare to the ground, placed his foot

inside it, then cinched it tight into his ankle.

'Not deer,' he said.

Harry stared at Jim's ankle in the snare.

'Bloody hell,' he said.

'Thought you might say that.'

Harry stared for a moment at the snare around Jim's ankle. Yes, he could see that it would snag someone, but it was hardly difficult to get out of, was it?

'Take it off, then,' he said.

Jim bent down and slipped the snare off his ankle.

'And there's your problem,' Harry said. 'It's not really going to hold someone for long, is it?'

'Depends,' said Jim. 'Put this in the right place, maybe with a sprung branch or something, and you've got someone being whipped off their feet. Catch your foot in it if you're in a hurry and you'll have a face full of dirt soon enough.'

Harry shook his head.

'I know what you're saying, but I've seen better ways to catch someone, if that's what they're trying to do.'

Jim shrugged.

'It's just a suggestion. I could be wrong. And I hope I am.'

'I do, too,' Harry said. 'Only way to find out what they're actually up to is to have a chat.'

He glanced at his watch. The afternoon was getting on now. Wherever the Bell twins were, he wasn't about to go wandering around the moors in an attempt to find them. That was a fast-track route to wasted hours, getting lost, and if they were still out here when daylight started to fail, ending up in Accident and Emergency with a broken ankle.

'What do you want to do?' Jim asked.

'Speak to these Bell twins,' Harry said, 'but it doesn't look like we're going to be able to do that any time soon, does it?'

'Not really, no,' Jim said. 'They could be anywhere out here and not be back for hours. Farmers don't keep normal hours.'

'Neither do the police, but even so,' Harry said. 'Looks like we'll be out here again tomorrow then, doesn't it?'

Harry was about to walk away from the pickup, but then thought better of it. He turned round, snapped a few photos of the vehicle and its contents, then climbed back into the RAV4.

'Come on,' he said, calling Jim over. 'Back to Hawes, I think, see how everyone else has done. We can come out again tomorrow.'

Jim opened the passenger door, but a whirl of black fur pushed past him to land with a damp thump on Harry's lap.

Jim quickly leaned in and grabbed Smudge.

'Sorry about that, Boss,' he said, and quickly clipped both dogs into the back of the vehicle.

'You may be,' Harry said, 'but she isn't, is she?'

Jim climbed in and they both looked over their shoulders to see Smudge and Fly staring at them.

'Not in the slightest,' Jim said.

Harry was about to head off when his phone rang.

'Grimm,' he said.

'It's Jen. Just wondering if you're done?'

'We are actually,' Harry said. 'You found anything interesting?'

'Only that the landlord has confirmed Phil's story.'

'So, why the call, then?'

There was a pause between Harry's question and Jen's answer, just long enough to have him look at Jim and frown.

'Jen?'

'You mind picking me up on your way through, then?'

'Why? Where's Matt?'

'He had to head off,' Jen said. 'Got a call from Joan.'

'He should've called me first,' Harry said, but Jen jumped in.

'It's my fault,' she said. 'I said I'd give you a call, but I got caught up.'

Harry could hear just enough hesitation in Jen's voice to know she wasn't being entirely truthful.

'When did he leave?'

'Not long after we arrived. Like I said, I was supposed to call.'

'Don't worry about it,' Harry said. 'I'll give him a call. We'll be with you as soon as we can.'

Harry hung up and was a little annoyed. He fully understood why Matt had headed off; his daughter was sick, he needed to be there, but there had to be a line, didn't there? If he'd called through, just to let him know, that would've been okay. Because then Harry would've known and he'd have called Jadyn or Liz or someone to go and grab Jen. Now, though, he'd been made to look like a DCI not entirely in control of his team.

He gave them all a certain amount of freedom, more than any team he'd ever worked with before, because that's what he'd quickly realised they needed. But had he let things go a little too far? And of all days for this to happen, the fact that Swift was around really didn't help matters. He would have to have words with Matt later, not only to get it sorted and to explain a few things to his generally excellent DS, but to show the rest of the team what he expected of them. That was fair.

'Right, let's get going,' Harry said. 'Sitting here staring at the scenery isn't getting us anywhere, is it?'

It was a rhetorical question, and he started the engine, shifted into first, then turned round to take them back down through the fields to fetch Jen.

CHAPTER TWENTY-SEVEN

Having stopped off at the farm on their way past, to leave a message with the Bell twins' parents that he wanted to speak to them, Harry picked up Jen in West Burton, then sped them back to Hawes. Jen seemed to enjoy herself in the back with the two dogs, but not half as much as the dogs themselves.

Back at the office, the rest of the team were starting to gather, the one absent person being Swift.

'Any news from him at all?' Harry asked no one in particular.

'Not a thing,' Liz said. 'It's been fairly quiet here, actually. No phone calls at all. Did a walk around and managed to include a chat with some of the parents outside the school as they were grabbing their kids.'

'Well done,' Harry said. 'Always good to show the human face of the police force. What about the photographs from Tuesday night? Swift said he'd call about those.'

'Those we do have,' Liz said. 'I've not looked through them yet. Thought you'd want to be on with that first.'

'Probably best,' said Harry. 'But first, let's have a run-through of where everyone's at, shall we? Jim, put the kettle on. I'll be back in five.'

Harry slipped out of the office and headed outside, phone to his ear.

'Matt, this is Harry,' he said when the call went through to voicemail. 'Hope everything's okay with the family. Just a friendly reminder, though, from your grumpy boss, that you should've given me a call as well. I don't want the team thinking I'm going soft in my old age, if you know what I mean. Consider this a friendly slap on the wrist. Next time, it probably won't be. But then, I'm assuming there won't be a next time, will there?'

Harry couldn't think of anything else to say, so said goodbye and hung up.

'Harry!'

A voice, loud and gruff and demanding attention, came at him from the lane leading back up towards the market-place. It belonged to a man who had the bearing of a Sherman tank, if said tank was also dressed in a tweed jacket and waistcoat and some properly fancy shoes.

'Dave,' Harry said, with a wave, as Dave Calvert strode over towards him. 'Home again, are you?'

Dave worked offshore, though Harry wasn't entirely sure doing what. So, he'd be away for a few weeks then, on his return, usually look Harry up and take him out for a few beers, or just turn up at his door unannounced, carrying whatever he'd decided they were going to eat that night. The fact that Grace was around hadn't made any difference at all. 'The more the merrier,' seemed to be Dave's happy place.

'Arrived home at the weekend. Saw you as I walked by so thought I'd pop over and see if you were around later.'

Harry frowned.

'It's been a difficult one this week, if I'm honest,' Harry said. 'Grace—'

'You've not broken up? If you have, you and I will be having words, that's for bloody sure! Are you mad? Grace is the best thing that—'

'No, we've not broken up,' Harry said. 'Why would you even think that?'

'You've a dark look in your eyes.'

'That's basically just the way I look.'

'Fair point,' Dave said. 'But you haven't, have you?'

'What?'

'Broken up?'

'No, we bloody well haven't! All that's happened is that Grace found a ...' Harry stopped himself from saying any more. The investigation was, as yet, not public, though he had no doubt that pretty much everyone in the Dales already knew. It wasn't so much that people gossiped, just that word got around without anyone really knowing how.

'I'll call Grace now,' Dave said, not waiting for Harry to even explain why he'd stopped mid-sentence. 'Check she's okay.'

'She's fine,' Harry said. 'You don't need to call her.'

'I'm her friend as well, Harry,' said Dave.

'That you are ... You know what, why don't you give her a call? I'm sure she'd appreciate it.'

'We'll arrange something for another night, then,' said Dave. 'I'll speak to Grace about that now, and we'll let you know.'

'How very kind of you both to keep me informed about your plans,' Harry laughed, but Dave was already heading off into Hawes marketplace with his phone to his ear.

Back inside the office, everyone was ready with their mugs of tea. There was just enough of the afternoon left to go through everything and sort out what was what for the next day. Plus, he'd be checking who was on duty tonight. He was a little concerned as to the whereabouts of Swift, but then perhaps the DSupt had headed back home. It was probably for the best, he thought, but then the door opened behind him and he turned round to see Swift enter, followed right behind by Matt.

'Got your message,' Matt said. 'Fully understood.'

'Good,' said Harry, as Swift came over.

'Can I have a quick word, Grimm?'

Harry gave a quick nod, handed the meeting over to Gordy, and led Swift out of the room and once again to the small interview room.

'So, how did it go?' Harry asked, as they both sat down.

When Swift answered, his words just tumbled out of him like children tossed out of a bouncy castle.

'I've got cancer,' he said, his words almost landing on top of each other. 'We think we've caught it early, but we don't know quite yet. Treatment starts tomorrow.'

Harry stared across the table at his superior officer. The man seemed to have shrunk a little since he had seen him earlier that day. He was fidgeting, too, wringing his hands together like he was trying to unscrew them at the wrist.

'I'm really sorry to hear that,' Harry said. 'I won't ask how you're doing, because the only answer you can rightly give is bloody awful. Whatever you need though, sir, you just have to ask.'

'I didn't go and see that Vince chap,' Swift said. 'I wanted to tell you on the phone, but I couldn't, so I came over here to tell you face-to-face. Then I couldn't do that either and ended up just forcing myself on you and into this investigation. I can only apologise.'

Harry had known something wasn't quite right from the moment Swift had called him, and things had only become weirder. Now though, it all made sense.

'I don't think that really matters right now,' said Harry. 'But from now on, I suggest you just tell me what's going on rather than letting things get out of hand. So, where've you been today, then?'

'Just driving around,' Swift said. 'Been up and down Swaledale a few times. It's beautiful over there, isn't it? There's a peace to that place and that's what I suddenly found myself needing. I should've called in, but time sort of just disappeared.'

'So, you're not retiring, then?' Harry asked.

'Oh, I'm still retiring,' said Swift. 'Of course I am. If I get through this, then the last thing I want to do is to celebrate still being alive by going back to work.'

'Probably for the best, then,' said Harry. 'And if I were in your shoes, I'd probably do the same.'

'Funny you should say that,' said Swift.

Harry cocked his head at this.

'Funny I should say what, exactly?'

Swift went to speak, but there was a knock at the door.

'Come in,' Harry called out.

Jadyn popped his head around the door.

'No, we don't need tea or biscuits,' Harry said.

'I wasn't offering,' Jadyn said.

'Then what is it?'

'Jen and Jim have found something,' he said. 'Jen said I should come and get you.'

Jadyn shut the door and Harry turned back to Swift.

'You were going to say something, I think,' Harry said. 'Before we were interrupted.'

'It can wait,' Swift said and stood up. 'It's just an idea of mine at the moment anyway, so probably good that I keep it that way.'

'If you think that's for the best.'

'I do.'

Harry led Swift out of the room and along to the main entrance.

'Thank you,' Swift said, turning to Harry as he made to leave.

'Nothing to thank me for,' Harry said. 'You just need to look after yourself and to let me know if and when you need anything.'

'I know I'm a crotchety old git,' Swift said, almost as though he'd not heard a word Harry had said. 'And I know I didn't exactly take to you when you first arrived.'

'Most people feel like that when they meet me,' Harry said. 'I'm an acquired taste, I think.'

'You are,' Swift said. 'But take it from me, you're also a bloody good copper.'

Then, before Harry could say anything in response, Swift turned on his heel and was out the door.

Harry almost went to follow him, but Matt was at the door to the main office.

'You're definitely going to want to see this,' he said.

Harry watched Swift for a moment, as he made his way into Hawes marketplace, then turned to face his DS.

'If it's food related, I'm going to be very unhappy.'

'For once, it's not,' Matt said. 'Looks like Jen's found

something on the footage from that scrap dealer we visited yesterday.'

'Really? What?'

Matt stepped back and motioned for Harry to come into the office.

CHAPTER TWENTY-EIGHT

'So, what am I looking at, exactly?' Harry asked.

'I was going through the footage again,' Jen said, as everyone gathered around behind her and Harry to see what she had found. 'I'd not seen anything new, but you never know, do you? It's always worth a second and third look at something, even if all it does is make you think about something else you might have missed.'

'Go on,' Harry said.

'Well, I'd gone over this bit a fair few times, like,' Jen continued. 'It's when the person who we think is the victim drives the stolen car out of the scrapyard.'

'I can see that right enough,' Harry said. 'So, what is it that's got you all excited, then?'

'This,' Jen said, and pointed to the top left of the screen.

Harry leaned in closer. He was staring at the disappearing rear-end of a car in black and white, and that was it.

'I'm still not seeing it,' Harry said.

'Here,' Jen said. 'Just along the road leading to the gates. See that vehicle there? Watch ...'

Harry did, and as the suspect's car drove past it, the vehicle Jen had pointed at pulled out after it.

Harry stood back up.

'So, someone drove off in their own car after the suspect's car had gone past. I can't see how this is in any way important?'

'It was Jim who spotted it,' Jen said, and she turned to look up at the PCSO.

'Here,' Jim said, and pulled out his phone. 'Remember earlier when we were up on the moors?'

Jim handed his phone to Harry. On the screen was a photograph of the Bell twin's Toyota Hi-Lux.

'Didn't realise you'd taken photographs as well,' Harry said.

'I'm glad I did,' said Jim. 'Meant I could check.'

'Check what?'

'The number plate.'

Jen paused the film and opened a screenshot she had taken of the vehicle in the security footage. She had zoomed in to view the number plate.

'It's a little blurry,' she said, 'but you can still make it out.'

Harry looked at the image on the computer, then at the one on Jim's phone. Then, to make doubly sure, he checked again.

'Bloody hell,' he said. 'That's the Bell lads.'

'It's one of them at least,' Jim said. 'We can't see how many are in the vehicle itself, but I think we can safely assume it's not their parents.'

'When was this?' Harry said, pointing at the computer screen.

Jen read the timestamp and date on the footage.

'It's later on the same night as the argument in the pub

with those poachers,' Harry said, then looked directly at Jim. 'And Gill.'

'What if Rob and Danny didn't go straight home from the pub after all, that night,' Jim said, 'but instead stayed around long enough to follow those poachers back home?'

'My thoughts exactly,' Harry said. 'If they did that, then they could easily have followed our victim home and found out where he lived. Then they'd have no problem following him again another night.'

'Like to a little woodland, perhaps,' Matt suggested.

'There's two of them, and we know from the forensics that Luca was attacked by at least two individuals.'

'And they're big lads, too,' Jim said. 'Someone like our victim wouldn't stand a chance against them. I can't think of many who would.'

Harry walked away from the computer.

'At the moment, this is all just conjecture,' he said. 'There's a very good chance that what we're doing here is putting two and two together and getting five.'

'That's definitely their vehicle, though,' said Jadyn.

Harry looked at the young constable.

'Did you find anything at the car wash?'

'We did,' said Gordy, and gave Harry a very quick run-through of what she'd learned from those she'd spoken to, and Jadyn's encounter with the young woman and the baby.

'So, they're all Eastern European, then?' Harry said.

'Romanian, Slovakian,' said Gordy. 'Everyone except the woman running the place, that is. She's definitely local.'

'Then we have a clear link with the victim,' said Harry. 'And the woman on the phone.'

'But that's about it, though,' said Gordy. 'They didn't offer me much at all, other than to say that they didn't know anyone called Luca, and that they were very happy at work, how well treated they were, that kind of thing.'

'What, they all said that? No one was disgruntled or anything like that?'

Gordy gave a nod.

'You think they'd been prepped?'

'Had crossed my mind,' Gordy said. 'The place was certainly doing a roaring trade, so it's obviously bringing in good money.'

'But is enough of it going to them, I wonder?' Harry said.

'How do you mean?' Jim asked.

'Places like that, they've a bit of a reputation. Cheap labour, pay in cash, that kind of thing.' Harry looked again at Gordy. 'Anything else? What about the young woman and the baby?'

'I think that gives us a good reason for another visit,' said Jadyn. 'The owner didn't seem to know who she was, and said she was going to look into it. Gave us some fluff about children not being allowed on the site. Don't know if it's relevant or not, but I also noticed bruising on the arms of a couple of the staff.'

'Part and parcel of the job?' Harry suggested.

Jadyn gave a shrug.

'Looked painful,' he said. 'I guess they might bruise themselves working around cars all day, but even so ...'

Harry frowned.

'A sign that discipline is meted out with heavy hands?'

'Maybe,' Jadyn said. 'Oh, and she lied.'

'What about?'

'You know how they all sounded like they'd been told what to say?' said Gordy. 'Well, they also all said how they'd been working there for months, and in some cases, well over a year.'

'So?'

'According to the manager, she has trouble remembering who everyone is because staff come and go a lot.'

'Well, that doesn't add up, does it?'

Gordy shook her head.

Harry now had to prioritise. The team had brought in a lot of information, but which should they act on first?

Gordy spoke again.

'If you're trying to decide what we do next, then I say that.' She pointed at the computer screen in front of Jen. 'We need to bring these Bell twins in urgently and find out exactly what they've been up to.'

'Agreed,' Harry said. 'There's been no call yet from the Bell farm, I assume?'

'Nothing,' Liz said.

'Well, give them a call now, please,' Harry said, then he remembered something. 'I forgot to ask, did that solicitor come over to give a statement?'

'Mr Palmer? Yes, he did,' said Liz. 'Wish he hadn't, though.'

'Why's that?'

Liz looked thoughtful for a moment.

'I'm not sure, really. He was about as threatening as Matt.'

'Hey,' said Matt. 'I can be threatening.'

A laugh fluttered through the room.

'There was something about him, though, he was—' Liz stopped talking and shook her head. 'No, you'll think I'm an idiot if I say that.'

Harry leaned in.

'I don't think anyone in this room is an idiot. Whatever it is you were going to say, say it.'

Liz shook her head.

'That's an order.'

'He was creepy,' she said, 'but not in a follow you home, murder you in an alley kind of way. This was different. He was very polite, very well dressed, middle-aged, and his shoes were really shiny.'

'Doesn't sound very creepy,' said Jim.

'Oh, I don't know,' said Jadyn. 'I've always found shiny shoes to be terrifying.'

Harry stared at Jim and Jadyn, shutting them both down. They apologised.

'No, they're right,' said Liz. 'Doesn't sound creepy at all, does it?'

'No,' said Jen. 'He sounds like a vampire.'

Liz jumped at this.

'That's exactly it!' she said.

'What, the solicitor is a vampire?' said Matt.

'No, but he reminded me of one,' Liz said.

'You know, you've got a point, actually,' Gordy said, jumping in. 'Had that Hammer House of Horror vibe, didn't he? All well dressed, but cold.'

Harry decided that the conversation had gone on long enough. As frightening as vampires were, or not, and as much as he respected everyone's thoughts and opinions on the team, they weren't here to discuss someone who sounded like every other solicitor he'd met in his life.

'Well, I'll read his statement later,' Harry said.

'It doesn't say much,' Liz said.

Gordy leaned in at this.

'I got the impression he was coming over to provide an alibi for our friend Vince,' she said.

'Well, he didn't,' said Liz. 'Oh, he talked for a good while, and I'm pretty sure the only reason he did that was because he liked the sound of his own voice. But anyway, what he said is that he advised his client to say nothing at the time, just so he could have a proper talk with him first.'

'So, does Walker have an alibi or not?'

Liz shook her head.

'His solicitor said that he met with Walker earlier that evening, to run through a few business whatevers, but after that, he was unable to provide any further details as to the whereabouts of his client.'

Harry was quiet for a moment.

'Well, we know he's not a fan of people being on his property, but he also doesn't seem to have the faintest idea about what Grace gets up to with this shoot he's paid her to set up, or indeed what land he actually owns.'

'It's suspicious, but not exactly the sound of a cell door shutting, is it?' said Matt.

'No, it isn't, and right now, those two Bell brothers are the ones worrying me the most. I need to make sure that if they're back home, they stay put until we arrive.'

'And what if they're not?' Gordy asked.

'Then we're all going to need to pack our walking boots,' Harry answered, then gave a nod to Liz.

Liz put the call through and spoke with Mr Bell, who insisted then on talking only to Harry.

'Mr Bell,' Harry said, his phone now on speaker so that everyone could hear, 'just wondering if those sons of yours are back down off the hill yet?'

'No, they bloody well aren't, as it happens,' Mr Bell said,

his voice echoing around the room with frustration. 'Been up there most of the day, now, buggering around with those daft cameras of theirs. When they do get back, they'll be getting thick ears, the pair of them, that's for damned sure.'

'So, they're still up on the moors? You're sure of that?'

'I haven't the faintest,' Mr Bell said, 'but I'm assuming so, yes. And if they're not down soon, then there'll be no tea for them, because the dogs will have it. And serve them right, too, if you ask me.'

Harry was finding it hard to believe Mr Bell was talking about two fully grown men and not a couple of naughty teenagers.

'Right then, Mr Bell,' Harry said. 'I'm on my way over. If Rob and Danny do happen to turn up in the meantime, can I ask you to keep them there, please, until I arrive?'

'And what if they don't happen to turn up?' Mr Bell asked.

'The team is heading over with me,' Harry explained. 'Bit of a search party, if you like. We'll head out and find them, I'm sure.'

'Well, you'll need to before the sun goes down,' Mr Bell said. 'Up there when it's dark, it's murder to walk around. You'll all end up with your ankles bust in rabbit holes or your heads cracked after a fall, you mark my words.'

'We certainly will, Mr Bell. Thank you.'

Harry hung up.

Matt raised a hand.

'You don't think this is more of a Mountain Rescue situation, do you?'

Harry shook his head.

'This is two farmers who know the land better than anyone else. They're up to something, that's for sure.' Harry explained then about the cameras he and Jim had found in the back of the Toyota Hi-Lux, and the snares.

'It's not looking good for them right now, is it?' Matt said. 'You don't think they're out laying more traps for poachers, do you?'

'Only way we can find out is to find them and bring them in,' Harry said.

'It's a bit odd that they've been out on the moors so long, though,' Jim said. 'Looking around up there, it didn't seem like there was much to be occupying them, even if they were putting down some traps. It's not an all-day job by any means.'

'Then let's get ourselves over there sharpish,' Harry said. 'The sooner we find out what's going on, the sooner we'll be able to have Rob and Danny answer our questions. Agreed?'

The team nodded as one.

'Good,' Harry said. 'Then get your stuff together and get moving!'

Arriving at the Bell farm about an hour later, Harry pulled up in the yard, followed by the rest of the team. Jadyn, Jen, and Matt had travelled over with Gordy, and Jim and Liz had jumped in the RAV4 with him and the two dogs. It had been a bit of a squeeze, but they'd managed it.

'You're here then,' Mr Bell said as Harry walked over to meet him. 'My two lads aren't, though. Daft sods. What the hell they're thinking, I don't know.'

'Have you any idea what it is they're doing up there?' Harry asked.

'There was a time I'd check up on them every day,' Mr Bell said. 'But that was years ago, when they were learning the ropes, like. So, to be honest, no. I've no idea at all.'

'And they've not been in touch all day?'

Mr Bell shook his head.

'We're not due to bring the sheep down yet, but they could be up checking them over, seeing if any are lame, or if they have flystrike, that kind of thing. But that doesn't make much sense either, because they've not taken any of the dogs with them, and you need a couple with you if you're to go gathering them in for an inspection. We'd usually do that by bringing them down into one of the lower fields, then we can set up some pens, that kind of thing.'

Mrs Bell appeared then, coming to stand beside her husband.

'When you do find them,' she said, 'you make sure you give them a bloody good hiding from me! A clip round the ear is too good for them; their hides need to sting!'

Harry decided it was best to offer no response to this, so just gave a nod and headed back over to the team.

'As we've only one four-wheel drive here, we'll have to do two trips to get everyone up to where we think Rob and Danny are,' he said.

'Not necessarily,' said Jim, and jogged over to chat with Mr Bell. Harry saw Mr Bell nod, disappear into the house, then return and hand something to Jim, who then walked back over to the team.

'And what was that about?' Harry asked.

Jim held up a set of keys.

'Mr Bell has kindly lent us the use of his other pickup. Just means that whoever rides in the back will have a bit of a bumpy ride.'

Harry smiled and looked at his team.

'Well, I'll leave it to you lot to sort out who goes where,' he said. 'But whoever's with me, Smudge will fully expect a tummy rub, I'm sure.'

Harry walked over to his vehicle and climbed in to find Gordy in the front passenger seat, reaching back to give Smudge's nose a scratch.

'Where are the others?' Harry asked. 'I can take two more.'

Gordy laughed, then pointed across the yard to the pickup. Harry looked over to see the rest of his team, including Matt, climbing into the pickup as Jim slipped in behind the wheel.

'Like kids, the lot of them,' he said.

'And you sound just like a proud father, or should I say mother hen?'

Harry narrowed his eyes at Gordy.

'Do I look like a mother hen?' he said, his voice quiet as it slipped through clenched teeth.

'Goodness no,' Gordy said, shaking her head with a little too much enthusiasm. Then she smiled and added, 'But looks aren't everything, are they?'

Harry dropped himself into the driver's seat.

'Hold on,' he said, keyed the ignition, then headed off, for the second time that day, out of the yard and up onto the moors.

CHAPTER TWENTY-NINE

When Harry saw the old yellow Toyota Hi-Lux in exactly the same position as it had been a few hours ago, his gut twisted just enough to let him know something about this wasn't right. He didn't know what, exactly, but for two farmers to go missing on their own farm? That just didn't make any sense at all. There was no way that they could be lost. This land was their home. They knew it better than anyone, so that wasn't even a consideration. What, then, was the reason for them to still be out here? What the hell had happened?

Harry pulled up next to the pickup and climbed out as Jim rolled up next to him. In the back, he saw Matt, Liz, Jadyn, and Jen looking a little more dishevelled than they had been back at the farm.

'Good trip?' Harry asked.

Matt was first to climb out.

'A bit of fun, that,' he said. 'Reminded me of being a kid.'

'Spent a lot of your childhood in the back of pickups, did

you?' Harry asked. 'Though I'll admit I'm nervous to ask why.'

'My dad had one,' Matt said.

'And he let you ride in the back, did he?'

Matt grinned. 'Still does.'

Harry was tempted to ask for more information, not least because Matt had never spoken of his parents before, but finding the Bell brothers was more important.

As he waited for the team to gather around, he had a quick look at the horizon through his old binoculars. The whereabouts of the twins was a mystery indeed, and he stowed the binoculars away.

'This here is the vehicle Rob and Danny came up here in,' he said.

'I recognise it,' Liz said. 'Most of us do, I think.'

'Amazed it's even road legal,' said Jen.

'It hasn't moved since Jim and I were up here earlier today,' Harry continued. 'And it strikes me as strange that these two seem to have vanished. Obviously, they haven't, but maybe with a few of us up here, we have a better chance of tracking them down.'

'A manhunt!' Jadyn said. 'Cool!'

'No, this is not a manhunt,' Harry corrected. 'We just need to find them so that we can bring them in for questioning, that's all. I've no reason to suspect that this is suspicious, but I would like them found.'

'Where did you look last time, then?' Matt asked.

'We didn't,' Harry replied. 'I figured it made more sense to come back with more bodies if we needed to. And here we all are.'

'Very sensible.'

'I'm glad you approve. Any suggestions on how best to go about this?'

Matt did a very good impression of looking deep in thought.

'Yes,' he said at last, then started to gesture at the land-scape before them. 'Probably best we leave someone here with the vehicles. The rest of us can spread out in a long line and just work our way along from where we are, up there to the left, then swing back along. That way we'll cover the area well enough, I think.'

'What happens if we don't find them?' Jadyn asked.

'Well, they're adults,' Harry said, 'And they should know this area better than anyone, shouldn't they? Still, I'm tempted to call out the Mountain Rescue Team.'

'I agree,' said Matt. 'The light is already starting to fail. Once it gets dark, I don't think any of us should be up here walking around. It'll be too dangerous.'

'Well, that's settled, ' Harry said. 'Matt, you lead everyone off. Just need a volunteer to stay with the vehicles.'

'I think someone wants it to be you,' Gordy said, and pointed at Harry's RAV. He turned to see Smudge's big, black head sticking out of the open passenger window, staring at him.

'That's decided then,' Harry said, and pulled out his binoculars. 'I'll stay here and keep a lookout. The rest of you, watch where you're going. If anyone sees anything, call me.'

Once the team had headed off, Harry firmly glued his eyes to his binoculars again, but saw nothing except for moor-land stretching off to touch the sky, heather mottling the land with ink blots of purple flowers.

Harry had no idea where the twins were or what they were up to, and he wasn't about to jump to any conclusions, either. But the fact that they were seen having a proper go at a couple of poachers, as identified not only by Phil Thwaite but Gill Mitchell, and all that they'd found in the back of their truck, Harry was keener than ever to get them in for a chat. The disappearance only added to his suspicions.

Having met Mr and Mrs Bell, though, Harry was finding it hard to see how the offspring of two such people could turn into the kind of men who would happily take away someone else's life, and in such a violent fashion. Doing something like that, it wasn't a heat-of-the-moment thing; it was cold and calculated and took planning.

If something had happened in the pub, he would have found that more believable, Rob or Danny or both of them spotting the poachers, seeing red, then letting fists fly. A man trap, though? Still, it wasn't as though there was a type when it came to being a murderer. Of course, there was plenty of profiling and whatnot, but one of the things Harry had learned over the years was that almost anyone was capable of murder. Still though, with Rob and Danny, he remained to be convinced.

'What do you think, then?' Harry said, sweeping around again with the binoculars before turning around to look at Smudge and Fly. Both dogs had their heads out of the window and were staring at him, their ears flapping in the cool breeze.

'You're right,' he said., 'There's probably a rational explanation for it all, isn't there? But we'll just have to wait and see.' He dipped his hand into his pocket and brought out a tin. He opened it and took out a few small chunks of dried sausage; dog treats he'd bought from the pet shop near the community centre. He gave the dogs one each. Both were surprisingly gentle in taking it from his fingers. Then, as he went in for another of the treats, something caught his eye.

At first, Harry thought it was just a lone sheep far off. It certainly wasn't one of the team because they were nowhere near where he was looking right now.

Bringing his binoculars up to his face, Harry swept the horizon to find that it wasn't a sheep at all, but a lone figure walking towards him. Right then, he couldn't make out any details. For all he knew, it was a lone hiker heading down off the moors to grab a bed and a pint at the nearest pub.

The figure stumbled, disappearing from view. Harry kept the binoculars on where they'd fallen. As he watched, the figure seemed to move in slow motion, pulling themselves to their feet, falling again, tripping as they moved forward.

Harry pulled out his phone.

'Matt?'

'Boss.'

'I've eyes on a figure coming out of the moors. You see them, too?'

'Where?'

Harry gave rough directions.

'We've not covered that area yet,' Matt said. 'Just a minute ... Yep, I see something for sure. No binoculars here, though. What have you got?'

'Not sure,' Harry said. 'Just someone on their own. Tripped a moment ago, struggled to get to their feet.'

'Could be a walker,' Matt said. 'Knackered after a day out on the hill. Probably trying to get down too quickly, dreaming of that first pint.'

Harry kept staring, binoculars in one hand, phone in the other. The figure was closer now, though still a good way off.

He could just about make them out, and one thing was very clear.

'Not wearing a backpack,' Harry said. 'So, that rules out a walker, doesn't it?'

'There are still some folk who head out with no kit on them,' Matt said, 'but yes, I reckon it does. You think it's Rob or Danny?'

Harry didn't answer right away. He was waiting to see if he could make out any other details. Then the figure waved, before once again dropping out of sight.

'Whoever it is, they're in trouble,' Harry said.

The figure was back on their feet and Harry could now see that it was a large man, half walking, half stumbling as he moved towards him. Then he spotted something else.

'Matt, he's bleeding.'

'What?'

'He's bleeding,' Harry said, urgency in his voice now. 'Probably from the fact that he keeps falling down. I can't make out exactly what's happened to him, but there's definitely blood on his face and clothes.'

'How far away from you is he?'

'A few hundred metres,' Harry replied, dashing round to the rear of his vehicle to open the door. He pulled out a bag, slammed the door.

'I've a first aid kit,' he said. 'Always carry one. Old habits and all that.'

'You can take the man out of the Paras,' Matt said, 'but you can't take the Paras out of the man, right?'

'Right.'

'I'm going out to him,' Harry said. 'Get everyone else back to the vehicles.'

'What about Rob and Danny?'

Harry took a final look through his binoculars. He could clearly see the man now, the blood on his face, what he was wearing, which was certainly not the gear of a walker, his feet clad in green Wellington boots, and a waxed jacket on his back. And he was a big chap, too, Harry thought.

'My guess is that this is one or the other,' he said. 'I'll call you when I get to him, and we'll work out what to do from there.'

Harry hung up the phone, checked the dogs were secure, then headed off across the moors, his eyes on the approaching figure. As he marched, the heather hindered his pace as it snatched at his ankles like it was trying to trip him up. And the ground wasn't flat, either, rising and falling in lumps, then cut through with sections of wet, black peat, which sucked at his feet.

Carrying on, Harry was momentarily shunted back in time, and he remembered marching across other moors, his body screaming at him to just stop, to take off all the kit he was carrying, and rest. But once he'd set his mind to something, Harry had never been one to just stop. That wasn't his way. Never would be, either.

The sound of someone panting was enough to drag Harry out of his memories of P-Company and he looked up to see the man now seemingly charging towards him, panic riven across his face.

Harry held up his hands.

'Stop!' he shouted. 'Stop! Police! I'm here to help! Stop!'

The man didn't stop. Instead, he charged into Harry, knocking him to the ground, almost as though he just hadn't seen him there. Harry landed hard on his back, but the soft ground broke his fall. The impact sent the man stumbling and Harry watched as he tried to keep on his feet, but his arms whirled, he stumbled, and then the ground took him.

Harry was up and over to him as quickly as he could, repeating who they were, that they were there to help.

'Back there!' the man said. 'Back there! Danny, he's in a right mess! I have to get help, I have to!'

'We can help,' Harry said. 'You need to calm down. Tell me what's happened to Danny. You're Rob, yes?'

The man stared through Harry, but his eyes eventually focused from under a fringe of scruffy black hair.

'Yes,' he said. 'I'm Rob. We need to help Danny! He's hurt, like. But it was an accident!'

Harry helped Rob to his feet.

'What about you? Are you hurt?'

Rob shook his head.

'No, I'm fine. It's Danny ... He's ...'

'The blood, though.'

'That's all Danny's,' Rob said. 'When he was hit, like, it went everywhere. I caught him when he went down and got more of it on me. We need to get to him before it's too late. Please! It's my fault, all of it. I'm an absolute bloody idiot.'

With Rob now back on his feet, Harry stared at him, holding the man's concentration. With Danny injured out there somewhere in the moors, he was the priority. The investigation would have to be parked for now and Danny and Rob's part in what had happened on Tuesday, if any, would have to wait.

'Rob, you need to tell me what's happened to your brother,' Harry said. 'You need to tell me where Danny is.'

Rob was shaking his head now, out of disbelief at what had happened, or out of fear, Harry really wasn't sure.

'Rob?'

The man seemed to sag then, as though the weight of what he'd just witnessed had in that moment become too much to bear.

He dropped to his knees.

Harry followed him down to the ground.

'Rob,' he said. 'What's happened? Where's Danny?'

Rob looked up at Harry, then raised an arm to send a pointed finger over Harry's shoulder and off across the moors.

'He's been shot,' Rob said.

Harry wasn't sure he'd heard correctly.

'Shot? Are you sure? How? What happened?'

'It just went off,' Rob said. 'It wasn't supposed to. It's a warning, that's all. But I did it wrong. It's my fault. He was too close. It's all my fault!'

Harry was having a job keeping Rob focused.

'We need to get to Danny now, Rob,' he said. 'If Danny has been shot, we'll need to call the air ambulance. I need a location.'

'There was a flash,' said Rob, 'then Danny was down and screaming. I ran for help. But I fell. Knocked my head I think.'

'What, you knocked yourself out?'

Rob shook his head, shrugged.

'I don't know. Maybe?'

Harry's mind was working overtime now. If Rob was concussed, he couldn't risk having him lead him to Danny because he was a casualty himself. So, now what?

'Can you give me directions?'

'Yes,' said Rob.

'Good, because I need you to stay here.'

'I'm coming with you.'

'No, you're not. You might have a concussion.'

Harry grabbed his phone.

'Matt?'

'We're nearly back at the vehicles.'

'I need you here,' Harry said. 'Suspected concussion. Bring Jen with you. She can come with me to try and find Danny.'

'On my way.'

'Bring the RAV4. It'll be quicker. And we're going to need the air ambulance. I don't know how long Danny's been out here or how bad he is. All I know is that Rob's saying Danny's been shot.'

'Shit.'

'My thoughts exactly,' Harry said. 'Move it, Matt.'

'Already am.'

Conversation over, Harry turned back to Rob.

'Tell me where Danny is,' he said.

CHAPTER THIRTY

A FEW MINUTES LATER, MATT AND JEN ARRIVED IN Harry's vehicle. Harry had Rob calmer now, and he had managed to provide detailed directions to where Danny was, which Harry had written down. As for Danny's injuries, that was all still a bit of a mystery.

Matt took over caring for Rob as Harry and Jen climbed into the RAV4.

'You can't drive across the moors,' Rob said, looking over at Harry.

'Watch me,' said Harry, and started the engine.

Rob tried to push himself to his feet, but Matt made it very clear he was to do no such thing.

'But you'll get stuck,' Rob said. 'Or bottom out. You won't make it.'

'We have to get to Danny quickly,' Harry said, starting the engine. 'Walking isn't quick.'

'And getting stuck won't do anyone any favours, will it?' Rob fired back.

'Is there another way, then?' Harry asked.

Rob was quiet for a second.

'Those directions I gave you, they're fine, but if you're going to drive, you'll have to just watch as you go. Be careful. There's an old cart track soon enough, so use that.'

Harry looked at the directions.

'That's not mentioned on here.'

'No, it isn't,' said Rob, 'because those directions are a straight line. You won't be able to do that if you drive, but you're right, you will get there quicker. Just use the footpath, follow that, and then you'll soon see the trees and that ravine. Just hurry.'

Harry said no more and set off, Jen beside him, the dogs in the back.

'Thought you'd have left those two daft sods with the other vehicle,' Harry said, as he threw the RAV4 forward, the vehicle bucking and bouncing as they raced on. Though perhaps *race* was too strong a word, he thought, as the thick heather covering the ground snatched the steering wheel from his hands, sending them sideways. He had the vehicle quickly under control, though, and pushed on.

'In the rush, I forgot they were even there,' Jen said. 'They were both fast asleep.'

'Check the directions,' Harry said.

'Just keep going the way you're heading,' said Jen, pointing through the windscreen. 'See that grey scar ahead, cutting across? I think that must be the old cart track Rob mentioned. We drop onto that, and head left I think.'

Harry focused on where they were heading. The front of the vehicle kicked upwards, and for the briefest moment Harry felt weightless as the rest of the vehicle followed, then they crashed back down, bounced, and carried on.

Harry was picking up some speed when the cart track

Rob had mentioned raced up to meet them and he nearly overshot it. But he managed to heave the vehicle round, control the rear-end as it spun out, and pointed them down the twin ruts cut into the moors.

'Doesn't exactly look well used,' Harry said, looking to make conversation.

'Probably been here centuries,' Jen said. 'The Dales are covered in tracks like this, scarring the place all over. They're so old that the fells don't seem to want to give them up, you know?'

'I can understand that,' Harry said. 'Scars tell stories, don't they? Even if you forget them, they're still an important part of who you are.'

Jen stared.

'Wow,' she said. 'That was a bit philosophical, wasn't it?'

'Yeah, sorry about that.'

Jen looked back out through the window.

'Looks like it twists and turns a fair bit, but in a few minutes, we should see a ravine drop away to our left, and a little bit of woodland.'

'And that's where Danny is,' Harry said, and drove on.

'You said he'd been shot,' said Jen. 'Any idea how?'

'None at the moment, no. Rob wasn't exactly clear about what had happened. We'll just have to see what's what when we find him.'

'Shot, though?' Jen said. 'What were they out here doing in the first place for that to happen?'

Harry thought about that, what he and Jim had found in the back of the Toyota.

'My guess,' he said, 'is that they've had a few problems with poachers in the past and that they're out here setting up a few traps to deter them.'

Jen's eyes went wide at this.

'So, you think they're responsible for what happened Tuesday night, then?'

'There's a connection, obviously,' he said, 'but it doesn't make sense, does it? I mean, that's not their land, is it? So, why the hell would they be over there in the first place?'

'But if they're out here setting up their own traps ...'

'Then they're bloody idiots,' Harry said, 'but that doesn't put them at the scene of the crime.'

'They were seen in the pub,' Jen said. 'And forensics reckon that there were two attackers, don't they?'

'I'm still not buying it,' Harry said.

'Is that your gut talking again?'

'It is,' Harry said. 'I've learned to trust it over the years.'

'There,' Jen said, interrupting Harry. 'You see it? Just ahead.'

Harry did see it, a ravine dropping off to their left, the thick green of trees huddled together against all weathers.

Harry pulled them to a stop and turned to face Jen.

'Right, let's go and find Danny,' he said.

'There's nothing else Rob said about how this happened?' Jen asked. 'How Danny ended up getting shot?'

Harry shook his head and made to get out of the vehicle. As he did, he turned back to Jen. 'You stay here.'

'I should come with you.'

'No, you shouldn't,' Harry said. 'We don't know what's down there, how Danny was injured. Anything. You stay with the vehicle. If I need you, I'll call. Your job is to direct the paramedics when they arrive. Understood?'

Jen gave a firm nod.

'Good,' Harry said. 'Let's just hope he's easy to find and not at the bottom of a cliff or something.'

Harry grabbed his first aid kit, slammed the door and headed off, phone to his ear.

'Matt?'

'Yes, Boss?'

'How are things there? How's Rob?'

'He's fine,' Matt said. 'I've checked him over. No injuries I can see other than a few scratches and scrapes. I still want him checked over, though, for a concussion, just to make sure. Mountain Rescue is on their way and Air Ambulance is aware.'

'Aware? What bloody use is that? Why the hell isn't it on its way?'

'There's only one,' said Matt. 'And it's currently on a job. Soon as that's done, it'll be over here sharpish. Mountain Rescue will make sure Danny is stable and guide them in when they arrive.'

Harry went quiet for a moment, thinking things over.

'Right,' he said, 'I need Gordy to head back to the farm to stay with Mr and Mrs Bell. She's our family liaison officer, so she's best placed there. Jen is staying with the vehicle to direct the paramedics to where Danny and I will be. Can you send Jim and Liz up to where we are? You've got the directions from Rob. It won't take them too long to head over on foot. All they have to do is follow my tracks, anyway, until they hit the old cart road, take a left, and follow along until you see where we've parked up. This is potentially a crime scene and it'll need securing.'

'And Jadyn?'

'I need him to go and speak with Gill,' Harry said. 'If he and Gordy head back down, he can drop her off, then go over to Gill's.'

'About anything in particular?'

'Yes, actually,' Harry said. Something had been niggling at the back of his mind since Tuesday night. He'd not really been sure why, but now another thread had decided to tie itself into a loose knot with what was going on. 'I know that Gill has an alibi for Tuesday night, a solid one, too, but there's a link there, and I think he might be it.'

'Really? How's that, then?'

'Something Grace said about Gill helping her and her dad put the pheasant pens up.'

'That doesn't mean anything by itself.'

'No, it doesn't, but it does mean that Gill knows the place and knew how to get there.'

'I'm not following you.'

'No, but I think someone may have been following Gill,' Harry said. 'And I need to know if Gill knew or ever suspected it.'

'Following him? Who'd be doing that?'

'The poachers,' Harry said.

CHAPTER THIRTY-ONE

With his instructions given, Harry hung up and stowed his phone, then headed down into the ravine. There was a small path to follow, leading from the cart track and down under the bows of the trees, but it clearly hadn't seen much use over the years; the way was a tangle of roots, the ground loose, and a number of times Harry stumbled. So, he took his time, conscious that the last thing any of them needed now was another casualty. Even a twisted ankle would be a problem here and rescuing him and Danny would be no easy task.

As he moved on, each foot carefully placed, and reaching out to use not only the trees, but the steep bank on his left to keep stable and upright, Harry noticed how the air was richer and heavier in the green gloom. It was as though the branches and leaves had kept it in close, and the trees' breath filled it with the sweetness of sap and an earthy note of mushrooms and mould.

Harry thought he'd been walking for at least fifteen minutes, and hadn't as yet seen any sign or heard a sound to give away Danny's location. But I must be close, he thought, and gave a shout.

'Danny?'

Harry's voice died as it hit the trees.

He tried again.

'Danny, this is DCI Harry Grimm. Your brother went for help. If you can make a sound to let me know where you are.'

Harry stopped, listened, and for a moment heard only the wind, the distant call of a bird of prey, then, as he was about to call out again, he heard a groan.

'Danny?'

Silence, then another groan, louder this time, and Harry was able to use it to direct himself to where it was coming from.

'I'm nearly there,' Harry said. 'Hold on, okay, Danny?'

Another moan and then Harry saw Rob's twin, lying just to one side of the thin path, covered in blood.

'Hello there, Danny,' Harry said. 'I'm Harry.'

He waved, smiled, made to step forward, at which point Danny moaned again, only louder this time, shaking his head.

'It's okay,' Harry said, holding his hands up to keep Danny calm. 'I'm here to help. I'm with the police. We've paramedics on the way, mountain rescue, and if my DS has anything to do with it, probably a mobile pie shop to help us all keep up our strength.'

Danny moaned again, shook his head, except he wasn't shaking it, was he? He was gesturing, off to his left.

Harry looked, couldn't see anything at first, but then caught sight of something that never looked right unless it was camouflaged properly: a straight line. He stared a little longer, allowing whatever it was to reveal itself. A few seconds later, Harry knew what he was looking at: the barrel of a gun at just below waist height.

For a moment, Harry didn't move. If that was what had injured Danny, then what was worrying Harry now was the how. It was clear there was no one else here, and yet there was a barrel, pointing out of the trees, and at his feet, the man it had shot.

Harry focused, went back to basics, the one rule being a detective boiled down to: look for something that shouldn't be there but was, or something that was, but shouldn't. And then he saw it, a thin wire, across the path.

Crouching down, Harry examined the wire, looked up at the barrel pointing out of the trees. He could see that both he and Danny were safely out of its line of fire. If this was a trap that the brothers had set to catch another poacher, then something had obviously gone very wrong indeed and they'd triggered it themselves. Harry would have to deal with all of that later, though how exactly, he wasn't entirely sure at that moment.

'Danny,' he said, 'you're going to be okay. I'll check your wounds and then when the paramedics arrive, they'll take you to hospital. Do you understand?'

Danny gave a nod, then moaned in agony.

Harry crawled over towards him. He could see that Danny's legs were bleeding badly, his trousers dark with the stuff. He had to check him over and get him stable. That he was still conscious was a good sign, though.

After quickly checking Danny over, to make sure there were no other injuries than those to his legs, Harry opened his first aid kit and pulled out a pair of scissors, cutting away Danny's trousers as quickly and carefully as he could. With the material eased away, he saw that the skin was pitted with small marks, like pinpricks. None of the wounds looked serious, but together, they'd managed to seep a good amount of blood. And there was no doubting Danny's pain.

After cleaning the area as best he could, Harry then pulled out a handful of haemostatic dressings, which contained an agent to promote blood clotting. These he placed over the worst of the bleeding, using smaller dressings to deal with the more superficial wounds.

Harry's phone rang.

'What?'

'Jim and Liz should almost be with you,' Matt said. 'Gordy's just called, and she's at the farm with Mr and Mrs Bell.'

'How are they?'

'From what I gather, Mr Bell is having a large whisky and swearing a lot and his wife is busying herself by putting together a few tins of biscuits and cakes for everyone, and by everyone, I don't just mean us, but everyone else who hasn't even arrived yet.'

'And where is everyone else?'

'Mountain Rescue is on the way. Gordy will direct them from the farm.'

'Air Ambulance?'

'No sign yet, but Mountain Rescue will already be coordinating with them, so we don't need to worry about that. What about Danny?'

'I've stabilised him,' Harry said. 'How's Rob?'

'He's calmed down, but not said anything yet about what's happened. Still in shock, I think. You have any ideas yet?'

'Right now, I'm not sure,' Harry said. 'But it looks like some kind of booby trap with a shotgun.'

'You can't be serious.'

'Oh, I'm serious,' Harry said. 'Danny's been hit in the legs. There's a wire across the path. He must've caught it with his foot. Looks like they set it themselves.'

'Absolute bloody idiots! You think this is like what Jim mentioned from the auction rooms?'

'What was that?' Harry asked, his mind still focused on Danny.

'The bloke he and Liz spoke to mentioned something like what you've just described. Called it a poacher's gun, I think. Basically, a shotgun on a swivel spike. You attach it to a few trip wires. Someone pulls on one of them, it swings round and—.'

'Bang ...' Harry said and glanced over to the barrel and the wires. 'That sounds very much like what I'm looking at right now. Though we won't be able to say for sure until Danny's dealt with, and we can have a proper look.'

'It can't be, though, can it?' Matt said. 'Anything like that is decommissioned before it's sold on, like Jim said.'

'That man trap on Tuesday night was new, remember? Modelled on the real thing.'

Harry stared down at Danny. The man's bleeding had slowed, but his face was pale as the moon and he was clearly still in agony. Had he and his brother really put up a poacher's gun? What the hell had they been thinking?

'Matt, keep me posted, won't you? Let me know when Mountain Rescue arrives.'

'What about the Air Ambulance?'

'I reckon I'll hear them, don't you?' Harry said.

Call over, Harry looked back at Danny.

'You've got a lot of questions to answer,' he said.

Danny opened his eyes then and looked up at Harry. He opened his mouth.

'No, not right now,' Harry said.

'Accident,' said Danny. 'It ... it was ... an accident. Not ... Rob's ... fault.'

'Well, either way, you're a pair of complete bloody idiots,' said Harry. 'But for now, focus on staying calm. Help is on its way.'

Harry was about to give Danny another check-over when his phone rang again.

'What is it now?' he said, answering the phone without bothering to see who it was.

'Boss, it's Jadyn.'

Harry could hardly hear the constable's voice.

'I'm a little busy right now. And you're supposed to be having a chat with Gill.'

'Yeah, that's why I'm calling.'

'What was that?' Harry asked. 'You need to speak up a bit.'

'I can't.'

'What?'

'I can't!' Jadyn repeated.

'Is there a problem? If he's not there, then leave a note for him to give us a call.'

'It's both.'

'What is?'

'This is,' said Jadyn. 'There's a problem and I don't think he's here.'

Harry rubbed tiredness from his eyes and turned away from Danny to continue speaking to Jadyn.

'What kind of problem?'

'It's Gill's house,' Jadyn said. 'When I arrived, the door was already open. I drove past to turn around and then ...'

Jadyn stopped speaking.

'What was that?'

'There's someone here, I mean there, Boss,' Jadyn hissed, the volume of his voice dropping sharply. 'At Gill's house.'

'Who?'

'I don't know,' Jadyn said. 'Someone. Well, *someones,* actually. I think there's two of them. There's a car parked outside.'

Harry's world stopped dead.

'What was that?'

'There's two people in Gill's house. And I don't think either of them are this Gill bloke.'

'You're absolutely sure of that?'

Jadyn didn't answer.

'Jadyn?'

'I've just seen someone else. I think it's Gill. Yeah, that's him, for sure.'

'What's he doing?'

More silence. Harry was worried now. Whatever was happening at Gill's house, it didn't sound good. And to have an officer there on his own made him nervous about what could happen next.

'Speak to me, Jadyn.'

'He's just appeared from around the other side of the car,' Jadyn said. 'Now he's disappeared again.'

'And these other two?'

'Still in the house, I think. Bloody hell!'

'What?'

'It's Gill, he's just scarpered, Boss. Jumped in a little red Suzuki I think it is and drove off. Just a minute ...'

'Don't you do anything foolish, Constable,' Harry said.

'The other two, they've just left the house in a hurry and jumped in their car. They're after him, I think. Shit!'

Harry heard a sharp crack through his phone, and recognised the sound immediately.

'They're shooting at me, Boss! With guns!'

Another sharp crack, and another.

'Jadyn?'

'I'm okay,' Jadyn said, but Harry heard fear in his voice. 'They've driven off after Gill. They hit the car, though. My windshield is a bit of a mess. I can still follow them, I think. I'll just have to drive with my head out of the window.'

Harry's gut reaction was to reply with, 'No, you bloody well won't!'

'I'll stay far enough back, it'll be fine.'

'You'll stay so far back you won't bloody move from where you are right now!' said Harry. 'Do you have the number plate?'

'Yes.'

'Good. Now call Gordy, give her that and anything else, and she can call it in. Last thing we need is a car chase through the Dales with bullets flying. And I'm not having you chase after people who've already taken potshots at you, even more so if the only way for you to drive at all is with your head out the door!'

'But what about Gill? What if they catch up with him?'

'You said he drove off; which direction? Back towards West Burton?'

'No,' said Jadyn. 'He drove straight past me.'

Harry remembered then what Jim had said about the lane in front of Gill's cottage.

'That doesn't lead anywhere except up into the hills,' he

said. 'My guess is he knows exactly what he's doing because they'll only be able to follow him so far before their car gets stuck.'

'If that's the case, then they'll be driving past me again, won't they?'

'No, they won't,' Harry said. 'Because you're getting out of there right now.'

'But I thought you said I shouldn't drive.'

'I did,' Harry said, 'but all I want you to do is to get out of their way so that when they do come back, they don't think it would be a good idea to take another potshot or two. Do you think you can make it back to the farm?'

'Yes,' Jadyn said.

'Good. Then no more talking. Move!'

Harry didn't give Jadyn a chance to reply and killed the call.

He looked back down at Danny.

'Really turning into one of those weeks, isn't it?'

CHAPTER THIRTY-TWO

'So, we've nothing on Gill at all? But he can't have just disappeared, can he?'

Harry was standing outside Gill's house, waiting for the arrival of Sowerby and the rest of the forensics team. On the other end of the phone was Gordy.

'For now, it seems he has,' Gordy said.

'But where could he have gone?'

'We think he doubled back. The lane he headed up on, well that leads nowhere really, but there's another rough track further up, and it looks like he cut across to that and then headed back down the dale again. But there's been no sign of him.'

'What about the two who were in his house and shot at Jadyn?'

'Well, we've found their car, but not the two who were in it,' Gordy said. 'Looks like it packed up on them as they were driving back down dale towards Middleham. No idea where they were heading, though. They could be anywhere by now and probably are. They must've had someone come and pick them up.'

'Forensics will want to take a look at it.'

'I've already run the plates. They're fake.'

'Stolen car?'

'Looks that way, yes.'

'What the bloody hell is going on here?' Harry said. 'We've gone from a murder in a woodland to drive-by shootings by way of poaching, a privacy-obsessed rich landowner, a scrapyard, a car wash, and two idiot farmers. And now we have a missing person to add to it all? None of this makes sense. None of it!'

'Don't forget Liz's vampire.'

'Believe me, I wish I could,' Harry sighed. 'How can it all be connected?'

'Your guess is as good as mine.'

'I don't want guesses. I want facts.'

'Actually, we have a lot of facts,' Gordy said. 'But like you said, none of it makes any sense.'

Harry checked his watch. The evening was turning darker by the minute, the sun having dipped below the horizon a good while ago now.

'Where are you?' he asked.

'Standing in the middle of a field, getting cold and hungry.'

'How's Jadyn?'

Harry heard Gordy laugh.

'Well, he's gone very quickly from the shock of being in a car being shot at, to the excitement of being in a car being shot at,' she said. 'He's buzzing.'

'Well, that isn't terrifying at all.'

'His vehicle has been picked up, so I'll drop him home and fetch him in tomorrow. What about you?'

'Well, we've got Gill's house cordoned off. Once forensics arrives, I'll send everyone home. I can handle things for this evening.'

'Matt, too?'

'Matt especially,' Harry said. 'Joan's back home with their daughter, so I want him there with them.'

Leaving Gordy to take Jadyn home and to the rest of her evening, Harry put his phone away as the sound of engines had him staring down the lane. He saw headlights and, a few moments later, two large white vans and a car pulled up in front of him. Further off, he saw the twinkling lights of West Burton and would very much have loved to take a wander down and into the pub.

The driver's window of the car lowered into the door with an electronic whirr.

'You know, we have to stop meeting like this,' Sowerby said. 'People will talk.'

'Sometimes, I just can't help myself,' Harry replied. He looked over at the two vans, then back at her. 'Everyone here, then?'

'I'm afraid so, yes,' said Sowerby, rolling her eyes.

Harry looked up and saw Bennett climb out of the front van. He approached Harry with another man, the crime scene photographer.

'Make yourselves at home, gentlemen,' Harry said, and pointed at Gill's house, then, to avoid talking to Bennett, turned back to Sowerby, who was now pulling herself out of her car.

'I hear you've had an interesting day,' she said.

'Well, it's not every day you have to go and find two brothers who've set up a device to catch poachers and ended up catching themselves.'

Harry thought back to Danny and Rob, both of whom were now in hospital. Rob was okay, but was being kept in for observation. Danny, on the other hand, was a little more serious, having been shot. Though not by shotgun pellets, as Harry had found out from the hospital.

'Rock salt, though,' Sowerby said. 'What the hell were they thinking?'

'They were thinking it would be enough to just sting,' said Harry. 'Rob replaced the shot in a 4.10 cartridge with salt crystals, thinking they'd just disintegrate on impact, scare the hell out of an unfortunate poacher, and that would be that. And he'd have been right, if Danny hadn't been so close to the damn thing when it went off.'

'It'll be an interesting one for the courts, that's for sure.'

'Well, seeing as Danny isn't pressing charges, right now, it's hard to see what will happen. They'll lose their gun licences, though. I'll be making sure of that.'

Sowerby pulled on her PPE and gestured at the house.

'Shall we?'

'Well, you can't go letting Bennett have all the fun, can you?'

Harry stepped back to let Sowerby walk past. On the way, he quickly ran through everything they knew, about Gill, about what Jadyn had witnessed.

'So, you think these two men are the ones responsible for what happened on Tuesday night?'

'It's a fair assumption,' said Harry. 'My guess right now is that they know Gill had something to do with the poacher they killed, though what or why, I've not a clue.'

'So, you think this is still about poaching, then?'

Harry shook his head.

'I don't know what any of it is about,' he said. 'But it's very quickly getting out of hand, that's for sure. It has to be bigger than poaching, though, doesn't it?'

At the cordon tape, Jen was waiting.

'How's life as scene guard, then?' Harry asked.

'A thrill a minute.'

Harry lifted the cordon tape to allow Sowerby to head on through to the house.

'Not coming?' she asked.

'I'm going to send the rest of the team home,' he said. 'Now, why don't you go and have fun with your favourite person?'

Sowerby scowled and walked off.

Harry called the rest of the team over to where he and Jen were standing.

'Right, I want you lot to head home.'

'But what about this?' asked Matt.

'This is easy and I can handle it on my own,' Harry said. 'I don't think there's going to be much here, anyway. Whoever those two were, they weren't here for long. There's no sign of any violence at the scene, so forensics won't take long. It'll be fine. Jim?'

'Yes, Boss?'

'You mind taking Smudge back with you? Then bring her in with you in the morning.'

'No problem at all. I'll give them both a good run when I get up as well, make sure they're properly knackered.'

Harry turned then to Liz.

'Tomorrow I'll need you to head to the hospital and take statements from Rob and Danny.'

'Will do.'

'Jen, I'll take over as scene guard and I want you and Matt in the office first thing so we can go through what we have so far with Gordy and Jadyn.'

'How is he?' Jen asked.

'I've a horrible feeling that he now thinks he's in a real-life episode of The Professionals,' Harry said.

Matt laughed. He was the only one who did.

'The Professionals?' Harry repeated. 'Bodie and Doyle?'

Liz, Jen, and Jim all stared back at Harry with blank faces.

'We're getting old,' Matt said.

Harry waved the team off and headed back over to the cordon tape. He had an awful lot to think about, and as he did so, he sent a text through to Grace to let her know he would text her later when he was on his way. Her reply confused him.

Sorry. Busy. Got company.

Really?

Came bearing gifts (a bottle of wine and chocolates).

Who?

A real gentleman, well dressed, too.

Harry laughed.

I'll see you both later, then. Give my regards to Dave.

With nothing much left to do other than wait for the forensics team to complete their job, Harry gave himself a moment or two to think back over everything that had happened so far. He needed to start making connections, but so far he'd come up with zilch. Well, not exactly zilch, but right now he felt as though all he had was a big tangle of events and somehow he had to tease it all out to make sense of it.

Walking away from Gill's house, Harry took a stroll up the lane, the lights of West Burton behind him. In front of him the black silhouette of Brown Haw rose so ominously and with such weight, it seemed as though at any moment it could just topple and crush him.

Everything had started with a murder, and one which on the face of it seemed to be connected to poaching. And maybe it still was. Whoever Luca was, he'd been out in those woods to take pheasants by nefarious means. They also knew that he was malnourished, had an Eastern European name, and that somewhere out there was a woman wondering where he was. That thought darkened Harry's already bleak thoughts about everything. If the woman on the other end of the call he'd made using Luca's phone was his next of kin, telling her what had happened was going to be horrendous.

And what of that other call Luca had made? Was that to the same person who had come out to him and applied a tourniquet to try and save him? Who were they?

Luca's name, the woman's accent, linked him to the car wash, as did the state of his hands, the damage they had received from water and detergent; Jadyn had made that connection, which had impressed Harry hugely. Luca's death, though, was about more than poaching. Harry was sure of it. A death like that, it was a message, but who had it been for, and why? Jadyn had mentioned he'd seen some bruising on the staff at the car wash. Was there a link there, too?

As for Rob and Danny Bell, Harry despaired at their stupidity. That had been a wild goose chase, hadn't it? Or had it ... They had followed the two poachers, one of whom Harry was pretty damned certain had been Luca. They'd followed them from the pub after the altercation with Gill, and then to the scrapyard. They'd waited and then trailed them once again. But where to? That was something for Liz to find out tomorrow, so he quickly sent her a text to tell her to do so when she headed over to get their statements in the morning.

And now they had Gill missing, having been chased off by two men who, it was safe to assume, were the ones responsible for Luca's death. They also needed to have another word with Mr Walker, even if it was only to pin down his whereabouts and remind him that being secretive with the police was never a good idea.

Harry turned back down towards Gill's house, his head throbbing from tiredness and overthinking. Then he remembered Liz's concern about the solicitor and shook his head. If the man turned out to be a vampire, he probably wouldn't be surprised, not with the way things had been going so far. And finally, there was Swift, what he was going through, and the fact that he'd left Harry with something clearly unsaid. As to what, Harry hadn't the faintest idea, but it was something else to worry about, wasn't it? Though it would have to get in line.

A shout pulled Harry out of his thoughts, and he saw Rebecca Sowerby walking towards him. She pulled her face mask off, and rubbed her eyes and yawned.

'That it, then?' he asked.

Sowerby laughed, the sound filled with weariness.

'A pathologist's work is never done,' she said. 'Nothing much to tell so far. Whoever they were, they weren't looking for anything at the house other than the person they then chased after. We're done inside and moving our search outside, do a sweep, check the shed, that kind of thing. And the garage.'

'There's a garage?'

'It's locked, but that shouldn't be too much of a problem.'

'Anything useful yet?'

'Hard to say. No real signs of any disturbance,' Sowerby said. 'Didn't even break into the place.'

'You mean Gill let them in?'

Sowerby shook her head.

'They probably let themselves in. The front door doesn't lock.'

'Of course it doesn't,' Harry said with a sigh, despairing at the trusting nature of the folk of Wensleydale. On the one hand, it was heartening to find such trust in the world, as it was a place where people were pretty sure no one was going to come round and have a rummage through their valuables, but on the other, he sometimes felt that some of them could do with a sprinkling of wariness in their lives.

Harry saw one of the forensics team drop a box off at the vans.

'A few items that may be of use, to help us draw a picture of the owner,' Sowerby said by way of explanation. 'I'll get a report to you tomorrow. Not sure there'll be much in it, but if there is, I'll let you know.' She went to head back to the house, then turned back to face Harry again. 'Looks like they took his guns, though.'

Harry felt the hairs rise on the back of his neck.

'Guns? What guns?'

'There's a gun cabinet under the stairs. Large one, too.'

'When you say large ...'

'It had room for six, but you know what people are like; always try to shove more in an already full cupboard. So, could've held eight at least, maybe more. It's empty.'

'Eight?' Harry said, almost despairing now. 'That's all we need.'

Sowerby stared over at him and shook her head.

'It isn't, is it?'

'No, it really isn't.'

'And there was this, too,' Sowerby said, pulling an evidence bag from a pocket. 'Which is proof I'm tired, because this is supposed to be in one of the boxes now in the van, not here, isn't it?'

'And what is that, exactly?' asked Harry, looking at the bag. As far as he could tell, all it contained was some rough scraps of material.

'Just some rough scraps of material,' Sowerby said, as though she'd read his thoughts, which almost made Harry laugh, and she handed him the bag. 'They were caught in the door of the cabinet, like they'd been yanked off when whatever they were part of was removed.'

Harry stared at the bag for a moment. There was something familiar about what it held, wasn't there? But what? Where had he seen something like this before? He shook his head, trying in vain to dislodge a distant memory, but it refused to shake loose, and he handed the bag back.

'Been a fun few days, hasn't it?' he said.

'Positive mental attitude,' Sowerby said, smiling. 'I'm impressed.'

Sowerby headed back to the house, leaving Harry alone, darkness gathering around his feet, the empty eyes of the windows in Gill's house staring at him. He had a strange feeling that they knew something he didn't, as though behind them were secrets, not just about what had happened inside those walls, either, but something else. He attempted to stare back at the house, challenging it almost, but all it gave in return was the silence of yet more unanswered questions, and a worry he couldn't shift. Not just about what had happened to Gill, but thanks to that last nugget of information from Sowerby, his small arsenal of guns.

CHAPTER THIRTY-THREE

Harry was on the shores of Semerwater. The sun was high and dripped liquid gold across the surface of the water. Around him rose the fells, an amphitheatre of emerald, the vivid greens dotted with the grey-white presence of sheep, their throaty calls to each other rolling through the air.

Out in the water, Grace stood waist-deep. She was smiling at him, calling for him to follow. And he would, in a moment or two, once he'd finished drinking it all in. Not just the beauty of the place either, but of the woman in front of him, mischief playing in her eyes and at the corners of her smile, her hair already wet from taking her first dip.

Harry stretched, the cold of the water already burning a ring around his ankles, the sharp stabs in his feet from the stones of the lakebed causing him to stumble. But he caught himself, arms out to each side for balance, tottering from foot to foot like a toddler learning to walk.

A buzz sounded. Harry looked around for a wasp, though surely a sound that deep and threatening was a hornet.

The buzz sounded again. Where the hell was it? He'd swat the little sod if it came too close. No way was some evil little bug going to ruin this moment with its arse-dagger.

The buzzing grew louder.

'Where the hell are you? Where?'

Then the water at his feet turned black, the sky split in two, and the brightest of lights burned into Harry's skull.

'Bollocks ...'

Harry sat up, rubbed his eyes, and reached for his phone, as a warm hand reached over and stroked his shoulder.

'Who is it?'

Grace's voice was all sleep and the promise of safety in her embrace, but there was no way he could ignore the call.

'It's Matt,' Harry said, and answered his phone.

'Sorry,' Matt said. 'It's early, I know, but we've just had a call come in from a couple of fishermen down on the Ure.'

'What about? And why are you telling me at,'—Harry checked his watch— 'Bloody hell, it's not even six!'

Grace shuffled in closer, wrapping an arm around him, her legs spooning his.

'They're up here on holiday,' Matt said. 'Couple of retired blokes fishing their way around the Dales. And this morning, when they walked down to a nice quiet spot on the river, they found an old red Suzuki Jeep, doors open, riddled with what they think are bullet holes.'

Matt's words lit a fuse in Harry that had him sitting up and awake better than any double espresso.

'That's Gill's,' he said.

'Can't see it being anyone else's, can you? I'm heading down there now. Want me to drop by and pick you up?'

Harry swung his legs out of bed.

'I'm over at Grace's,' he said.

'I'll be there as soon as I can.'

Call over, Harry placed the phone back on the bedside cabinet and reached a hand round to rest on Grace's hip.

'Sorry,' he said.

'Don't be,' Grace replied. 'It's the job, not you.' She sat up. 'You okay?'

'Tired,' Harry said.

'Coffee and bacon, then?'

'You stay in bed. I'll sort myself out.'

'And miss the opportunity to wave off my brave detective? Not a chance of it!'

Matt arrived just before seven.

'You look terrible,' he said.

'I always look terrible.'

'There is that.'

Grabbing a quick goodbye kiss from Grace, Harry followed the DS to his vehicle and climbed in.

'Where are we going, then?'

'The fishermen, they're just out of Aysgarth, Hawes' side. There's a lane as you're leaving which heads down to the river.'

'Not far, then.'

'Not at all. You could walk.'

'I could, but I don't think I will.'

'No, I won't either, then. Good decision, that.'

'Mine usually are.'

Having only just driven out of Carperby, Matt took a left down a road which very soon became a lane, the drystone walls on each side moving slowly inwards, pinching the road just enough to turn it into a single lane.

'Have you been to Aysgarth Falls, yet?' Matt asked.

Harry shook his head.

'Not yet, no. It's on the list.'

'You've a list?'

'Of course I haven't,' Harry said with a laugh. 'But if I did, it would be on it, right at the top.'

'Can't believe you've not been yet. They can dry up almost completely during a hot summer, so my advice is to wait until a storm's been through; the falls are spectacular when the river's in spate. Pretty bloody terrifying, too, I might add. Don't half make you feel small.'

'And you're telling me this why?'

Matt slowed down as the lane widened again, only to sweep under the shadow of woodland and to head downwards, thin strands of grey shadow falling in their path.

'Wind your window down.'

Harry did, thinking it easier to just go along with whatever Matt was on about.

Matt slowed down even more.

'You hear that?'

'What?'

Matt glanced at Harry.

'Well, stick your head out, then!'

'I'm not a bloody Labrador!'

'Humour me.'

'I do that more often than you seem to realise,' Harry said, but found himself leaning his head out of the window.

'Well?'

Harry could hear something now, a quiet rumble, low and thunderous.

'The bridge is just up ahead. I'll stop a moment on the other side, give you a proper look.'

The woodland cleared a little and Harry saw the bridge, then Matt was rolling over it and pointing off to their right.

'There you go,' he said, slowing down to a stop. 'Aysgarth Falls. There's a bit of water in them, but like I said, get down here when we've had a wet one, and you'll really feel the power of the place.'

Harry gazed past Matt to the falls. The DS was right, they were impressive. He remembered something Jim had mentioned.

'That Robin Hood movie was filmed here, wasn't it? With Kevin Costner.'

'Here and up at Hardraw,' Matt said.

Harry remembered swimming there with Grace a while ago. God, that had been cold. Fun though.

'Interesting though this is, can we crack on?'

Matt drove on.

When they arrived out the other side of Aysgarth, Matt turned off the road to head down a thin gravel track. There was barely enough room to squeeze his vehicle down and nowhere to pull over if they happened to meet someone coming the other way.

A few minutes later, the lane turned right and Matt pulled over beside a small section of woodland.

'The fishermen are through there,' he said, pointing over at the trees. 'River's nice and sheltered.'

'What about Gill's Suzuki?'

Matt pointed over to a large stone barn.

'Just over there, behind that,' he said.

Harry followed Matt through a gate and on towards the barn. And sure enough, there was Gill's Suzuki.

Harry stopped dead.

The vehicle looked sad and forlorn, the driver's door hanging open, the window smashed. He saw other damage to the bodywork, holes everywhere, the windscreen a shattered mess.

Harry pulled out his phone and looked at Matt.

'You know what this means, don't you?'

He then spoke into the phone.

'Me again,' he said, then quickly explained to Sowerby where they were and what they were looking at, the pathologist yawning a little too obviously as Harry gave her the location.

CHAPTER THIRTY-FOUR

HAVING CORDONED OFF WHERE GILL'S SUZUKI WAS
parked, Harry had then wandered down to the river to have a
chat with the two fishermen who had found it earlier that
morning.

Matt was scene guard, and Harry had had a quick chat
with Gordy to let her know what was going on and what he
wanted the rest of the team on with. Liz was heading over to
speak with Rob and Danny. He wanted Gill's gun licence
checked up on as well. He also thought it would be sensible
to have someone out to check up on Danny and Rob's
parents, and to do a bit of door-knocking around Aysgarth,
considering what had happened the night before and what
had been found. There was always the chance that someone
had seen or heard something that could make all the difference to a case.

When forensics turned up he didn't want to get in
Sowerby's way, or talk to Bennett, so heading over to chat
with the two fishermen seemed like a good idea. Apparently,

they'd seen no one about. The sight of the vehicle, and what had happened to it, had obviously given them a scare; one of them was already sipping enthusiastically from a hip flask and the other couldn't stop eating chocolate.

'Not something you expect, is it?'

'No, it's not,' Harry said, speaking to the man with the hip flask who had introduced himself as Geoff, as if that was more than enough for anyone.

The other man had been a little more forthcoming, giving their full names.

'And you're absolutely sure you saw no one down here, then, Mr Hunter?'

Geoff shook his head.

'Not a soul. Nice and peaceful, isn't it? Never been here before. We'll come again, I'm sure.' He held the hip flask out to Harry. 'Damson gin,' he said. 'Homemade.'

'Bit early for me,' Harry said.

Geoff took another sip.

'Not driving, I hope.'

'We came in my car,' said the other man, a Mr Timothy Fletcher. 'Geoff's is a bit of a shed, really. Mine's got heated seats.'

'Make you feel like you've wet yourself,' said Geoff. 'Can't see the attraction myself.'

Harry asked them both to tell him as much as they could about what it was they'd seen, and just when he thought they had finished talking, Geoff then added, 'I caught a hat.'

Timothy immediately apologised to Harry.

'Ignore him,' he said. 'He says hat, but it's little more than a ball of wet, muddy fur. Hardly relevant to whatever happened over behind that barn, is it?'

'Where is it?' Harry asked.

'I nearly threw it back in,' answered Geoff. 'Dragged it in on the end of a hook. Thought I'd caught a big one, then I thought it was just a dead rabbit.'

'That's because it is,' said Timothy, glancing at Harry and rolling his eyes.

'But you've still got it?'

'It's over with my gear,' Geoff said. 'Just a minute ...'

Twisting the lid back onto his hip flask, Geoff jogged off towards the river and their fishing gear, and returned shortly.

'Here you go,' he said, holding a matted ball of wet, muddy fur. 'Like I said, I thought it was a rabbit, but it's definitely a hat.'

Harry pulled a pair of disposable gloves from a pocket, along with an evidence bag, and took the thing from Geoff.

'I wouldn't go trying it on,' Geoff said, as Harry teased it out.

'Can you show me where you found this?'

'Just over there,' Geoff said, pointing to the riverbank just along from where he and Timothy were set up for the day. 'My cast went wrong, you see, a gust of wind threw it back, and it got a bit tangled in the reeds. I managed to get it loose and found that thing on the end. Definitely not a fish.'

Harry knew he'd seen the hat before, Gill had been wearing it when he and Jim had gone to see him. And now, here it was, having been dragged from the river not more than a couple minutes' walk from his ruined four-by-four.

'Thanks for this,' Harry said, and stuffed the hat into an evidence bag. 'I have your contact details, so if we have any questions, or need something clarifying, someone will be in touch.'

Instructing Geoff and Timothy to gather up their

fishing gear and leave what was now a crime scene, Harry walked back to Gill's Suzuki. As luck would have it, Sowerby was there, waiting for the photographer to finish up.

'Here,' Harry said. 'This was found over by the river. I think it belongs to the owner.'

Sowerby took the evidence bag and held it up.

'It's dead, yes?'

'Ignoring the fact it's been in the river for a fair while, it's a hat made from rabbit fur,' Harry explained, 'or I would assume so. Gill, who owns this Suzuki, was wearing it when I last saw him.'

'And you're sure that this revolting-looking thing is the same one?'

'I can't be absolutely sure, no,' Harry said, 'but I doubt there are too many homemade rabbit hats around, do you?'

'Not sure I'll get much from it,' Sowerby said.

'Neither am I, but it's a worry all the same.'

Sowerby frowned.

'We're standing next to a bullet-ridden vehicle and it's this you find to be a bit of a worry?'

'There's really only one way it ended up in the river,' Harry said. 'And that's with Gill still wearing it.'

'That's a bit of a leap.'

'It is, but I think we need to do a wide search, from the vehicle to the river,' Harry said, then caught Sowerby's stare. 'Sorry, don't mean to tell you how to do your job.'

'Good,' Sowerby replied, and Harry heard that hard edge the pathologist still had, though he didn't see it half as often as he had when he'd first arrived in the Dales. 'And we will be doing that anyway, as a matter of course.'

Harry looked over at the vehicle as the forensics team got

288 DAVID J. GATWARD

to work, the photographer now done. Bennett was there as well.

'He's quiet,' Harry said.

'I told him if he didn't stop trying to undermine me, I'd throw him in the river.'

'That'll do it.'

'I've not finished my report on yesterday, I'm afraid,' Sowerby said, pulling a facemask down from where it had been resting on her forehead. 'The team is still collating everything.'

'How could you have?' Harry asked. 'That was only a few hours ago and here we are once again.'

'Found some fingerprints, though.'

'You did?'

'I've got someone checking them this morning. If we get a match, we'll let you know. And if there's anything else to pass on, I will.'

Harry was only half listening. His mind was back on the river and the hat Geoff had found.

'We're going to have to call in the divers, aren't we?'

Sowerby's question stuck itself firmly in the front of Harry's mind.

'Yes,' he said. 'We are.' And with that, he left Sowerby to get on.

'AND YOU'RE ABSOLUTELY sure about this, Grimm?'

'I am, sir,' Harry said, having put a call in to Swift later that morning. Forensics had been busy, not just with the vehicle, but with a search along the river, covering where the hat had been found, what looked like the entrance point that Gill had taken, and the opposite side, too, on the off chance of finding evidence of him having clambered out.

'Evidence so far looks like the driver of the vehicle was chased to the river, that he entered the water, and that's about it.'

'But he could be anywhere.'

'He could,' Harry said, 'but Aysgarth Falls aren't too far away so ...' The gravity of what he was saying weighed heavily on his mind.

'So, you think the body could be there?'

'Could be, yes,' Harry said. 'Though, it could just as easily have washed over. There's enough water in the river to send someone a good way along.'

'I'll make the call, then,' Swift said.

'How are you doing, sir?' Harry asked, the question out before he'd really had a chance to think about it.

'I'm fine, Grimm,' Swift replied.

'About what you said, I appreciate how difficult it was for you to tell me.'

'Difficult? Why would it be difficult?'

'It's a lot you're going through and dealing with, sir, and if there's anything I can do to help ...'

'I'm sure there isn't, but thank you.'

Swift is back to his usual curt self, Harry thought, but then maybe that was for the best. Everyone coped with things differently, and perhaps he'd surprised himself with how open he'd been. Still, though, Harry couldn't help but wonder about what Swift had been about to say when he'd seen him the day before.

'I'll let you know as soon as I hear about the divers,' Swift said. And with that, he ended the call.

Harry checked his watch. The morning had almost gone,

as though the events of the previous night and that morning had squeezed it to nothing. Lunch was racing towards him and Harry thought it was probably sensible to head back to Hawes. There was nothing more to do here, not now that the forensics team was nearly done. There would be a wait for the call from Swift, and then another long wait for the divers to head out to join them.

Between now and then, he would need the crime scene manned. That wasn't a job he was volunteering for, mainly because he found divers to be a strange bunch. Probably because he just couldn't see the attraction of parading around in all that gear, the weight and bulk of it making them look like walking tugboats with legs, then throwing themselves into the dirtiest, murkiest water, to look for anything from drugs and weapons, to bodies. They did a good job though, and he admired them for it, just had never really seen the attraction.

Harry's phone buzzed.

'That was quick, sir,' he said.

'I think things have been a little quiet for the team over the last week or two,' Swift replied. 'A rare thing, really. Anyway, they jumped at it and are on their way. They're travelling up from their base of operations, down near the Humber, so it'll be a couple of hours, I should think.'

'That's great,' Harry said. 'When you headed off yesterday, sir, I think you were about to say something to me. It sounded important, and I was just wondering what—'

But Swift wasn't listening because the line was already dead.

Shaking his head, Harry put his phone away. Then, with a wave to Sowerby, he headed over to Matt. A quick call through to the office and he had Jen on her way over to replace Matt as Scene Guard. Jim would follow on after, once Harry and Matt were back in Hawes, to help liaise with the diving unit.

About twenty minutes later, with Jen now on site, and with the mention of lunch, the DS was all too happy to whisk them both away from the Ure and back up the dale.

CHAPTER THIRTY-FIVE

WITH LUNCH BOUGHT FROM COCKETT'S, AND WITH Matt already eating as they made their way back across the centre of Hawes, Harry entered the office at the community centre with Matt close on his heels.

As Harry had requested, Jim had brought Smudge into the office with him and his own dog, Fly. Now heading down dale to join Jen at the crime scene in Aysgarth, he would drop Fly back at the family farm in Burtersett so that he wouldn't have to worry about having the dog down by the river.

Gathering the rest of the team together, Harry sat down to speak with Liz about her visit to the hospital to chat with Rob and Danny. As he did so, Smudge leaned against his leg and thumped her tail on the carpet, staring up at him through her big brown eyes like he'd been gone for months.

'Rob and Danny, well, they're not exactly on speaking terms,' Liz said.

Harry was still stunned by the men's stupidity in setting up the homemade gun trap.

'How were they with those statements?' he asked. 'And I'm not really that interested in what happened up on the moors right now, more what happened the night they had that barny with the poachers in the pub.'

Liz leaned back in her chair.

'They tried to deny it at first,' she said. 'I told them to stop talking bollocks and pointed out that we had footage of them, in their vehicle, at the scene, and that things could very easily get bad for the pair of them if they didn't get to the point sharpish.'

'And those were your actual words, were they?' Gordy asked.

Liz grinned and looked at Harry.

'I've learned from the best,' she said.

'So, what did they say after that, then?' Harry asked.

Liz checked her notes.

'Like you suspected, they didn't actually leave the pub and head home. Instead, they waited in their pickup and followed the poachers.'

'Did they give a reason why?'

'I doubt it was to apologise,' said Matt, showing a little too much of the food in his mouth in the process.

'Funnily enough, Rob dared to suggest that was the reason,' said Liz. 'But I don't think Danny was in any mood for messing around, not after what had happened. He kind of just shut Rob down and told me straight.'

'Told you what, exactly?' Harry asked.

'That they planned to follow the poachers home and, to quote Danny here, "Slap them around a bit, like, so that they'd never poach on our land again." He also added, "the bastards."'

'At least he was honest,' Harry said. 'So, what happened,

then?'

'They followed the poachers to the scrapyard, the one Jen and Matt visited. They parked up, because they weren't really sure what was going on. Then, when they saw one of them break into the place, they thought they'd stick around to see why.'

'They really know how to waste an evening, don't they?' said Jadyn.

'When they saw the car drive out of the scrapyard, they followed it home.'

Harry latched onto this.

'So, we have a possible home address for Luca?'

'We do.'

Harry almost fist-punched the air.

'That's brilliant, Liz, well done.'

'Thank you.'

'So, what did they do when they arrived at the house? It must've been the middle of the night.'

'I think they got cold feet.'

Harry was baffled.

'After all that, they got cold feet? Why? And where exactly is home for the two they were following, just out of interest?'

'Over in Richmond,' Liz said, handing Harry the address, a page torn from her notebook. 'They saw a woman and a baby at the door. Also, Rob said they saw a few other people coming and going from the property. I think they thought it was going to be just two on one. They hadn't counted on there being others.'

'Or a child, either,' Harry said. 'Seems they've got some sense, then.'

'Not too much, though,' Liz said. 'The next day, Rob

was still riled up about it and off early to go and wait outside the house. He wanted to get the one they'd followed alone so he could "have a word." That didn't happen though, because he saw him picked up by a minibus. Which he followed.'

'I'll give him points for being a tenacious sod,' said Matt.

'Where did the minibus take him?'

'Guess ...'

'No,' Harry said. 'I'm not in the mood.'

Liz gestured to Gordy and Jadyn.

'The car wash visited by our very own DI Haig and PC Okri here, that's where.'

Harry sat up at this.

'Seriously?'

'I've the address here,' Liz said, tapping her notebook. 'Rob parked up and watched the minibus unload. Then he walked over to, as I said earlier, "have a word."'

She made air quotes around those last three words.

'He needs to have a word with himself if you ask me,' suggested Matt.

'He didn't get very far, apparently, and ended up having a blazing row with a crowd of staff and the woman running the place.'

Harry said, 'And this would be the staff and manager who told our very own DI that they had never heard of anyone called Luca?'

'Indeed, it is.'

Harry clapped his hands down on his thighs, stood up, and looked down at Matt, who was busy wiping crumbs from his chin.

'If you don't mind me saying so, Detective Sergeant, that car of yours is looking a bit dirty,' he said, walking over to wash his mug and throw away the paper bag which had carried his now-consumed lunch.

Matt rose to his feet.

'Well, we can't be having that now, can we?'

'No, we most certainly can't.'

'What will people say?'

'Here's the car wash's address,' Liz said, ripping another page out of her notebook.

Harry took the address and looked over at Gordy.

'I want you to head over to the address Rob gave Liz. If it is Luca's home, then my hunch is that the woman and baby mentioned are the same ones Jadyn saw at the car wash the other day.'

'And the woman whose voice you heard on the phone,' Gordy said.

'You read my mind,' Harry said. 'Which means ...'

'Don't worry,' the DI said, her face already showing the distant cloud of sorrow at what she would have to do if their assumptions were correct. 'I know what it means.'

'I'm not giving you the job because I don't want to be the one to pass on the news about Luca's death. I just think that it might come easier from you.'

'Not a problem at all.'

'Also, with the car wash, they've seen you already. But if I turn up with Matt, here? That'll have everyone on edge, won't it? And people on edge make mistakes, say things they shouldn't. Oh, and take Jadyn with you. He saw the woman, so recognising him might also play in your favour.'

Gordy made to stand up, but Liz spoke again, so she sat back down again.

'I also checked up on Gill Mitchell's gun licence, if

you're interested. Which you will be, because, well, it's a bit strange, isn't it?'

'Strange how, exactly?' Harry asked. 'I'm guessing that the empty cabinet wasn't there just to hold a couple of air rifles and a pea shooter.'

'Not exactly, no,' Liz said. 'But his licence says he owns two air rifles, so points for that. Both are FAC-rated, though, which is why they're on the licence, so not exactly back-garden plinking guns.'

'FAC? Oh, right, firearms certificate, you mean. What else?'

Liz read through a list of other guns, which included both shotguns and rifles.

'Quite the collection,' Harry said. 'Why the hell would Gill need all of that?'

'Different guns have different uses,' said Matt. 'A 4.10 is a great ratting gun. Those air rifles are perfect for clearing rabbits out at a considerably longer range than your normal legal-limit gun. The rifles, well, he's got calibres there that'll allow him to take anything from a squirrel or a fox right up to a deer.'

Harry shook his head, as much in rage as in anger.

'And right now, we can only assume that they're all now in the hands of our two killers. Not good at all.'

'Come on, then,' Matt said. 'Best we get that car of mine cleaned, then, don't you think?'

'I do,' Harry growled.

'And we'll be off to that address,' Gordy said, getting to her feet.

Jadyn jumped to his and was at the door in a beat.

'Wait a moment,' Harry said, and looked back at Liz.

'You said the gun licence was strange, but none of what you've just told us strikes me as all that weird.'

'His name is, though.'

'His name? What's strange about being called Gill?'

'Nothing, if that was his name.'

'But everyone calls him that,' Harry said.

Matt agreed.

'They do. No one calls him anything else that I know of. And he's been around the Dales for years. That's his name; Gill Mitchell. Not sure what Gill is short for, though.'

'I checked up on that,' said Liz. 'Could be Gilbert, even William. Except it isn't, because his actual name is Alasdair.'

'Alastair? What's that got to do with Gill?' Harry asked.

'No, not Alastair, with a T, but Alasdair, with a D. I looked it up and that's the Scottish spelling.'

'So, Gill Mitchell is actually Alasdair Mitchell? Then why the hell is he called Gill?'

'Must be some kind of nickname, though why or from what, I've no idea,' said Liz. 'Strange, right?'

Harry let out a long, deep sigh.

'This whole damned week has been strange,' he said, and pushed back out into the day.

WITH LIZ STAYING PUT to run the office, Jim and Jen over dealing with the divers, and Gordy and Jadyn heading to the address Liz had provided, Harry and Matt were just arriving in Richmond itself when Harry's phone buzzed.

'It's Sowerby,' he said, looking over at Matt, as the DS slowed down for the bridge. Over to their right, Harry saw Richmond Castle, another place he'd not visited yet, and something else to add to that list, he thought. 'Hope she's got some good news. We could certainly use some.'

'Odd, isn't it,' said Matt, 'that we consider anything a pathologist says to be good news, considering what we deal with?'

Harry answered the phone.

'So, what've we got?'

'A couple of things, actually,' Sowerby said. 'A bit of extra information from the crime scene on Tuesday. We have dog hair.'

'Not something I'm going to get all excited about, if I'm honest,' Harry said, then he paused. 'Though the woods aren't public access, are they? And the only dogs down there would be Grace's, and they're Spaniels. So, what have we got?'

'Well, I can tell you that the animal is black,' Sowerby said. 'Breed is something that'll take a while longer to ascertain.'

'Grace doesn't have a black dog.'

'Well, we have black dog hairs,' Sowerby said. 'And they're specifically at the crime scene rather than anywhere else. By which I mean we didn't find any traces anywhere else, just where the body was. Very localised distribution.'

Harry remembered the dog Gordy had encountered at Walker's house; it was black, too, a definite link.

'What else?'

'First, we found something in the shed behind the house.'

'Found what?'

'I'll send you a photo,' Sowerby said. 'You know what they say. A picture paints a thousand words.'

'Or you could just tell me,' Harry said, as his phone

buzzed to let him know the photo had already arrived. 'Just a minute, then ...'

Harry opened the photo, showed it to Matt.

'Finding one of those is strange enough,' the DS said. 'But two in the same week?'

'And you know me and coincidences,' Harry said, as ahead, the car wash came into view. He went back to the phone. 'And you found this in the shed?'

'We did,' Sowerby said. 'My guess is that this is the one used to model the one used in the murder. You heard anything from the diving unit yet?'

'No, I haven't,' Harry said.

'I never really know if I want them to find anything or not,' Sowerby said. 'Particularly if there's a missing person involved.'

'I know what you mean,' Harry said. 'Anything else?'

'Yes,' Sowerby said. 'We think your man had a military past.'

Harry then remembered the way Gill had stared at him when they'd first met. The scars had caught his attention, but thinking about it now, there had been recognition in his eyes, hadn't there? He'd looked at him through the eyes of a soldier, had seen scars like that before.

Harry asked, 'Did you find some medals or something?'

'Medals, no, but some faded black and white photographs in a wallet, and a beret. They were in the vehicle by the river.'

'The beret; what colour is it?'

'That's important?'

'The Commando beret is green,' Harry said, 'and the only way you'll have one of those is if you're in the Royal

Marines or pass through the commando course. My beret was maroon because I was in the Paras.'

'I think sometimes you still are,' Sowerby said. 'Anyway, it's neither of those colours.'

'So, what is it then?'

Sowerby told Harry.

'You still there?'

'I am,' Harry said.

'You went quiet there.'

Matt pulled into the car wash.

'Right, thanks for the call,' Harry said, still thinking about that beret.

'No problem. Oh, and you know that locked garage?'

'Yes, what about it?'

Sowerby was quiet for a moment.

'He had another car,' she said eventually. 'The garage was dry, by which I mean almost hermetically sealed, which would explain why the car was in such good condition. He clearly looked after it. I mean, it's spotless.'

'What other car?'

'A little MG,' Sowerby said. 'No idea what model. But it's a beauty, all red paint and chrome and leather.'

'Really?'

'Really,' Sowerby said. 'Anyway, I'd best be off. Promise to not call me tomorrow night, won't you? I need to get at least some sleep this week.'

Conversation over, Harry stared again at the photograph of the mantrap Sowerby had sent through. It being where it was certainly suggested something, or it was supposed to, anyway. But it just didn't sit right in Harry's head, not now, not after everything that had happened at Gill's house. And particularly not after what Sowerby had just told him about Gill's military past. Then he had an idea and quickly forwarded it to Jim with a short message to check with the auction rooms in Leyburn.

Someone in the car wash waved Matt forward.

'Cash only,' the DS said, glancing over at the menu of services provided.

'They always are,' Harry said, and pulled out his wallet.

CHAPTER THIRTY-SIX

THE HOUSE WAS A TERRACE ON A STREET SO NARROW that Jadyn wondered if the cars parked nose-to-tail along it only ever saw the sun when they were driven away by their owners.

'We'll have to park further along and walk back,' Gordy said, as they drove past the address Liz had acquired from the Bell twins.

Jadyn looked at the house as they drove past. The windows were grubby and hung with net curtains, upstairs and down. The front door was scuffed and peeling, the window it had once contained now boarded up with chipboard, damp and grey.

When they came to stand in front of it, Jadyn felt no sense of being in front of a home. Buildings obviously didn't have emotions, but this one seemed depressed, he thought. There was no welcome here, and Jadyn had the odd feeling that the place was almost trying to hide from view. That if it could, it would sink back, out of the street, and let the houses on either side close in to give it something to hide behind.

'No bell,' Gordy said, clenching her fist and giving a sharp rap-rap-rap against the door.

Jadyn stood as still as he could, leaning close to the door, trying to hear any sound from inside.

'I don't think anyone's in,' he said.

Gordy tried again, with the heel of her fist this time, and on the third strike, Jadyn saw something, a twitch in an upstairs net curtain.

'I was wrong,' he said, and pointed upstairs.

He looked left and right, saw a small alleyway leading between two houses to the back of the row.

'Go,' Gordy said. 'Call if you need backup and don't do anything daft.'

Jadyn jogged down the street and turned into the alleyway. It was strewn with rubbish, and he had to pick his way carefully through.

At the back of the houses, he saw that a shared access path led along, so he followed it until he was outside the correct house.

'I'm in position,' he said, speaking to Gordy on his radio.

He heard Gordy knock on the door again and call out for someone to answer.

Jadyn wasn't sure what they could do. If no one answered, then they couldn't exactly break down the door. They'd probably have to just wait it out, which meant a rather dull day ahead, and an uncomfortable one, too.

Gordy knocked again. Still nothing. Then, as Jadyn was thinking it was probably sensible to head back around to the DI, the backdoor opened and there in front of him, her face lit with surprise, was the woman he'd seen at the car wash, and in her arms, a baby.

'Hi,' Jadyn said. 'I mean, hello, I'm Police Constable—'

The woman stepped back, her eyes wide with what to Jadyn looked very much like terror, and tried to slam the door, but he managed to step forward just enough to put a hand up to the door and stop her.

'Gordy!' he shouted. 'She's here!'

The woman then tried to push past Jadyn.

'Please! Let me go! Let me go!'

But Jadyn stayed his ground. Then the baby started crying, and the woman pushed harder, just as DI Haig arrived at the scene.

'Please,' she said, stepping forward, her hands out in front of her to calm and reassure. 'My name is Detective Inspector Haig. This is Constable Okri. We just want to talk, that's all, I promise.'

The woman pushed again at Jadyn and the baby screamed louder still.

'Doesn't sound like the bairn's enjoying it much, does he?' Gordy said. 'If we pop back inside, I'm sure he'll calm down.'

The woman pushed again, but there was less effort this time.

'What's his name?' Jadyn asked.

'Stefan, after my father,' the woman said.

'He's a handsome chap. Loud, too.'

The woman's fear broke for a moment at Jadyn's comment, and she smiled.

'He is louder at night,' she said. 'No sleep. Never. Very difficult child. But yes, also handsome.'

Gordy was now at Jadyn's side and showed her ID.

'Can we come in?'

The woman's shoulders sagged, and she stepped back.

'Yes,' she nodded. 'Please ...'

Jadyn stepped back to allow Gordy in first, then followed on behind.

The first thing that struck him was the smell. There was a note of vanilla in the air, he noticed, as though someone had tried and failed to tackle it with a scented candle. Damp, that's what the smell was, he realised, and he saw black patches on the walls, the ceilings, and wondered just how cold the house got for it to be like that. Was there no heating? No, there was, because there were radiators on the walls, but a brush with his hand told him it wasn't on and he guessed it probably hadn't been for a very long time.

'Please, through here,' the woman said, and led them on, past a door to a small kitchen where, even with a glance, Jadyn could see that every work surface was covered with crockery and tins and packets of rice and pasta. But the amount of crockery just didn't make sense; this was a small terrace house, so who lived here? The next room answered that question.

The space had clearly once been the lounge. Small, yes, but probably cosy with the fire lit. But that was boarded up now and where sofas and comfy chairs would once have sat, there now stood three bunk beds, one against each wall, the wall facing the street, with the net-curtained window, the only one without. Beneath the bunks were suitcases, and the floor was strewn with clothes.

'I ... I am sorry for this,' the woman said. 'I have not had time to tidy.'

'How many people live here?' Jadyn asked, the question out of his mouth before he had a chance to stop it.

The woman shook her head.

'I do not know. There are three bedrooms upstairs, and

this one. Sometimes thirty maybe? It depends. People, they come and go.'

'Thirty?'

'Sometimes, yes. But not always.'

'And you ... this is your room?'

'Me and Stefan, yes,' the woman said. 'We share it with his father, and three others. They are all good with him, with Stefan. He is happy.'

The woman smiled, though the act itself seemed to tire her out on the spot and before Jadyn knew what he was doing, he had reached out and taken the baby.

'Thank you,' the woman said, and sat down on one of the bunks.

Jadyn stared at the tiny human now in his arms. He couldn't remember the last time he'd held one, or if he ever had. He must have done it at some point, but he had no reference for the experience that he could think of.

'Hello,' he said, and bounced the baby in his arms.

Stefan stared at Jadyn, his yelling abating just enough to allow him time to reach out and grab the constable's nose.

'It doesn't come off,' Jadyn said. 'At least I don't think it does.'

The woman smiled.

'He likes you.'

Gordy said, 'We know Stefan's name, but not yours.'

'Elena,' the woman said. 'Elena Romanescu.'

'You said that you live here with Stefan's father?'

At this, Jadyn saw a flash of worry in Elena's eyes.

'Yes,' she said. 'But he is ... Luca is not here.'

Jadyn caught Gordy's eye as an icy hand reached in and squeezed his heart.

'I have not seen him for three days now,' Elena said. 'Is that why you are here?'

Gordy looked up at Jadyn.

'Perhaps you should take Stefan outside for a moment?'

Jadyn understood.

'Come on, Stefan,' he said. 'Let's go and see if we can spot a pigeon or two. Did you know that when a pigeon coos, what it's actually saying is, "My poor foot's bleeding"? My dad told me that when I was a few years older than you. And it's all I can hear in my head now, every time I hear a pigeon.'

Jadyn knew he was rambling, but it was keeping Stefan calm and occupied and that was what mattered.

Then a scream from the room at the front of the house chased Jadyn and Stefan outside and Jadyn couldn't help but squeeze the little man in his arms a little tighter than he had before.

CHAPTER THIRTY-SEVEN

Back at the car wash, Harry knew something was up. The manager, Michelle Knight, was tripping over herself to be helpful, while at the same time trying to make excuses to get the hell out of dodge.

'Honestly, you've caught me at a bad time. I'm just heading out. I'm sure the rest of the staff will be more than happy to speak to you.'

Harry and Matt were in the office, standing in front of the desk, the woman on the other side. She was busying herself with locking drawers and shutting down her computer.

'Well, we won't take too much of your time, I'm sure, Ms Knight,' Harry said.

'It's Mrs,' the woman said, and flashed a look outside. A moment later, one of the workers came in and told her there was a call for her.

'I'd better get that.'

'I'm sure it can wait,' said Harry.

'It's important.'

'Really?' Harry said. 'I would've thought that an important call would surely come through to your office phone, yes?'

'We have another phone outside. Round the back, I mean.'

'If that's so, then how does this gentleman here know there was a call at all? I'm sure he's been out front there since we arrived.' Harry looked at Matt. 'Wouldn't you agree, DS Dinsdale?'

'I would,' Matt said. 'In fact, when we arrived, he was busy washing that four-by-four that's still out there now.'

'You mean that one he's gone back to washing again?'

'That very one.'

'But I do need to go,' Knight said. 'Perhaps you could call back again later? Tomorrow, maybe?'

Harry shook his head.

'No, I think today would be best.'

He grabbed a chair and sat down, then stared up at Knight.

'Please,' he said, and gestured to the chair on the other side.

At last, the woman sat down.

'So, how can I help?' she asked. 'We had two of your officers here the other day. I'm sure there's little else that I can add to what—'

'Luca,' Harry said, interrupting.

'Pardon?'

'When did you last see him?'

'I don't know who—'

'We know he was here a couple of weeks ago. And I noticed that you have security cameras out on the forecourt, so that should confirm it, shouldn't it?'

'Should it?'

'Well, if he was here, then yes, it should. And this is where you will need to help me and Detective Sergeant Dinsdale here, Mrs Knight, because it is my understanding that yesterday you and your staff told my fellow officers that you had no idea who Luca is.'

'I don't ...'

'And that doesn't add up, does it? Because we know he was here. We know, because we have a witness to the fact. We also know that there was an altercation, shall we say, on your forecourt, between yourself, your staff, and a man who had followed Luca here from where he lives. Ring any bells?'

Knight's mouth opened, but she shut it again, quickly.

Harry leaned forward, resting his arms on the desk.

'I'm going to give you some friendly advice,' he said. 'The way I see it, right now, you're in a lot of trouble.'

'But I haven't done anything! I only work here!'

'And the argument *I was only following orders* doesn't really stand up in a court of law, either.' Harry let that sink in for a moment, then said, 'Withholding information from the police under any circumstances is never a good idea, and I'm sure you can understand that.'

'Of course I can. I'm not an idiot.'

'I never said you were. However, withholding information when those circumstances are murder? Well, that ups the ante a little, wouldn't you say?'

Harry was fairly sure that if he had listened carefully enough, he would have been able to hear the blood drain from Knight's face.

'Murder? What are you—'

Harry had no idea if the woman in front of him knew anything or not, but that wasn't going to stop him from pushing to try and find out. She had to know something, for sure, even if she didn't realise it herself. And right now, all Harry could see in his mind was Luca's body in the mortuary —the bruises, the severed leg, the cold post-death mutilation by the pathologist—the cold evidence of his terrible death right there in front of him.

'Where did you go yesterday, Mrs Knight?'

'I went to speak with the— Wait, what?'

Harry had changed tack and it had caught her off guard.

'You left as soon as my officers arrived. And you tried to do the same just now.'

Harry didn't pose it as a question, just a statement of fact. He said nothing more, instead allowing the silence to grow, waiting for Knight to fill it.

'I had to go and speak with the owner,' she said.

'About what?'

'Business things.'

Harry looked over at Matt.

'You hear that? Business things,' he said. 'Sounds important, doesn't it?'

'Very. Definitely important enough to have to rush off for two days in a row.'

Harry's eyes were back on Knight.

'So, you're not the owner, then?'

'Of course I'm not.'

'You just work here.'

'Yes.'

'So, who is?'

'So who is what?'

'The owner,' Harry said.

'I don't like him, you know,' Knight said then, almost blurting it out. 'He doesn't take any interest in anything I do.'

'I didn't ask if you liked him. I asked who he is.'

'And the staff?' Knight continued. 'Where does he find them? That's what I want to know. He never tells me. They can hardly speak English, any of them, which I don't have a problem with, obviously, if that's what you think, but it doesn't make it easy for me. I've learned to keep my head down.'

'And yet you rushed out to see him yesterday and wanted to rush out to see him today. Why was that?'

'Because I have to, that's why!' Knight said. 'His solicitor has made that more than clear, let me tell you. And I'm not exactly in a position to argue. I have a mortgage, just like everyone else.'

Not exactly everyone else, not yet anyway, Harry thought, but now was not the time to be reminded of those unsigned documents, particularly after what Knight had just said.

'His what?'

'His solicitor,' Knight repeated. 'And it's usually him I have to speak to, more often than not, anyway. Like I said, he doesn't take much interest. The owner, I mean.'

'And you've still not given me his name.'

'I'm sure I have.'

'You heard any names, Detective Sergeant?'

'Not a dicky bird,' said Matt.

Harry stared at Knight, raising a questioning eyebrow.

'Walker,' Knight said. 'The owner's name is Vince Walker.'

BACK AT THE HOUSE, Jadyn had been called back into the room by Gordy and he'd handed little Stefan to Elena.

She had taken the baby from him with a gentleness formed of a love broken and smashed by the news Gordy had delivered, confirming that their victim was the same Luca, and that Elena had been the woman who'd answered the call Harry had made from Luca's phone.

Leaving Gordy to deal with the fallout, and to gently ask Elena some more questions, Jadyn took himself out of the room and, instead of going outside, headed upstairs. On entering the first room, he immediately wished that he hadn't.

The room contained four sets of bunks, all of them occupied, as were the two sleeping bags on the floor. Ten people, all clearly so tired that not only had they not heard any of the commotion from downstairs, they didn't even wake when Jadyn stepped on an empty plate and sent the cutlery flying with a clatter into the steel leg of one of the bunks. He backed out and checked out the other rooms, ducking his head in only to find the other rooms empty of humanity, but just as crowded, with bunks and suitcases and the scattered remains of food eaten in a rush. The bathroom was enough to give him nightmares, and he headed back downstairs to find Gordy standing in the hall.

'It's the same upstairs,' Jadyn said. 'Only worse, if you can imagine that.'

'I can,' Gordy said, and Jadyn saw a shard of flint behind the DI's eyes and was glad then that they were on the same side.

'What did she say?'

'I don't know where to begin.'

Gordy turned and made her way to the back door.

'We're going to need someone here,' she said. 'I think it had better be me, for now, until the others get here.'

'But they're busy,' Jadyn said.

Gordy shook her head.

'No, I've just spoken with the DCI, and he agreed with me.'

'Agreed with what?'

'This situation, it's not just murder. So, I've just come off the phone with Harrogate. They're sending a team down to help.'

Gordy walked past the kitchen, heading outside. Jadyn couldn't help but look in once again, drawn by the horror of it, imagining Elena somehow having to cope in a place like this, unable to understand how or why she was here at all.

'If you ask everyone upstairs, they'll tell you the same,' Gordy said, breathing deep the outside air.

Jadyn did the same, trying to force the fetid air from inside the house out of his lungs.

'Tell me what?'

'They were promised a new life,' Gordy said. 'Safety, security, work, a future. Then, when they arrived, their passports were taken as insurance. Then they were brought here and given work. Only first, their wages have to pay off the debt they owe for being brought here in the first place. And without their passports, they can't go home, can't go anywhere. So, they're trapped, given barely enough money to buy food, and provided with the kind of accommodation that even rats would shun.'

'They're illegal?'

'Illegal doesn't cover it,' Gordy said. 'They're slaves.'

In that moment, Jadyn's world shifted. He'd always been the one to see the positive, to find hope, to look on the bright side. But this? Just what the hell was this, that someone could treat people in such a way? Slaves? Elena was a mother, and how old was Stefan, anyway? Probably not even one!

'Do we know who's responsible?' Jadyn asked.

'And do you know why Luca's dead?' Gordy asked, Jadyn's question not even registering.

Jadyn shook his head, wasn't sure he wanted to know the answer.

'Because someone cared, that's why. Because someone tried to help them, to give them food, to look out for them. And because of that ...'

Gordy's voice crumbled.

'Because of what?'

'The pheasants,' Gordy said. 'This is all because of those bloody pheasants.'

CHAPTER THIRTY-EIGHT

MATT HAD ALREADY LEFT THE OFFICE AND WAS SITTING in the car waiting for Harry. They had finished their not entirely enjoyable conversation with Mrs Knight, which had become an extended meeting involving a rather interesting look at the security footage from the cameras at the car wash. This had confirmed not only Rob Bell's visit, but also Gill turning up in his MG, establishing a clear link between him and Luca before the incident at the pub. And with that done, Harry had then been on the phone with DI Haig.

'She also confirmed that little call you made from Luca's phone,' Gordy said. 'She didn't know who you were and hung up.'

Harry had forced himself not to think about what Luca's wife and child would now be going through, and after further discussion with the DI about what had been uncovered, had agreed that they needed additional help brought in, not just to the house, but to the car wash as well. That help had now arrived, which meant that they could head off to do something else.

This wasn't simply the murder of a man over the poaching of some pheasants. Far from it, though Harry still wasn't quite sure how everything fit together. In many ways, he felt as though he had all the pieces of a jigsaw in front of him. He'd managed to find all of the edge pieces and put them together. Inside these, he could see other pictures emerging, but it was the whole picture he just couldn't see, and the pieces that would help him pull it all together lay scattered around to frustrate him.

So, the delightful Vince Walker owned the car wash. And considering the house he lived in, Harry had found it difficult to see how the man could afford such a place with the proceeds of just one. But, as Mrs Knight had then pointed out, it wasn't just one, was it? No. There were numerous car washes across the north of England. In fact, Vince's business stretched all the way up to the Scottish borders, with what they now assumed could be hundreds of people living in the worst conditions, to work for a man with, according to Gordy anyway, the worst taste in art.

Modern-day slavery, and the only reason they'd stumbled on it at all, was because someone had been so hungry that they'd taken up poaching to stop themselves from starving. Except that wasn't entirely the case either, was it?

Harry headed over to the car and climbed in.

'So, we think Gill was helping them, then?' Matt said.

'If it hadn't been for Sowerby finding that other car of his in the garage, we'd have never known it was him on the footage from the security camera,' Harry said. 'Gill clearly knew who Luca was before he saw the Bell twins lay into him and his friend at the Hare and Hounds.'

'I asked Jim if he knew Gill had that old MG,' said Matt.

'He knows him better than the rest of us, and he had no idea about it at all. Strange, really, isn't it?'

'It is, and it isn't,' said Harry. 'If all Gill ever did was take it for a drive to a car wash and back now and again, and never tell anyone about it, then it's easy to see how.'

'So, you think that's how he and Luca got to know each other?'

'Not according to his wife, Elena, no,' Harry said. 'She told Gordy that Luca had been going out poaching for months. A few from the house would go out together and see if they could bring some extra protein back, something free. Elena said that one night, after Luca had been out, there was a knock at the door. No one dared answer it. When they did, they found a bag on the doorstep. Inside were half a dozen rabbits.'

'Gill?'

Harry gave a nod.

'My guess is that he did the same as the Bell twins and followed Luca home. But whereas Rob and Danny were baying for blood, Gill saw the place, the people living there, maybe the child as well, and took pity on them.'

'Luca still went out poaching, though.'

'Apparently so. And Gill would leave food for them every week. Not always on the same day, but there would be a knock and they'd find something inside to eat.'

'He's quite the good Samaritan, isn't he?'

'I don't think Gill knew anything about where they worked. He just happened to recognise them one day, when he took that car of his out for a spin and stopped off to have it washed. Luca probably recognised him as well. At which point, I think someone, somewhere started to get nervous.'

'How so?'

Harry was quiet just long enough to quell the storm of anger in his mind at what was now being uncovered.

'Those people, poor bastards like Luca, they live in fear,' he said. 'That's how it works. That's how someone like Walker can keep them employed, because he knows they won't tell. They do their job, terrified of being sent back home, or worse, and he reaps the benefits. And if anyone steps out of line, talks to someone, looks like they might break and let the cat out of the bag ...'

'He sends a couple of heavies around so he doesn't have to get his hands dirty.'

'But why was Gill here yesterday?' Matt asked. 'He must've headed over just after you and Jim had gone to speak to him.'

'And got back before it all kicked off at his,' Harry said. 'Unless ...'

'Unless what?'

Harry thought again about that man trap and what Gill had been up to. The man trap linked him to the murder, didn't it? But that just didn't sit with what they now knew Gill had been doing. Had Gill been followed home? Or had he arrived and found someone already at his house trying to set him up? Maybe even kill him, make it look like a suicide?

Harry's head was hurting, a swirling storm of thoughts and ideas and conspiracy theories swirling around in his head.

Matt started the engine.

'Let's go and pay Mr Walker a visit then, shall we?'

'Yes,' Harry said, his fists clenched. 'Let's.'

. . .

JIM AND JEN were at the river. The arrival of the dive team had been exciting at first, mainly because Jim had never worked with a dive team before. They had been kind enough to answer all of his questions, and had even given him the name of a contact of theirs who would happily give him some advice on taking up diving if he should ever want to.

Which he didn't.

Now, with the divers all getting on with the search of the river, which was a long, laborious, and clearly very dangerous job indeed, there wasn't, and hadn't been, much for either him or Jen to do. He'd done as Harry had asked, and given the auction rooms in Leyburn a call, forwarding them the photograph Harry had sent him. And they'd come back to confirm that the man trap found at Gill's looked very much like the one they had sold to Mr Vince Walker. Though wouldn't be able to say for sure, until they saw it in person.

'How long do you think this is going to take?' Jim asked, as Jen stretched out her arms and yawned.

'It'll take as long as it takes,' Jen said.

'Do you think they'll find him? Gill, I mean.'

'We don't know that he's even in the river.'

'No, I suppose we don't.'

Jim couldn't accept the idea that old Gill might be dead. That he was mixed up in any of this at all was a shock, but being shot at and then chased into a river? It was hard to take in. What on earth had he got himself involved in?

The man trap also bothered him. That made no sense at all. Gill had always struck him as a man of principles, someone who understood the countryside, who hunted carefully, and never thought lightly of a life taken. He prided himself on a clean kill, ensuring the animals he took never suffered. So why the hell had that man trap been found in his shed?

'Movement,' Jen said, giving Jim a nudge and distracting him from his thoughts.

She was pointing over at the river.

Jim looked up to see a diver being helped up the bank.

'He's got something with him,' he said. 'What is it?'

'I can't tell,' Jen said.

Jim forced himself to stay where he was instead of racing over to find out what the diver had found. He also didn't want to come across as a total idiot if it turned out to be nothing more than a gnarly old fence post or something.

Eventually, one of the dive team came over. She was a tall woman who wore a face that said she didn't spend much time indoors, the evidence of long days out in all weathers etched into her skin like scuff marks on a church floor.

'You asked us to keep you posted on anything we find,' she said.

'Boss's instructions,' Jen said.

'Well, we've found something.'

'We saw,' said Jim. 'What is it?'

'A rifle. Actually, we've found two. Just fetching the other one up now.'

'Do you know what type?'

'They're clearly air rifles,' the woman said. 'PCP. Expensive pieces of kit.'

'But why would they be in the river?'

'No idea,' the woman said. 'Our job is to find stuff. It's your job to work out how it got there.'

'I'm just a PCSO,' Jim said.

'As far as I'm aware,' the woman said, 'there's no such thing as just a PCSO.'

'Where were they?' Jen asked.

'Together, about a hundred yards downstream.'

'No other weapons, then?' asked Jim.

The woman shook her head, then turned to head back to the river.

'I'll let you know as soon as we find anything else.'

When she was gone, Jim looked at Jen.

'Bit odd that, don't you think?'

'Is it?'

'Remember that list we got from Liz of all the guns on Gill's licence? Why would only the air rifles be in the river? What about everything else?'

'Not as valuable?'

'Oh, they're valuable alright,' Jim said. 'You wouldn't just throw them away, not unless you simply didn't need them.'

'And why wouldn't they need them?'

'I think it's more why they would need everything else,' Jim said.

Jen folded her arms and stared at the PCSO.

'If the ones who shot at Jadyn have them, then Harry's right to be worried, isn't he?'

Something still wasn't fitting together in Jim's head, though. Not just that the air rifles had been found and nothing else had, but about what he'd been told about the cabinet. Plus, there was that man trap, too, wasn't there?

'I need to check something,' he said. 'Back at Gill's.'

'What do you need to check? Harry told us to stay here, liaise between the divers and him.'

Jim climbed into his Land Rover.

'I won't be long.'

'Harry won't be happy.'

'Harry doesn't need to know.'

Then, before Jen had a chance to persuade him otherwise, he started the engine, and headed away from the river, back up the track, to make his way over to Gill's.

WHEN HARRY and Matt arrived at Vince Walker's house, everything Gordy had told them about the place had still not been enough to convey how truly bloody awful it was.

'Ignoring everything we now know,' Matt said, 'that house is reason enough for us to arrest him, charge him, lock him up, and throw away the key.'

Harry could not have agreed more. That such a place had been allowed baffled him. Yes, the original house was still there, but as for everything else? The best thing would be to have it all pulled down, and soon.

Matt pulled up and turned off the engine.

'Gordy mentioned a dog,' he said.

Harry unclipped his seat belt and pulled a tin out of his pocket.

'What's in there, then?' Matt asked. 'A dog-taming genie?'

'Smudge's training treats,' he said. 'Meat and cheese. High-value stuff. It'll have the dog eating out of our hands, I promise.'

'Either that or actually eating our hands,' Matt said.

Harry climbed out and headed for the front door, Matt stepping in behind him. The door was open and Harry stepped inside. Really, he should have announced his arrival, but he was much more in the mood to give Mr Walker a surprise. It was the least he could do.

Walking on, they passed the art Gordy had told them about, though art was, in many cases, not the word Harry would've used to describe any of it. Abomination seemed more apt.

'You hear something?' Matt asked.

Harry stopped, listened.

'Singing?' he said.

'I'm not hearing things, then.'

As they walked further into the house, the singing grew louder until at last they emerged into a huge room of glass, at the centre of which sat two enormous sofas on either side of an idiotically sized coffee table. The rug beneath it Harry imagined Smudge would've taken to all too quickly and then been next to impossible to prise from. On one of the sofas was Vince Walker, on the other, a huge dog. The dog turned its terrifyingly large head to stare at them. Vince was swinging around a large bottle of what Harry assumed was something alcoholic. He was also completely naked.

'Come in,' Vince said, calling over. 'Don't mind if I sing, do you?'

Of all the things you're doing right now, Harry thought, singing is not the one I'd say that I mind.

'Mr Walker, I'm Detective Chief Inspector Grimm, and this is Detective Sergeant Dinsdale. We need to ask you a few questions.'

'Let me guess,' Vince said. 'Is it anything to do with me being stark bollock naked?'

'No, it isn't,' Harry said. 'Though, I would appreciate it if you could go and put on some clothes.'

'I've got two more guesses, and then I'll get dressed.'

'No, you'll get dressed now. And Detective Sergeant Dinsdale here will accompany you, just to make sure you don't have any other ideas, like running away, perhaps.'

'Two more guesses,' Vince repeated. 'Two.'

Harry eyed the dog.

'Do I need to be concerned about that?' he asked.

The dog slumped down on the sofa and closed its eyes.

'Not at all,' Vince said. 'He's actually a big softy. No use as a guard dog at all. Probably because I spoil him. Don't I, Thor?'

The dog's thick tail wagged with all the energy of a dead fish being dropped on concrete.

Vince stood up and placed his hands on his hips. Harry immediately wished that the man would sit down again. There were things no one should ever see, and it turned out that Vince was most of them all in one go.

'Right then, my second guess ...'

Vince tapped his chin thoughtfully. The movement had a very undesirable effect on his belly, as well as other places Harry wished he could burn from his memory forever.

'Is it anything to do with the fact that I didn't win the lottery at all and have been lying about it all this time?'

Harry's patience had worn thin.

'Right, that's enough,' he said, and made to walk over to Vince, but Vince had other ideas, leaping up onto the sofa to brandish his bottle like a club. The clear contents spilled out, down his arm, and onto the floor.

'One more guess!'

There was pissed, and then there was whatever this was, Harry thought, because between Gordy meeting him and now, the man had clearly lost his mind.

'Mr Walker ...'

'Would it have anything to do with the fact that I killed a man with a man trap?'

Vince laughed then, the sound of a bird trapped in the jaws of a hungry predator, threw the bottle at Harry, and in the process tumbled from the sofa to land squarely on his head on the rug.

Harry ran over and dropped down onto his knees next to Vince, convinced that the idiot had broken his neck, only to find Vince still conscious and giggling like a child.

Matt came over.

'Right now, I really don't know what to say, Boss.'

Harry pulled out some cuffs and clipped them onto Vince's wrists.

'Do you think that was a confession?'

Harry climbed to his feet and stared down at the naked drunk on the floor.

'Yes,' Harry said.

'Really? The man's pissed and naked,' said Matt.

'He is,' said Harry. 'And it's almost as though he knew we were coming, don't you think?'

'But who told him? And why?'

Harry was thinking exactly the same thing when his phone rang.

'How are the divers doing, then?' Harry asked, hearing Jen's voice on the other end of the call.

'That's why I'm calling,' Jen said.

'They've found something?'

'Two guns about an hour ago, but they've just pulled out something else.'

Harry felt the air around him turn cold.

'What?'

'It's a body, Boss,' Jen said. 'They've found a body.'

CHAPTER THIRTY-NINE

Leaving Matt to help the very drunk and very naked Vince Walker into some clothes, before someone from Harrogate dropped by to pick him up and get him processed, Harry raced over to Aysgarth, skidding to a stop in the field near the dive unit's vehicles. Opening his door, he saw Jen walking over to meet him.

'Where's Jim?'

'On his way back,' Jen said.

'On his way back? But he's supposed to be here, as per my orders. And on his way back implies that he isn't.'

With Matt's own behaviour as well, Harry was beginning to wonder if he was getting soft and needed to be a little harder on the team than he had been.

'He went before I could do anything to stop him. Said he needed to check something over at Gill's.'

Harry took a deep, slow, calming breath.

'Well, I'll deal with that when I need to,' he said. 'For now, tell me what we've got.'

'Ambulance is on its way. Forensics has been informed.'

Harry immediately felt for Sowerby. This week it was as though she'd been attached to Wensleydale by an invisible length of elastic, always twanging her back just when she thought she'd escaped.

'The body, Jen,' Harry said. 'Who?'

Jen clenched her jaw for a moment before speaking.

'Well?'

'We don't know,' she said.

'What?'

'It's definitely not Gill. Male, mid-thirties, well built.'

'And he drowned in the river?'

'Hard to tell.'

Harry was confused.

'Is it? Why?'

Jen stared at Harry clearly having difficulty answering his question.

'I need to know, Jen.'

'Because most of his head's missing, that's why.'

Harry wasn't sure he'd heard right.

'His head? What? Has it been bashed in by the river or something?'

Jen shook her head.

'Looks like it wasn't there to begin with. The consensus from the dive team—and it sounds like they've got experience with this kind of thing, certainly more than me, anyway—is that whoever he is, he took a bullet to the head before being thrown into the river.'

'But there's no blood anywhere near here,' said Harry.

'There is further downstream,' said Jen. 'Looks like he was shot walking along the far side of the river.'

'And we're sure it's not Gill?'

'They can't identify him, obviously,' Jen said, 'and there's nothing on the body to help with that either, nothing in the pockets, no driving licence or credit cards or anything, but they know for sure that he's not the age Gill was, I mean is, I mean ...'

'I know what you mean,' Harry said.

'You think it's one of them?' Jen asked.

'The two who shot at Jadyn?'

'Yes.'

'Can't think it would be anyone else.'

'And do you think it's the same two who we want for what happened over in Carperby?'

'That, I'm not so sure about,' Harry said. 'Because right now, we've got someone who's just gone and confessed to that, and the evidence really does point their way even if he is the most ridiculous idiot I've ever met. And I've met a few, that's for sure.'

The sound of an engine approaching had Harry turn from Jen and look up the lane towards Aysgarth. He saw Jim rolling down towards them.

Harry walked over to meet him as Jim brought his vehicle to a stop.

'You've some explaining to do,' Harry said, unable to disguise the anger in his voice. 'When I give an order—'

'The gun cabinet,' Jim said, 'did the forensics team actually say it was broken into?'

'What?' Harry said.

'Over at Gill's. The cabinet.'

'Sowerby told me it was empty when they found it.'

That hadn't been strictly true, had it? Harry thought. Sowerby had found those strange scraps of material caught on the door and now, when he came to think of it, he did recognise them, didn't he?

'The key was still in the lock,' Jim said.

'So?' said Jen. 'Maybe it was open when those two arrived and they just helped themselves.'

Jim shook his head.

'No way I'm buying that. I know Gill. He would never leave his cabinet open. Ever.'

'Maybe he did just this once,' Harry suggested, thinking about those scraps of material, and that beret Sowerby had found. 'Everyone forgets.'

'Not Gill,' Jim said. 'Just not in his nature. He was a stickler for treating a gun with respect. It was almost an obsession.'

'I'm not sure what you're getting at,' Harry said, but he was beginning to get an idea of it all himself.

'I'm saying that the only reason the gun cabinet was open was because Gill left it open. Except that Gill would never leave a gun cabinet open.'

'That makes no sense,' Jen said.

'I think Gill took his guns with him,' Jim said. 'I also think that man trap in his shed is complete bollocks, Boss, if you don't mind me saying so. It just doesn't fit.'

'Look,' Harry said. 'We know that there were two people at the crime scene, yes? Two people murdered Luca. What if one of them was Gill? He knew the land. He'd set those pens up with Grace.'

Considering what he now knew about Luca and how Gill had tried to help him and all the others, Harry knew that he was talking nonsense, but right now he was playing devil's advocate, forcing not just Jim and Jen to think, but himself, too. Because the beret, the scraps of material, the missing guns, and now a dead body in a river, it was all leading somewhere he really didn't want any of them to have to go.

'You can't believe that, Boss, you just can't,' said Jim. 'You met him, right? You met Gill. It's impossible.'

'So, where is he, then?' Harry asked. 'Where the bloody hell is Gill?'

But Harry knew, didn't he? Not exactly, as in a location, but he knew where Gill was almost certainly.

'I've no idea,' Jim said. 'All I'm saying is what I've just said, that if that gun cabinet was found empty, then it was Gill who emptied it, and that the man trap in his shed had nothing to do with him. Nothing. It was planted there. Had to be. And my money is on it being done by those two who were at his house, one of whom is already dead, and the other who, like Gill, seems to have disappeared.'

Harry thought for a moment, then looked at Jen.

'Where's the body?'

Jen pointed across the field.

'Right, best I take a look for myself, then, isn't it?'

Leaving Jen with Jim, Harry jogged over to where the dive team had placed the body while it waited for collection. It would then get taken to the mortuary and then be introduced to Sowerby. But Harry needed to have a look right now. Would it confirm his suspicions? He wasn't sure it made any difference, not now, not with what was clearly at play.

Arriving at the body, Harry showed his ID. He didn't need to see the appalling wound the body had suffered; he'd seen enough of those in his time as it was. No, what interested him more was at the other end.

Crouching down, Harry reached out and pulled back a white sheet to reveal the footwear the body had on. He saw a pair of sturdy boots. He quickly took a photo of the tread on the sole of each boot, pulled back the sheet, then forwarded the photographs to Sowerby, with a request to compare not only with any prints they may have found at the crime scene on Tuesday night, but also with the stomp marks Harry had seen himself on the body at the mortuary.

Her response was almost immediate.

They match. Where?

Harry texted back to let her know about the body from the river.

You caught one, then.

Looks like it.

What about the one that got away?

Harry didn't know how to answer that because after what he'd just learned from Jen and Jim, he had a horrible feeling that somewhere out there, a very well-trained hunter was tracking their prey.

'Boss?'

Harry turned to see Jim walking toward him.

'Yes?'

'I'm sorry,' Jim said. 'For just heading off. I had a hunch, and ...'

'I know what you had,' said Harry.

'I've known Gill since I was a kid,' Jim said. 'It can't be him. I know it can't.'

'It isn't,' Harry said, hearing an almost desperate tone in the PCSO's voice. 'Gill was helping Luca.'

'He was?'

Harry gave a nod.

'And I'm beginning to think that he still is, at least in the only way he knows how.'

'I still don't know what you're getting at, Boss.'

Harry didn't want to say anything else, so he sent Jim back over to Jen. Then he was on the phone to Matt.

'Where are you?'

'Nearly to Harrogate. Why?'

'Has Walker said anything else? Confessed again, maybe?'

'Nothing,' Matt said.

'I'm pretty sure that he didn't do it,' Harry said. 'Divers pulled a body from the river just now. Male, mid-thirties. I think it's one of the two who shot at Jadyn and who killed Luca.'

'Drowned, then?'

'Apparently not,' Harry said. 'Someone took his head off with a bullet.'

'That'll do it,' Matt said. 'Who, though? And where's his friend?'

'Running for his life, I'd think,' Harry said. 'Which is why everything is leading me to think that even if Walker may be involved in all of this somehow, he certainly didn't kill Luca. He's nothing more than a pawn.'

'A chess metaphor?' said Matt. 'Dreadful game, Boss. Hardly compares with the darts.'

'Regardless, I think someone has been moving him around a very big board,' Harry said. 'I think someone has been using Walker, probably for a very long time, and I think that whatever it is he's been used for, it's all now come to an end, so they've fitted him up well enough to have him confess to a murder he didn't commit. But I don't think everything has gone to plan, and they've come up against something absolutely bloody terrifying.'

'Terrifying? How do you mean?'

'I mean,' Harry said, 'that when you take a sand-coloured beret, scraps from a ghillie suit, and missing guns, what do you have?'

'A ghillie what?'

'And that's where he got his nickname, isn't it?' Harry realised then, more pieces falling into place, the jigsaw growing clearer and clearer. 'Gill; it's short for ghillie.'

Matt was silent.

'It's the Scottish word for gamekeeper,' Harry explained. 'And if you remember what Liz said, Gill's real name is—'

'Alasdair, with a D,' Matt said.

'The Scottish spelling of the name,' Harry said, then went on to explain. 'I think Gill is old-school ex-SAS. I think that nickname of his stems from his Scottish past. Maybe he had relatives who worked the estates up there or something, I don't know. And remember that Bog Myrtle that Phil had in the front of his Land Rover on Tuesday night, back at the wood? That was from Gill, too, wasn't it? He told us that, how Gill had given it to him, that it was from Scotland.'

'You're like an elephant,' Matt said. 'You don't forget anything, do you?'

'Sowerby found scraps of material in Gill's gun cabinet,' Harry continued. 'I recognised them when she showed me, but I couldn't quite work out why. But when she told me about the beret, that's when I remembered. They were scraps from a ghillie suit, also known as a sniper suit. And if Gill was still into some deer stalking, which judging by the guns on his licence he was, then that's as good a reason as any to own one.'

'You can't be serious.'

'When have you known me to be anything else?'

'True.'

'There's still something or someone—perhaps both—bigger at play here, and Walker is the key. Somehow, he's been persuaded to take the fall for this. And we need to know who's behind it and what they have on him.'

'And Gill?'

'My guess is he's responsible for the body in the river, is now after the other killer, and potentially has an even bigger target in his sights. What they did to Luca, the fact that they tried to fit him up for it, it seems like he just can't forgive that.' Another thought crossed Harry's mind. 'The tourni-quet,' he said. 'And that other phone call of Luca's, the number I called where whoever answered it was just silent.'

'Gill?'

'Too bloody right it was.'

'So what now?'

'The only one I think who can help us is Walker.'

'But he's still pissed,' Matt said. 'And fast asleep.'

'Then what say we sober him up?'

'Not sure I like the sound of that.'

'I want you to take him to the mortuary,' Harry said. 'I'll call Sowerby now and meet you there. And I need to call Gordy, too.'

'And what do we do until you arrive?' Matt asked.

'Pray that he doesn't wake up.'

CHAPTER FORTY

Vince Walker started to stir when Harry arrived to help Matt lift him from the rear of the car they'd been picked up in. The two uniforms in the front weren't exactly sure that Harry's plan was entirely above board, but the look on Harry's face had been enough to persuade them it was probably best to just let him get on with it and wait it out in the car with a sausage roll and a can of Coke each.

'I can smell him from here,' Sowerby said, as Harry and Matt half carried, half dragged Vince down various corridors until they came to the mortuary.

Having kitted themselves and Vince up in PPE and Wellington boots, Harry dabbed some vapour rub under his nose, then handed the pot to a thankful Matt, who did the same.

'You really think this will work?' Sowerby asked, as Harry stowed the vapour rub. 'It's not exactly following procedure, is it?'

'Bollocks to procedure,' Harry said. 'Vince here needs a

cold, sharp shock, something that'll bring him to his senses and also help us hopefully stop any more killing.'

'And this was the best plan you could come up with?'

'It was the only plan I could come up with. And it wasn't exactly beating its way to the door through a crowd of other plans, now, was it?'

Sowerby led the way out of the transition area and Harry and Matt followed, Vince doing his best to walk now, his feet tripping over themselves.

'I'm gonna puke,' Vince said.

Sowerby whipped an evidence bag from a pocket and pinned it over Vince's mouth. The man heaved then, filling the bag with a violent torrent of steaming liquid.

The vapour rub did its job, managing to disguise the reek of the vomit just enough to make it bearable.

Vince convulsed again, but his stomach was empty, and he dry heaved, the action so violent his body went rigid and he was almost on tiptoes.

'Where the hell are we?' he asked, lifting his head.

Sowerby headed away to dispose of the bag of vomit.

'Can you stand?' Harry asked.

'What?'

'Stand. On your feet.'

'Of course I can bloody well stand on my own two feet. Watch!'

Vince pushed Harry and Matt away and stood there in front of them, swaying horribly, his face ashen.

'Ta-dah!' he said, lifting his hands into the air as he cheered.

'Well done,' Harry said. 'Now, let's have you sitting down, shall we?'

Vince looked around and Harry saw the man's brow crease with confusion. Then he laughed.

'Something funny, is it, Vince?' Harry asked, as he sat the man down on a stool in front of a stainless steel table covered in a white sheet.

'This place,' Vince said. 'It looks like a morgue. Like you see on TV on those cop shows.'

'Give the man a coconut.'

Vince's face creased with confusion.

'I don't like coconut.'

'It's a prize,' Harry said. 'For being so observant. And Vince here, really is very observant, isn't he, Detective Sergeant?' Harry said, glancing over at Matt, who was now on the other side of the table and standing next to Sowerby.

'Very,' Matt said. 'Nothing gets past him.'

'You want me to let you in on a secret?' Harry said, leaning in close to Vince.

'A secret? Aye, why not?'

'You're right. This is a morgue.'

'Mortuary,' Sowerby said. 'Sorry, but you know, this isn't the US, and, well ...'

Harry glanced up at her, saw her mouth the word *sorry* again.

'I should be a detective,' Vince said. 'Nothing gets past me.'

'Is that so?'

'It is.'

'Then what do you think this is in front of you?' Harry asked, and he gestured towards the shape hidden by the white sheet on the stainless steel table in front of them.

Vince stared, narrowed his eyes, leaned forward to get a closer look, then reached a finger out and poked the sheet.

'I've not a clue,' he said.

'Take a guess,' Harry said, the words hissing through gritted teeth as he thought back a few hours to when he and Matt had found the very naked, and very drunk, Vince at his house. 'And you like guesses, don't you, Vince? Remember? Shall I give you three? All you have to do is think about where we are, right now, and what that just might be under that sheet.'

Harry stood back and waited, watching the cogs turn in Vince's mind.

Vince looked at each of them in turn, his eyes eventually falling back on Harry.

'It's not, is it? I mean, it can't be. I ... I touched it ...'

'Yes, you did,' Harry said. 'You touched it. But what did you touch, Vince?'

Vince tried to mouth the words.

'You'll have to speak up,' Harry said. 'Come on, Vince. Three guesses, remember? But I don't think you're going to need them, are you?'

'It's ... it's a body ...'

Harry dropped his hands firmly onto Vince's shoulders, and gave a nod to Sowerby who, on Harry's signal, swept back the white sheet to reveal the cold, lifeless body of Luca Romanescu.

Vince actually screamed and tried to run, but Harry had him pinned to the chair.

'Do you know who this is?' Harry asked.

'Fuck no, of course I don't!' Vince said. 'What is this? Why am I here?'

'You're sure you don't know him?'

'I said no, didn't I? God, cover him up, will you? I mean, what the hell happened to him?'

Harry looked over at Matt.

'You happened to him, apparently,' Matt said. 'And in various horrific ways, too, I might add.'

'What?'

'You did this.'

'No, I fucking didn't,' Vince said, the words firing out of him with the shock of what he'd just been accused of. His head was shaking, his whole body joining in, denial seeping from every pore.

'You confessed to this,' Matt continued. 'You confessed to the murder. This is what you did. To another human. How's that make you feel, then? Like the big man in the room, is that it?'

'I didn't do this!' Vince said. 'I didn't. This wasn't me! Why would I? Why would anyone? I didn't do it!'

'But you've already told us that you did,' Harry said. 'That's why we arrested you.'

'I know, but ...'

'But what, Vince?' Harry said. 'Why would you confess to doing this and then tell us you didn't? You can understand that might be somewhat confusing, can't you?'

Vince was still staring at the body.

Harry gave a nod to Sowerby.

'He was beaten,' Sowerby said, then pointed at various injuries on the body. 'Three broken ribs, internal bleeding. He fought back, which is why there are so many bruises and lesions on his arms. His leg was severed by a man trap. He died in agony, and he knew there was no way he was going to survive.'

'But ... but what about all those other cuts and stuff?' Vince asked. 'That big one on his chest, the line around his face ...'

Sowerby explained in detail what she had done to Luca's body, the cut into the chest cavity, the removal of the face, the brain.

Harry pulled out his phone and flicked through to the pictures Gordy had sent to him as he had driven over to the mortuary.

'His name is Luca Romanescu,' Harry said. 'This is Elena, his wife.'

Vince stared at the photo on Harry's phone, but said nothing.

'And this is Stefan, his son.'

'Jesus ...'

'If you ask me,' said Harry, leaning in, 'even Jesus would have trouble forgiving you for this. And even if he wanted to, I reckon I could be persuasive enough to make him change his mind, don't you?'

'But I ... I didn't ...'

Harry was towering over the cowering figure of Vince, fully aware of just how to make himself seem terrifying when he needed to.

'You didn't what?'

'I didn't do this.'

'But you told us you did, Vince,' Harry said. 'You murdered Luca, didn't you? Beat him half to death, cut his leg off, left his wife without a husband, his son without a dad. I mean, that's forever stuff, Vince. Stefan will never know his dad. Ever. He'll be haunted by it forever, not just because his dad died, but because his dad was murdered. By you.'

'He wasn't! I didn't fucking murder him! I didn't! I'd never do this!'

Harry spun Vince around in his chair, away from the

body and dropped his face down in front of him, their noses almost touching.

'The thing is, Vince, I believe you. I really do. I just don't think you're the kind of person who could do this.'

'I'm not.'

'You're a good actor, Vince. You've played the role well. But I think it's time you stopped playing, don't you? Because I'm not interested in the actor. I want the director, Vince. That's who I want. You're the monkey and I'm here for the organ grinder.'

Vince's eyes flickered up at Harry and they were filled with a desperate hope.

'Organ grinder? What are you talking about?'

'Luca was murdered, supposedly for poaching. But that wasn't actually the reason, was it? You see, I think he was killed to send a message. What was done to him, that would get around, wouldn't it? Luca had stepped out of line. He knew the rule—to stay quiet, talk to no one—but he had a family to feed, so that's what he did. And because of that, he had to die.

'I'm not sure you ever thought this day would come. Where you'd have to step into the spotlight and take the big fall, but it did, and so you did. Except, other things are in play now, because sometimes, it's impossible to be completely in control.'

Vince looked so confused that his face gave the impression that he was in pain.

'Luca's death was one thing, but we've another body now, Vince. And I have a feeling that unless we move quickly, there will be more. I don't know how many, because I don't know exactly who else is involved, or why, but that's where you come in, Vince. You can stop this.'

'I can't stop anything.'

'Yes, you can.'

'I can't!' Vince shouted, spit flying from his mouth. 'I can't! They'll kill me! That's what they said.'

'Who?'

'I had no choice! I was bankrupt. Yes, I had all those businesses, but I liked a flutter, if you know what I mean? Kept on, didn't I? Trying to win big, hoping to pay it all back, but I couldn't. So, they offered me a loan. And I couldn't pay that back either, but I think they knew that's what would happen. That was their plan all along. I had no choice. The offer they made was too good. You'd have said yes, too, you know? Anyone would.'

'What did they offer?'

'I'd still be the owner on paper, be paid to live like I was still raking it in, but they'd run things from then on. They said it was the perfect business for what they wanted, that I'd have nothing to worry about. Just to keep my mouth shut, play the role. It was too good to be true.'

'Yes, it was, wasn't it?' Harry said, spinning him back around. 'And look where you are now, Vince.'

Vince refused to look up. He fell quiet, a faint sob escaping.

'They'll kill me.'

'No, they won't,' Harry said. 'We'll protect you.'

'You can't.'

Harry gently lifted Vince's face so that he had no choice but to look at Luca again.

'Whatever it is that you've done, it's nothing compared to what happened to Luca,' Harry said. 'They did this, not you.'

'They'll get to me.'

'No, they won't. Not if we get to them first.'

Vince shook his head.

'I can't ...'

Harry pulled out his phone again, showed Vince the photos of Elena, of Stefan.

'For once, Vince, don't think of yourself. Think of them, the family Luca left behind. And tell me who did this?'

Vince sighed then, and his whole body sagged, all hope gone, all resistance.

'Okay,' he said. 'I'll tell you ...'

CHAPTER FORTY-ONE

Having left his car in the multi-storey, the man wheeled his small carry-on-sized luggage behind him, across the road and into the airport. The crowd was thick, and he didn't really like that very much, because he had never been a fan of being physically close to anyone, and that went for anything romantic as well. Other people were an annoyance, a necessary evil, cattle.

The vast building he was now standing in at least gave him that sense of anonymity, because even though it was crowded, no one knew who he was, and he liked that. Which was why, despite everything that had happened, he was actually rather looking forward to arriving at his destination.

The house would be cool when he opened the door to let the sun in across the flagstone floor for the first time in months. The only food in the place would be what he had in the cellar: some of that speciality sausage, hanging from the beams, the cheese he'd sealed away to carry on ageing, and the wine in the rack. Heaven! His mouth watered at the thought of it.

He looked up to check on his flight, saw that everything was on time, and so joined the queue, patting his pocket just to reassure himself that he had his passport. Then he pulled it out to double-check that it was the right one. He knew it was, and he also knew that if it wasn't, then his day would become considerably more frustrating, but still he checked. Yes, it was the right one. Good.

The queue moved slowly but constantly, and soon the man was at the desk, checking in.

The woman at the desk, whose smile was candy-coloured and played around her words like her lips were dancers or lovers even, picked up his passport and ticket.

'Going away for long, Mr—'

A hand slipped around the man's bicep.

'Palmer,' said a voice in the man's ear.

The woman at the desk looked confused.

'No, I think you have the wrong man,' she said. 'This is Mr Paterson.'

The man turned his eyes from the woman to the man holding his arm. He was small, older than him by a few years, and was holding up a little wallet to identify himself as a member of Her Majesty's Police. He looked tired. The grip wasn't very strong either, and the man was sure he could easily pull himself out of it. But there was something in the man's eyes, wasn't there? A fire that still burned white hot. Also, he was accompanied by two other, considerably larger men who stared at him, almost like they were silently daring him to just try to pull away and make a run for it. And they'd like that, wouldn't they? the man thought. Running after him, chasing him down. He wouldn't give them the pleasure.

'Come on,' the smaller man said.

The man took back his passport and ticket as the smaller

man pulled him away from the desk. The wine, the sausage, the cheese—that would all have to wait, he thought.

Outside, one of the two larger men opened the passenger door to a nondescript car with grey paint and alloy wheels. The smaller man who had not let go all the way from the check-in desk now did so, to pull out a phone and lift it to his ear.

'Grimm?' the small man said. 'It's Swift. Just thought you'd like to know we got him.'

The man took a seat in the back of the car.

Swift hung up and looked at Palmer.

'You're nicked, mate,' he said, and that fire behind his eyes burned just a little hotter.

BACK IN HIS FLAT, Harry placed his phone down on the table in the kitchen. It had been, in almost every way, a week to remember and yet, at the same time, one to forget. He was exhausted, the entire team was in fact, and still his mind was a whir with what they'd uncovered.

When Vince had told them who had been running things, Harry had called Swift immediately. They had a description and, like it could when it wanted to, the force went into overdrive. Not least, because it then turned out that Palmer, if that was his real name, was a wanted man and linked to various organised crime gangs, all of which had their grubby hands stuffed firmly into the drugs trade.

Palmer, Vince's "solicitor," was caught in his car by CCTV, and the consensus was that he was heading to the closest airport at Leeds. And Swift, perhaps in some last attempt to be part of the big chase before retiring, had pulled every string he could to have himself be there to make the arrest. Judging by the sound of his voice on the phone, Harry guessed he'd rather enjoyed it.

Harry had also already been given an update on what Palmer had been up to. Drug money can't just be spent, it has to be laundered. So, to do that, Palmer was the go-to man. He would identify legitimate businesses that could be used, take them over, and run them as a front.

The businesses were always the kind that dealt in cash, such as fast-food vans, cafés, and car washes. Then all he had to do was have people pose as customers and use the drug money to pay just a little too much for what they'd asked for, be it a burger or a shampoo, wax, and polish.

With the car wash business, the criminal side of things was darker still, with people ferried in on the ghosts of promises of a better life, only to find themselves trapped and enslaved and living in squalor. Palmer, and his network of connections, were the worst of the worst, and Harry was rather stunned that it had now somehow all been brought down by his little team in the Dales.

If Palmer had kept his nerve, if he had just left Luca alone, then he would probably still be trading and getting rich by ruining the lives of others. But he'd messed up. In trying to use Luca's death as both a warning to tell people to stay quiet or else, and to rid himself of Vince who had, perhaps, become a liability or maybe just an irritation he could do without, he had unknowingly set up his own downfall.

But there was still something that bothered Harry. Because although Vince was now in protective custody, and Palmer was soon to be behind bars, they still had two missing persons. Palmer had brought in two heavies happy to dish out violence. Beating staff to keep them in line hadn't worked, so they'd gone a step further with Luca. Now one was dead, the other in the wind. And Harry had a horrible feeling that soon, the body count of two would rise to three. There was also the unspoken thing that Swift had yet to mention, and Harry's gut told him what it was, that with him retiring, Swift was going to push Harry to take his place.

'Penny for your thoughts?'

Harry looked up to see three faces staring back at him. One was covered in black fur, a large pink tongue hanging from its mouth. As for the other two, one he had fallen in love with, and the other was almost terrifying. It was the terrifying one that had spoken.

'Sorry, Dave,' Harry said. 'It's been one of those weeks. And I've said that rather a lot these last few days.'

'It has,' Dave said. 'And now it's the evening and you've a job to do, haven't you?'

Dave tapped the tip of a huge, meaty finger on top of a pile of documents on the table.

'I need to read through it all again,' Harry said. 'And I'll be honest, I'm a little tired.'

'Bollocks you do,' Dave said. 'Here.'

Harry looked up to see Dave holding a pen.

'You've read it all a dozen times, I bet,' Dave said. 'So stop buggering around and just get on with it!'

Harry took the pen, then looked at Grace.

'Hey, don't look at me,' Grace said. 'This is your decision and yours alone.'

'Sign!' Dave bellowed.

Smudge's tail thumped on the floor.

Harry pulled the lid off the pen and slid the papers over.

'Welcome to the Dales, Harry,' Dave said, his stern face now broken with a smile.

'And if it's all the same with you,' Grace said, 'I'd prefer it if you didn't leave.'

Harry dropped his hand to the papers and started to write.

EPILOGUE

HARRY WAS SITTING IN HIS FLAT STARING AT BOXES. Some were full, others were empty, none of them were doing a good job at holding his attention. With the house now bought and contracts exchanged, he'd decided to crack on with packing up his stuff, even though he didn't really have much to pack, and there was still more than enough time before he would move out. That there probably wasn't enough money to buy all the furniture he would need was another problem entirely, but he would worry about that at another time.

The only other occupant of the room was Smudge, and she was fast asleep on the sofa, her favourite way to spend a Saturday morning.

Deciding that the boxes could wait, Harry made his way to the kitchen to make a coffee. There was also some cake in a tin courtesy of Arthur, Grace's dad, and that absolutely needed finishing off.

Outside, the weather was certainly getting up, a wolf's

howl of wind cutting through the sound of the kettle heating up.

With a coffee made, Harry sat down at the table and took a moment to just breathe. The sequence of events surrounding Luca's murder was still on his mind. Not just because the whole case had grown into something stretching beyond the borders of Wensleydale, or because so many people were involved, but because among all the numerous loose ends the case still had, all of them being tied up by numerous officers far and wide, there was still one that was bothering him.

No, there were two: the still-undiscussed suggestion by Swift that he might be putting Harry forward for his soon-to-be-available job, and the whereabouts of Gill Mitchell and Luca's other killer.

Harry sipped his coffee, ate some cake, stretched to the sound of his back popping disturbingly. There was no movement from Smudge.

Harry attempted to ponder for a moment the idea of becoming a Detective Superintendent. The fact was, that no matter what Swift said, assuming he was ever going to say anything about it at all, Harry knew he would never be considered. And that wasn't just down to who he was and what he was like, either. There were hoops to jump through, and he would have to jump through a few more before he'd even get the chance to consider a superintendent role.

Not that he was going to consider it anyway. There had been more than enough change in his life of late and he rather fancied a little bit of time to just be somewhere he had decided to call home, doing something he loved and, for whatever reason, was good at. The pay hike would be nice though, he thought as he went to drain the last of his coffee and there was a knock at the door.

Harry made his way down the hall and opened the door to Ben, his brother.

'I know you don't live here anymore, but you still have a key,' Harry said.

'Seems rude just walking in,' said Ben, then he winked. 'I mean, you could be up to anything, couldn't you?'

'No, I couldn't,' Harry said, and stepped back out of the way to allow Ben in. 'You here for that box, then?'

While gathering together his own stuff, Harry had come across a few bits and bobs of Ben's and sent him a message to come and collect it whenever he wanted.

'I am,' Ben said, and handed Harry a pile of letters and leaflets and junk mail. 'Posty was just on her way over, so I saved her the trouble.'

'You shouldn't have bothered,' Harry said. 'This lot is for the bin.'

Harry followed Ben into the flat, where they were greeted by Smudge.

'She misses me, I see,' said Ben.

'We both do.'

'You big softy.'

'Not at all,' Harry said. 'I just appreciate how you always cleaned the bathroom and did the washing up.'

Ben laughed and spied the small box Harry had packed for him.

'I bet it's all junk,' he said, picking it up.

Harry was shuffling through the mail, wondering if any of it wasn't junk.

'Probably,' he replied. 'How's Liz?'

'She's great,' Ben said.

'So, you're still enjoying living together?'

'It's early days, I know, but yeah, things are going well.'

'I'm pleased.'

'I know.'

Back at the door, Ben stepped out into the wind. It whipped around him, like it was trying to knock him off his feet.

'I miss this place, though,' he said.

'No you don't,' said Harry.

'No, you're right, I don't,' Ben replied, then with the box stuffed under one arm, he reached over and pulled Harry into a tight hug.

For the briefest of seconds, Harry was too stunned to know what to do, and he just stood there, the letters and junk mail in his hands, his arms hanging by his side. Then, he reached up and returned the gesture.

'See you, Harry,' Ben said, and headed off.

'You will,' Harry replied, and watched his brother walk on into Hawes.

Back inside the flat, the door closed behind him, Harry walked through to the lounge and slumped down next to Smudge, chucking the junk mail onto the coffee table. He'd put it in the recycling later. But then, as he sat back, with Smudge leaning over to rest her head in his lap, he saw something on top of the pile.

Reaching over, he picked up a postcard. Flipping it over, he saw that it was genuine, the stamps on the back clearly from somewhere beyond the shores of England, the picture on the front of a sun-kissed beach. The address written on the card demonstrated just how Hawes worked, Harry thought. Instead of his full address, he saw his name, the town itself, followed by 'Wensleydale, North Yorkshire,

United Kingdom.' No mention of the flat or where it actually was in Hawes, and it had still found him.

Dear Harry ...

Harry was confused. He didn't exactly have many friends, and certainly none that he was aware of who were on holiday abroad. And the friends that he did have, he was pretty sure they wouldn't send him a postcard in the first place. The writing was very small and very neat. He read on.

I'll keep this short, one soldier to another.

Then, Harry knew. Not only who this postcard was from, but why it had been sent in the first place.

I did my best to help them and look after them, but I failed at that, didn't I? I'm sure you've got that in hand, though. You strike me as someone who gets a job done. Much like me, if you know what I mean.

I think I do, Harry thought, a stone sinking in his stomach.

I know you found the one by the river. Sorry about the mess. The other slipped away. But I found him. And by the time you've read this, he won't be able to hurt anyone else, I promise.

Bloody hell, Gill, Harry thought.

I won't be coming home. Fancied a holiday anyway. One last trip for these old feet of mine. All the best, Gill

Harry sat back, the postcard still in his hand. Then he read the PS ...

Sell the car. Give the money to Luca's wife and son. Thanks, Harry.

Outside, Harry was sure that the wind howled a little louder.

Don't miss out on the next up-all-night Harry Grimm Crime thriller *Unquiet Bones*

JOIN THE VIP CLUB!

WANT to find out where it all began, and how Harry decided to join the police? <u>Sign up to my newsletter today</u> to get your exclusive copy of the short origin story, 'Homecoming', and to join the DCI Harry Grimm VIP Club. You'll receive regular updates on the series, plus VIP access to a photo gallery of locations from the books, and the chance to win amazing free stuff in some fantastic competitions.

You can also connect with other fans of DCI Grimm and his team by joining The Official DCI Harry Grimm Reader Group.

Enjoyed this book? Then please tell others!

The best thing about reviews is they help people like you: other readers. So, if you can spare a few seconds and leave a review, that would be fantastic. I love hearing what readers think about my books, so you can also email me the link to your review at dave@davidjgatward.com.

ABOUT DAVID J. GATWARD

David had his first book published when he was 18 and has written extensively for children and young adults. *Fair Game* is his eleventh DCI Harry Grimm crime thriller.

Visit David's website to find out more about him and the DCI Harry Grimm books.

 facebook.com/davidjgatwardauthor

ALSO BY DAVID J. GATWARD

THE DCI HARRY GRIMM SERIES

Welcome to Yorkshire. Where the beer is warm, the scenery
beautiful, and the locals have murder on their minds.

Grimm Up North

Best Served Cold

Corpse Road

Shooting Season

Restless Dead

Death's Requiem

Blood Sport

Cold Sanctuary

One Bad Turn

Blood Trail

Unquiet Bones

The Dark Hours

Silent Ruin

Dead Man's Hands

Dark Harvest

Milton Keynes UK
Ingram Content Group UK Ltd.
UKHW041431300824
1448UKWH00022B/51

9 781917 001106